Crossing Hearts

Sara looked at him wonderingly. "Then you're going back to England when the war is over."

"Yes. I thought you were planning to do the same?"

"I was."

"Then why should I come back to the United States?"

Their eyes met and held for a long moment, and all at once Sara was aware of a deep feeling of joy that swelled within her heart and gave wings to her being. It was as if, in that one shared look, they had discussed their future and decided it.

"You'll wa... that touched Rob's ... ften the craggy planes of ...

"Of course ... e the one who's going ... the one with all the growing up to do...

"No. No, that isn't true." Rob's smile was gone, replaced by an intensity that seemed to shiver through her. Taking one of her hands, he turned it over and kissed the inside of her palm. Gently he closed her fingers around it as though he would have her hold the kiss there forever.

Then he reached out unexpectedly to take her face in his hands and press his lips to her lovely, laughing mouth . . .

      .   **.**   **.**

"Emma Gordon transports us effortlessly back in time, bringing a vanished world into brilliant focus. I was both enthralled and enchanted by her lyrical descriptions of scenes and places. *Crossing Eden* is a first-timer's triumph!"

—ßeverly Hughesdon, author of *Song of Songs*

Crossing Eden

Emma Gordon

This title first published in Great Britain 1992 by
SEVERN HOUSE PUBLISHERS LTD.

This edition licensed by Severn House Publishers Ltd.,
produced by Magpie Books Ltd., and published by Parragon
Book Services Ltd. in 1994

A copy of the British Library CIP data is available
from the British Library.

  ISBN 0-75250-103-8

Printed and bound in Great Britain

To my mother

We did not, in the innocence of youth, know then that we had left Assyria behind and were brashly crossing Eden.

E. Skoda, 1905
Letters from Abroad

Contents

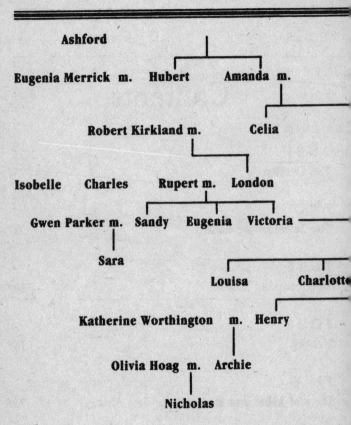

```
        Ashford
                              ┌─────────┴─────────┐
Eugenia Merrick  m.  Hubert          Amanda  m.
                                              ┌──────┴──
                  Robert Kirkland m.        Celia

Isobelle    Charles    Rupert m.  London
                    ┌──────┼──────────┐
Gwen Parker m.  Sandy  Eugenia  Victoria ──────
        │
      Sara
                                    ┌──────────────┴──
                              Louisa        Charlotte

        Katherine Worthington   m.  Henry
                              │
            Olivia Hoag m.  Archie
                        │
                    Nicholas
```

Note: Only the characters relevant to the work are listed here.

and Warburton Family Tree

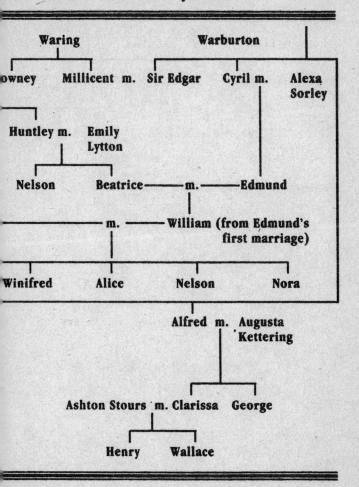

Waring   **Warburton**

...owney   **Millicent** m. **Sir Edgar**   **Cyril** m. **Alexa Sorley**

Huntley m. **Emily Lytton**

Nelson   **Beatrice** ——— m. ——— **Edmund**

——— m. ——— **William (from Edmund's first marriage)**

Winifred   **Alice**   **Nelson**   **Nora**

Alfred m. **Augusta Kettering**

Ashton Stours m. **Clarissa**   **George**

Henry   **Wallace**

ONE
The Garden

Chapter One

May, 1937
Rose Cottage, Millham Cross, Kent

A meadowlark, nut brown against the brilliant green of the garden, flitted down through the budding elm branches to land upon the high stone wall. Fluffing its damp feathers against the drizzling rain, it began to warble a tentative song, then bolted away, alarmed by a sudden movement beyond the border of wild-growing roses. A gate creaked and a tall figure in an olive-green mackintosh and Wellingtons came striding down the path. It was an elderly woman with a strong-boned face, brandishing a pair of pruning shears, her fine, intelligent blue eyes alight with determination.

Halting beneath the dripping branches of the single acacia tree growing in the middle of the daisy-sprinkled lawn, she began to attack the thick ivy snaking its way about the trunk. Her jaw clenched and her breath came in short, exerted gasps, but it was clear that she was enjoying herself.

"There!" She stepped back, surveying with grim satisfaction the pernicious green fingers she had calmly snipped to bits. Nothing left but debris, and she'd need only a moment to throw the handful onto the compost heap before going in to drink her tea.

Normally she left the pruning to her gardener, Mr. Brockman. But somehow it seemed that the nearer London Ashford approached her seventy-fifth birthday, the more unwilling she became to relinquish all of her chores to that overworked little man. Besides, since it was raining, she had given him the afternoon off, and it certainly wasn't his fault that she had succumbed to the sudden whim of destroying those detestable vines as she peered from her kitchen window while waiting for the water to boil.

Mr. Brockman would scold, of course, but London was used to that. She knew perfectly well that he never really meant a word of what he said. Actually, her daughter, Victoria, could be far more tiresome whenever it came to admonishing her mother not to take on so much work in the garden. Poor Victoria simply didn't understand, as London suspected Mr. Brockman did, that this unruly little garden with its crumbling walls, overgrown herbaceous borders, and capricious rambler roses, had intrigued her from the first moment she'd moved into the abandoned lodge-keeper's cottage at Bellehurst nearly two months earlier. Taming a neglected garden was a task she enjoyed; a challenge that she wasn't about to give up no matter how old she became.

I'm afraid Victoria's nothing more than a meddlesome prig, London decided disloyally. *Why, if I were to give up gardening I'd have nothing left. Nothing save reading, writing my letters, doing embroidery—and the grave. And Lord knows I'm not ready for* that *quite yet.*

She stooped to gather the trailing vines, then made her way slowly to the compost pile behind the shed. Here, she discarded them neatly and paused for a moment to admire the scilla budding beneath the hawthorn hedge. Very soon now the entire garden would be in bloom, though regrettably not until after her birthday party, which was scheduled for Sunday next and at which her entire, illustrious family—Ashfords and Warburtons alike—would gather.

"Bah," said London. Her back had begun aching a little and so she returned to the house, crossing the terrace and entering the kitchen by way of the little door cunningly concealed beneath an archway of trailing roses.

Here, she was greeted by the cozy warmth and the delicious smell of the scones she had put into the oven to heat. The kettle sang softly to itself, and London measured out the tea before adding the water, suffusing the air with the rich aroma of fine, dark Assam. While it steeped, she went to the larder, took out butter and a crock of jam, and seated herself at the oak table from where she could admire the lovely view of her garden through the neat rows of mullioned windows.

Frowning, she noticed suddenly that she had left her secateurs lying in the grass beneath the acacia tree. With a sigh, she fetched her mackintosh and set off across the wet lawn, her boots squelching as she walked. A bird's song greeted her as she bent to retrieve the precious tool.

Straightening, London heard someone calling to her from beyond the garden gate. It would have to be the delivery boy with the groceries she'd ordered from Hurley's market in Millham Cross. Life had certainly become much more convenient ever since Mr. Hurley had purchased himself a delivery van.

"Come in, dear, come in!" she called, cupping her hands. Her voice was firm, without the tendency to quaver one might expect from a woman of advanced years. "You'll find the money on the hall table. I'm afraid Mrs. Putney isn't here to help you unload. I've given her the afternoon off—"

She was interrupted by a laughing voice from beyond the lilacs blooming in purple profusion along the terrace wall: "Oh, Grandmama! It isn't the greengrocer. It's me!"

Startled, London let the pruning shears fall to the grass. None of her grandchildren—and she had quite a few—ever called her anything but "Granny" or "Gran." Besides, her son-in-law, William, had herded them off to a point-to-point somewhere in the west country and they weren't expected home until evening. For the life of her she couldn't imagine who had come to see her on such a dreary day—and had the temerity to address her in such an archaic manner. She saw the garden gate swing open, and then someone was coming across the wet grass toward her, a slim figure in a dark gray raincoat, whose features were obscured by a rather ridiculous floppy hat. The hat had fallen back a little, revealing a youthful face filled with joyous laughter.

Dear God, Sandy!

London caught at the tree to prevent herself from falling. She felt herself reeling, falling into some distant heart of darkness where a host of memories reared up their unwanted heads to engulf her. How well she remembered that wealth of shining hair, the color neither red nor gold but somewhere in between, and those eyes, Sandy's eyes, so wide and deeply blue that you could almost believe the very sky was reflected in them.

Don't be a fool, she told herself fiercely, grappling for some semblance of sanity. It couldn't be Sandy. Sandy was dead—

"Grandmama?"

The absurd little hat had fallen off entirely, and London realized all at once that the worried face peering up at her was a woman's, not a man's. Instantly her heartbeat slowed. Thank God the shock was fading and reality was once again taking a firm hold upon her brain. This wasn't her long-dead son Sandy, but his daughter, Sara, hurtling into her life with all her usual abruptness. She must have traveled all the way from New York without so much as bothering to cable.

"Why didn't you let me know you were coming?" London inquired peevishly. "Or at the very least ring up from the city? I would have sent Mr. Brockman or Francis to fetch you. How on earth did you get down?"

Still laughing, Sara Ashford brushed the damp curls from her face, looking not in the least repentant. "By bus. One of the locals brought me up from the village."

"In a horse cart, I imagine." London stooped and groped for the shears, trying to collect herself and get over this uncanny turn done to her heart. She was, she decided grimly, getting far too old for such staggering surprises. "I know perfectly well there's no taxi to be had on a weekday afternoon in Millham Cross."

"You're quite right about that. At least Mr. Sidlow was kind enough to bring me all the way to the gate. And from the smell of it, I think the last thing he'd been hauling in his cart was potatoes, not manure."

London's lips twitched. "How very fortunate for you." Carefully she dried off the secateurs and tucked them into the pocket of the work apron she wore beneath her mackintosh. "Naturally we weren't expecting you. My birthday isn't until next week."

"I know. I'm sorry. I should have rung up from London when I arrived, but I did so want to surprise you. Do you realize how long it's been since we've seen each other?"

"Sixteen years," London responded dryly. "You've grown far too thin since I saw you last. Neglecting yourself, as usual. Most young women nowadays do. And of course I imagine you haven't slept a wink since leaving New York."

"Oh, Grandmama!" Laughing, Sara threw her arms about the old woman, not in the least put off by her tone. It was, she knew, her grandmother's way of coping with such a tremendous shock. Besides, even as a child she had never feared that formidable bark. "On the contrary, I slept magnificently last night. At the Savoy, no less. Mother made all the arrangements. And I had my own cabin aboard the *Berengaria*, too."

"In that case you won't be needing a nap."

"No. Only a towel and a cup of tea."

"Well, then, come inside. The kettle's on. We'll have us a lovely chat, and I promise not to make a single one of those trite remarks people are always making whenever they haven't seen one another in a dreadfully long time."

London hung the secateurs away in the wooden shed that was cleverly concealed by a mass of rhododendrons growing in the far corner of the garden. "Even though you really are the image of your father."

There. She'd said it. Just as casually as if it hadn't mattered that her heart had nearly stopped beating when she'd first seen Sara running across the lawn and had foolishly, unforgivably, mistaken her for her long-dead son, Sandy.

"Well, you certainly haven't changed one bit, Grandmama."

London, in the process of pulling off her boots by the

terrace door, looked up in astonishment. "Good heavens! Should I have?"

Sara was silent for a moment, considering. Age certainly hadn't stooped those once-proud shoulders or faded the sharp intelligence and will burning in her grandmother's blue eyes. White-haired, tall and regal, she looked exactly the same to Sara, and so she dimpled and said, "No, I suppose not."

Once inside the house she was not permitted to help with the tea or lay the tray, but was ordered instead to bring in her luggage and refresh herself in the bathroom. Watching her vanish down the hall, London was suddenly glad that she had observed her usual, though admittedly pointless, ritual of putting out fresh guest towels and a new cake of White Windsor that morning. She hoped Sara would be pleased with the bath, which was done up in shades of cool green and rose, the walls and floor luxuriously tiled, the fixtures gleaming.

Victoria was the one who had insisted on making the guest bath so grand while the cottage was being remodeled, despite her mother's protests concerning the unnecessary extravagance. London wondered now if Sara would remember that there hadn't even been a bath—let alone hot-water plumbing—either here at the lodge-keeper's or up at the manor house when she had lived there as a child.

Her hands shook a little as she measured another scoop of loose tea into the pot. Obviously the girl's arrival had affected her far more than she cared to admit. Well, for heaven's sake, why shouldn't it? Cheeky thing, claiming she had only meant to surprise her!

More like sending me into a decline, London thought, but she was smiling as she left the kitchen and crossed the low-beamed hall to the parlor.

There, she found Sara standing by the open French windows looking out into the garden. A gramophone stood on the spindle-legged table beside her, with London's newest possession, a wooden wireless set, accorded the cramped shelf beneath it. But Sara had elected not to switch either of them on.

London nodded approvingly. She, too, preferred drinking her tea with only the gentle sea-sound of the rain falling through the high branches outside. In fact, the oak-beamed parlor with its cozy inglenook fireplace was by far her favorite room for sitting quietly and doing nothing at all. It was a charming room, decorated in shades of cream and pale blue, and despite the heavy beams and stone hearth, it managed to convey a pleasing femininity with its chintz draperies and hand-flocked paper. The old furniture smelled comfortably of lemon wax, and Sara had removed her hat and coat and was peering outside with the restful air of one surrounded by the familiar.

London paused for a moment in the doorway, her Wellingtons discarded in favor of comfortable house shoes, the work apron for a tweed skirt and knitted cardigan. She stood there without announcing her presence, drinking in the wonder of her long-lost granddaughter come home at last. Time might have stolen the cheeky moppet with the rag curls and grubby knees, but, oh, what a lovely young woman had taken her place! Fashionable too. Sara's traveling costume was made of dark green linen with a smartly tailored jacket that flared gently over her hips. The close-fitting skirt revealed her long legs and boyishly graceful form—an athletic form, slimly pleasing. The way Sandy's had been.

Sensing her grandmother's eyes upon her, Sara turned with a welcoming smile, then hastened forward to take the heavy tray from her. "Goodness, Grandmama! Don't tell me you haven't any help?"

"Not today, dear. Mrs. Putney asked for the afternoon off, and of course I said yes, not dreaming you were coming."

"Is that all? Just Mrs. Putney?"

London looked surprised. "Who else should there be? Mr. Brockman does all the heavy gardening, and I can always ring up the house if anything special needs doing. Provided your aunt and uncle aren't entertaining, of course, because then I've got to endure the usual lecture about how not a single one of them can be spared."

"By that do you mean the servants? But aren't they yours to begin with?"

"Well, yes, I suppose they are. But now that I'm living here at Rose Cottage it seems rather silly to keep them hanging uselessly about. Besides, Mrs. Putney is very efficient at tidying up, and prefers working alone.''

London was pouring tea as she spoke. The silver teapot was the same one she had used when Sara was a little girl, as were the wafer-thin blue-and-gold Royal Worcester cups. The tea was Indian, the sandwiches made of cucumber spread with Gentleman's relish or hard-boiled egg and anchovy. And there was also the much-loved pastry tray, filled, just as Sara remembered, with ginger cookies, buttery scones, and Grandmama's unforgettable fruitcake, darkly moist and steeped with rum.

An unexpected lump rose in Sara's throat at the sight of it. She knew that this elaborate tea was her grandmother's way of letting her know that she was welcome. Her earlier brisk-ness in the garden had merely served to mask her shock. Fruitcake and tea was a homier, and far more loving, way of revealing her heart.

"Rose Cottage?" Sara said now, mainly to cover her own feelings.

London's smile was rather defensive. "Well, why not? The roses are everywhere, and I couldn't stand having every-one refer to the place as 'the lodge-keeper's' after I moved in.''

"I can imagine," Sara teased. "You always were such a pretentious old thing. But why did you do it? Move down here, I mean? Surely Aunt Victoria couldn't have begrudged you a quiet wing of your own?''

"That's just it, my darling. I'm afraid peace and quiet fled Bellehurst for good when your Great-uncle Charles died last year. He left both your aunts quite a tidy sum, you see, and ever since they inherited money and a title, Victoria and William have developed a real passion for entertaining. It seems the house is always filled with guests at weekend.''

"But the house is yours!" Sara pointed out indignantly. "Bellehurst was never part of the entail, and I remember distinctly Grandpapa leaving it to you when he died! Surely you've every right to insist on some privacy?''

"My dear girl, I rarely insist on anything these days, and it isn't as if I've given them the house, for heaven's sake.

I've only stepped aside for a time. Victoria's inheritance can't last forever, though to be honest, I do enjoy living here. It's much more private than Bellehurst ever was and, strange as it may seem, I get a great deal of satisfaction from watching Victoria blossoming as a hostess. I know it's dreadfully disloyal of me to be saying so, but she never . . . well . . . *excelled* at anything before. Of course, it wasn't really her fault. She's had a very difficult life until now."

"Yes, I know," Sara said unrepentantly. "Your letters were always frank. It couldn't have been easy making a go of it with five children crammed into that dreary townhouse of Mother Warburton's."

"And all of them so dreadfully headstrong and spoilt!" *Not to mention as painfully dull and unhandsome as their father*, London wanted to add, but wouldn't.

"But it couldn't have been easy for you either, abandoning Bellehurst after all these years!" Sara insisted.

"Nonsense. I've always been a Bedouin at heart, and it's better for an old woman like me to take herself off to the relative seclusion of an abandoned cottage than try to make herself pleasant to every new face appearing at the supper table night after night. I simply haven't the energy to act amiable anymore."

Sara had to laugh. "You always were an ill-tempered old thing, Grandmama."

"Yes, wasn't I?"

In truth, London found it difficult to explain, even to her granddaughter, that she simply did not care to live at Bellehurst any longer now that her husband, Rupert, and his brother, Charles, the most recent Ashford heir, were gone. While Rupert had been dead for many years now—nearly fifteen, wasn't it?—his younger brother Charles had somehow always served to keep his memory alive. Even though Charles had visited Bellehurst only rarely, preferring his office and his West End clubs to the isolation of the Kentish countryside, something of the old order seemed to have gone with his passing.

London thought herself too old these days to care what happened to that big house on the hill, or to protest the elaborate lifestyle adopted by her daughter and son-in-law now that they styled themselves the Earl and Countess Ladbroke.

For with old age comes indifference and the freedom to admit to oneself, quite without feeling the least bit disloyal, that one's own daughter and son-in-law were nothing more than a disagreeable pair of snobs. Let them do as they pleased with the house and the grounds; spend their days hobnobbing with that hard-drinking, objectionable set of friends they had recently begun drawing around them. Victoria's inheritance could go only so far, and since the family firm was presently suffering from the same economic malaise as the rest of the country, one couldn't count on squeezing extra money out of the accounts much longer. And because William's mother, Beatrice, was still very much alive and clinging hard as ever to her own purse strings, it didn't seem likely that additional funds would be forthcoming any time soon.

The thought made London smile somewhat grimly. It would be interesting to see what would happen once the money ran out.

Sara, meanwhile, had been thinking about the former occupants of Rose Cottage, and had managed to conjure up the vague recollection of a balding little man whose wife's ample apron pockets had always yielded a cache of sticky-sweet chocolates. "What happened to him?" she asked now.

London's thoughts were drawn up short. "Who, dear?"

"The lodge-keeper."

"Oh, Mr. Skelton. He finally died last year. Why, he must have been close to ninety and deaf as a sign post. William decided not to replace him, seeing as the gates were always left open anyway. Most sensible of him, I suppose, though I did so hate to see another of the old ways coming to an end. Still, I'm delighted to be living in Mr. Skelton's house, surrounded by his lovely garden, with no one to disturb me but the cows and the birds."

"What happened to Mrs. Skelton?"

London's brow furrowed. "I believe she went to live with a sister in Gloucestershire after her husband died. The children are grown up and moved away too." She smiled suddenly, a mischievous smile that highlighted the sharp, clean bones of her face and revealed something of the great beauty she had been in her youth. "The youngest daughter, Mirabelle, is working in the kitchens at Chartwell now. Mrs. Skelton was positively scandalized. Mr. Churchill, you see, thinks nothing of roaming his house in the nude."

Sara choked on her scone. "Grandmama!"

They laughed together, wickedly, at the thought of awkward, blushing Mirabelle being subjected to such horrors.

"What about Aunt Eugenia?" Sara asked. "I assume she's coming for the party?"

"You know perfectly well that one can never outguess Eugenia," London responded tartly. "She hasn't let me know one way or the other as yet. We quarreled the last time she was here, you see, and for all I know she may have fled to the Far East with some of those odd cronies of hers."

"What was the quarrel about?" Sara inquired with interest. She knew that Grandmama and Aunt Eugenia understood one another very well and that any dissent in the family usually took the form of disagreements between Grandmama and her priggish younger daughter, Victoria.

"Nothing serious, really," London said breezily. "Eugenia objected to my moving here. She was convinced that William had somehow driven me out of Bellehurst and into Rose Cottage."

"Eugenia has never really cared for Uncle William, has she?"

"Eugenia has never really cared for any man. Not even, I think, the two she married. One of them was quite useless, as you well know, painting those horrid blue landscape scenes that no one would buy. And Sir Reginald certainly made a hash of it by taking a stand against women's issues in Parliament. Surely he must have known before he married her that Eugenia would hound him to his grave for that. Still, she's obviously much happier now that she can lead the life of a respectable, and well-heeled, widow."

Sara smiled. "Some women aren't interested in cluttering their lives with men."

"Is that how you see it?" London inquired shrewdly.

A faint trace of color crept into Sara's cheeks. "This isn't the beginning of a lecture, is it?"

"Certainly not. You know it's not my way to pry."

"No," Sara agreed with a laugh. "You've always preferred going straight for the jugular. So let me assure you, Grandmama, that I'm not pining for anyone."

"Really?"

"Yes," Sara said firmly.

Silence fell between them, although London couldn't help thinking that her granddaughter's reply had sounded rather defensive. Was it possible that she was hiding something about her past? An unhappy love affair, perhaps?

Despite their active correspondence over the years, Sara had never written to her about anyone special. Nevertheless, London knew perfectly well that Sara's mother had, over the years, paraded a veritable army of American bachelors in front of her only child. More than likely Gwen and Sara had disagreed over who was suitable and who was not. And Sara, no doubt wearied and disillusioned by such arguments, seemed to have chosen to live her life without romance.

To London, this was a tragedy. She knew that Sara was the sort of woman who would thrive in a loving, bustling household—a lifestyle London was convinced that the girl had missed ever since leaving Bellehurst as a child. She wondered how to broach the subject without appearing meddlesome.

The china clinked as London stirred cream into her cup. Wearily she leaned back in her chair and allowed the warmth of the tea to soothe her. She would have to let William and Victoria know, of course, that Sara was here. But not just yet. Time enough to ring the house later—after dinner, perhaps, when they had returned from their point-to-point and she and Sara had had the chance to share a cozy meal together. There was ham in the icebox and some leftover ragout that wouldn't take but a moment to heat. And after dinner they would open a bottle of Charles's excellent claret, and she would ask Sara all the latest news from abroad.

She would have to see that Sara stayed at Rose Cottage during her holiday, London decided firmly. Not up at the house sharing one of those dark little garrets with some decaying aunt or boring cousin the way Victoria intended. She could sleep in the guest room, the one with those pretty pink curtains and Eugenia's old canopied bed. London felt sure it would suit Sara far better than forcing her upon the rest of the family when they arrived.

London couldn't help shuddering every time she thought of the fuss Victoria was making over her birthday. She didn't like to appear ungrateful, but since when did turning seventy-five mean that one had attained such an all-important milestone in one's life? Stubborn as always, Victoria had refused to pick up on the gentle hints dropped by her mother: that London had grown accustomed to the solitude of Rose Cottage and had no desire to interrupt the quiet, predictable routine of her days with a party that seemed likely to rival King George's recent coronation. All those people, the elaborate entertainment, the food, the wine, the liquor and ale, when money really was so very dear these days despite the reckless manner in which William was spending it.

But to her surprise, London had lately discovered that she no longer cared. In fact, she would even go so far as to say that she welcomed the idea of having her far-flung, fractious tribe assembled beneath her roof once again. And all because she suddenly felt charged with the oddest sense of purpose and optimism. As though only good things could come of seeing those long-forgotten faces again. Whatever could have gotten into her to make her feel this way?

"Grandmama?"

London slowly opened her eyes to find Sara's lovely face smiling into hers. The girl's red-gold hair made a cloud about her narrow shoulders, and she looked slimly graceful in her traveling jacket and tailored skirt despite the fact that both were still slightly damp. "What is it, my darling?"

"Would you mind if I took this scone? It's the last one."

"Not at all, dear. I've had quite enough."

With a sigh London settled back in the armchair and allowed the peaceful warmth of the room to enfold her once again. Her favorite granddaughter was home. What else could possibly matter?

Chapter Two

Victoria Warburton banged down the receiver of the telephone on her nightstand and passed a trembling hand through her disheveled brown hair. Her huge, satin-covered bed was littered with glossy magazines and nibbled pieces of chocolate. Pushing them aside, she drew her expensive shantung silk dressing robe about her plump body. Its color, a deep, scarlet red, did not suit her, but Victoria had a passion for brightness and did not care whether she looked well in it or not. Besides, no one save her husband, and the maid who tiptoed in to turn on the radiators first thing in the morning, ever saw her in it anyway.

From the big, sumptuous bath connecting Victoria's bedroom with William's came the sound of gargling and someone spitting into the sink. A vulgar sound, truly, though after twenty-odd years of marriage, Victoria Ashford Warburton had grown quite accustomed to her husband's objectionable habits. She had even learned to ignore the more loathsome ones among them, including that guttural *arghh* he made whenever he rinsed the tooth powder out of his mouth and spat the remains into her expensive marble basin.

Most of the time, that is. Tonight, however, the terrible sound was somehow impossible to ignore. Victoria found that she had to fight the impulse to storm into the bath and slap William right across his foam-smeared mouth and afterward, with one sweep of her arm, send his toiletries crashing down from their rows of expensive glass shelving.

Fortunately for both of them Victoria had far too much self-control to indulge in such madness. In fact, she had

16

always prided herself in possessing more than the average person's share. One couldn't help but build endless reserves of patience after living for years under the same roof with one's mother-in-law in that horribly cramped townhouse off Saint James's, and afterward with one's own mother here at Bellehurst.

Thank God that impossible old witch (Beatrice, of course, never darling Mama) had decided to remain behind in London when Mama had finally extended her long-awaited invitation to move Victoria's ever-increasing brood of children to Bellehurst, thereby bringing a much-needed measure of peace into Victoria's harried life. Furthermore—and Victoria would only admit this to herself in the most private of moments— she had been more than a little relieved when Mama herself had announced similar plans to move out of Bellehurst several months ago, although not, like the sensible Beatrice, to some lovely little flat in Mayfair. Instead she had calmly announced her intention of taking up residence in Bellehurst's oldest outbuilding: the lodge-keeper's cottage at the outskirts of the park, which had been abandoned half a year or more ago upon the ancient keeper's death.

Victoria had been deeply shocked and aggrieved at first. That ghastly little hut had dark, poky corridors and long-neglected rooms! Surely nowhere else in all of England could one find a more unsuitable domicile for a baroness, a woman who had, in her youth, been the toast of the county and a great favorite at court. What on earth were people going to think?

But Mama had been adamant, and Victoria, after agonizing at length over the matter, had gradually come to realize the advantages of keeping Bellehurst all to herself, with Mama still conveniently nearby. And once Victoria had accepted her mother's decision she had also managed—as she always did—to convince William to spare enough money to have the ramshackle place properly painted and papered, and fitted with real baths as well as wired for electricity and a phone.

"But whatever shall I do with one of those?" Mama had asked, genuinely astonished when Victoria had proudly told her the news.

Victoria's smile had faded. "Why, ring up your friends, your children, anyone you wish."

"It's only a three-minute walk up to the house, which is certainly no trouble at all should I have anything of importance to say to you or my grandchildren. And as for calling my friends, I shall always prefer seeing them face-to-face."

Victoria had only just held her temper. How typical of Mama to be so stubborn! And how unfair of her to bring up the subject of those endless visits to her friends and acquaintances when she knew perfectly well that it was presently such a sore point between them! Why, only last month William had purchased Mama a motorcar of her own, a Bentley no less (though admittedly used), and Mama had actually been so ungrateful as to refuse it outright—and turn down William's kind offer to teach her to drive!

She was far too old to begin learning now, London had insisted, and besides, there was nothing in the least wrong with her dogcart and the little hackney mare that pulled it, though to be honest she had admitted that Jessamine was beginning to look a little scruffy these days and seemed to have lost the spanking gait of her youth.

"And when you grow too old and frail for a pony and cart?" Victoria had demanded, by now thoroughly vexed. "What then?"

Her mother had smiled sweetly. "Then I shall buy myself a bicycle."

"A—a bicycle?" Victoria had gone very pale. "At your age?"

"Why, yes. I'm not exactly in my dotage yet, dear. Or I could always ask dear Mr. Brockman to squire me about."

Victoria had very nearly groaned aloud. Henry Brockman, Bellehurst's gnarled gardener, was even older than Mama and quite an abominable sight with his unkempt hair, missing teeth, and oft-patched, baggy clothing. A relic, in one word, and as such quite unsuited to support the image Victoria wanted everyone in the family to convey now that she and William had inherited at last.

Henry Brockman, indeed! Ludicrous, laughable, to picture *a gardener* driving Mama around the countryside—just like the late queen bowling through Windsor park with that horrid, shaggy, drunken Scottish servant she had so revered, John Brown. And she, Victoria Ashford Warburton, who happened to bear that same, revered queen's name, was not about to be made a similar laughingstock or have people whispering behind her back that the new Countess Ladbroke's elderly mother was clearly eccentric or—worse—grown senile!

"There are more and more cars crowding the roads around Millham Cross every year," Victoria had tried one last time. "It could prove dangerous for you in that slow-moving carriage! Supposing there was to be a head-on collision in one of those narrow lanes?"

London had soothingly patted her daughter's cheek. Strange, she had mused, how petulant Vicky could still look at her great, grown age of forty-seven. "I'm quite familiar with the roads around Millham Cross and assure you that I won't be in any danger of having an accident."

And of course Mama had ended up having her way about the car, simply by refusing to take it out of the garage despite their endless pleading, until William had lost patience and ordered it taken to Tunbridge Wells to be sold. Thank God Mama had at least relented in the matter of the telephone, if only because she thought it might prove useful in the unlikely event she fell ill or had an accident.

Though with calls like this one, Victoria thought now, staring hatefully at the small black box sitting innocently on her cluttered nightstand, perhaps it would have been better to leave Rose Cottage in the same, primitive condition in which the Skeltons had left it!

Swinging her bare feet over the edge of the bed, Victoria slipped into her mules, the new ones with the gold heels and silver boa trim she had purchased at Harrods—and was annoyed to find them just a little tight. Surely she wasn't putting on weight again? Why, with all this planning for Mama's party and the endless running up and down the stairs after her children, the servants, the hounds that William had recently decided were so fashionable to keep, one would think she would be worn to the thinnest of frazzles by now!

Unless. . . . Oh, no! That was a thought too horrible to

contemplate. She was forty-seven, for heaven's sake, far too old to be bearing more children! But even as Victoria rushed to the bedside mirror to convince herself that it hadn't happened again, she could already hear the hateful taunts of her sister, Eugenia, who had already gone through that inevitable, fortunate change of life and had managed despite two marriages and (so Victoria suspected) a most promiscuous lifestyle, to fail to conceive so much as once.

"Oh, come off it, Vick!" Eugenia had harped during a particularly gruesome Christmas visit fifteen years ago. Victoria had an excellent memory for dates and never forgot anything, including the fact that she had been rushing about that night in a feverish attempt to assemble her recalcitrant offspring in the icy hall and muffle them in scarves, mittens, and hats; William honking impatiently in the Daimler outside as he waited to drive them to Millham parish for Christmas service; Mama already seated in the back with a tartan throw over her knees and Eugenia, as usual, not lifting a finger to help despite her sister's obvious distress.

"The Victorian age is over, haven't you heard?" Eugenia had lectured from the sweeping double staircase that met at the top of the gloomy, raftered hall where she had come to see them off. Eugenia never attended church herself. "It died more than twenty years ago with that prudish, pig-headed, plump old queen you so revered! Lots of women these days use contraceptives to limit the size of their families."

Victoria remembered clearly how hot with embarrassment those words had made her and how she had tilted back her head in order to stare hard, and a trifle' enviously, at her sister's narrow waist, which was clearly revealed in a shockingly close-fitting cream sweater and a pair of blue woolen slacks.

The year was 1922, and Victoria herself was dressed in the height of formal fashion: pale blue crepe dress falling in soft folds to the floor, her dark hair piled high in back-sweeping puffs in the same elegant style (so Victoria imagined) as the oh-so-imperious Queen Mary. And until today Victoria had never seen a woman wearing slacks before; would never have imagined that such a person could actually be received at Bellehurst, even if that woman was Mama's other daughter.

"Do you?" she had demanded despite herself, momentarily forgetting the presence of her children. "Use them, I mean?"

"Why, of course, silly. Have been for ages."

Victoria had raised her chin, its terraced folds of flesh quivering indignantly. She always seemed to get just a little heavier with every child she bore although, God be thanked, there hadn't been another since Nelson's birth two years ago. "Well, I for one refuse to descend to such utter depths of depravity!"

"Depravity? Don't be such a cabbage-head! It's the only sensible course for a woman saddled with a husband like yours."

Hot color had rushed to Victoria's cheeks; she was well aware that William and Eugenia couldn't abide each other, but that certainly didn't give Eugenia the right to make crude remarks about William's fondness for, well, the sexual act.

"It's a wife's responsibility to be dutiful," she countered stiffly.

"Dutiful—ugh! There's another of your grotesquely outmoded Victorian concepts! Do us all the favor, Vick. Next time William goes off shooting in those dreadful Norfolk bogs, call me. I'll arrange for you to see someone at the Harriet Stovall Clinic and be properly fitted with a Dutch cap. If you're discreet, William will never know you've got one."

"I'll do no such thing!" Victoria exclaimed, trembling with indignation, unwilling to admit that she didn't have the vaguest idea what a Dutch cap was.

"Suit yourself," Eugenia had said with a shrug, tossing her fashionably shingled black head for emphasis. "Just don't say I didn't warn you."

Two weeks later Victoria had discovered that she was pregnant for the fifth time. And it was then that she had moved her growing family to Bellehurst because Beatrice's townhouse simply couldn't hold them anymore.

Now, as Victoria recalled the wrenching agony of that

last cesarean birth despite the fact that she had been heavily chloroformed at the time, and admitting candidly to herself that Nora, her youngest daughter and the only one still living at home, could sometimes be the most exasperating of her difficult brood, she could not help examining herself with growing trepidation in the mirror. But the reflection in the glass showed only the familiar, smoothly-padded contours of her body beneath the expensive scarlet silk of her dressing gown.

Victoria could scarcely control her sigh of relief. She could not understand why she should still be cursed with the ability to bear children when most of her friends—even those years younger—had long ago declared themselves free of that hated monthly burden. William had always said (rather unkindly, Victoria thought) that she was an admirably fertile female. And while other women were first alerted to their "delicate conditions" by increasing nausea, fainting spells, or headaches, for Victoria it had always been a minor gain in weight, a barely perceptible tightening of her corsets and, later, her more modern feminine undergarments, several days before that dreaded, all-confirming cessation of her monthly menses.

"Was that the phone I heard before?"

Victoria whirled as her husband lumbered from the bathroom with a dark blue sheet wrapped about his midriff. Victoria scowled. At present she could certainly not credit William, the second Earl Ladbroke, with cutting a particularly fine figure of a man of fifty-three, not with that untidy, thinning blond hair or with his small, clipped mustache still smeared with tooth powder, and certainly not with that extra padding of fat spilling grossly over the top of his carelessly knotted towel.

For some inexplicable reason all of Victoria's resentment came surging back at the sight of him. "I just had a call from Mama," she said tightly. "It seems that Sara has arrived unannounced from America and that the two of them spent the entire evening alone together without so much as bothering to inform us she was here. Furthermore, Mama insists that Sara stay with her at Rose Cottage, despite the fact that she is fully aware of how hard it was for me to arrange decent, workable accommodations for everyone in the family! Sara was supposed to share the Blue Room with Eugenia, and now"—Victoria's lower lip quivered—"now she's gone and ruined everything!"

William, who had been standing before the mirror examining his receding hairline with ill-concealed annoyance, did not even bother turning about. "Who's Sara?"

Oh, really, it was all too much! How could William be such a dolt and pretend not to know, when Victoria had complained often enough how unfair it was that Sara Ashford, that curious, red-headed American creature, should continue to remain Mama's favorite grandchild even after years and years of separation, and especially after Victoria had presented Mama with five beautiful, blue-blooded English grandchildren of her own?

Naturally it was because Sara was Sandy's daughter, and Sandy, being Mama's only son, had always been her favorite child. Never mind that Victoria was the only child who had remained Mama's constant and abiding companion during the lonely years following Papa's death; her one great comfort during Uncle Charles's final illness; her sole confidant and provider in her own advancing age. And wasn't Victoria the one working her fingers to the bone to make Mama's seventy-fifth birthday an occasion to remember?

Uttering a choked cry, Victoria fled the room, her golden heels slapping across the thick carpet. Sometimes life could be so grossly unfair!

"Oh, dear," said London, cradling the phone in the hall at Rose Cottage far more gently than her daughter had done in the state bedroom at Bellehurst.

Sara appeared in the kitchen doorway, a dish towel in her hand. "What is it, Grandmama?"

"I'm afraid Victoria didn't sound at all pleased when I told her you'd be staying here. I keep forgetting how hard she's worked trying to squeeze everyone under one roof rather than putting them up at the Paxton Hotel."

Sara's expression softened. "I wouldn't worry too much, Grandmama. I remember Aunt Victoria always getting worked up about something, but that it always blew over quickly."

"Yes, thank goodness for that."

"I've finished the dishes. How about some tea?"

Smiling, London rose and smoothed out her skirt. "No, thank you, although you're a dear to suggest it." She yawned and glanced at the clock, surprised to discover how tired she felt considering it was only half-past nine. But it was a kindly sort of tiredness, assuaged by the unexpected warmth that Sara's presence had brought into the house. London had never considered herself lonely before, but tonight she had to admit to being filled with an unreasonable happiness of the sort she hadn't experienced in years. Surely this outspoken American girl, with her unaffected chatter and her remarkable resemblance to her father, had to be responsible?

On impulse, for she was not usually a demonstrative person, she kissed her granddaughter's cheek. "Good night, my darling. Sleep well."

"I'll be up soon," Sara promised.

"No need for that, if you aren't tired. Sit up and read, or play the gramophone if you wish. And for heaven's sake, don't worry about disturbing me. I sleep like a log."

"All right then, I will stay up, if you don't mind. I'm not really sleepy yet."

"Not at all. Good night, my darling."

London's bedroom was located at the top of the stairs, under the eaves where, every spring, the swallows arrived to dip and wheel in joyous flight around the nests they built deep amid the ivy. It was a small room, the ceiling descending at a sharp angle toward the windows to accommodate the steep slope of the outer roof. It was Victoria who had decided that the walls should be painted a deep yellow and who had selected the brightly flowered blue curtains sewn by Millham Cross's able seamstress, Mrs. Bodkin, despite her mother's objection to the colors.

To her surprise, London had loved everything about the finished room. She felt safe here, cosily surrounded by her most prized possessions: her antique escritoire, her armchair and reading table, even the canopied trestle bed brought down from the big, gloomy third-floor bedroom at Bellehurst, which she had occupied ever since abandoning the state bedchamber upon Rupert's death in 1921.

On the mantel of the fireplace, rather incongruous amid the pretty feminine furnishings of the room, stood a grouping of hand-blown glass vases and perfume bottles whose colors embraced nearly the entire dark end of the spectrum: violet, indigo, hazy lavender, and the same deep blue of the sky that had always reminded London of Sandy's laughing eyes.

They were very old, these bottles, the glass crazed and cloudy, some of the delicate handles chipped in places, or some missing a stopper or a spout. Victoria had been secretly relieved when London had insisted on taking them with her. Victoria found them ugly old relics, fit only for the dustbin, but they were extremely dear to London, inasmuch as they were the only personal possessions she had brought into her marriage to Rupert Ashford more than fifty years ago.

Now, as she lay in bed with the coverlet draped over her, London listened to the sighing of the wind beyond the old-fashioned, hand-blown panes and tried to ignore the aching of her bones that always reminded her, whenever the weather was damp, that she really wasn't young anymore.

The house was very quiet. Sara had not turned on the music as London had expected. Instead she could hear the girl moving about in the kitchen below, then the back door creak, and a moment later the faint clumping of boots on the wet path.

Everything changes, London thought with a sudden smile. And nothing does. Even as a child Sara had always loved to take solitary walks, never daunted by the darkness or the weather. Doubtless she was on her way up the hill to see how the manor house would appear through the scudding clouds, and to see what, if anything, had changed, and what remained the same. At least from the outside.

Already drifting into the light sleep of old age, London had to smile a little at her own self. How well she still knew her granddaughter's heart despite the long years without her! It was almost as if she could feel Sara's eagerness, the burning expectancy one couldn't help experiencing when looking upon something that hadn't been viewed for a very long time. Like the house you were born in, or a beloved face you had thought gone from your life forever.

Like Sara's face, London thought sleepily, and the man who had revealed himself tonight in shadowy, breath-robbing glimpses whenever Sara had tossed her head or laughed just so. Or later, in that aching moment when the fire had burned low and the single lamp on the end table had shed its light at just the right angle to illuminate the fine, clean line of Sara's brow and cheek. Oh, yes, London remembered that profile very well—and of course that smile, the way it had always dazzled everyone with its warmth.

How nice to know that she hadn't forgotten; that it could move her still, after all these years. Time, it would seem, really did have a way of dimming the terrible pain of loss, leaving only a sweetness that one could savor without rancor in thinking back on the days when London herself had been young and happy and passionately in love.

TWO
The Jewel in the Sand

To an honorable man, a gracious wife is as
fortunate a find as a jewel in the sand.

Old Arab Proverb

Chapter Three

1879
Algeria

White-washed houses, shaded by pepper trees, lined the great boulevards that cut wide swaths through the ancient Arabic city. Beyond them, along the steep hills rising above the curving length of the harbor, there were no trees save for an occasional pomegranate planted in a sheltered terrace garden, or a jujube whose sun-blasted branches offered little in the way of relief from the molten heat simmering in the twisted alleyways. To the Arabs of the city, relief from the hot transparency of evening could best be sought in the market *sugs*, which were roofed by planks and canvas or reed wattles, or perhaps in the dim cafés, although most of the inhabitants of this teeming city preferred conducting their lives outdoors.

For Alex MacLaughlin, sitting on the terrace of a hotel room overlooking countless other white terraces descending in an unbroken line down to the seafront, there was little relief to be found from the oppressive heat. Clouds hung low over the distant Atlas range, promising cooling rain, but no rain had fallen in six months or more, and it was not likely that the drought, or the plague of insects accompanying it, would end any time soon.

From the streets below drifted high-pitched music and the calls of the vendors selling their wares. The heady scent of perfume blended on the hot wind with the smell of incense and the pungent aroma of a hashish pipe. Donkeys brayed, women trilled in ancient languages as they bartered for goods, and a pair of Frenchmen, obviously drunk, passed beneath the hotel wall singing a vulgar dance-hall song in an unsteady, discordant key. Farther off, the racket from the shipyard mingled with the ever-present whining of mosquitoes and the constant droning of the flies.

From his terrace Captain MacLaughlin did own to a fine view of the sea: azure where the sun lingered in molten colors upon a horizon smudged here and there with the bluish smoke of ships, darker mauve within the confines of the buoys serving to mark the boundaries of the harbor. Earlier, he had purchased a pot of ginger tea from a Sudanese café, and now he sat sipping the sharp contents in thoughtful silence, flicking away the flies that settled on the cup rim while the hot breeze blew through the open collar of his shirt.

He was twenty-eight years old, the son of a wealthy British nabob, born in the sumptuous Indian city of Calcutta. From the very first the East had drawn him; not the genteel world of the British Raj that was inhabited by his parents, but the exotic, teeming, polyglot darkness of Calcutta's alleys and bazaars. Sent to Eton as a youth, ostensibly to follow in his father's footsteps, Alex had learned instead to shoot, play rugby, ride to hounds, and smoke and gamble—and to develop a healthy dislike for his pretentious countrymen that was to last throughout the course of his life.

At eighteen he was back in India, determined to make a career of fostering understanding between the British military and the teeming Hindu millions who inhabited the land. His hope was to advance the lot of Easterners while refusing to pander to the Raj, but his ambitions did not sit well with his father, who showed his displeasure by refusing to pay for his son's commission in a crack regiment. Thus, inadvertently, the way was opened for Alex to join John Company's Indian Force.

Now, after having spent the last eleven years of his life serving the Force in British India, Alex had attained the rank of captain in the Forty-first Bengal Lancers and could profess himself greatly contented with his life and still enamored of his career.

At present he was a long way from home, but Alex could not own to feeling the least bit uncomfortable at finding himself in Algiers. He was, after all, well accustomed to the heat and noise of Eastern lands, and the alien lives led by North African Muslims did not differ markedly from those of their Hindu counterparts in India. In fact, Alex was compelled to admit that he had felt considerably more out of place during his recent visit to England than he did here in Algiers.

In the courtyard below a pair of camels began to fight. Alex had to smile as their keeper forced them apart with a heavy stick and a string of colorful oaths. His knowledge of the Arabic vernacular was casual at best, but sufficient to enable him to appreciate most of them. With a contented sigh he settled back against the hot stones, his booted legs crossed on the terrace wall before him.

He was not a tall man, only slightly above medium height, but one who carried himself with unusual grace. Sinewed arms and broad shoulders gave evidence to a physique hardened after long years of riding patrol on the rugged Northwest Frontier, which served to give him the impression of considerably more inches. His hair was coal black and his eyes, like his mother's, a deep blue, while the square chin and ruggedly carved features of his sun-bronzed face—too harsh to be considered handsome—were the legacy of his Scottish father.

Alex had not seen his parents for two years or more. It had been his intent to return directly to Calcutta after being granted six months' leave following the recently ended Afghan conflict, in which his regiment had played a crucial role. But fate, in the form of an unexpected death in Kabul, had sent him instead to England. He had gone there on a mission of mercy, which had in turn set into motion yet another curious string of events that now found him sitting on a stifling Algerian rooftop sipping the burning dregs of Sudanese tea and biding his time until tomorrow, when the primitive wagon he had engaged would depart for the African interior and what would probably prove the strangest undertaking of his life.

The camels in the courtyard had finally been beaten into submission. Immediately the hot, still air came alive again with the strange Eastern music of the *sugs* and cafés. The blinding blue of the evening sky was thinning to violet, and from the minaret of a nearby mosque came the cry of a muezzin calling the faithful to prayer.

"*La ilaha illa Allah; wa-Muhammad rasul Allah.*"

"There is no god but God," repeated Captain MacLaughlin softly, "and Muhammad is his prophet."

How easily, automatically, the words fell from his lips. It was a habit acquired after years spent patrolling the Northwest Frontier with only his Muslim *jemadar*, Muhammad Atok, for company. It shouldn't be at all strange that some of the teachings of Islam should have rubbed off on him, and considering his reasons for coming to Algiers, Alex had to own that perhaps he had come to believe, a little, in the deeply rooted Islamic belief that a man's fate is cast at birth and, once written, cannot be rubbed out.

His lips twisted at the thought. Bloody rubbish. Fate had nothing to do with bringing him here—friendship and greed had done so. He was honest enough with himself to admit that the lure of one hundred pounds British sterling had certainly whetted his appetite for Arabic adventure.

Three months ago, at the end of June 1879, Captain Alexander MacLaughlin of the Forty-first Bengal Lancers, had paid a courtesy call on one Powney Warning, second Baron Ladbroke, of Bellehurst, Millham Cross, Kent. Not since his brief tenure at Eton had Alex been back to England. The memories, naturally, had dimmed with the years, and nearly everything he now knew of that thriving, powerful, prestigious seat of the British Empire had been garnered from the homesick memoirs of the weary, expatriated British wives whose menfolk served either the British military or the Honorable East India Company in Peshawar and Calcutta—and also from the works of Byron, Keats, Coleridge, and others whose poetry had filled many a frigid night by the campfire in some lonely outpost beyond the Khyber pass.

Nevertheless, none of those lyrical posturings or his own, dim memories of public-school life had prepared Alex for the dazzling green of the Kentish countryside. Because the railway from London to Tunbridge Wells was still under construction, he had been obliged to ride horseback the entire distance down narrow lanes flanked by oak trees of immense age and size, the road itself worn deep into the earth by centuries of oxcarts and coaching wheels.

The clean bite of an easterly wind had accompanied him across hills that climbed steeply toward emerald summits only to slope abruptly into valleys where tidy villages of thatched-roof cottages nestled against the silver ribbons of winding rivers, and fields of grain lay with neat, checkerboard precision beneath a hollowed expanse of pearl-gray sky. It was a land of flowering meadows and small stone bridges, neat farmhouse and cottage gardens, orchards groaning with the yields of plums and cherry trees, and the strange, conically shaped oasthouses where the harvested hops were dried in kilns.

It was early evening when Alex's weary mare finally turned through a pair of wide-standing, wrought-iron gates that separated the pastures stretching along the hedge-grown lane leading from the village of Millham Cross into Bellehurst's meticulous park. Just beyond the gates, in the middle of the neatly scythed lawn, sat a small, ivy-grown house of mellow brick, with countless tiny, old-fashioned windowpanes set beneath an overhanging tile roof.

Apparently the lodge-keeper was not at home, for no one emerged in response to his calls, and Alex did not linger. Instead, he urged his mare down the lane, which by now had taken on the unmistakable characteristics of a proper drive: broad and smoothly graveled, neatly edged with brick, it ran for a mile or more along an avenue of ancient beeches. Above their lush crowns the sprawling rooftops and chimney pots of the house had come into view, and the mare, sensing that oats and warm bedding lay near, lengthened her stride to a steady trot.

The dying sun had set fire to the upper windows of the house and to the walls of the main block and pair of rambling wings running east and west of it. At first Alex thought that they were white-stuccoed in the manner of the palaces of British nabobs sprawling along the reed-grown banks of the Hooghly River, but now he saw that they were built entirely of native limestone, the color so unusually pale that the entire facade seemed to glow in the fading daylight.

It was difficult to guess either the age or the architectural style of the house, because it seemed to have been thrown up without rhyme or reason over the course of the years: a wing here, a corner tower there, remodeled often to suit the taste of its owners. Unlike most of its Victorian counterparts, however, it had not been embellished in recent years with up-to-date stained glass or the mock-Tudor appointments currently so popular with the countrified gentry. Instead it maintained a surprisingly Elizabethan air with its twisted chimney stacks, sharply gabled roofline, and huge, iron-braced door that led from the wide stone steps down to the circular drive.

The overall effect was nonetheless pleasing, and on the eve of Captain MacLaughlin's arrival, Bellehurst had managed to enjoy some fifty years of unparalleled prestige in the county—although not all of those years had been kind. It was 1879, a time when the golden age of the English country house was drawing to a close. The reasons were numerous: a hard-hitting agricultural depression that seemed destined never to end, and the growing importance of London townhouses, whose popularity had been influenced by the free-spending lifestyle of the Prince of Wales. In addition, the once widely loved Queen Victoria, widowed nearly eighteen years before, was now living such a sequestered life at Windsor that her reclusive behavior, and the irresponsible antics of her oldest son, were lending momentum to a powerful political movement calling for an end to the monarchy.

Closer to home, Lord Ladbroke's wife, Amanda, and both his children, Celia and Huntley, were long dead, while Powney Waring himself was now an old man stooped with age. His interest in farming had long since waned; by the time Alex MacLaughlin showed up at his door it had been a decade or more since he had last ridden to hounds. Added to the old man's increasing sense of isolation was the bitter blow of losing his only grandson, Nelson, Huntley's eldest child and heir, during the recently ended Second Afghan War.

It was in the frigid winter passes of a hostile land half a world away from the cultivated beauty of Kent that Lance Corporal Nelson Huntley Waring had died after being ordered to march with his regiment under cover of darkness across the rugged mountains near Fatehabad to attack a closely guarded border fortress and so open a crucial route for the British army through the treacherous Khyber pass. While fording the swollen river cutting through the Lagman Valley tragedy had struck: an entire column of Bengal Lancers had been swept away from the current, many of them still clinging to the backs of their frantic chargers. Among the bodies found floating in the downstream eddies the following morning had been Alex MacLaughlin's longtime adjutant, Muhammad Atok, and his good friend and junior officer, the loyal, likable Corporal Waring.

Barely a month later a peace treaty had been signed between His Highness Muhammad Yakoub Khan, Amir of Afghanistan, and the Indian viceroy, Lord Lytton, on behalf of Her Britannic Majesty, Queen Victoria. Alex, recovering in the Rawalpindi infirmary from a broken collarbone suffered during the campaign, had written Nelson's grandfather informing him that he was in possession of the boy's belongings, entrusted to him on the eve of the disastrous Lagman march because Nelson had not wished them to end up forgotten in some dusty Peshawar cubbyhole.

Alex went on to say that he would be leaving for London as soon as he was mended in order to deliver a number of dispatches to the Foreign Office. With six month's leave due him he had wanted to bring Nelson's effects to Bellehurst should the baron have no objections.

Powney Waring had replied promptly, urging Captain MacLaughlin to avail himself of the first steamer shipping out of the East once his own affairs were settled. His tone had been autocratic to be sure, but Alex had assumed that had been because the first, raw grief of the baron's loss had not yet been assuaged. Indeed he had still been obsessed with the details of his grandson's death when Alex met him.

Alex arrived at Bellehurst from London tired and ravenously hungry. Announcing himself to the elderly manservant who opened the front door, he was brought upstairs without first being given the chance to wash away the grime of the long journey or soothe his parched throat with tea or stronger spirit. Thinking he was being led directly into the baron's presence for an interview, he was greatly startled to find himself brought instead to his own room, which lay at the far end of a long and gloomy corridor.

"Mrs. Waring, the baron's daughter-in-law, is currently away in London with her daughter," admitted the servant, perhaps detecting something in Captain MacLaughlin's expression that suggested an explanation might be in order. "Lord Ladbroke himself has already retired. I was asked to apologize for both the ladies' absence and his. He hopes you have no objection to taking supper in your room?"

"None at all." In truth, Alex would have liked to object quite strenuously. He was unaccustomed to such rude welcomes and found it extremely odd that Nelson's mother should be gone from Bellehurst at a time when her son's belongings were expected to arrive via personal courier from India.

But there was little sense in taxing the elderly manservant with this, or with complaining about the largely unappetizing fare that was brought to his room after what seemed to him an unconscionably long wait. "I suppose I've no one to blame but myself," Alex decided aloud once the servant was gone, and left the supper tray untouched, feeling annoyed with himself and the world in general.

Night fell swiftly, and his room remained unwelcomingly dark despite the small lamp burning on the bedside table. Crossing to the window, Alex drew back the drapes but could see nothing through the blackness. Cold air streamed through the cracks, and Alex scowled, letting the curtains fall back into place. Lowering himself onto the lumpy iron bed set against the far wall, he crossed his arms behind his head and tried to ignore the dampness penetrating every nook and cranny of his room. The exhilaration that had held him in thrall earlier while riding through the crisp northern air had faded, leaving behind an odd sense of alienation. Thankfully he was weary enough, despite his annoyance and the unaccustomed cold, to fall without difficulty into sleep.

He awoke at dawn with a headache pounding behind his eyes. Peering from the window he saw that clouds had blown inland overnight, causing the temperature to drop even further with the suddenness characteristic of northern latitudes. Glimpses of the park through the tiny, leaded panes revealed a thick fog hanging over the wych elms, and by the time Alex had finished the tea, butter scones, and eggs that constituted his breakfast, an icy rain, unlike the warm downpour of Indian monsoons, had begun to fall.

Feeling exceedingly cross and in no mood for pleasantries, Alex followed the same elderly manservant down an interminable series of long corridors before he was at last ushered into a sumptuous antechamber blazing with heat and light. Here, a skeletal old man wearing an outmoded silk dressing gown and a curious caxon wig that had not been fashionable since long before the Prince Consort's time, sat near the roaring fire regarding him with an equal measure of hostility.

"Sit down, Captain," the baron said curtly. "It was good of you to come."

Alex thanked him, and a heavy silence descended while the baron gave his young visitor a long, assessing look from flinty black eyes that were set beneath a pair of slashing white brows. His thin, hard mouth worked spasmodically, then curved all at once into a humorless smile. "Yes, yes, I think you'll do quite nicely."

"Sir?"

"Would you care for tea, Captain?" The baron's voice wheezed asthmatically whenever he spoke.

"Thank you, no. I had tea at breakfast."

"So you did. So you did."

Again a lengthy silence fell. Alex shifted restlessly in his chair. On his knees lay the box he had brought with him from Peshawar containing the last of young Nelson's personal effects, but as yet the baron had not asked for it or even acknowledged its existence. Instead he leaned forward in his chair and, as though he considered his visitor hard of hearing, began to talk loudly and dispassionately about his headstrong daughter, Celia, who had set out for India in the company of an aunt many years ago and had managed to incur her parents' wrath by falling in love with the British commander of a dashing Indian regiment and marrying him without consent.

"Disinherited her immediately, of course," the baron concluded. "Shameless piece of baggage." He uttered a bitter laugh and then coughed, and a fine spray of spittle flew from his lips.

Alex suddenly understood. The old man was senile. Surely that would explain the odd treatment Alex had received since his arrival and the fact that neither Nelson's mother nor his sister Beatrice were here to greet him. More than likely the old man had simply forgotten to tell them that Alex was expected. Feeling somewhat more charitable toward his host, Alex straightened in his chair and tried to show some interest in the old man's garbled tale.

"That was shortly before the Sepoy Mutiny of 1857," the baron was saying. "Were you living in India then?"

"I was just a boy," Alex answered. "We saw no trouble in Calcutta. Neither the Hindus nor the Muslims living there raised arms against us."

"Then you were certainly lucky, Captain, lucky indeed! My daughter and her husband were not so fortunate."

"I take it both were killed?"

The skeletal head shook vigorously back and forth. "No, no. My sister Millicent and her family were butchered in Delhi, but Celia took shelter in the British Residency at Lucknow. Her husband commanded the residual forces there. They spent nearly a year in hiding but both survived. And with the British army once more firmly in control of India, Colonel Kirkland's career prospered. A year or so later Celia was expecting her first child."

"You must have been very pleased," Alex said politely.

The baron's flinty eyes blazed. "Pleased? Bah! My wife and daughter-in-law urged me to relent—wanted Celia to come home to have it—but I still wouldn't forgive her. As it turned out, I never had another chance."

"I assume she died in childbirth?" India, Alex knew, was littered with the graves of countless Englishwomen and their newborn babies.

The baron nodded, his face averted so that Alex could not guess his thoughts. "It was a girl. Celia insisted she be christened 'London' before she died. God in heaven, what a silly name! Kirkland must have been out of his mind to allow it."

But Alex felt only a rush of sympathy for poor, unknown Celia, who had undoubtedly been dreaming of the cool of that faraway English city as her child labored to be born and the grinding heat of India slowly sapped the last of her strength. In view of her suffering he found the name entirely understandable.

"The girl survived," the baron continued, wheezing and clearing his throat. "She was raised by one of those Indian ayahs who lived with them in Lucknow where her father commanded the Thirty-fourth. But I refused to acknowledge her existence until 1870, when her father met with an accident on military maneuvers in the Punjab. After his death I had no choice but to welcome the orphaned creature to Bellehurst."

Which he had admittedly done unwillingly. Arrangements had finally been made through acquaintances in Delhi to send the girl north in the company of a French couple known to the baron. On the way, they had made a brief stop in Algiers, where Monsieur Tavernier, as chief engineer of an artesian drilling crew, had been asked to assist in the installation of new equipment.

"Two weeks later we heard there'd been a fire aboard the steamer *Charlotte Dundas* while at anchor in Algiers," the baron concluded. "Although it was confirmed immediately that the Taverniers lost their lives, the Algerian authorities were unable to substantiate a rumor that my granddaughter had been ashore at the time. I made a few inquiries of my own but met with no success. So I simply dismissed the matter out of hand.''

Alex said nothing. He was trying hard to keep outrage from showing on his face.

''Think me heartless if you will,'' the baron continued, regarding Alex shrewdly, ''but at the time I really didn't care. The gel's mother was long dead to me, and I had other things to worry about. There was a depression on and my farms were losing enormous sums of money. On top of that, here was Nelson, my only grandson and heir, suddenly clamoring to attend Dartmouth because France was under siege and he had some wild notion that we'd be plunged into war once Mad Willy was crowned emperor of Prussia. The last thing I wanted was another soldier or a sailor in the family, by God!''

''I suppose I can't blame you there, sir,'' Alex murmured.

''Bloody well not!'' The baron was clearly agitated. His parchmentlike skin had taken on a mottled hue and his lips trembled. ''I'd already lost my son Huntley in a coaching accident years before and wasn't about to risk losing Bellehurst to some objectionable in-law should something happen to my grandson and heir! Nothing left but Warburtons, you see. My sister Millicent had married into their cursed family and I'd just as soon hang every last one of 'em at Tyburn than let 'em get their hands on my money!''

Looking at the crabbed old man, Alex didn't doubt it. But he was growing increasingly bored and found it difficult to keep his mind from wandering.

''I suppose you want to know what the Kirkland girl has to do with all this,'' the baron said sharply.

Alex tried hard to stifle a yawn. ''It crossed my mind.''

''Well, then, let me tell you. The simple truth of the matter is that there's no one left now that Nelson's dead. Just me, and Nelson's mother, Emily, and Beatrice, Emily's other child. My granddaughter.'' The way he said it made it clear that he had no particular feelings for the girl. ''Not exactly a brilliant future for the Warings, eh? Eh?''

Serves the old man right, Alex decided crossly. Perhaps if he'd shown young London Kirkland just a hint of compassion years ago he'd not be so desperate to save his sinking empire now. If one could call it that. Alex found little to commend in this dark, creaky hunting lodge or the Waring fortune, which, he supposed, must have dwindled considerably over the years in the hands of this doddering old man.

"I need the girl," the baron rasped.

Alex looked up, frowning. "Sir?"

"I need London Kirkland. To keep Bellehurst alive. Oh, not the girl herself, but I've a husband in mind for her, you see. A nephew on my wife's side. Disgustingly dull and scholarly fellow I'd never have considered until it occurred to me that he could easily bring a fecund young wife into the marriage. But he wouldn't have anything to do with me either, arrogant sot, until I dangled Bellehurst's library in front of his nose. I've got a collection of rare medieval manuscripts, you see, and he's keen on researching the life of some obscure Italian pope."

Alex found it difficult to conceal his sudden contempt. "Aren't you forgetting something, sir?"

"Eh? What's that?"

"Nearly eight years have passed since your granddaughter was reportedly drowned in Algeria. How can you be certain she's still alive?"

Powney shrugged. "I can't. But I'm willing to gamble that she is. That's why I need someone to go to Algeria for me. Find out what happened to her. Bring her back if she's still alive so I can marry her off t' my nephew. Someone previously unconnected with the family and who knows how to be discreet. And that, my dear fellow, is where you come in."

Alex sat up with a jerk. "I, sir?"

"Now, now. No need to look so alarmed. I give you my word you'll be handsomely compensated. Handsomely indeed."

"I assure you," Alex began coldly, "that I have no—"

"One hundred pounds. Fifty up front and fifty when you return with her. Or with sufficient proof she's dead. All travel expenses paid, of course."

Alex's lean face was suddenly wiped free of all expression.

One hundred pounds. His officer's pay wouldn't cover that sum in a year. In several years. His mind raced ahead to everything he could buy with that sort of money. A pair of oxen and the skilled labor needed to dig drainage ditches so that his district could finally be freed of the sewage-born diseases that plagued the peasants, the villagers, and the troops quartered in Alex's barracks. A missionary school. Or perhaps he could approach his commanding officer and the District Resident about opening a medical clinic for Britains and Hindus alike. Major Thompson was a fair and forward-thinking man who would, Alex knew, lend a sympathetic ear.

And as for the girl, this long-forgotten granddaughter of Powney Waring's . . . Certainly Alex owed it to her cousin and his friend, Nelson, a forthright and honest fellow, to warn her of the objectionable conditions awaiting her here, so that she could make up her own mind concerning her future. Provided he even found her.

"Then it's settled," said the baron.

Alex looked up into the old man's eyes. And had the swift and uncomfortable suspicion that the baron was not at all as senile as he would have others believe. Alex frowned and opened his mouth to protest, but the baron, perhaps sensing his intent, rose stiffly to his feet.

"Well," he said in a tone that brooked no argument, "now that that's settled, how about a drink and a look at that box you've brought."

And without waiting for Alex's reply, he limped to the bell pull to ring imperiously for brandy.

Chapter
Four

The primitive van serving as the garrison mail wagon left Algiers shortly before dawn the following morning. It was driven by two swarthy Calabrians whose French was even more execrable than Alex's and who appeared to find great enjoyment in abusing the spavined, bad-tempered donkeys that pulled their vehicle. Alex rode in the back amid a heavy cargo of barrels, water kegs, mailbags, and crates in the company of a dark-skinned Sudanese whose left foot was missing a toe. Alex knew this to be a sign of servitude, and since he had always abhorred slavery, he found the Calabrians' constant, tasteless jokes concerning the man's race and appearance making it difficult to keep his temper in check.

His patience was to thin even more as the miles wore on, and he and the Sudanese were bounced about in the back of the van for hour upon endlessly jarring hour. Their destination was a primitive French outpost of barely twenty souls known to the Arabs as Hassi Ban Anit, lying fifty miles or more south of El Djelfa in the blue shadows of the Atlas Mountains. Alex was on his way there because he had discovered, while making discreet inquiries in Algiers, that an elderly French missionary, supposedly accompanied by an orphaned English girl, had traveled there nearly nine years before and had never returned.

Alex had been unable to discover the girl's name, or why she had left Algiers rather than seeking help from the French authorities. No one knew the answers. The men who had served the local government in those days had been recalled to France or were long dead or seemed unable to remember anything of importance concerning the sinking of the steamer *Charlotte Dundas*. Small wonder that Powney Waring, writing letters from faraway England, had fared little better.

Eventually Alex, too, had dropped his inquiries. Like all Eastern cities, Algiers was administered in a routinely haphazard fashion, and Alex was well familiar with the futility of battling indifferent bureaucracies. Nevertheless, he considered himself fortunate in having stumbled upon such a slim lead in the first place, and he supposed London Kirkland would be able to enlighten him herself concerning any unanswered details when—if—he met up with her in Hassi Ban Anit.

Indeed, he had left Algiers congratulating himself enormously on his skill at picking up the trail of Powney Waring's missing granddaughter so easily, but as the villages grew more and more remote and the unexpectedly lovely, heather-covered landscape grew more mountainous and barren and the trail soon became scattered with huge, bald, monochrome rocks whose presence slowed the van to a jolting crawl, he began to wonder if perhaps his mission was not, as had at first seemed apparent, turning out to be some harmless sinecure.

By nightfall of the sixth day every bone and muscle in Alex's body ached, and the dust had settled thickly in his clothing and hair. The wagon had rattled on and on for endless miles that day along a twisting dirt road lined with ancient trees, climbing higher, and higher still, into the snow-capped Atlas Saharien. The air was sharply cold and heady with the fragrance of the heather that bathed the valleys below in a brilliant fuchsia color. It was impossible to believe that the simmering heat of Algiers and the calm blue of the Mediterranean lay less than two hundred miles to the north.

When Alex lay down to sleep that night, his head cradled on a mail sack, he found, despite his weariness, that his thoughts kept turning time and again to tomorrow's forthcoming descent from the tortuous terrain of high hills and the crumpled red boulders lining their pinnacles to the valley floor glimpsed far, far below just before darkness had fallen. His

lips thinned every time he envisioned those plunging preci-
pices and the barely functional brakes of the donkey cart.
Why hadn't he thought to buy himself a horse in El Djelfa in
order to ride alongside it? *In'shallah*. It was all in the hands
of God.

For some strange reason the thought amused him and he
dismissed with sudden indifference the likelihood of plunging
to his death. And when he drifted off to sleep at last he found
himself dreaming pleasantly of the comforts he had left behind
in the civilized world rather than of the hardships lying ahead.
Dreaming not only of the proper beds and hot, well-cooked
meals he had enjoyed in Europe, but of the luxury of the
Turkish baths built in the ancient, classical quarters of Algiers
which he had, in his infinite arrogance, dismissed as frivolous
on the day of his departure. He supposed he'd never be so
unwise as to make the same mistake again.

"Master, it is time to awaken." The Sudanese, Umbilli,
nudged Alex's sleeping form with his foot, then sank back
on his haunches and unscrewed the goatskin flask.

Lifting his head, Alex peered groggily through the faint,
colorless morning light at what appeared to be a grove of
twisted cypress trees lying beyond the expanse of rusty sand
that rose and fell to the swaying of the vehicle.

"Hassi Ban Anit," said Umbilli.

They had crossed the mountains at last and before them lay
the red wilds of the Grand Erg. Behind them the mountains
lay shrouded in low-hanging clouds, and far away to the south
brooded the vast desert, its endless miles of deep, driving
sand the color of crumbled brick in the dawn.

The village of Hassi Ban Anit lay several miles to the east,
at the southernmost edge of a small oasis, its few lowly huts
made of clay and reed wattles. Apricot and fig trees spread
their thinning branches over the baldly thatched roofs, and
wood doves fluttered uneasily as the wagon approached. It
was difficult to tell which of the huts, if any, were inhabited
by Frenchmen. According to the Calabrians, the mail and
supplies were to be dropped off in the house of one Issuf Wad

Muhammad, who would arrange for their delivery via camel to the French fortress some three miles back amid the rugged mesas. No wheeled vehicle could possibly make it through.

On the far side of the oasis Alex noticed a small group of nomadic Arabs quartered beside their camels. The blue smoke of cooking fires hung low in the sky, and he could see several figures in flowing burnooses moving about in the swiftly rising light.

"Umbilli," he said, addressing the Sudanese in the halting Arabic he had managed to perfect during the course of the journey, "I have a favor to ask."

"As you wish."

Despite the hospitality for which they were famed, Alex was well aware that desert Arabs did not make friends easily with *roumi*—foreigners—particularly Europeans. But they were quite willing to exchange a pound of coffee for a bit of gossip with a Sudanese slave, and when Umbilli returned a half hour later to the shade tree beneath which Alex waited, he was grinning broadly.

"Well?" Alex was impatient. The Calabrians had driven off to the house of Issuf Wad Muhammad rather than wait for him to conclude his business, and he was suspicious of their promise to return for him once they had finished their own.

"They have heard of the girl whom you seek," Umbilli said importantly.

Alex froze. It was something of a shock to hear as much, because he had not really expected to find her quite so easily. "Well? What did they say? Where is she?"

Umbilli grinned. "They said, and I repeat it exactly to you: *'Jamila, wa-lakin ghali jiddan.'* "

Alex swallowed his growing irritation. "What the devil does that mean?"

" 'Handsome, but very expensive.' "

"What is? The information concerning her whereabouts? How much do they want?" Alex dug in his pockets for a few coppers, but Umbilli stayed him with a gesture.

"No. They mean the girl herself. She is the one worth the great cost."

Alex regarded him blankly.

"It is said she is quite beautiful despite the fact that she was born with fair hair—which the Arabs consider unlucky— and that her bridal portion is accordingly high."

"Her bridal—? Good bloody Christ! I haven't come to marry her myself! Didn't I tell you to make that clear to them?" With the utmost effort, Alex managed to control his temper. "Will they take me to her?"

"No. I have asked. She is under the protection of one Ali Wad Zarim of the Tuareg tribe, who rules much of the land you see before you to the south." Umbilli made a sweeping gesture with his arm to encompass the chain of high, sandy mesas lying blood-red in the morning light that swept for mile upon endlessly scorching mile toward the great dunes of the Sahara. "The Arabs fear the Tuareg. As do I. The Tuareg fear no one. Not even the French."

"Then at least find out how I can get to their encampment."

Umbilli inclined his head. "I am certain it will be granted."

As a cavalry officer, Alex MacLaughlin was accustomed to spending long days in the saddle. While serving as a recruit in the Indian Force he had quickly grown bored and disillusioned with the petty daily life of the military compound at Peshawar. As a result he had asked for—and been granted— a transfer to one of the regiments patrolling India's Northwest Frontier. Skilled with a lance and gifted at tracking, he had quickly proven himself a natural guide, and as a result had spent the past eight years of his life riding patrol on the border with only his horse and, occasionally, Muhammad Atok for companionship.

Because of his broken collarbone and subsequent journey to England, it had been many months since Alex had last sat a pack horse, but now he could not, in all honesty, say that he enjoyed even a moment of the six-odd days it took to ride from Hassi Ban Anit to the Tuareg encampment on the far side of the Jim' Umma range where, supposedly, he was to find London Kirkland at last.

As the long, hot days passed with numbing slowness he amused himself by trying to recall everything he knew about

the Tuareg people, though his knowledge was scanty. Umbilli, born into servitude in a hostel in Algiers and therefore
not of the desert himself, had not been able to tell him much,
and the Calabrians had merely laughed and made slicing
motions with their fingers across their throats from ear to ear.

They were wandering Berbers was all Alex had learned;
more fair-skinned than their Arab counterparts, their caravans
controlled much of the lucrative desert trade. According to
Umbilli, they were wont to call themselves the masters of the
Sahara, and it seemed that few cared to dispute it. They were
an educated, enlightened, and wealthy people who spoke the
ancient tongue of their ancestors and preferred to roam the
desert, grazing their flocks on the richest vegetation, while
the oases they owned were farmed in their absence by black
serfs in return for a small share of the crops.

Quite an organized and industrious tribe, Alex thought
grimly. What the bloody hell was London Kirkland doing in
their midst?

For perhaps the hundredth time that day he fingered the
small package crackling in his vest pocket and very nearly
laughed aloud recalling that it contained the betrothal ring
Powney Waring had given him just before he'd departed
Bellehurst. What on earth was that vain old reprobate going
to do if his granddaughter turned up married to some Tuareg
chieftain? She would be seventeen now, certainly of an age
to marry whomever she wished according to the standards of
any North African country. And certainly old enough to have
found her way back to England on her own by now had she
wished to do that too.

The thought made Alex feel uncomfortable. Admittedly he
had taken a strong dislike to the baron and could find little to
commend in the old man's description of his dry-as-dust
nephew, Rupert Ashford. Perhaps the Kirkland girl would be
better off after all married to some handsome Tuareg youth,
although Alex hoped fervently that he would not be called
upon to make *that* particularly unpleasant decision.

Alex had slept little during the past six nights, having been
warned in Hassi Ban Anit of the danger of sleeping too long
on the sand without suitable bedding, because it was at night

that scorpions and horned adders emerged to hunt. He had been further assured that the Tuareg encampment lay less than a week's journey away, and for that reason he had declined to purchase a canvas bedroll or the services of a guide, thinking he could find the way himself. And he had certainly made good time thanks to the fact that the heat hadn't slowed him down as Issuf Wad Muhammad had predicted. Why should it, after a lifetime spent in India?

Nevertheless, Alex had to own that he had developed a healthy dislike for this North African land; the shifting sand that made the landmarks described to him so difficult to locate; the incredible sense of isolation; the stale water and the objectionable diet which had wreaked such havoc on his bowels ever since leaving Algiers.

Should London Kirkland not be here, Alex had already decided, he'd give up this madcap adventure, return the fifty pounds Baron Ladbroke had given him by way of an advance, and consider himself heartily glad to be done with the whole, objectionable thing.

At that moment his mare pricked her ears and, without warning, lengthened her stride along the uneven trail. Shaken out of his lethargy, Alex lifted his head and felt an absurd twinge of relief at seeing the distant glow of campfires ahead. They were larger and clustered closer together than those of herdsmen, telling him that he must have reached the Tuareg settlement at last.

The compound lay on a barren hilltop along a sandy wash filled with the tracks of countless goats and bordered by a stand of acacia trees. A number of veiled men and wide-eyed, whispering women emerged from their leather tents to stare at him as his horse plodded up the last, rocky slope. Lifting his hand, Alex called out the traditional Arab greeting even though he had been warned that most Tuareg tribesmen spoke nothing but Tamahaq, their own, incomprehensible language.

Nevertheless the response was instant and encouraging, for in the desert, where there are no inns, a stranger is never turned away when seeking shelter for the night: "Welcome, and may your coming be well-omened!"

His horse was led away and a small boy hurried forward

with a bulging goatskin flask. Lifting it to his lips, Alex drank
and drank. The water was cold and unbelievably sweet.

Suitably refreshed, he made it known that he wished to be
taken to one Ali Wad Zarim and was immediately led to a
tent on the outskirts of the *zariba*. Here, a tall, bony man in
a dark blue veil that covered his entire face but for the eyes,
emerged from between the cloth drapes to meet him. Extending his hand, Alex repeated the traditional greeting. He
was much relieved when Ali Wad Zarim shook hands warmly
and then addressed him at length, not in Tamahaq, but in the
proper Arabic of the Koran, without the vernacular that Alex
had found so difficult to understand while conversing with
Umbilli and the Muslim-born Algerians.

Nevertheless, he knew better than to state his business
immediately. Hospitality had to be established, for generosity
was the foremost hallmark of a desert nobleman. A weary
stranger must first be offered drink, food, and rest. Traditionally, a camel should have been slaughtered and a great feast,
lasting three days or more, planned and executed before Alex
would be permitted to state his purpose. But because he
was a foreigner, and because there seemed about his thin,
unshaven face a sense of urgency, Ali Wad Zarim merely
uttered a few curt words to the women gathered in the shadows behind him, sending them hurrying away.

"Come," he said. "We will talk after tea."

Alex was led into the tent and given a seat on one of the
sumptuous, hand-stitched rugs spread over the hard-packed
ground. Behind him stood a grouping of low beds made of
tamarisk wood decorated with fancy leathercraft in which,
presumably, the nobleman slept with his principal wife and
unmarried daughters. A circle of glowing embers burned near
Alex's feet, and these were stirred to fresh life by a dark-
skinned youth who added more of the precious wood before
scurrying away.

While Ali Wad Zarim himself boiled the tea, a woman in
deep blue cotton robes moved silently between them laying
out trays of boiled dates, bread, and spoons for the communal
pot of *tikhammazin*, which Alex discovered was pellets of
wheat flour boiled in goat butter. The woman did not cover

her face as did the Arab females of the north or those who had watched Alex with shy, dark eyes from the doorways of the huts of Hassi Ban Anit. Apparently only Tuareg men veiled themselves before strangers, a habit that was strictly observed, for even while they ate and talked quite amicably together, Ali Wad Zarim did not remove the vast length of his *tagilmust*, his heavy headcloth, but discreetly lifted his spoon and water cup to his lips beneath it.

Once Alex's initial hunger had been sated and a pot of cardamom tea had been set before him, he listened as the nobleman talked of the Tuareg way of life and his growing concern that it was dying. Ali Wad Zarim's greatest fear was the conquests of the French, who were pushing their way ever southward into the desert and taking away the tribesmen's swords and spears as they came. Soon, said Ali Wad Zarim, they would doubtless replace the Tuareg camels with the strange moving machines—Alex realized he meant railway cars—that he himself had seen in the shipyards of Algiers.

The Tuareg could not, he passionately maintained, sacrifice their flocks or their freedom, for without them they were nothing. It saddened him to know that, while his people had managed to resist French invasion for many years, the swords and spears of the Tuareg were losing out at last to European firearms. And yet, surprisingly enough, he bore the white men no malice.

"We have always accepted the decisions of Allah with grace," was all he had to say on that score. "I can only offer prayers that He will not forsake us."

"God is generous," Alex agreed.

"Ameen," Ali Wad Zarim responded solemnly, but Alex thought that beneath the heavy veil he was smiling his approval.

In the next moment, however, the bronze-colored eyes narrowed beneath the twisted headcloth, and Ali Wad Zarim set aside his teacup with a decisive rattle. "Now you must tell me what brings you here, a foreigner who insists on traveling the desert alone."

Alex told him, wasting no words, and the nobleman listened, nodding his head from time to time or holding up a bony forefinger in order to end the flow of talk and so ask a polite question. And afterward there was silence while the wind stirred the sand outside the tent and the many noises of the night came to them: the grunting and gurgling of the hobbled camels, the bleating of a goat, the murmur of voices elsewhere in the encampment, the sudden, shrill wailing of an infant from a distant tent.

"You have been told the truth," said the sheikh at last. "The girl lives here, by Allah's blessing. But she is not at present among us."

Alex's brows drew together. "I do not understand."

Ali Wad Zarim smiled faintly. "Do not be concerned. She is away for a short time only. Once, the Tuareg made their living plundering the caravans of other tribes, but the Frenchmen and their laws, and especially their firearms, have made it difficult for anyone to be a successful bandit nowadays. As Allah is my witness, I am certain that one day our plundering will be outlawed altogether. That is why many of us have taken to transporting salt for our livelihood."

"Salt?"

Ali Wad Zarim nodded impassively. "My nephews travel the distant route to Agadès and back, my sons to the salt mines in Bilfha. It is four hundred miles, a very long journey."

"And London—the girl?" Alex amended, knowing the name must sound foreign to the sheikh as it rolled off his tongue.

"She has gone with the caravan to Bilfha. I have permitted it on occasion because—*ya yimma!*" He spread his hands, and once again Alex had the impression that the bronze-colored eyes were smiling. "She is unlike any daughter of my own loins. There is a certain . . . restlessness about her at times, and I find it wisest then to send her away. If she were married—but no, I do not wish that because of her blood. That is why I have set the bridal portion so high for her. While she is genuinely dear to my heart, I thank Allah that my own sons and nephews are promised to their cousins. In this way, too, the Tuareg will remain pure and may yet not die."

"I understand." Alex was silent for a moment. "But you say she has gone to Bilfha."

The sheikh nodded.

"When is the caravan expected back?"

"As God wills. They left six days ago."

There was a moment of stunned silence, then Alex surprised Ali Wad Zarim by throwing back his head and giving vent to a great roar of laughter. *Good bloody Christ!* was all he could think. Another two months—perhaps three, if he failed to catch up with them right away—that he must remain in this godforsaken land? He should have known! Why in God's name hadn't he demanded a thousand pounds, or two thousand, from that crafty old bastard rather than a mere one hundred?

Chapter Five

Despite the haste with which he set off in pursuit of the Bilfha caravan, Alex was not prepared for the swiftness with which he actually found it. In centuries past, the salt caravan camels had numbered among the thousands, mainly for the sake of safety, but, as Ali Wad Zarim had explained, they were now divided into groups according to speed. Those journeying to Bilfha, in fact, were considered the fastest inasmuch as they were able to travel well into the night thanks to Zarim's oldest son's ability to navigate not only by the sun, but by the stars and moon.

Nevertheless, a caravan heavily laden with supplies could not possibly travel as fast as a lone, and quite determined, British horseman. Originally Alex had refused Ali Wad

Zarim's offer of a guide. He was accustomed to traveling alone, and with the niggling reminder that his leave was fast running out, he did not wish to waste further time waiting while a suitable guide was selected and made ready for departure.

In the end, however, he had agreed to take along two youths chosen by the sheikh, one of them old enough to have already adopted a man's complicated *tagilmust,* the other still wearing the simple *chechia* headdress of a fifteen-year-old boy. But both wore the indigo robes of their tribe, which had long ago dyed their skin the unearthly shade of blue that had earned the Tuareg the sacred name of Blue Men. Neither of the pair spoke a word of Arabic, but it didn't really matter to Alex, as he was in no mood for conversation. With the Tuareg boys astride a pair of off-white bull camels, the saddles placed before the withers in Tuareg fashion, and Alex riding his hard-mouthed bay mare, the three of them set off across the plains before the sun was so much as a faint streak of red on the distant horizon.

Recalling every unpleasant detail of his journey from Hassi Ban Anit, Alex expected the trek to be difficult, and it was. But early on the evening of the sixth day, when they had ridden less than ten hours across a vast, rust-colored plain broken here and there by silvery tufts of reeds, they came across the sudden green of an oasis on the far side of a wadi. Here there were figs, tamarinds, and oleanders, and everywhere the shaggy, bleating presence of goats. A trio of Arab herdsmen was preparing a meal over a cooking fire beneath the shade of a feathery palm, and on the far side of the oasis a great herd of camels was being couched for the night by another, larger group of shouting, scurrying men.

Wiping the grit from his eyes, Alex questioned Abboud with a glance, and received an answering nod in return. And so, with the whooping boys galloping their camels before him, Alex guided his mare into camp.

"Peace be upon you, and may your coming be well-omened."

Alex could see at once that the tall young man in the indigo blue *gondurah,* the long cotton robe of the desert, who strode forward to greet him, was the son of Ali Wad Zarim. Not only was the resemblance between them quite striking (from what little Alex could see of the proud features hidden beneath the folds of the robe which the young man had, as custom dictated, pulled over his head in the presence of a stranger), but his height and bearing proclaimed that Sadu, like his father, was an *imaheren*, a prince of the desert.

"Peace be unto you," Alex responded, dismounting and bending to slap the dust from his clothes.

"From which tribe are you?" Sadu inquired.

Alex subdued a grin. Thanks to the miles of thorn scrub through which he had ridden from Hassi Ban Anit, his breeches had been in tatters when he had finally arrived at the Tuareg encampment. Ali Wad Zarim had graciously loaned him one of his own blue-dyed robes, and a headcloth and cowl to protect him from the glaring sun, and Alex had not removed them since departing the hilltop *zariba* six long days ago. It amused him now to think that he had been mistaken for a fellow Arab.

"I am *Ingleezi*," he replied honestly.

"Ah," said Sadu, as if that explained everything.

Naturally the news that a European had arrived in their midst traveled swiftly throughout camp despite the fact that every herdsman and slave was busy unloading camels or hurrying about with saddlebags and goatskins or building fires while shouting and swearing to the accompanying snarls and stamping of their weary beasts. An Englishman, sent to them by Ali Wad Zarim himself, could mean only one thing, and Abboud and Habjur were delighted to repeat the tale of his arrival at the *zariba* and his inquiries into the whereabouts of the chieftain's foster daughter to anyone who would listen, for rarely had the youths found themselves the object of so much attention.

But while they embellished their story more and more colorfully for the sake of every newcomer, Alex remained politely reticent with Sadu, his host. Time must be set aside first to observe the customary greetings, to slake his thirst at the well, and then to settle himself on a palm mat and drink the three customary cups of sweetened tea offered to him and to each of the veiled, blue-tinged men who gathered to receive him. If London Kirkland was somewhere in the camp, Alex suspected that she would come to hear of his presence soon enough.

But despite Sadu's gracious welcome and the soothing effect that both the tea and the camp gossip had upon him, Alex's nerves remained taut. Perhaps that was why he heard the faint drumming of hooves on sand several seconds before the others did. Leaning back discreetly, he turned his head in the direction of the wadi. By now a velvety darkness had fallen, and only the campfire and the faint glitter of stars illuminated the veiled faces of the men who squatted around him. But Alex, whose eyesight was keen, had no trouble spotting the lone figure approaching at a gallop from the direction of the plains, long robes streaming like a banner in the wind.

The camel, a huge, fawn-colored bull, was brought to a dust-raising halt just beyond the circle of light made by the fire. Even before it began to kneel, its rider had leaped to the ground and strode toward the gathered men with the same graceful movements characteristic of an *imaheren*. But Alex saw at once that this was a woman. Her face was veiled and she wore the long, indigo-dyed robes of the Tuareg, although hers was belted in female fashion with a sash of bright embroidery about the waist. Her bare feet and ankles were very slim and browned, and when she paused before the mats upon which Alex and Sadu sat, she spread her feet boldly and threw back her veil, fixing them both with an arrogant stare.

Alex MacLaughlin peered unbelieving at this bronzed young Amazon. London Kirkland's face was striking in its fine-boned beauty. Wide at the forehead and pointed at the chin, it boasted a pair of lovely, tilted eyes as deeply blue as the robes she wore, and a long, straight nose that bore an uncanny resemblance to a certain proud old buzzard Alex had recently met in England. Nevertheless, he thought she was the most stunning woman he had ever seen.

"Dear God," he said softly in English, "you're not at all what I expected."

"And what did you expect, *Ingleez*?" London Kirkland

countered. Her voice was low and husky, her English words bearing only the faintest trace of an Eastern accent.

Alex didn't know. He could sense the interested eyes of the others upon him. "I'm not really sure," he admitted inadequately.

London Kirkland laughed, a sweet sound filled with the magic of youth, and Alex had the sudden, inexplicable suspicion that she laughed that way quite often. The thought did not sit well with him at all. Even the most unimaginative of minds would have been able to draw the conclusion that she was happy here and that she had been accepted without question by the Tuareg tribe.

Alex thought again of the ring in his pocket. There was still time to throw it far across the wadi, where no one would ever find it, and notify Lord Ladbroke from Algiers that he had been unsuccessful in his efforts to find the girl. Suddenly the extra fifty pounds promised him was inconsequential when compared with the freedom and happiness he would take from this woman.

It was a tempting solution but for the nagging reminder that he had given the baron his word and that he was not one to accept his responsibilities lightly. There was also Ali Wad Zarim's dry remark about the purity of Tuareg blood to consider. Alex frowned, realizing that the situation was not as simple as he had supposed. There could be no future for London Kirkland here among the Tuareg, and yet her future with her English relatives seemed equally unfortunate.

"Have you come to take me back, *Ingleez*?"

The question caught Alex unawares. He had some considerable experience with women, but had never encountered one quite so direct. In India, ladies of the British Raj did not address unmarried men unless they were properly chaperoned, their faces hidden discreetly behind fluttering fans, and even then their conversation was limited to nothing more than the exchange of a few coy innuendos.

"Couch your camel." The sudden command came from Sadu, who could not possibly have understood their exchange but had nevertheless felt compelled to interrupt it.

Alex looked at him with new interest. So Ali Wad Zarim's

handsome son was not entirely impervious to this English girl! Was this the reason his father had set her bride price so unrealistically high?

London turned away from Sadu with a toss of her head. Deference to males of the household was clearly not a Tuareg trait. "Will you come with me, *Ingleez*? I think you have many questions to ask. And there is much I, too, would like to know."

Alex rose from his mat, half expecting a violent protest from Sadu. But the men of the circle continued to sip their tea as though nothing was untoward, and Sadu himself ignored them.

Eastern nights are never entirely dark, and a faint violet light hung over the vast land, turning to deepest scarlet the pool of glowing embers behind them. With a jerk on the lead rope and a clipped command, London brought the camel to its feet, and Alex walked beside her as she led it away down the dune. The camel was clearly impatient to graze, and a Negro boy appeared out of the darkness carrying a piece of twisted hemp with which to bind the animal's legs. Together he and London worked quickly to hobble the beast, while it snarled irritably and lashed out with its hooves.

Finally London slapped it sharply on the rump. "Be still, you son of the uncircumsized!"

Grinning, the boy joined in by jumping up to punch the camel's rubbery nose. Enraged, the beast gave a great roar before gurgling up a stream of noisome green cud which it spat at them with astonishing accuracy. Both London and the boy managed to leap aside just in time, while Alex, watching from a safe distance, burst into laughter.

Disheveled and laughing a little herself, London crossed to him while the hobbled camel was led away. "Let us hope the same never happens to you, *Ingleez*! We have no water for washing here."

"My name is MacLaughlin," Alex told her helpfully. "Captain Alexander MacLaughlin of the Forty-first Bengal Lancers. And I think I can move quickly enough if the situation warrants."

London's blue eyes widened at his words, and her slim

hand flew to her throat. "The Bengal Lancers? Then you—you haven't come from England! You are a *sahib*, like my father, not—"

"You misunderstand me," Alex interrupted quickly, annoyed by the sudden blaze of hope in that unguarded face. "I haven't come to take you back to India. Your grandfather in Kent sent me to find you."

London turned swiftly to adjust her headcloth, which her struggles with the camel had knocked askew. If Alex hadn't known better he would have sworn she was trying to compose herself. For some reason the thought made him angry, and for the first time in his adult life he found himself speaking without thinking first. His emotions dictated his words.

"Listen, you don't have to come back with me if you don't want to. How old are you now? Seventeen? Not exactly your own mistress under English law, but certainly of an age to know your own mind. I've brought along a betrothal ring from your grandfather's nephew, but you're under no obligation to accept it."

London turned slowly to look at him, and Alex was aware of a sudden queer blow to his heart. In that moment he wanted to touch the lovely face framed by that unmistakably Arabic headcloth.

"Now you, I think, misunderstand me," London said quietly. "If I must leave here, then I would greatly prefer returning to India to live. But it seems I have no choice."

"Even if I were to tell you—"

She shook her head to interrupt him. "There is nothing you could say that would make me disobey my grandfather's summons. The Tuareg may not be devoted followers of Islam, Captain MacLaughlin, but my foster father, Ali Wad Zarim, made certain that I was given the chance to read and study the Koran. And one of the things it teaches us is the Islamic virtue of *sabr*, the capacity for endurance and acceptance. You've traveled a long way to find me. If you have a betrothal ring with you, then I will accept it. Without protest."

"*In'shallah* you mean?" Alex asked, annoyed.

"Yes, as God wills."

"Even though you are happy here?"

"Surely there is happiness to be found elsewhere in the world? With a husband who, I think, seems disposed to treat me kindly?"

"I cannot guarantee that." Alex was thinking as he spoke of the baron's obsessive desire to see his granddaughter produce a new heir.

London's voice held a faint trace of scorn. "Surely you know that few things in life are guaranteed, Captain?"

"But you've no idea what Rupert Ashford is like!" Alex persisted rather violently.

She seemed genuinely surprised. "Does it matter?"

Alex's mouth thinned as he grappled with his mounting frustration. He had forgotten that nearly all Tuareg girls were promised to their first cousins at birth. In view of this, the idea of an arranged marriage would not seem strange to London Kirkland.

"I will accept the ring and return with you willingly," London repeated as the silence between them lengthened, addressing Alex's broad back. "I've always been aware that I'd have to leave the desert someday." Her lips curved unexpectedly. "I just didn't think it would take eight years."

Alex looked around at her with some astonishment. "Then why didn't you try returning to civilization on your own?"

She shrugged her slim shoulders. "What for? As you said, I've been happy here. As I was in India. But the Koran also tells us that it is blasphemous to attempt defying one's destiny. That's why I feel I must come with you, now that you've found me."

Alex opened his mouth to speak, but she laid her hand on his arm. "Please," she said urgently, "it's kind of you to warn me, but I'm already well aware of the sort of man my grandfather is. I haven't forgotten how he treated my mother so many years ago, and that he never made any attempt to contact my father after her death. But he is still family, all that I have left. And surely this Rupert Ashford cannot be so very bad. He agreed to marry me, didn't he? Considering my unconventional upbringing and the fact that, for all he knows, I could very well be a broken-toothed old she-ghoul?"

Alex held up his hand in the gesture of a swordsman acknowledging defeat. "How soon can you leave?"

"Oh!" She opened her eyes wide and laughed at him. "I can't possibly abandon the caravan until we return from Bilfha! Every one of us is needed here, including me—however strange that may seem to you." Something in his face compelled her to add merrily: "And I daresay Sadu will find something useful for you to do too."

"Good God, you can't mean—"

She took his arm and drew him away. Her touch was gentle, and at once Alex felt drawn into her world. "Come, Captain MacLaughlin. Darkness is the best time for fiction, and they will have begun telling tales by the fire. I will translate them for you so that you may enjoy them as well. *Kan ma kan*—'There was, there was not'—is how they all begin."

Only with difficulty did Alex manage to keep his mixed emotions in check. But as he walked with her back toward the fire he couldn't help thinking, certainly not for the first time, that bringing Lord Ladbroke's orphaned granddaughter home from Africa was certainly not proving to be a harmless sinecure.

Chapter Six

London came awake with a start. For a long moment she lay staring at the familiar ceiling of her bedroom at Rose Cottage without knowing where she was. The long-forgotten heat and the smell of dust and camel dung seemed more real to her at the moment than the softness of the feathery bed

upon which she lay and the fragrance of the scilla blossoms
on the table beside her. The room was very dark. Outside in
the cold night a pheasant screamed.

Sitting up, London swung her bare legs over the side of
the bed and shook off the last vestiges of her dream. She
could hear her granddaughter Sara moving about in the room
next door preparing for bed and realized that it must have
been the girl's return from her walk that had awakened her.

London smiled a little to herself, feeling nothing but gratitude toward Sara, whose presence in the house seemed to
have unleashed this long-forgotten flood of memories. How
well she could remember the confusion she had felt as a young
girl sitting in the darkness outside her tent long after the fires
had died and the men had gone to sleep! In those days, she
had known nothing about England save what she had read in
the books her mother had left behind in the bungalow in
Lucknow when she died. Books with mysterious titles like
Middlemarch, *Jane Eyre*, and *Vanity Fair*, which London,
ten years old at the time, had struggled to read despite the
fact that the style had seemed so very ponderous; the words,
the people, and the passions that stirred them much too alien
for her to understand.

A long-forgotten Arabic saying sprang suddenly to London's mind: "We live in ignorance and Allah is the all knowing."

She smiled at the thought, thinking how apt it was, and
became aware that the sky beyond her window was no longer
black, but ablaze with countless stars. The moon had set and
the night had grown very still. Even the night birds no longer
shrilled, and from Sara's room there was nothing but silence.

How still it had been, too, on that long-ago night when
Alex MacLaughlin had first appeared in her life! As still as
now, although London could clearly remember sitting in the
cold desert sand listening to the faint snores coming from the
distant tent of old, fat Wad In Tom, Sadu's personal vassal,
who never left his master's side.

It had been Sadu, London recalled, whose unmistakable
interest in her had made her realize, even before Captain
MacLaughlin's appearance, that the time had come for her to

leave Algeria. For Wad In Tom had confided in her that Sadu was secretly trying to amass the large herd of camels and cattle required to pay the bridal portion that Ali Wad Zarim had set for her.

By leaving Algeria at once, London had made certain that neither she nor Sadu had brought shame to the house of Ali Wad Zarim or insulted the untarnished name of Khadija Sata, the beautiful cousin on Sadu's mother's side whom Sadu was expected to marry. Regrettably, the leaving had not been easy, despite the haste in which London had accomplished it. First off, there had been the unfinished business of the journey to Bilfha. And then there had been Alex. Even now she could vividly recall their first days together.

Dawn had broken in a hot, translucent light on Alex MacLaughlin's first morning with the caravan. The camp had come alive with the protests of camels being loaded with baggage and the shouts of the small boys running here and there with saddlebags and goatskins. London remembered lighting the cooking fires and relishing the noise and confusion that erupted following the great silence of the night before.

She remembered Alex standing with his arms folded across his chest surveying the bustling scene below. Abboud had hurried toward him with a small cooking pot, and Alex had accepted it gratefully—until he happened to glance down and saw that it contained a grayish gruel made of pounded millet and greasy lumps of goat meat. Shuddering, he had set it aside.

London had walked toward him, her long robes rustling. "Shame on you, Captain MacLaughlin!" She wagged a slim finger in his face. "The first lesson the fasting of Ramadan teaches those of us who are fortunate is that to a hungry man, yesterday's bread crusts can taste like cake."

Alex scowled. "I thought the Tuareg were not devout Muslims?"

"No, but all who travel the desert soon learn the wisdom of Islamic teaching."

She watched as he grudgingly tasted a spoonful of gruel, then hid her smile at the expression on his face. She couldn't help thinking how different he was from the officers of her late father's regiment. Although time had dimmed most of her memories of India, she could still remember the jovial, bewhiskered 'career soldiers' who had lifted her high onto their shoulders and pranced about her father's study in the Lucknow residency neighing like horses and making her squeal with laughter.

She was old enough at seventeen to understand that most of them had cared little for India and the dark-skinned millions who inhabited it, and that they had drunk too much and talked far too loudly because of it. But Alex MacLaughlin did not really resemble those red-faced, overindulgent, talkative men. Like the Bedouin, he was sun-bronzed and lean, with a physique hardened from a lifetime spent outdoors.

This gave London an odd sense of comfort. Surely her grandfather couldn't be so very awful if he had been wise enough to choose the likes of Captain MacLaughlin to escort her home?

In the next moment London had great cause to doubt her grandfather's wisdom as Alex, taking a deep draft from his water flask to wash down the mouthful of gruel, gagged unexpectedly and spat violently into the sand.

"Good God!"

Lips compressed, London peered over his shoulder as he poured more of the water into his palm. Nothing emerged but a greenish sludge in which a few suspicious-looking black hairs floated peacefully.

London couldn't help it. She burst into laughter. "It seems the goatskin you purchased in Hassi Ban Anit all too recently covered a goat, Captain!"

Alex's lips twitched. "I suppose this is what happens to uninitiated *roumi*, eh?"

"Never mind. We've plenty of others, and the wadi is rich with water. And I wouldn't worry so much about being a foreigner. Sadu has charged me with looking after you, so you can't possibly run into further trouble."

"Oh, he has, has he?"

London tried to look grave. "Yes. Have you ever ridden a camel?"

Alex's brows twitched into a sudden frown. "Elephants and bullocks, yes. But never a camel. Don't forget I have a mare—"

"Who will die if she is forced to carry you the entire distance to Bilfha. That is why Sadu has loaned you one of his riding camels."

"Kind of him," Alex murmured.

"Come," said London, taking his arm.

He followed unwillingly, feeling certain that Sadu would not waste the opportunity of making him look foolish. His suspicions were confirmed when he found a tall youth awaiting him at the bottom of the ridge with none other than the balking bull camel London had addressed yesterday as the misbegotten "son of the uncircumsized."

"We must hurry," London said, looking around her and seeing that most of the baggage animals were already loaded.

Alex's lips thinned. "Very well, if we must." He was not surprised to see that a number of tribesmen had gathered around to watch the *Ingleezi's* first attempt at saddling a camel. What was further obvious to him—and to everyone else—was that the enormous beast simply did not wish to be saddled. Alex held tightly to the chin rope while the youth shouted "Deh! Deh!" and attempted to sling the heavy leather saddle onto the creature's back. At once the camel gave a blood-curdling roar and spat up a thick stream of disgusting green cud. Alex held on grimly even though some of the foul-smelling stuff had splattered his robes.

The watching men began to shout advice, and amid the confusion Alex caught a glimpse of London's smiling face. Gritting his teeth, he turned back to the task with a ruthlessness heretofore unknown to him. Fortunately the saddle was soon slipped into place and the wide girth tightened about the camel's middle. Forcing the animal to kneel, Alex stepped onto the curve of its neck as he had seen the Tuareg do, and pulled himself up into the oddly shaped saddle. Wiping the sweat from his brow he glanced down at the watching men and saw in their expressions a dawning respect. But it was a hollow victory, for London had disappeared, and Alex himself was faced not only with the stench of camel sick rising from his robes but the prospect of a long day's march ahead of him before he could wash and change.

The moment the caravan set off, however, Alex found the awful smell instantly relegated to the least of his worries. It was a torment merely to breathe the smothering dust kicked up by the lead camels while at the same time attempting to protect his uninitiated derriere from his mount's bruising gait. The sand beneath him was blinding, the dunes seeming to shift and give way beneath every step, while the hot horizon shimmered like water in the distance, hurting his eyes. There was no sound save the relentless cadence of plodding feet and the occasional cry of the rust-red birds that stared from amid the boulders, their beaks agape.

"Be grateful you have the opportunity to ride, Captain," London said, drawing alongside some time later and noticing the harsh lines that scored Alex's face. "When we return from the mines loaded with salt we must walk."

Alex did not reply to this immediately. Like the Tuareg, he had drawn a veil over his mouth and nose to protect him from the stifling dust. But above it his eyes had narrowed. "Can you tell me one thing, Miss Kirkland? How in the name of God did you ever end up here?"

"Are you making fun of me, Captain? Or do you truly wish to know?"

"I confess to a certain measure of curiosity. This isn't exactly the sort of life which a child raised in the peaceful environs of an Indian cantonment could possibly thrive on. And how the devil did you reach this place to begin with? We're hundreds of miles from Algiers."

London's brow furrowed. "I'm afraid I can't remember. It happened so long ago."

It seemed that she could recall little more than the unbearable heat and the stench of coal smoke aboard the French steamer that had brought her to Algiers, and how the noise of the engines had prevented her from sleeping on the night of their arrival. In addition, she had come down with some sort of fever, and although the doctor who examined her had diagnosed nothing more than a harmless childhood ailment, Madame Tavernier had kindly arranged for London to spend the night with French acquaintances in the relative cool of the city. Only much later had she learned of their deaths.

"There was great confusion in the city at the time," she told Alex now. "Word had reached Algiers that the French and Prussians had declared war in Europe, and that the British were planning an invasion of the Sudan. There was great concern that the war would spill over into the rest of northern Africa. I was staying in the home of a French cleric at the time, and he was the one who sent me inland, fearing for my safety if an invasion should come. Fortunately, he happened to know of a missionary departing for the south, and as there were already a number of refugees in his party, no one thought it odd that I came along."

Not far from Wa' Ulima, however, the party had encountered a caravan of nomadic Kababish who had unknowingly been carrying the cholera with them. Father Brant had been the first to die, and the other Europeans had swiftly followed suit. Only London had been spared, and she was given shelter by a family of devout Muslims who had considered her survival an act of Providence. But they were Fellahin, poverty-stricken tillers of the land who could ill afford another mouth to feed, and when another caravan had passed through the area several months later, arrangements had been made for London to accompany them.

"Their leader happened to be Ali Wad Zarim's uncle," London concluded, "and since he had several daughters my own age, I ended up staying with him. When all of them were married off, I went to live with Ali Wad Zarim."

"Why didn't you stay with the uncle?"

"Because of Bikkela, his wife. From the moment of my arrival she was convinced I was a she-ghoul in disguise and that I had cast a spell on the men of her family."

Alex expected London to laugh, but she regarded him seriously with her great blue eyes. "Don't look so skeptical, Captain MacLaughlin. The Tuareg and the Arabs all believe in the existence of genies and ghouls. In the Tamahaq language they're known as *kel asuf*, and Bikkela wore two amulets, not one, to protect her from their—from my—magic."

"Hmm," said Alex. He knew that India, too, was steeped

in centuries-old beliefs concerning the existence of vengeful gods and goddesses. "Do you believe in them, Miss Kirkland?"

"No."

An appreciative smile lit his eyes. "Well, I must say I'm reassured." Alex understood that the girl's assimilation into English was going to prove difficult enough without the staid Victorian Warings discovering that she believed in evil spirits. He wondered suddenly if she could write and read, and, asking her as much, was rewarded with her clear, delightful laughter.

"In four languages, sir! English, Arabic, Tamahaq, and Hindustani."

"Hindustani?" Alex was skeptical. "After all these years?"

"Dost thou think I would forget the mother tongue of my ayah's people?" London inquired archly, switching in an instant to the familiar, liquid language of Hindustan. "I brought with me a number of books when I left Lucknow, and spent many hours committing them to memory so that I would never forget." She sobered instantly seeing the look on Alex's face. "What is it? Have I offended in some way?"

"No." Alex's tone was curt. He did not wish her to know that he was beginning to consider her a thousand times too good for the likes of Rupert Ashford, and that he was growing increasingly disgusted with the selfish miscreant who was her grandfather and who wanted her back only so that she could produce the sons that would keep his name alive.

Furthermore, and more disturbing to Alex's mind, was the thought of London struggling to adhere to the strict tenets of the insufferably prudish society governed by the frumpy, widowed queen who had ruled Great Britain for the last forty years. Surely the closed world of England's landed gentry would seem nothing short of horrific to her after the freedom of the desert?

But how to make as much clear to her? The first time Alex had tried, London had politely but firmly dismissed his warnings, and he could no more argue against her belief in the wisdom of *sabr* than he could make her understand the

vast difference between the free-living Tuaregs and the obses-
sively moral citizens of the gloomy island country she had
never seen.

He wanted to protect her from it all. He felt he understood
her far better than any other Englishman would.

Bloody hell! Alex thought. *What does it matter?* If he
valued his sanity, he'd do his best to put this entire, distasteful
episode out of his mind as soon as possible. But he knew that
he couldn't. London Kirkland had endeared herself to him
with her quick wit and innocent charm. Slowly, she had
captured his heart and he was determined to help her as best
he could. He had no other choice.

It was twilight when the caravan reached Bilfha at last, and
camp was made with the camels couched for the night in salt-
silvered sand that shimmered in the moonlight. Despite the
weariness of the travelers their mood was light, for the caravan oasis was rich with vegetation—and water. Not water
lying fallow in muddy wells, but flowing deliciously clean
through narrow canals and plunging into a gorge of deep
puddles and pools. The air was wonderfully cool beneath the
feathery palms that grew thickly around the deep wadi before
unfurling into the vastness of the vanishing sand.

The caravan was met by a delegation of Kanuri, the Negro
workers of the mines, who greeted the weary travelers with
overflowing goatskins and bowls of cheese by way of welcome. Tents were pitched for the first time in many nights,
and Alex, ignoring the gaunt salukis growling at his heels,
threw himself down on his bedroll, feeling truly sated after
the luxury of a good wash, all the water he could drink, and
the treat of freshly cooked camel meat that had been provided
by the Kanuri.

But morning brought the blasting heat of the rising sun and
the grinding toil of mining the salt. Pits were dug and filled
with water to loosen the salt, and then the moist mass was
poured into wooden molds to dry. As soon as they hardened,
the mushroom-shaped blocks—each of them weighing forty
pounds or more—were removed from their frames and carefully wrapped in layers of protective straw.

When enough blocks had been gathered, Sadu ordered the

camels loaded and roped together. Even the strongest among them staggered a little beneath the weight of the half-dozen blocks they were expected to carry. The handlers were warned not to halt for even a moment, thus giving the exhausted beasts the chance to kneel and pitch their loads over their heads.

It was not a pleasant way to travel. The Tuaregs walked to spare their camels and ate all of their meals on the move. No longer was the caravan indulged with meat braised on open fires or fresh dates gathered near the wadi. Now there was only the passing of a communal pot filled with an unfailingly tasteless gruel of water, millet, and goat cheese.

But for the keening wind the silence was unnerving. No one laughed or sang or even bothered to speak, and if one of the camels decided to show its displeasure by spitting its cud at its handler, no one paid the least attention. Nor did anyone laugh when Alex, lagging a little behind his own camel, was painfully bitten on the buttocks by the bull behind him, although normally the Tuareg derived great enjoyment from the inexperience of their *Ingleez* companion.

Darkness fell, but Sadu seemed in no hurry to call a halt. Only when the younger boys began to stumble in their weariness did he even allow the cameleers to ride. No command was given. Instead, Sadu merely grasped the lead camel by the hide and ear and sprang lightly onto its back. Instantly and just as silently the others followed suit, nothing in their impassive faces betraying their relief.

The camels managed to carry them for another hour or more before approaching that life-threatening point of irreversible fatigue. Again, Sadu seemed to know just when that moment had arrived, and quickly gave the command to halt. No tea was brewed that night. Instead, the camels were hobbled, and beds were scooped out of the sand, in which the weary caravanners collapsed and slept like the dead. On that first day they had traveled more than thirty miles from the salt mines of Bilfha.

Chapter
Seven

Five endlessly hot and difficult days later the caravan reached the Faraji oasis. Darkness had already fallen and the twinkling fires of a nomad camp welcomed them as they descended the last long slope toward the palm trees, which stood swaying in the light desert wind. Numerous tents had been erected on both sides of the cool wadi, the distinctive structures of sticks and goatskins known as *beit shaar*— houses of hair—easily identifying the nomads as a peaceful tribe of Berbers.

Poor as these herdsmen might be, however, their generosity toward the newcomers was legion. Even before the Tuareg camels stumbled wearily into camp, pots of heavily sugared tea were being brewed and a freshly slaughtered cow had been lifted onto the spit, filling the night air with the delicious smell of roasting meat. Despite the fact that his stomach was growling with hunger, Alex took his time stripping off his dusty robes and joining the other men in the wadi. He could scarcely subdue a groan of pleasure as he slid into the cool, clean water.

Later, dressed in fresh robes, his dark hair drying crisply about his head, he walked down to the fire to accept his portion of meat. Tearing into it with bare hands and teeth, he paid little attention to the others. Only when his hunger was sated did he look about the assembled faces for London.

The last five days had been unspeakably difficult, and he had not exchanged a single word with her out on the trail. Only on a few occasions had he even managed to catch a glimpse of her as she brought up the rear of the caravan,

leading an off-white camel by the chin rope, her face heavily
veiled against the stinging sand. Once or twice she had caught
his eye and waved to him, seemingly unaffected by the killing
pace, and Alex had been further impressed with this remarkable young woman.

He spotted London on the far side of the fire, surrounded
by the bleating goats of the Berbers and the dun-colored
donkeys that roamed freely through the camp. Alex frowned,
seeing that she was deep in conversation with Sadu, who
stood leaning against the trunk of a palm with his arms crossed
before him. Even from this distance and despite his concealing veil, Alex could clearly see the impatience on the nobleman's face.

London herself seemed equally irritated. Alex watched as
she lectured Sadu at length and then, with a toss of her golden
head that needed no interpretation, turned and stalked away.

Straightening, Sadu returned to the fire and reached for a
piece of meat. Squatting on his haunches, he took a bite and
then lifted his head. For a brief moment his dark eyes met
and held Alex's. There was no mistaking the hostility within
them. Apparently the argument had had something to do with
him, but surely Sadu must remember that London had a
bridegroom awaiting her in Kent!

A hand fell on his arm. Alex whipped about to find the
elderly tribesman Ali Abjur regarding him intently. "You
would do well to tread carefully, my son."

Alex stiffened. Had the old man also seen the glowering
look on Sadu's face? How many others had borne witness to
it? He swallowed a mouthful of grapes and forced himself to
speak lightly. "Careful of what, uncle?"

"If you eat too many of those, you will be running to the
wadi all night."

Alex threw back his head and laughed, his tension ebbing
instantly. "Wise advice indeed! I will be sure to heed it."

He did not glance again in Sadu's direction, and when the
meal was over made a point to withdraw without speaking to
anyone. Eventually the camp itself grew quiet as the others
sought their beds, but despite the welcome silence and his
own weariness, Alex found that sleep eluded him. Lying on

the soft bedding with his arms crossed beneath his head he stared at the tent hangings stirring in the breeze and thought about Sadu—and Rupert Ashford, the man Powney Waring had described as a dry-as-dust scholar interested only in inheriting Bellehurst's sizable library. Rupert did not sound at all like a suitable husband for London Kirkland.

"Alex?"

He sat up swiftly, without bothering to reach for his rifle, already knowing who it was crouching beyond the flaps of the tent. Swiftly he untied them and held them aside. "Did anyone see you?"

"No. I was very careful."

London pulled the heavy veil from her head and shook out her hair. The long yellow braid fell down the back of her robe nearly to her hips. Her teeth were chattering a little with the cold—or perhaps with fear—but when her gaze met Alex's she managed a shaky laugh. "You must think me impossibly forward, coming here so late at night."

Alex's expression softened. "Not at all. I take it you had something private to discuss with me? Something that could not be said under other eyes?"

The relief on her young face was so obvious that Alex was aware of an odd cramping in his heart. "Come," he said gruffly. "You'd better sit down."

London lowered herself onto the knotted carpet beside his bed and Alex, staring down at her bent head and tightly clasped hands, was aware again of that odd tug at his heart. He frowned and said abruptly, "I saw you arguing with Sadu near the fire tonight. I assumed—"

London's head came up. "There is nothing between Sadu and me," she said quickly. "While it is true that he has shown . . . interest in me of late, I am promised to another. Just as Sadu is expected to marry his cousin, Khadija Sata. He knows that as well as I do."

"But he certainly seems unwilling to accept it. What the devil did you say to him to make him look so murderous?"

London's chin lifted. "I merely informed him that you and I will be parting company with him when the caravan leaves Faraji the day after tomorrow."

"Oh? When was I consulted about this?"

London ignored his tone. She had already learned that Alex's dark coloring and craggy features could make him look terribly daunting whenever he frowned, but that he was not at heart an unkind man. Not by any means. "When the caravan leaves Faraji it will head south to Al Mardah," she explained. "There the salt will be bartered in the markets for millet, sugar, tea, and cloth. The men will attend songfests and—and take their leisure with the women of the village. They will not hurry in their celebrating, and it may be many days before they consider returning to our *zariba*. Forgive me, but you've seemed rather . . . impatient of late, and I thought perhaps you would prefer parting company with them here."

Alex's mouth twisted and he remained silent. There seemed nothing to say.

The cooing of a dove sounded from somewhere amid the thorn scrubs in the darkness beyond the tent. London's head came up at the lovely, liquid song. Her eyes shone. "Listen! Did you know that the Arabs believe a dove speaks when it coos?"

"What do they think it says?" Alex asked softly.

She smiled at him. "Surely you can hear it? *Uzkuru Rabbakum.* Remember your God."

Alex's mouth twitched, and London turned away abruptly, thinking he meant to laugh. "Do you know," he said unexpectedly, "I've finally come to understand why you're so reluctant to leave the desert."

London's lovely mouth trembled. How had he known? She had never revealed her pain in words to him, had tried hard to keep her own faith in the belief that fate had dealt her a kindly hand. This man, this Alex MacLaughlin, had traveled half the world to make certain her destiny was fulfilled by bringing her home to marry Rupert Ashford. Surely she could not refuse him now? And surely it was far better that she be removed forever from Sadu's jealous orbit?

But Alex was right: it was proving far harder than she had imagined to bid farewell to all she held dear. Unexpectedly, tears welled in her eyes, and she turned her back on him, ashamed.

"Oh, London—" Alex spoke half in anger, half in despair.

"Please," she said in a muffled whisper, "go away."

"I'd like to oblige you, but I'm afraid I can't. This is my tent."

A laugh broke from her that ended on a sob, and Alex reached out his hand to her. He meant for it to be nothing more than a gesture of reassurance, but the moment he touched her, everything changed between them. Startled, London turned and lifted her face to his, and Alex stared at her for a long moment without speaking. Seeing the tears that glistened on her long, spiky lashes in the dim starlight, and the trembling of her softly parted lips, his own mouth thinned in response and then, unexpectedly, he bent his head and kissed her. Tasting the salt of her tears he drew her into his arms. She stiffened, but only for a moment. Then her body seemed to melt against the length of his. His kiss was comforting, and this man, who only days earlier had been a stranger, now seemed as familiar as the stars she gazed at every night.

Alex whispered her name against her mouth, and she opened her eyes to look at him, her head tipped back against the crook of his arm. His eyes were dark in their intensity, and she yearned for his touch once again.

Just then a jackal howled somewhere in the hills and the sound startled both of them. Releasing London abruptly, Alex turned his back on her and put a hand over his eyes. For a long moment neither of them spoke. The dove in the thorn scrub flew away with a muffled flapping of wings. The silence closed in again. Then Alex said, without looking at her, "I'm sorry."

London wondered why. She herself had been deeply moved by what had passed between them. Smoothing back her hair, she went to stand near the entrance of the tent, drawing back the flaps so that she could look outside. She knew that she would go mad unless she thought of something to say to break the taut stillness. After a long moment she whispered tremulously, "What will happen to me in England? With the

people there, I mean? How do you suppose they'll treat me—
a woman raised among Arabs?''

Alex turned to see her staring out into the night. The moon,
which had been standing high in the sky earlier was beginning
to set. But the night was not so dark that he could not see the
lovely lines of London's body through the clinging fabric of
her robes as she stood with her back to him, her silky hair
falling to her hips.

He turned away quickly, forcing himself to consider her
question carefully before answering. He wished passionately
that he was not so acutely aware at the moment of being in
love with her. Although what difference it would have made
was not entirely clear to him. Only the fact remained that he
was falling in love; that he must have been for some time
without realizing it—until he had kissed her and known the
heart-stopping pleasure of holding in his arms the one woman
who would matter above all others.

Alex's lips thinned to a grim line. Yes, he loved her, but
the knowledge brought only a sinking sense of despair unlike
anything he had ever known. London Kirkland was betrothed
to another, and he, by virtue of a solemn oath and the urgings
of his own heart, had cast his lot with the army of the British
Raj. Neither of those facts were alterable. Nor would he
change the future to suit him even if he could. He knew that
he could never ask London to endure the oppressive life of a
British cantonment even for his sake, because the lot of a
soldier's wife in India was worse, so much worse, than anything Powney Waring had planned for her in England.

He had seen as much for himself in the garrisons of Simla,
Peshawar, Lahore—oh, the dozens and dozens of other cities
spread across the vast Indian Empire. Garrisons in which the
same suffering, the heartbreaking separations of wives from
husbands, the heat, the illness, the incredible loneliness and
boredom played itself out with frightening regularity. And he
knew suddenly that he would never view again with detach-
ment the sight of those countless graves containing the bodies
of women who had died in childbirth, that were scratched
everywhere into the iron-hard Indian soil.

''Alex?''

London's tone was faintly perplexed, and Alex realized that he had still not answered her question. He said now, in a voice that was not entirely steady, "P&O steamships have been carrying British tourists to the Middle East for decades now, but I'm afraid your countrymen still know very little about Arabic lands. Their contact with the locals is limited to boatmen and hoteliers in the larger cities, their history learned from hired guides."

"By that do you mean the dragomans?" London asked scornfully. "They know nothing about history, only legends and fanciful tales!"

"Just the stuff to fascinate wide-eyed Europeans," Alex agreed. "Who, by the way, have cast themselves in the role of apostles of civilization to the rest of the world."

"Apostles?"

"Prophets, fakirs, anyone condescending enough and arrogant enough to believe that they have the moral obligation to bring enlightenment to the backwater lands of the East." Alex's tone was suddenly bitter, and London, who was beginning to understand him very well, knew that he was thinking of India.

She was silent for a moment, considering this. Then she said slowly, "What you mean to say is that all of them in England, even those who have traveled abroad or served in India or the Foreign Office, will have a very distorted view of Eastern lands—and of me. They will have already convinced themselves that I've been held captive all these years in a jeweled mosque suffering at the hands of a brutal warrior sheikh, that sort of thing, right?"

Alex frowned, torn between tears and the desire to laugh. He forced himself to speak calmly. "Fortunately for you, a number of British subjects have spent their lives among the Bedouin. Sir Richard Burton, for one, and Gordon Laing, Lady Anne Blunt, Jane Digby . . . oh, a dozen others, so it won't be as if you'll be viewed as an eccentric novelty. One thing you most certainly will be is presumed an instant expert on the Middle East, and you'll be labeled a total dullard by polite society if you don't talk at length about your experiences and display strong opinions that confirm everything they've come to believe from the romantic literature of their time. And I promise you, travel accounts are quite the rage in England at the moment.''

There was an underlying earnestness to Alex's lightly spoken words that London could not fail to hear. He was trying to tell her what she must do and how she must behave when she arrived in England. There was a chance she would be accepted because she came from an old, respected family, provided she behaved the way they did and not like a foreigner or an innocent led astray by unenlightened savages. And she must make certain to publicly condemn the inferiority of those unenlightened savages at every turn. Betray them, in other words, and portray the likes of proud, university-educated Ali Wad Zarim as nothing more than a dirty, dark-skinned bazaar dacoit. London knew that at this, at least, she would fail.

Alex saw her head bow for a moment and knew the heaviness of the burden she had taken upon herself. His heart ached, and yet he had to own to a certain measure of relief—and pride. He had not misjudged her the first time they had met: London Kirkland had a core of steel; she would survive where other women in her difficult position would most assuredly fail. There was a great deal of the tough old baron in her, and a great deal of the Bengal cavalry colonel who had been her father.

"Come," he said, holding out his hand. "Sit by me. We may never have another chance to talk like this."

London did not answer, and Alex saw that she was still standing by the tent flaps, making no move to obey him. "London?"

She turned her head and slowly came to him. Letting Alex draw her down beside him, she leaned her head against the warm curve of his arm. There were tears in her eyes, but in the darkness Alex did not see them.

They had not intended to fall asleep. For hours they sat together talking of the East, its legends, its glorious past, and most of all its uncertain future. Toward morning a cool wind had begun to blow with a soothing rustling sound that had eventually lulled them into a deep and dreamless rest, London with her head on Alex's chest, his arms warm about her. Neither the paling sky nor the first faint stirrings from the other tents had awakened them.

It was the camels that had eventually done so. A number of the hobbled beasts had strayed overnight in their quest for fresh grazing, and their disagreeable complaints as their handlers rounded them up could be heard throughout the oasis and the desert beyond. Alex was the first to open his eyes at the sound of those ill-tempered snarls, but still he lay without moving, his harsh cheek pressed against the shining softness of London's hair.

Soon from the cooking fires closer to the wadi—and nearer his own tent—came the pounding of pestles on wooden mortars as the coffee beans were ground by the early-rising *iklans*. Alex's dreamlike composure shattered the moment he realized what the sound meant.

"Good God!"

He was unaware that he had spoken aloud, but his words roused London, who moved sleepily, then tried to draw away from him. Alex would not let her.

Her eyes flew open and she turned her head to look at him. "Alex?"

He covered her mouth with his hand. "Be still!"

Someone was fumbling with the tent flaps, and Alex quickly drew the rough blanket over London's head. She held herself perfectly still, and Alex knew a flash of admiration for her, aware that few other women would have grasped the dangers of the situation so quickly.

The sound of a deep-throated laugh made him turn his head. It was Ali Abjur, heavily veiled and robed in indigo muslin, standing in the pale light streaming through the doorway of the tent. Wagging a gnarled finger, he inquired in halting Arabic if the young *Ingleez* intended to sleep all morning while there were chores to be done in the camp outside?

Alex did not answer him. Instead he drew back the blanket a little and, lifting a handful of London's long blond hair, looked directly into Ali Abjur's startled eyes. He could only pray, as he had never done before, that he had not misjudged the kindly old man.

"Wah!" Ali Abjur exclaimed beneath his breath. For a long moment there was silence. Then, suddenly, the old man reached beneath his robes and withdrew a long, curving sword.

Oh, God, Alex thought in disbelief. *He means to kill us. And after nothing happened between us!*

Swinging the weapon down in a vicious arc, Ali Abjur cut the tent pole neatly in half. Instantly the heavy leather walls collapsed on top of them, and Ali Abjur set up a loud screaming for help. Alex could only lay there, too stunned to move. Had the old man taken leave of his senses? Did he wish to attract the attention of the entire camp?

Apparently so, for Ali Abjur's screams grew more high-pitched and hysterical, and he began to thrash about under the leather skins like a fish impaled on a pike. By now men were hurrying from all directions, but the old man's wild flailings effectively prevented them from removing the collapsed hangings and thereby freeing him.

Thankfully, Alex had by now understood Ali Abjur's intent. While the tent continued to buck and heave and the men shouted at Ali Abjur and at each other, he worked his way swiftly from under the blankets. There was no time to search for the best way out; London must go immediately, while the others were still distracted. There was barely room for her, but she managed to wriggle through the small opening Alex made for her by lifting up one side of the leather. Then she was gone, her lightly running footsteps drowned in the shrillness of Ali Abjur's screams.

Sadu was understandably furious when both men were freed at last and Ali Abjur confessed sheepishly that he had thought the *Ingleezi* was robbing him. Could the old man not see that the tent had merely collapsed? Had such a minor mishap really been reason enough to screech like a she-ghoul and disturb the others, who had more important things to do?

Ali Abjur nodded and looked grave and eventually the others drifted away, shaking their heads at the old man's foolishness. Alex himself had not spoken at all, only stood with his arms crossed before his chest attending Sadu's blistering lecture while looking carefully at nothing. Not until Sadu had brushed past him, shoulders rigid with disgust, did Alex straighten, his set mouth twitching. Ali Abjur's gaze met his.

"It would seem we have escaped serious harm," Alex observed.

"God's mercies are many," Ali Abjur agreed blandly.

Searching through the rubble of the fallen tent he picked up his sword and returned it lovingly to his belt. Then he saluted Alex gravely and sauntered away, for all appearances quite pleased with himself and the world.

Chapter Eight

When Alex and London arrived in Algiers, they found letters waiting for them at the British consulate. Two were for Alex and one was for London, written by her grandfather and posted from Kent less than four weeks ago. She did not open it immediately when Alex handed it to her in the lobby of the hotel where she was to stay until arrangements could be made for her departure. Instead she watched as he crossed to a secluded alcove behind the front desk and, leaning against one of the graceful columns set amid the greenery, slit open the first of his own with his thumbnail.

A desultory summer heat lay over the city, and the lobby was deserted but for the two of them. The huge, white-washed colonial hotel lay within sight of the sea, and the arched windows, cut high along the domed ceiling, revealed glimpses of placid water and hot blue sky. Woven tapestries covered the walls, interspersed here and there with brass lanterns and mirrors. Moonflowers grew in cachepots standing about on the polished tile floor, filling the air with heavy perfume.

London was oblivious to the beauty around her. She studied Alex's face while he read his letter, her heart filled with an aching love that had grown more intense as their journey progressed. She had not been able to look her fill of him very often; certainly not during the last few days while their camels had plodded over the difficult miles and the hot wind had flung blinding grit in their eyes.

There had been time only for a brief farewell from Ali Wad Zarim at the *zariba*, because Alex had been hot with impatience to leave for Algiers. Although a songfest had been planned to celebrate London's departure and her approaching marriage, Ali Wad Zarim had taken one look at her exhausted face and Alex's thin-lipped countenance and had declared rather forcibly that it would probably be wisest to place the girl under the protection of her future husband as soon as possible.

While the wives and numerous aunts and cousins who came to call wrung their hands and lamented the fact that there was to be no festival, London remained as adamant as Alex. There was, she stubbornly maintained, no reason at all to celebrate her marriage, since her bridegroom was half a world away, and surely the women of the encampment would be kept happy enough planning the nuptials of Sadu and Khadija Sata instead?

There had been a great deal of laughter and good-natured jesting in response to this, because the girl in question was herself present. And after the women of the *zariba* had cheerfully borne Khadija away, London had returned to the private quarters of Ali Wad Zarim in order to witness the counting out of her bridal portion: a bulging sack of silver coins presented by Alex MacLaughlin in place of the usual bridal dowry, in view of the fact that neither Lord Ladbroke nor his nephew, Rupert Ashford, owned a herd of camels.

Afterward, Alex had presented London with her betrothal ring, which was delicately fashioned of gold and a single ruby as red as pigeon's blood, that he withdrew from a small packet tied with twine. It was a lovely thing, and London did not know that it had been entrusted to Powney Waring after Celia's death with the request that he present it to her daughter when the girl came of age.

The knowledge undoubtedly would have done much to ease London's heartache, because she had little that belonged to her mother to remember her by, and certainly nothing as personal as Celia Waring's betrothal ring. But Powney in his arrogance, or perhaps because of the forgetfulness brought on by old age, had neglected to mention as much to Alex.

Alex had slipped the ring onto London's slim finger, and London had lifted her face to his, her eyes shining with a look that, like her mother's in a similar moment years before, conveyed her love quite clearly. And Alex had looked back, steadily, as if in that moment no one else existed in the tent or in all the world but the two of them.

He had said softly, in English, "If you should ever need me, whatever the reason, send this ring to me and I will come. Unless I am dead, I will come."

London's vision had blurred, but her voice was steady. "I will."

They had left some two hours later accompanied by a Heratin slave from the southern Sahara who was a serf of Ali Wad Zarim's, and a glowering woman of astonishingly ample proportions who seemed capable of, and certainly quite willing to, protect the virtue of her mistress from an entire tribe of marauders should the need arise. London had carried nothing with her save the few articles that fit into her saddlebags: a change of clothing, a few battered books in English and Hindustani that had once belonged to her parents and which had survived the ravages of time and insects, and a surprisingly beautiful collection of glass perfume bottles, presumably quite old, that had been looted from Abidjan by an ancestor of Ali Wad Zarim's and which he had presented to her upon her completion of Koranic instruction.

The wife of Ali Wad Zarim had wept openly while the women of the *zariba* set up a wild trilling that had keened in the ears of London and Alex and their companions and stayed with them long after the lowing of the cattle had faded and the small encampment on the hillside was lost from view.

Now, in the hotel lobby that was breathlessly hot and swarming with flies, and with the Heratin and the Tuareg beldam put up elsewhere in the city because in Algiers Europeans and Moslems lived strictly apart, London stood silently and looked at Alex. She wondered, as she had done so often in the past, if he was in love with her.

There had been times when she was convinced that he was, and times when she had doubted both herself and him. After all, he had not tried to touch her once since the night he had kissed her in his tent at the Faraji oasis, and on nearly every occasion since then he had addressed her curtly—as though her presence were an irritation and he wished himself heartily rid of the weight of responsibility she represented to him.

By now Alex had finished the first letter and was unfolding the second. Glancing down at it, he straightened abruptly, and a look crossed his face that London had never seen before. She crossed to him quickly. "Alex, what is it?"

He looked at her, frowning a little. "Oh, sorry. What did you say?"

"I asked about the letter—that one there. Is it bad news?"

A faint smile tugged at his mouth. "Bad news? No. I've been summoned back to Calcutta. It seems I'm to be given a new assignment. With the Indian Civil Service, no less."

"You can't be serious! You wouldn't really consider leaving the military?"

Alex laughed and his eyes glowed. "Not unless they cashiered me! But I'm not leaving it. I've merely been reassigned. To Jhulapore."

"Jhulapore? Where's that? I've never heard of it."

"Neither have I. It's a small kingdom in Rajputana and, according to this letter, boasts a fairly large community of Europeans. I've been asked to take command of the guard of troops accompanying the new British resident there."

And of course he'd accept the appointment. That much was clear from Alex's expression, and London remembered enough about the Indian Civil Service to know that only officers who had distinguished themselves brilliantly in the course of their military careers were offered a position on the staff of a government resident. It was the sort of promotion her father would have called a "plum commission."

She asked quietly, "Will you take it, then?"

"I'd be a fool to refuse."

London stood very still, her face wiped free of all expression so that Alex would not be able to read her innermost feelings, because she was suddenly so ashamed of them—and of her own, foolish dreams. It had been absurd—insane!—of her to imagine that he would take her with him when he returned to India to live. Like her father, Alex was a career soldier, tied until death to Her Majesty's foreign service. And further, and quite unlike Robert Kirkland, he was one of those rare men to whom the army meant everything. And she herself was already betrothed to another.

"The only problem," Alex was saying slowly, "is that I've been ordered to India immediately." Over the letter, his dark eyes met hers.

"Then don't trouble yourself with me," London said quickly. "I'm sure the British consul can be trusted to arrange a suitable replacement. Perhaps a lady of family who might also be able to help me with my wardrobe? I can't exactly arrive at Bellehurst dressed in native robes, can I?"

"No," said Alex, who hadn't given the matter any thought until now. "I'll admit it's not a bad idea. You certainly can't afford to make a spectacle of yourself, can you?"

London did not return his smile, and Alex added gruffly, "I insist on making the arrangements myself, not the British consul."

"But if they're expecting you in Calcutta—"

"It's the least I can do for you," Alex interrupted. "I want to do it."

London nodded and turned away. Tight-lipped, Alex crossed to the hotel desk and rang the brass bell so insistently that the attendant dozing in the back office dropped his fez in his haste to answer.

The night was to prove very hot and still, and London could not sleep. Hour upon restless hour she rose from her bed, brushed aside the netting, and went to stand at the window. The moon had risen, and the buildings of the city were bleached white by its ghostly light. There were few people about, and it was so quiet that London could hear the chirping of insects in the garden below and the scuttling of the lizards that hunted them.

Prowling through the hot darkness, she crossed to the nightstand, lifted the porcelain ewer, and poured herself a drink. As she put the glass to her lips, she suddenly spotted a fat black beetle floating in the water. Normally she was accustomed to—and quite unafraid of—the countless odious insects that dogged one's life in the desert, but tonight, her nerves taut, she could not prevent herself from shrieking and letting the glass fall to the floor, where it shattered on the hot tiles.

Instantly there came the sound of a door opening and closing across the hall, and then a low but insistent knock upon her own. Drawing her *gondurah* over her head, London unlocked the door and stepped aside quickly to let Alex in.

"I heard you cry out," he said. "Are you all right?"

"Yes. I dropped a glass. Be careful, don't cut yourself."

Together they cleaned up the jagged pieces, then straightened and stood looking at each other. Alex was wearing nothing but a pair of thin cotton trousers knotted loosely at the waist. In the faint moonlight, London could see the gleam of his smoothly muscled chest and the crisp, curling darkness of his hair.

"You'd better go," she whispered, afraid of his nearness and what it did to her. "Someone must have heard you—"

"No one heard me."

"Please," she whispered. Her eyes met his in the darkness, and she saw the same need she felt mirrored there. Even as she put out her hands to push him away, he pulled her roughly against the length of his body so that her palms slid across his chest and her arms curved about his neck where they locked themselves fiercely about his naked back.

"Oh, God, London—" Alex's mouth was on hers, hungry, insistent, and she was caught up in the fierceness of his desire and her own, urgent loneliness and pain. They staggered together to the bed, crossing lifetimes with every step, and then they sank together into the softness of a shared embrace, the voluptuousness of skin against skin.

Alex's dark eyes glowed as he buried his face in the clean, scented profusion of London's unbound hair. "Oh, God," he whispered, his heart twisting into a knot of unbearable longing.

"Alex—"

His name was no more than a breathed caress against his throat. He could feel the steady beating of London's heart and the slender warmth of her young body pressing against his own. Gently, almost reverently, he pushed aside her robe so that she lay naked in the moonlight beneath him. He lifted his head and his eyes met hers. There was a long silence.

At last London threaded her fingers through Alex's hair and brought his head down to hers. Shifting his weight, Alex covered her body with his. Then he, too, was lying naked in the dark, and nothing mattered but the rough warmth of his body upon her own and the way his kisses deepened as he felt London beneath him. Slowly, tenderly, he began to make love to her. London gasped at the brief stab of pain that was the ending of her girlhood, and Alex paused, his lips caressing London's closed eyelids, her cheeks and brow, until she sighed and relaxed once again. Only then did he resume the gentle assault that took him slowly into the womanly core of her. He could not withhold a groan as, untutored and instinctively, London arched her hips to meet his thrust. Alex burrowed deeply into her, half lifting her with his hands beneath her buttocks.

"Oh, God," he whispered again.

Their heated movement sent ripples of pleasure pulsating through him. His tongue grazed hers and she trembled at the hard, demanding touch of his mouth. A throbbing ache was beginning to build within her, and London strained toward it, toward Alex, until the pleasure grew and she seemed to teeter for a timeless moment on the edge of oblivion. And in that moment she was swept away in a shattering release that was like nothing she had ever envisioned or imagined. She felt herself drowning in the wrenching glory of it, and she cried out as reality faded, taking her consciousness with it.

London sailed the following morning aboard the steam-packet *Princess Louise* in the company of a stout, talkative Englishwoman named Muriel Armitage, who had professed herself delighted to offer the girl a berth in her cabin. Mrs. Armitage was the elderly widow of a former East India Company director who had traveled extensively throughout the East. Although her command of Arabic was execrable and she seemed to harbor those rosily distorted views of Eastern lands that Alex had warned London to expect from her fellow countrymen, she was kindhearted and gay, and sufficiently skilled at sewing to declare with confidence that Miss Kirkland should have no worries on the score of owning several adequate gowns by the time she arrived in England.

There had been little ceremony surrounding London's departure. After a morning spent in the clothhandler's *sug* with Mrs. Armitage purchasing lengths of muslin, cashmere, and silk, she met Alex on the pier near the water steps, where the harbor boat waited to take them across to the anchored packet.

Alex was looking tired and cross, and he all but ignored Mrs. Armitage when she offered her hand to him in farewell. Ignoring the shock on her kindly face, he pulled London off to one side of the pier and for a long moment stood looking down at her without speaking. London was wearing the indigo robes of the Tuareg tribe because these were the only clothes she owned, but at least she had heeded Mrs. Armitage's advice and abandoned her headcloth and veil in favor of a bonnet. Beneath it her fair hair was drawn back into a heavy chignon, as was the current Western fashion, and it occurred to Alex that she looked like a charming English tourist tricked out in souvenir attire.

He turned his head away suddenly, grappling with the urge to take her arm and flee with her into the crowded alleyways of the city. How many times during the sleepless nights since leaving Al Betain had he dreamed of doing just that? Even last night, still wrapped in the tangled embrace of sated love and slipping at last into the inscrutable sleep that neither he nor London could hold at bay, he had imagined himself renouncing all he knew in order to keep that which was dearest to his heart.

But he knew that he could not. In all likelihood he would be dismissed from his regiment the moment it was discovered that he had run off with the affianced wife of a British gentleman. The Army Act was grimly plain on the score: *Cashiered for conduct unbecoming the character of an officer*.

And what sort of life could he offer London then, out of work, without prospects, unskilled and unable to support her on anything but the largess of his father—who would never tolerate his son's actions in the first place and who would, promptly and understandably, cut Alex out of his will? Nor would London's grandfather tolerate the collapse of his carefully laid plans, and Alex was not entirely certain London would ever be safe from the old man's wrath were the unthinkable to happen.

"God is a great deviser of stratagems, you know."

"What?" Startled, Alex looked around to find London smiling at him, a calm, sweet smile that tore at his heart.

"Go to Calcutta," she said softly. He stared at her. "Go, and perhaps one day it may be that God will smooth your way back to me."

"And if I never see you again?" Alex asked.

"We live in ignorance, and Allah is the all-knowing."

"Those idiotic Koranic quotations!" Alex burst out. "How can you believe in them? Be so accepting? It may be that we never—"

London's hand covered his mouth so that he could not utter another word, and her lovely, tear-brightened eyes looked steadily into his. After a long moment his own gaze dropped, and he kissed the warm palm that was pressed to his lips.

"I must accept them and believe in my fate, as you, too, must believe in yours. Goodbye," she whispered.

Alex's mouth twisted. "Oh my heart's love, my life—" His voice broke and London turned from him with a pained gasp.

"London, wait—"

But she was gone, her lightly running footsteps fading on the rough planks of the pier, the deep indigo of her robes melting into the dazzling blue of the harbor.

Chapter Nine

The telephone shrilled from the hall. London, who had drifted to sleep in her armchair, awoke with a start. For a moment she sat there, confused. Alex and the exotic land of her youth had seemed so very real. How well she could remember the pain of leaving him. It had not been easy to give him up, but now, surrounded by all that had come to mean serenity and security for the last sixty years, she couldn't help but give thanks for the good fortune she had been granted.

The telephone jangled again. This time, London opened her eyes and struggled to rise. Sara, sitting across from her, laid down her magazine. "Don't bother, Grandmama. I'll get it."

"No, let me. I've been sitting long enough and have grown quite stiff."

The hall was filled with shadows and seemed very dark after the soft brilliance of the parlor. London groped for the receiver, then put it to her ear. "Rose Cottage."

"Mama."

"Victoria! What a pleasant surprise. We haven't heard a thing from you all day."

"I've been frightfully busy." Over the phone, Victoria sounded somewhat defensive. "Don't you remember? We're giving one of our little parties tonight."

"Do you really think that's wise, darling? With all the work you've been doing for my birthday?"

Absurdly, Victoria felt tears sting her eyes. She couldn't remember the last time she had heard her mother sound so concerned about her. Taking a deep breath she forced herself to speak brightly. "No trouble at all. Mrs. Jakes has done everything splendidly, as usual. I was hoping you and Sara would come."

"Oh, I'm afraid not, dear. I'm simply too tired. And as for Sara . . ." There was a pause as London turned from the phone. She was back almost immediately. "Sara says she prefers begging off too, if you don't mind. We've both been gone all day."

"You've been out making calls," Victoria said flatly. "I should have known. I've been ringing the cottage since morning."

"Oh, yes. We had a marvelous time." If London noticed how reproachful her daughter sounded she paid no attention. "The Olwyns are back from their Spanish jaunt and insisted we stay for lunch. The Beckwiths had us in for tea. And Sir Frederick wouldn't hear of letting us leave without offering a round of drinks. Everyone was delighted to see Sara, as you can imagine. No one's laid eyes on her since we buried your father. And I'm pleased to discover that at least one of my grandchildren doesn't feel the least bit embarrassed about riding around the countryside in a pony cart."

Alone in her spacious bedroom, Victoria gripped the receiver tightly and briefly shut her eyes. "Mama, William and I would like to see Sara too. She's been with you for three whole days now, and we've yet to lay eyes on her. Why don't you come up after dinner? I'll send Francis down with the car."

"That's awfully kind of you, dear, but really, it can wait until tomorrow, can't it? I'm certain Sara isn't up to meeting another set of strangers after such a hectic day. We'll come after breakfast. No need to send the car. We can walk."

"All right, Mama. Good night."

"Good night, dear."

"Thank you," Sara said, the moment London rang off.

"What for?"

"You know."

They smiled at one another in perfect understanding.

The following morning dawned fresh and clear, without a hint of rain. Beyond London's walled garden the sun drew sparkling fingers across the river that wound its lazy way through the daisy-sprinkled meadow. To the west, checkerboard farms stretched beneath pristine skies toward hills dappled green and gray by lazy clouds. A warm wind ruffled the bare treetops and rippled through the fields of budding corn, and London, standing on the terrace of Rose Cottage with her granddaughter, sighed as she looked about her.

"What an absolutely marvelous day! I'm so happy we decided to walk to the house. Oh, good morning, Mr. Brockman."

The gnarled gardener, appearing around the high stone wall with a spade in his hand, solemnly raised his cap. "Mornin', your ladyship, Miss Ashford. Best keep to the path. Scilla bulbs beginnin' to shoot."

"We wouldn't dream of stepping on them," London assured him, smiling. "Have you noticed the viburnum starting to blossom?"

"Saw it last week." He doffed his cap again and disappeared with a great deal of rustling behind the lilac shrubs.

"Pretentious little man. It probably isn't true, but he'd rather die than admit I've stolen a march on him. I can't imagine why all English gardeners possess such perfectly horrible temperaments. No matter. Come along, dear."

Sara, who had lingered on the terrace sniffing the warm scent of earth and growing things, had to run to catch up with her. "Isn't it quicker to go up the drive?"

"It is, but I thought we'd check on the cows first, if you don't mind."

The grass squelched beneath their shoes as London led the way along the uneven fence line toward the fields. Here the sound of an occasional car wooshing past was drowned by the droning of bees and the twittering of thrushes. Soon the thatched roof of Rose Cottage vanished behind a grassy rise, and the undulating gold-green of the meadow—dotted by the woolly red humps of cows—lay ahead.

"Red Devon cattle," London said. She paused near the gate to look at them, her hands thrust into the pockets of her trench coat; a man's worn black coat, Sara had noticed, which, coupled with the crushed felt hat crammed onto her head, gave her grandmother the look of a charming ragamuffin. Only Grandmama could pull off such a strange ensemble with total panache and not care a fig what anyone thought, Sara decided, smiling.

"We've only ten head now," London was saying. "William wanted to sell off the entire herd after your grandfather died, but I wouldn't let him. Times were hard then, almost as bad as they are now, what with so many men on the dole. 'One can never be too self-sufficient,' I told William at the time. The milch cows were too labor intensive, of course, so we settled on the beef cattle and one or two Friesians. The children needed their milk, after all, and I did so enjoy my butter and cheese of a morning."

"Surely you can get all of that from Mr. Hurley's store nowadays?"

"Where's the fun in that? Besides, you'd be surprised to learn that we actually turn a profit. Our surplus is sold to the Paxton Hotel, and anything left over goes to Tuesday market. And even if they did cost money I wouldn't consider selling them. Empty barns are so wasteful, not to mention depressing."

"What you really mean is that you've never gotten the herding instinct out of your blood, have you?"

Startled, London was forced to laugh. "I never thought of it that way, but yes, I suppose you're right. At least cows are much more agreeable than camels."

A half-grown calf, pink nose snuffling, stretched its neck cautiously over the fence. Sara leaned over to scratch its back.

"Come," London said, waving her hands to shoo it away. "It's late and Victoria will be waiting."

Far from it. While London and Sara were making their way slowly uphill toward the manor house, Victoria Warburton lay scowling bad-temperedly in a boiling hot bath, hating herself, her husband, the sight of her own naked, spreading body stretched out in the tub, and wishing truculently that she hadn't drunk so much champagne the night before.

Not that William was aware of her smoldering anger. She was much too good at hiding it. And in all fairness she couldn't really complain about everything last night. The party had been fun, the champagne had flowed freely until well into the morning hours, and Victoria recalled with considerable pride the many compliments paid her on the excellence of her table. Truly she would have enjoyed herself immensely if only Freddy Lansworth hadn't made that silly, off-hand remark about Merrick stock.

Poking her big toe out of the water, Victoria twisted on the hot-water tap, uncaring of how wasteful she was being. Frowning, she tried to remember how they had got on the subject of stocks in the first place. Now that she thought back on it, there had been far too much serious talk at dinner to begin with. Victoria liked parties best when people danced, traded harmless gossip, and shared uncomplicated prattle that had nothing in the least to do with Fascism, Burma or India, or those Zionist issues that confused her completely.

But last night someone had been going on and on about Mussolini and Abyssinia, and Victoria, bored to distraction, had turned to Freddy and inquired if anything was new in London that season. Whereupon Freddy had snapped his fingers as though remembering something important and, catching William's sleeve, had told him, in Victoria's presence, that he'd approached his senior partners and, yes, they were definitely interested in buying Merrick stock.

Later, near the buffet table, Victoria had asked William what Freddy meant. William had said it was nothing, that he was thinking of selling some of her father's shares and that he'd made an overture to Freddy's boss at Pearce, Brendle and Goldwaithe in Knightsbridge concerning a possible transaction.

"Oh, William, are you sure?" Victoria had asked. It scared her a little whenever William made decisions involving the family business. Not that she didn't trust him. She did. She just wished that he was a bit more like her father had been: old-fashioned and traditional, not so quick to pounce on every new money-making scheme or investment bandwagon that rolled his way.

"Of course I'm sure," William had said a trifle impatiently. "The price is right and PB&G seems more than willing. Besides, since when have you objected to raising ready cash? You never complain about spending it."

And he had left her without another word, embarrassing her with his rudeness, although no one else, thankfully, had heard. Victoria had watched him walk over to the Charles Midfords and begin chatting them up, looking urbane and well-groomed in his tweed jacket and flannel trousers, his thinning blond hair sprinkled with oil. Something very akin to dislike had flared inside Victoria as she looked at him. But maybe that was only because she hated it whenever he used hair oil, because she couldn't help thinking that it made him look like a classless bounder.

Nevertheless, the feeling of dislike hadn't diminished come morning. In fact, Victoria was more upset with William than ever. She had inherited her shares in the Merrick Company from her father, and felt that she was being disloyal to his memory to consider selling them. And perhaps, from a purely financial point of view, it would be a little unwise.

The Merrick Company had been founded by Rupert Ashford's younger brother, Charles. A visionary as well as a university-trained scientist, Charles had spent years experimenting with distillates, and his hard work had paid off when his research with ether had yielded the highly profitable invention of an automatic ice-making machine. Being Victoria's only paternal uncle, he had inherited the Ladbroke peerage when Rupert died and consequently been elevated for his research to an earldom, but he had rarely stayed at Bellehurst, preferring the excitement of his London offices and laboratory to the quiet routine of the country.

Victoria suspected uneasily that her mother would not approve of William's plans for selling her stock. Not that Mama ever offered advice or interfered in any way in her children's affairs, even though Victoria sometimes wished she would.

In the past few months a nasty suspicion had begun forming in Victoria's mind that her mother didn't care a fig what she and William did anymore, and sometimes she secretly wished that Mama would prove her wrong, if only—

The far-off ringing of the doorbell and the mad barking of the dogs roused Victoria from her unhappy reverie. "Oh, bother." The water sloshed as she rose and drew on her robe before stepping from the tub. She had forgotten that Mama and Sara were expected after breakfast. Catching sight of her face in the steamy mirror she saw that it was pale and rather puffy, with dark circles beneath her eyes. Nothing a little makeup wouldn't hide. Her lower lip protruded at the thought, and sudden tears pricked her eyes. Not that it mattered. No one seemed to take notice of her these days anyway.

While Victoria dressed and put on her makeup, feeling for all the world immensely sorry for herself, her mother was at the same moment opening the heavy front door and letting herself in without waiting to be asked. Sara followed, her heart thumping with anticipation. Even though she had been in Kent for three whole days, she had yet to set foot inside the house, which she had not seen since her grandfather's death so many years ago.

The moment she did, she found herself enveloped by the much loved and long-forgotten scent of a well-kept country house; a scent that had always made her think of old, polished wood, starched linens, lavender sachets, and lemon wax. She looked around eagerly, but the stone-flagged lobby with its glass door was new and awoke no memories.

"Come along, dear," said her grandmother, and Sara followed her into the hall. In her childhood it had been known as the Great Hall and had been used often for some social function or another because, in those days, the Ashfords and Warburtons had been an enormous family which spent nearly every holiday together.

Structurally, Sara saw that little had changed since her grandfather's funeral. The wide, double-hung staircase still floated upward to a landing brightened by curved windows of hand-blown Venetian glass and walls paneled in beautifully burnished oak. The massive pair of marble fireplaces still faced one another across the polished tile floor. But the hall itself was empty, its function apparently given over to nothing more than storage.

In alcoves that had once housed the lovely, ornate furnishings of the Regency era there remained only a jumble of umbrellas, croquet mallets, cricket bats, and shooting sticks. The great brass cachepots that had always been filled with fresh flowers from London's conservatory were now overflowing with dog leads, discarded field glasses, and badly crushed deerstalker caps. And in place of the lighthearted talk of men and women who had flocked inside on the morning of a hunt, dressed in colorful coats of harrier green and sumptuous habits of blue and black, there was nothing but silence.

A door in the far corner opened suddenly, revealing a white-haired man in formal black attire whose very demeanor oozed hauteur. "Good morning, madam. Lady Ladbroke is upstairs dressing. She asked that I show the two of you to the drawing room. Miss Nora is still down at the stables."

"And where is my son-in-law?"

"His Lordship left early this morning for work. Mr. Spencer was kind enough to drive him to London."

"I see. And my grandson?"

"Master Nelson returned to school yesterday afternoon."

"Without bidding his granny farewell, hmm? Well, I suppose that's not unusual. No need to escort us, Curwen. I know the way."

"Of course, madam."

"Who was that?" Sara whispered, following her grandmother across the polished length of the hall.

"Curwen, William's immensely haughty house steward."

"What in the world is a house steward?"

"I'm not exactly sure. Some sort of glorified butler, I think. Your uncle makes a great fuss over him, and Curwen, in turn, revels in his role. Pompous snob. In my day, a butler was enough."

They stepped through the imposing set of double doors leading from the back of the hall into the drawing room. Here, Sara was delighted to see that the elegant bow windows remained, still opening onto their lovely view of garden and river, although they were shorn now of their heavy drapes and had been double-glazed, presumably at great expense. The furniture was new: sofas, upholstered commodes, and scanty Hepplewhite pieces were scattered everywhere, lamentably doing little to complement the heavy Turkish carpet on which they stood and which, in its own turn, did the elegant room an injustice by covering nearly all of the lovely parquet floor.

"Nelson is up at Oxford," London was saying, divesting herself of the worn raincoat that Curwen had eyed with alarm in the hall and tossing it casually across the nearest chair. "Victoria insisted he attend Eton first, although I can't imagine why. Westminster was good enough for your father. Oh, my, I'm truly exhausted after our little walk." She sank gratefully into a capacious armchair.

"I remember Grandpapa always saying that public schools were only good for gaming, cockfighting, and drinking," Sara said, curling up opposite her on a dainty settee.

"Your cousin Nelson is a case in point."

"I don't remember him."

"No. He was barely an infant when you came for your grandfather's funeral, and Nora hadn't even been born."

Sara said nothing. From her grandmother's letters she had drawn the conclusion that Victoria and William's only son was something of a disappointment to the family. Wildly irresponsible and utterly ambitionless, he had shown himself at a surprisingly early age to harbor little more than a passion for fast cars and women. It was widely believed that his career at Magdalen college would not last through the final term. The Ladbroke heir. In a way Sara was sorry for him.

The door opened just then, revealing Sara's aunt standing dramatically on the threshold. Shawled, bejeweled, and very elegant in dark blue brocade of Parisian design, she was fatter than Sara remembered, and her glossy chestnut hair had grayed considerably. Nevertheless she was artfully made up and not at all unattractive, and Sara felt a small pang as their glances met. Victoria had inherited none of her looks from her mother, tending instead to resemble her tall, dark father. Now, well into middle age, that resemblance had grown almost uncanny. Sara could feel her throat constrict, because it almost seemed to her that those were Grandpapa's blue eyes peering out at her from Victoria's fleshy face, and his warm smile hiding behind those full, cosmetically brightened lips.

But the cry of pleasure and the gushing words of welcome were Victoria's alone as she hurried forward to press her plump, powdered cheek to her niece's. "Oh, my darling, how grown up you look! And so very like Sandy! You must have given Mama quite a turn when you showed up. Didn't she, Mama?"

"Yes," London said dryly. She had not bothered opening her eyes since Victoria's arrival.

"Oh, I can't wait for William to see you! And Nora. Mama must have told you that Nora lives at home. I'm afraid Nelson left yesterday with a friend from college, but he should be back in time for the party." Victoria's hands flew to her cheeks. "Oh, silly me! I forgot William's gone back to work. The Spencers spent the night and took him into town early this morning. But don't you worry. He'll be back at weekend with Mother Warburton."

I am counting the days, London thought irritably. She was in something of an evil mood because the walk up to the house had tired her more than she had expected.

"Would you mind if I took a look around the house, Aunt Victoria?" Sara asked eagerly. "I would so like to see it, especially the nursery."

"Oh, heavens! Didn't Mama tell you? We remodeled those antiquated rooms ages ago!"

London turned to Sara with a frown. "Surely I mentioned it in one of my letters?"

"Yes, you must have. I'd forgotten. But I don't care, really. I'd still like to go up."

"Do you suppose it could wait, dear?" Victoria had crossed to the sideboard and was pouring herself a Schweppes lime and gin. "Everything's so dreadfully muddled at the moment. You remember, don't you, that the family's coming next week, and of course several of the guest rooms are still occupied after last night."

"Oh, but I don't mind . . ."

Victoria came back around the sofa and patted her niece's cheek. The bracelets on her wrist clinked against her glass. "I'm sure you don't. But I'd much rather—" She broke off, seeing the sudden disappointment that clouded Sara's face. Unable to help herself, she relented. God, the girl looked like Sandy. "Perhaps when Nora comes in."

There was a scuffling in the hall just then, and the panting and whining of highly strung dogs accompanied by the noisy laughter of a young girl. Boot heels echoed on stone as Nora Warburton strode inside. She was a tall, rather alarmingly muscular girl of fifteen, her chestnut hair fashionably crimped and worn tucked beneath a black velvet crash cap. Brick-colored riding breeches hugged her athletic legs, and although she couldn't be considered beautiful, hers was an interesting face, with lively brown eyes and a smattering of freckles across a very retroussé nose.

Stooping to kiss her grandmother's cheek she turned next to Sara and held out her hand. "Hullo! Curwen said you were here. I'm sorry, but there wasn't time to change. I'm schooling Madrigal for the hunt trials next week." She tilted her head to one side and regarded Sara quizzically. "I don't recognize you at all from your photographs. I was hoping I would. Have you seen the house yet?"

Sara shook her head.

"Oh, Mummy!" Nora did a pirouette on her boot heel. "May I take her upstairs?" Without waiting for an answer she tugged on Sara's arm. "I've got a new gramophone and heaps of records. What kind of music do you listen to in America? Do you play tennis? Or squash? I've had no one to play with since Nelson went away to school."

Sara tried hard to warm to her. She remembered Nora's older sisters only vaguely and not altogether fondly. She had never written them after she'd gone to America to live, nor they her. Strange to think that they were married now, with children of their own.

"We'll be down in time for lunch, Mum," Nora called over her shoulder.

There followed a whirlwind tour of the house which left

Sara with the dazed impression that she had just completed a long and exhausting journey. Nora took her downstairs to see the kitchen, which was modernized now, with tile counters, an enormous refrigerator, and an electric oven replacing the huge, gleaming Black Eagle range with its japanned coal bucket and polished metal appointments. They went through an enormous, cluttered pantry which had once held both the laundry and stillroom, until those had become obsolete after Millham Cross opened a commercial laundry and grocery of its own.

Then upstairs. Sara caught a quick glimpse of her old room. It was newly papered and painted, and unrecognizable. The nursery was now a suite of modern bedrooms joined by a sumptuous, tiled bath. She also saw the dark, poky warren of rooms and corridors beneath the eaves where the house-maids had slept and Sara herself had played as a child. These remained very much the same, only musty now from long disuse and crammed from floor to ceiling with furniture that had originally belonged to Sara's grandparents and which her aunt and uncle had deemed unsuitable after they had moved in.

"Mummy swears she's going to have the secondhand man hump them away to be sold," Nora said, "but she never gets around to it. Poor darling, she's much too busy for anything these days. Look, here's the dumbwaiter. Nobody uses it anymore. Gran once told me Cousin Henry locked you inside when you were little. Is it true?"

"Yes." Sara reached out to turn the winch, but the gears had not been oiled in years and refused to budge. "It wasn't so bad really. Another time, he stopped a meal on its way down to the dining room. There used to be a suit of armor hanging in the Great Hall, and Henry took off its head and put it on the tray. The housekeeper nearly had a heart attack when she opened the door."

Nora did not laugh as Sara had expected. She merely looked disapproving—and very much like her mother when she frowned. "We'd better get back. Mummy's planning an early luncheon in the garden. Most of the guests slept in late."

"Oh." Dismayed, Sara looked down at her plain blue skirt

and white sweater and the walking shoes she had worn for the hike up to the house. "I wasn't aware there'd be visitors."

"There always are. No need to worry. *I* don't intend to change."

A brightly striped awning had been erected on the lawn, and when Sara came downstairs she found a dozen people gathered beneath it helping themselves to an array of dishes spread buffet-style on the table. A pair of maids in smart black uniforms handed out plates and filled glasses under the watchful eye of Curwen, who stood scowling amid the shadows.

Sara's aunt introduced her around, and Sara was surprised at the attention she received. Almost everyone seemed to know who she was and where she lived and were eager to ask questions about America. But they made no effort to hide their surprise at the fact that she was still unmarried, while the frank admission that she worked for a living raised eyebrows all around.

"One of those new breed of women," someone remarked in Sara's presence.

"Should that surprise you? Bellehurst was always awash with radical females before William married into it and had the good sense to put his foot down."

"Eugenia was always the worst of them."

"Isn't that the truth! What a frightful bore she was! No sense of fun at all."

A smothered laugh. "I'll bet the Ashford girl's no different."

Sara walked away, her slim shoulders rigid. Looking around for her grandmother, she realized suddenly that she had not seen her since coming outside with Nora. After making a few inquiries of the maids, Curwen, and her aunt, she went indoors, down the long, carpeted hall, and through the glass doors leading to the conservatory.

Here, the warm, loamy smell of soil mingled with the subtle fragrance of flowers. Gardenias, carnations, chrysanthemums, and lilies blazed against the deep green backdrop of cropped lawn beyond the windowpanes. Sara found her grandmother sitting on the potting bench in the far corner near the pump, her eyes closed, her face so white and still that Sara was instantly alarmed.

"Grandmama! Are you all right?"

London's eyes opened and she smiled. "Of course I am. I was only resting. It's so warm and lovely here."

But Sara was not convinced. She thought of the long hike they had made across the pasture earlier. Perhaps it had been too much. Looking again at her grandmother, she was suddenly able to see beyond the smoothly unlined face and realize for the first time that her grandmother was *old*. Seventy-five. Few people lived that long, and those who did were rarely so lucid or energetic.

"Can I get you something to drink? Would you like to go upstairs and lie down?"

"Heavens! Whatever for?"

"Because you could probably use a little rest."

Hearing the concern in her granddaughter's voice, London made a deliberate effort to sound bracing. "I'm fine, dear, really. Just a little tired from our walk. Victoria knew I was coming here. Didn't she tell you?"

"Yes, but—"

"I spend several mornings a week in here pruning and repotting, watering the seedlings, that sort of thing. Mr. Brockman refuses to let me do more. He's fiercely proprietary when it comes to his plants, you know. As a matter of fact, I was getting ready to cut back a few pinks just before you came in, but decided to sit down for a while first. The sun felt so good on my face."

Sara could feel herself relaxing. There had been no reason to panic. Her grandmother was in excellent health. She did not have a groggy heart about to give out or a faulty valve in her brain getting ready to burst. "Grandmama!" She spoke a little breathlessly because the thought of either one happening was so awful. "Why don't you let me fetch you something from the buffet? You could eat in here."

"So soon after breakfast? Do I look ready to starve?"

The calm voice was so reassuring that Sara grudgingly laughed. "Not really."

"Then sit beside me for a moment." London moved aside

the trugs and shovels and Sara sat down, crossing her long legs before her.

"What do you think of it?" London asked.

"It's all very strange," Sara answered at once. "Everything's so familiar, yet so different. So many things that I've forgotten have come back to me just from being inside the house, smelling the furniture polish, seeing the old portraits on the walls, even hearing Aunt Victoria's voice. I know every twist and turn of the corridors, every creaky place on the stairs, and just about every rock and shrub on the grounds, but I don't feel a part of it any more."

"That will come. Are you glad you're here?"

"Yes, very."

"I warned you that things had changed."

"I know."

"Not that change isn't a good thing. William and Victoria remodeled extensively after they got their hands on Charles's inheritance. With my approval, I'll have you know. The kitchen was admittedly archaic, and the baths badly needed redoing. My moldering antiques had long outlived their usefulness too. Your uncle arranged for some sort of professional person to come down from London to do the decorating. At hideous expense, of course."

"Uncle William's tastes are very different from yours."

"Bah!" London spoke without rancor. "Your uncle is the very epitome of gothic haughtiness. Do you know he actually had his earl's coronet placed on the canopy of his bed after Charles died? I always thought it a great pity he wasn't born two hundred years ago, when being an earl really meant something."

"What a wicked thing to say!"

"Yes, isn't it?" Smiling, London rose to her feet and linked her arm through her granddaughter's. "Come. The pruning can wait. I've decided to eat something after all. Whatever his faults may be, I cannot criticize my son-in-law for the quality of his table."

Later, when they were home again, Sara made tea while London went upstairs to change into a comfortable housedress and sweater. Returning to the parlor, she found Sara laying out the cups and silverware. The room was filled with the cozy smell of warming scones and steeping tea. Behind Sara, through the terrace doors, the sun was hanging low, sending fingers of deep golden light streaming inside and setting her granddaughter's hair ablaze.

"Your father's hair was the same color," London remarked. "Red and yellow all at the same time."

Sara set a bowl of plump, greenhouse-ripened strawberries and a jug of cream onto the table. She smiled. "I still say it's a good thing you named him Sandy."

"I always expected he'd be born dark, like his father."

"Oh? Was Grandpapa dark in his youth? I thought he was more chestnut-haired, like Victoria and Eugenia. Before it turned white, anyway."

London looked away. "Did Victoria strike you as being somewhat nervous today?" she asked unexpectedly.

Sara considered. "Not really."

"I can't help feeling she was hiding something from me."

"What do you mean, Grandmama?"

"I don't know. Just a feeling I have. Victoria was never good at keeping secrets."

Sara reached over to steal a berry from the bowl. "I'll bet it's got something to do with your birthday. Maybe she's planning some sort of surprise."

"Heavens, I hope not. Having the entire mélange of Ashfords and Warburtons gathered together beneath one roof will be shocking enough as it is."

"Sit down, Grandmama. I'll pour. And I wouldn't worry. Victoria will confide in you sooner or later if anything is troubling her."

"Yes," said London. "I suppose you're right."

Later that night, after Sara had gone to bed, London lingered downstairs setting the parlor and kitchen to rights. There were dishes on the drain board to be cleared away and coffee to grind for breakfast. Her flowers needed watering, and she wanted to give the floor a final sweeping. It took a long time, because she was tired and found the work went easier if she moved slowly. The floor was the worst; bending to brush up the crumbs and dump them into the dustbin, she felt positively light-headed.

Tomorrow, she promised herself, she would spend the entire day resting in bed or lounging on the sofa catching up on letters or ringing a few old friends to hear their news. Surely Sara would not begrudge her some time alone? It would do the girl good to get out on her own too. Fond as they were of each other, they certainly didn't have to spend every minute together.

Turning off the lights at last, she stood for a moment before the kitchen window. A pale crescent moon was rising into the blackness of the sky, and it was so quiet that she could hear the faint murmur of the river flowing through the meadow beyond her garden. She thought again of Sara's well-meant advice. Sadly, it wasn't quite as easy as that. She doubted that any mother ever stopped worrying about her children, no matter how grown-up they were. And it still hurt unbearably whenever those children were sad or in pain, even if they had deliberately brought some of their troubles upon themselves.

For instance, London had been aware for some time of a growing coldness between her daughter and son-in-law, although Victoria went to great lengths to conceal it from her. Or was that only a fretful mother's imagination? Perhaps Sara was right in saying there was nothing to worry about. Perhaps something like this was bound to happen after twenty-odd years of marriage to the wrong man.

The wrong man. London's heart squeezed at the thought. How could anyone ever be sure of having found the right one? Had she herself ever known? Even now, with the past long dead and buried, the truth continued to elude her, refusing to unravel from all the emotions, events, and consequences that made up the many threads of her life. Perhaps it never would. And perhaps it was better that way.

THREE
The Rounded Moon

These pearls in ancient gulfs were bred
each softly luscent as a rounded moon,
Then plucked they were from Eastern beds
and strung upon an English thread.

—from James Russell Lowell

Chapter
Ten

1879
England

It was October, a month of ruby sunsets and vivid azure skies, of brisk, northerly winds and hawthorn berries showing red amid the hedgerows. Bellehurst's fields and forests wore their autumn colors: the cherry trees tinged with scarlet, the beech and chestnut trees brilliant with gold. In the garden, chrysanthemums blazed and the roses shed their petals like tears upon the paths.

London stood on the terrace with a basket of flowers over her arm. Her hair was windblown and her cheeks reddened by the frosty air. A mantle of deep green velvet fell from her shoulders. Beneath it she wore a cream-colored gown and the frilly, spreading skirts and bustle that were current English fashion. She had turned her head and was looking toward the stables, which lay amid the copse of trees on the far side of the circular drive. An unexpected gust of wind lifted the wide brim of her hat, and she put up a hand to catch it. The lovely feminine gesture of raised arm and long, graceful neck did not go unnoticed by the man standing at the terrace windows watching her.

Rupert Ashford was thirty-six, a quiet man who preferred scholarly pursuits and the comforts of home and hearth to the gaiety of city life. He was tall and always impeccably dressed and not unhandsome, with a wealth of wavy chestnut hair and neatly trimmed whiskers. Men pronounced him amiable, while women were less inclined to flirt with him than treat him as an older brother.

London, who had been seasick during the voyage to England and as a result had lost considerable weight, had not made a favorable first impression on her family. But Rupert considered the girl a beauty, and her quietness—which he had put down to shyness—had earned her his unqualified approval. As a rule he disapproved of noisy, headstrong women, and London's listlessness, which he attributed to the strain of adjustment, aroused in him a strong desire to protect her. Even now, a full month after their marriage, he found it hard to believe that this golden-haired child-woman was actually his wife.

Opening the terrace door, he stepped outside. London whirled guiltily and, unaccustomed to her wide-spreading skirts, stumbled and nearly fell. Rupert moved quickly to catch her. "Careful!" Stooping, he retrieved the flowers that had fallen from her basket. "Sorry. I didn't mean to startle you. Who did you think it was?"

"The gardener."

London had already learned that no one in the household was permitted to pick flowers from Mr. Bozman's borders; never mind that Bellehurst's gardens were fairly bursting with an overabundance of late-summer blooms. He had already explained to her, irately and in a largely incomprehensible dialect, that flowers were never to be cut, but allowed to go naturally to seed and then turned under for mulch.

But London, enchanted by colors and blossoms she had never dreamed existed beyond the monochrome world of the desert, went on picking them anyway. Only now she did so furtively, whenever Mr. Bozman was elsewhere; snipping the flowers randomly from the end rows in the hope he wouldn't notice.

"You'll get all of us in trouble," Rupert warned, taking the basket from her.

"Not unless he catches me. Which he won't. I planned it like a camel raid."

Rupert gave a hearty laugh. Considering London's stillness and her halting command of the English language, he had at first been inclined to accept the family's pronouncement that Celia's daughter was blessed with little intelligence. But lately he had begun to suspect that beneath his wife's silent facade lurked a very lively and quick-witted spirit. Regrettably, he had no idea how to encourage it. God knows he was not the dashing sort who could sway anyone with the force of his charm.

"There you are! I've been searching everywhere for you!"

Both of them turned to find London's cousin, Beatrice Waring, standing in the doorway, scowling with unconcealed dislike. Although Beatrice had at first dreaded London's arrival, she had been greatly relieved to discover her a thin, nondescript creature with an outlandish wardrobe and a silent, put-offish manner that could not possibly endear her to anyone. But she had not been prepared for the sympathy London had aroused in the bosom of her own mother, Emily; her grandfather, the baron; and even, startlingly enough, her fiancé, George Warburton, to whom she had become engaged earlier that summer despite her grandfather's violent protests.

Beatrice herself had no sympathy for this foreign-born daughter of Aunt Celia's, whose looks and mannerisms she considered utterly bizarre. It would only be a matter of time, she believed, before London made some shocking social faux pas that would drag the family name down into ridicule. Something had to be done immediately to prevent this. Because Emily seemed not to share her daughter's fears, and the baron himself was too old and indifferent to care, Beatrice took it upon herself to provide for her cousin's Western education. Subjects as diverse as Victorian discipline, class protocol, and the stately routine of a large country house were included in her hastily organized instruction. Nor was London's marriage overlooked, for Beatrice was determined to see her cousin converted into a dutiful, well-trained wife, and every night, when London withdrew, exhausted, to her room, it was to find yet another chapter of *Mrs. Beeton's Book of Household Management* or *Enquire Within About Everything* lying open on her bedstand.

Strangely enough, London did not care. She had already dismissed her stout, unattractive cousin as being no better than Bikkela, the shrewish wife of Ali Wad Zarim's long-suffering uncle. Thus it was a simple matter to turn upon Beatrice's lectures a totally deaf ear, as though her cousin were talking to someone else and not to her. There was so much else for London to think about, to learn and grow accustomed to and struggle to understand. Yes, she was annoyed with Beatrice Waring's silliness, but she paid it no real mind, and in a way was glad for the girl's irritating presence, as it somehow served to keep her own thoughts from growing idle and dwelling where she had no wish for them to.

"It's nearly three o'clock," Beatrice was saying now, peering accusingly at the wooden trug London carried, which was, she knew, crammed with flowers cut illicitly from Mr. Bozman's precious borders. "Surely you remember we're having visitors for tea?"

"Yes. Grandfather already told me he wants me there."

"Not only are you to be present," Beatrice said coldly, "you're expected to act as hostess. Do you remember what that means?"

"Of course," London said coolly. "It means I'm supposed to pour."

Without another word she tilted her chin and went inside. But she forgot as she did so to hold aside her wide skirts, which meant that Beatrice was forced to flatten herself against the door in a most unladylike manner. After London was gone, Beatrice looked down. There were grass stains on her spotless white bodice, and the lace on her sleeve was crushed. Her heart began to burn with hot resentment. She was older than London by nearly three years. She had been born in this very house. Why hadn't Grandpapa given *her* the honor of presiding over tea? Surely he must realize how much he'd offended her by giving London the privilege?

Of course not. He was far too crabbed and mean to care about his granddaughter's feelings—or anyone else's! At least Beatrice could find some comfort in the fact that he appeared to terrorize London equally as often as the rest of the family. Everyone at Bellehurst was afraid of him, including Emily, and no one ever escaped his brusque tongue and cold, condemning eyes, not even his precious, newfound granddaughter.

Beatrice's furious expression faded into puzzlement. Oddly enough, London appeared not to mind. In fact, she never failed to smile sweetly at the dreadful old man whenever he cursed her and called her names, and always answered him in the kindly manner of an adult humoring a cross and sickly child. This, of course, infuriated the baron, and confounded Beatrice, who could not understand how *anyone* could treat Lord Ladbroke with such indulgent affection. Thank heaven George had agreed to set up a private establishment for the two of them in Mayfair when they married!

Less than a year, Beatrice reflected dreamily. Less than a year until she could escape the oppressive atmosphere at Bellehurst and finally become Mrs. George Warburton. She had chosen the month of May herself, and pressured her mother into writing the Archbishop of Canterbury to inquire into the matter of a ceremony at Saint Margaret's.

"You'll have to accept her sooner or later, you know."

Beatrice had forgotten all about Rupert. Now she turned to find him standing on the terrace with his hands in his pockets, watching her. She stiffened. Rupert Ashford was everything she disliked in a man: dull, bookish, a constant source of irritation because he was always quoting in Greek or Latin from some impossibly obscure piece of work she didn't recognize or understand. He knew nothing about the gentle art of flirtation, of making polite talk and paying pretty compliments, of making a woman feel . . . well, like a *woman*.

She eyed him coldly. "I haven't the slightest idea what you mean."

"No. I didn't think you would."

For some reason the blood coursed to Beatrice's cheeks at his tone, which annoyed her considerably. Absurd to think that this tedious old man could possibly say anything to offend her. "Excuse me," she said with icy dignity, "I must prepare for our guests." With head held high, she brushed haughtily past him.

London, meanwhile, had crossed to the hall, where she stood arranging her flowers in a huge brass cachepot taken down from the marble-topped commode. She worked quickly, not wanting the housekeeper to catch her. The fact that she had to perform such an innocent task in so clandestine a fashion annoyed her. She had already decided that she would never grow accustomed to the number of servants employed here at Bellehurst or the fact that they were expected to do every little thing for the family.

There had been servants and slaves at Al Betain, of course, but they had worked the fields and tended the goats while London and the wives and daughters of Ali Wad Zarim had prepared the meals and cared for themselves and their households alone. Beatrice, however, had made it clear that every person on Bellehurst's sizable staff had specific chores to perform and that London must never, ever interfere with them.

The gardener in his green baize apron, the housemaids in their black dresses and starched white caps, the cook and her staff, and especially the housekeeper and butler, all lorded over a private domain in which the family was blatantly unwelcome. Responsibilities were clearly defined, right down to the actual ownership of initialed dustpans and the rooms in which they were to be used; the polishing cloths and bottles of beeswax and turpentine that were numbered and kept in separate cupboards according to the furniture they were meant to clean; the tissue paper, silk dusters, and French chalk that were assigned to various housemaids, each of whom jealously guarded her right to wash the high ceilings, rub clean the brocaded walls, or prepare the dance floor before a ball.

This was especially true of the vases and cachepots, which were considered the housekeeper's property and which she alone kept filled with bouquets clipped from a special cutting bed in the far corner of the garden under the strict supervision of Elias Bozman. London had quickly discovered that even Aunt Emily, although mistress of the house, would never dream of suggesting that she put together the simplest of floral arrangements.

"But I'm not Aunt Emily," London decided aloud, stepping back to admire her handiwork.

The lilies and mums that now spilled in charming profusion over the lip of the cachepot added a lovely dash of color to the otherwise austere hall. London wished that she had thought to cut some roses, for she loved their scent and graceful shape best of all. But few of them were still blooming at this time of year, and she did not care for the fat hips that waited, devoid of petals, for the cold clip of Mr. Bozman's shears.

From deep within the walls of the house came the urgent jangling of bells. London looked up. The butler's summons, no doubt from the baron's rooms. She remembered suddenly that the family was expected to be punctual for tea. The vicar and his daughters were joining them from Millham parish, and a few of the neighbors had been invited as well. No one of any real importance, Aunt Emily had explained. It was merely another chance of allowing London to adjust slowly from the colorful, casual life of a Tuareg *zariba* to Bellehurst's orderly world.

Not that the family would be able to keep her shut away from the rest of that world much longer. The county was still in an uproar over London's wedding, which the baron had insisted on keeping private despite the fact that Bellehurst had been swamped with letters, cards, and calls from people who had wheedled, pleaded, demanded invitations. So great had been the furor, in fact, that the baron had finally taken to his bed in a rage, and poor Emily, upset and confused, had turned to her daughter for help.

This, quite understandably, had maddened Beatrice, because by then it seemed that all England had heard of the existence of Lord Ladbroke's "other" granddaughter. The fact that the girl had been raised by Arabs and ordered home from Algiers without anyone in the family being consulted had set tongues wagging nearly as much as the announcement of her hasty betrothal to the baron's nephew. Everyone, including the Prince and Princess of Wales, had clamored to lay eyes on her, and it was all poor Beatrice could do to keep them at bay.

To her credit she had succeeded quite admirably, for the wedding had indeed ended up taking place *en famille*, as the baron had wished. If London was aware of the efforts Beatrice had expended, or suspected the gossip and speculation her marriage had aroused, she did not say. She rarely said anything to anyone, in fact, and beyond her delight in Bellehurst's flowers, showed little interest in the world around her. She was dutiful toward her newfound family only because Ali Wad Zarim had taught her to be so, and if her grandfather wished her to pour tea and make herself agreeable to Mr. Wynstaffe and his unattractive daughters then she would do so, calmly and without protest.

Tucking a last, straying flower into the vase, London lifted her skirts and went quickly upstairs. Her bedroom lay on the second floor of the high-waisted house, with the servants' wing to the east and the nursery, schoolroom, extra suites, and attics quartered above. It was the baron's late wife, the wealthy Bath heiress Amanda Ashford, who had been instrumental in remodeling the small country retreat her husband had inherited, and insisting before her death that it be modernized with Rumford stoves in all of the fireplace openings and colza-oil lamps for light instead of candles. Earth closets had been added to the ground floor and water closets above, and London's bedroom boasted a tiny bathroom all its own, fitted with a gilded washhand stand that was filled daily with hot water from the kitchen by way of copper ewers and cans.

As London stepped inside, she found Lucy, her personal maid, struggling to pour out the last of these. Damp ringlets clung to the girl's thin face, and she smiled breathlessly at her mistress. "I thought you'd be wantin' to wash, ma'am, seein' as you've been down in the garden again."

Wordlessly London stripped off her gloves and unpinned her hat. Shaking out the heavy volume of her hair she went to stand before the looking glass that took up one entire corner of the blue-and-gold dressing room which separated her bedroom from Rupert's in what was pompously known as Bellehurst's State Suite.

"You'll like the vicar and his daughters, ma'am," Lucy went on, accustomed to her mistress's silence and ignoring it. "He's ever so much better than the last one we had. All fire and brimstone about sin whenever he was on the pulpit and then sly, pattin' hands when he was visitin' the women-folk of the parish." She clucked her tongue disapprovingly as she went about laying out towels, soap, and fresh undergarments from the cupboard. "Which dress will you be wantin' to wear?"

London shrugged. "The blue one, I suppose."

"The figured jaconet 'ud be better."

"Very well. Bring it here."

London watched silently as Lucy crossed to the enormous mahogany wardrobe. She had quite a large trousseau by now, paid for by her grandfather and purchased in London. Every gown was suited to a particular purpose: balldresses of white muslin barred with silver basketwork; pale blue or rose watered silk overlaid with tulle and flounced in silk or velvet ribbon; morning dresses of delicately hued merino and taffeta; evening dresses of moiré antique, silk brocade, or embroidered muslin more ravishing than anything London had ever seen. There were jewel-toned dresses intended for outings, walks, and teas, and it was one of these, in a lovely tea-rose yellow, that Lucy took down from the wardrobe and laid carefully across the bed.

London, meanwhile, had removed her morning dress and was brushing her hair. Once the heavy golden mass was pinned up and out of the way, she stood quietly while Lucy laced her corset and slipped the billowing gown over her head. Tugging the padded skirts to rights, the maid stepped back to admire the result.

"There!"

London's gaze followed Lucy's to the cheval glass and for a moment she was tempted to laugh. She wondered if she would ever grow accustomed to the way she looked. Gone forever was the girl in the flowing blue robes of the desert, whose shining hair had fallen in a single braid nearly to her knees. In her place stood the very ideal of a Victorian maiden: pale, demure, her waist so tightly laced as to restrict proper breathing, her heavy hair twisted and secured with combs to the top of her head.

It dawned on London suddenly that she was thinner than she remembered. The lovely, rounded body that Alex MacLaughlin had claimed with such heart-stopping delight had grown angular and boyish, and it seemed as if her cheeks were too hollow and her eyes too large for her face. She, who had spent a lifetime out in the sun, was now so pale and worn that were Alex to see her, he would probably never recognize her.

London gave a faint sob of pain at the thought of Alex and quickly put a hand to her head. Lucy was instantly beside her. "Oh, ma'am, what is it? Are you sick? Should I send for Mrs. Emily?"

"No, no, I'm fine. It's just this wretched corset." London sat down abruptly on a chair. "You'll have to loosen it, I'm afraid, otherwise I won't be able to eat a thing." She forced herself to smile reassuringly as Lucy quickly removed the gown and untied the laces and shoulder ribbons of the offending undergarment. "I'm still not used to this thing. I'd better not eat so much at tea."

"Oh, go on with you, you never touch a thing says Cook," chided Lucy. "And it won't be the food makin' things fit too tight. It'll be the baby, won't it?"

Frozen silence.

"Why, I'm sorry, ma'am. Maybe I shouldn't've mentioned it. But everybody knows downstairs. We're ever so glad for you, too."

The silence remained. Lucy's face reddened. "I suppose you're wonderin' how I know. I just guessed. It wasn't too hard, not after waitin' on you these past two months, both of us bein' women and all. My mum had her last one this summer, that's how I know all about it. I've got eleven brothers and sisters." She smiled tentatively. "I figured you was holdin' off tellin' Mr. Ashford until you were sure, because he isn't actin' like someone what knows he's going to be a father, is he? Nor the baron neither. A great-grandfather, I mean."

"How is it that the others know?" London spoke in a difficult whisper.

"Eh, well, I sort of let slip to Mrs. Garroway, and she can't keep a secret no ways."

"Mrs. Garroway? The cook?"

Lucy nodded. "Her son Pat be married to my oldest sister Liza. And soon as Liza knew, so did everybody else. I hope I didn't make you angry, ma'am."

"No," said London. "No, I'm not angry." She dismissed the girl and went to stand by the window. Closing her eyes, she leaned her forehead against the cold glass and tried hard not to think. She did not want to think. Not about anything. But somehow the image of a man's thin, sunbrowned face rose before her, and suddenly it was as if she could smell the hot desert air once again, see the palm fronds swaying in the breeze, and feel Alex's hands, so tender and sure, roving her trembling body.

A child. Had she been so wrapped up in her own private misery that she hadn't even noticed? Of course not. All at once she realized that she had known all along, but had let the suspicion linger in the back of her mind, where she had taken to hiding everything and anything that might remind her of Alex.

I mustn't let Rupert know, London thought wildly. Rupert was good and kind and didn't deserve to be hurt. And she had no intention of letting Alex's son—not for a moment did she doubt it was a son—suffer the shame of questionable parentage. No one must ever suspect that she hadn't conceived him during that awkward encounter on the night of her marriage to Rupert. Least of all Rupert himself. And Alex too. Alex must never know.

The tears that London had stubbornly held inside since Alex had last touched her on the waterfront in Algiers were suddenly swelling in her throat, scalding her eyes and sliding hotly down her cheeks. It was impossible to stop them. She felt as though they were welling up from her very soul and bringing with them the fluttering, dying pieces of her heart. She pressed her hands to her mouth in a desperate effort to still her choking sobs while the tears continued to drip onto the pane, mingling there with the raindrops running down the far side of the glass.

Chapter Eleven

The news that he was soon to become a great-grandfather had a very curious effect upon the aged baron. Bedridden with sciatica since the damp onset of autumn, he seemed all at once to forget his pain and, to the dismay of the collective household, insisted on rising from his bed. Reclining in an armchair with several shawls layered about his bony shoulders, he held court throughout the day, demanding endless interviews with London, with her physician, Dr. Carne, with Rupert and Emily, and sending his valet, Kingsley, on numerous and quite mysterious errands.

He explained nothing, snapped furiously whenever anyone was foolish enough to ask him a question, and generally behaved in such a manner as to fill his future son-in law, George, with mounting trepidation.

"He means to change his will, by God!" This dire pronouncement was made on a cold November evening shortly before eight o'clock as George and Beatrice sat alone in the drawing room of the spacious Palladian town house, located on a quiet, cobbled street just off Saint James's, belonging to George's widowed mother, Augusta Warburton.

Beatrice and Emily had arrived in London a week earlier to visit friends, go shopping in the West End, and attend a modest dinner party given by George's older sister Clarissa in honor of Augusta's sixtieth birthday. Unfashionably punctual as the Warings always were, Emily and Beatrice had been the first to arrive, but for once Emily had remained undaunted, and even contrived to turn the parlor over to Beatrice and George for what she hoped would prove a brief, romantic interlude.

George, however, had not behaved in the least like an ardent suitor should. Rather than taking advantage of the moment to make love to his future wife, he had wasted no time in tasking Beatrice with the underhanded scheming of her doddering grandfather. "Why else would he insist on all this secrecy?" he continued now, pacing up and down before his startled fiancée's eyes. "Why else would he spend all his time plotting with Rupert Ashford and your cousin and that imbecile Kingsley unless he means to cut me out?"

He glared at Beatrice, clearly expecting an answer, and she smiled at him bravely, trying hard to swallow her disappointment. She had not seen George since London's wedding, and of course she had been expecting a far warmer reception than this.

Smoothing the folds of her bronze-green satin dress, she strove to sound calm and bracing. "George, dear, be reasonable. You don't really think Grandpapa means to change his will in favor of Rupert Ashford, do you? How can he? London is his *daughter's* child. I'm his son's."

George paused in his pacing to throw her a look of utter contempt. He was a heavyset man, well over medium height, with a florid face presently taut with anger. "You think that makes a difference, do you?"

"Of course it does," Beatrice responded calmly. "The entail is clearly—"

"Spare me the lecture, please! An entail in the hands of a good lawyer is full of bloody holes these days, thanks to the recent acts!"

Hot color flooded Beatrice's cheeks. George had never spoken to her like this before. "What do you mean? What acts?"

"Oh, never mind. You'd never understand. And it isn't just the entail. There's the estate itself to consider, and the personal wealth he's amassed over the years thanks to the stock your grandmother left him when she died. God, I bet the old rutter made thousands on New River alone! The money's his to dispose of as he pleases, Beatrice, never forget that. And I wouldn't put it past him to favor his nephew and that infidel granddaughter of his just because he doesn't approve of our engagement. All because they're presenting him with a great-grandchild before we can.''

The heat rose higher in Beatrice's cheeks. "George, really—''

"Oh, bloody hell, forget it! What time is dinner?''

"Clarissa plans to serve at ten. She's asked the Hurleys and Lord and Lady Siddons.'' Beatrice gazed at him anxiously. "Are you going somewhere?''

But George was already gone, slamming the door behind him as he went. Beatrice pretended not to notice, but her lower lip quivered. She had never realized before how quick-tempered George could be. Although perhaps it wasn't fair to judge him just now. He had every right to be upset.

"All of us do," Beatrice assured herself aloud, "what with Grandpapa behaving so unreasonably of late.''

As a matter of fact, the atmosphere at Bellehurst had grown so intolerable in recent weeks that Beatrice had been only too glad to flee for a time. Not only because of her grandfather's impossible behavior, but because of the ridiculous fuss everyone was making over London's pregnancy, going on and on about it, even Emily and the servants, until Beatrice had thought she would scream.

Regrettably, she had not found any real escape from her cousin here in London either. Wherever Beatrice went, people were forever asking endless questions about her. Why, only yesterday George had returned in a temper from Marlborough House to report that the Prince of Wales had pressed him relentlessly about meeting this "mysterious Arab beauty.'' Perhaps George would care to present her at court?

Beatrice had very nearly fainted at the news. London invited to Osborn House for a meeting with the queen? Dear God, it was unthinkable! After all, it had taken weeks just to teach the wretched girl to use a knife and fork at meals! How on earth was she ever going to learn the proper protocol required to make her curtsy to the queen?

Shuddering at the thought now, Beatrice came quickly to her feet. Since it didn't seem likely that George was going to return, she might as well join the others in the parlor. Pausing for a moment before the mirror, she made certain that their unpleasant exchange had not left some sort of telltale mark upon her. She saw that her diamond hair clasp was askew and spent some time fussing with it before she was satisfied.

It was terribly important that Beatrice look her best tonight, because word had it that Anne Marie Siddons was planning a fancy-dress ball which, it was rumored, would eclipse even the extravagant celebrations marking the recent end of the Zulu war. Naturally Beatrice coveted an invitation for herself and George and was determined to see that she got one tonight.

There was only one problem: the annoying fact that Lady Siddons had behaved extremely coolly toward Beatrice when they had first been introduced at Covent Garden the other night, as though she hadn't liked her. But Beatrice took comfort in the thought that Clarissa Warburton had also made a point to invite Amelia Hurley to the party tonight. Since the Hurleys and the Ashfords were connected by marriage on Beatrice's grandmother's side, and Amelia Hurley and Anne Marie Siddons were themselves first cousins, Beatrice had already decided that she need merely suggest to Amelia—

Cousins.

Beatrice's racing thoughts froze, then backtracked swiftly and seized upon the obvious. But of course. Why hadn't she thought of it before? She didn't need that snidely pompous Amelia to intervene in her behalf! She would procure an invitation all by herself—by promising to arrange for the "mysterious" London Ashford to make her first public appearance at the Siddons's fancy-dress ball—in Arabic costume no less.

Beatrice's eyes gleamed as she envisioned her own heightened importance for bringing off such an unprecedented coup. Lady Siddons would surely crow with triumph while London, she felt supremely confident, would not think to refuse.

* * *

Back home in Kent, London was enjoying the delicious quiet that had settled over Bellehurst with her cousin's departure. Perhaps it was merely her imagination, but it seemed as if the entire household had suddenly become more relaxed and cheerful. Even the baron had abandoned his frantic activities and returned to his bed like a dutiful patient, although he continued to demand regular interviews with Dr. Carne concerning the progress of his granddaughter's pregnancy.

He need not have worried. London was feeling extremely well. The nausea that had plagued her during the early weeks was gone, and she quickly found herself filled with an abundance of energy and purpose. These she directed toward planning her baby's future, determined to see that the boy was accepted without question into the world in which he would be born. Regrettably not the Tuareg world, but this strange, bustling, Victorian world of Empire, machines, enterprise, and money, all played out on a scale so lavish and grand that London doubted she herself would ever grow used to it.

After some reflection she had come to realize that she could assure acceptance for Alex's son only if she became part of that world herself. Neither her family's name nor her husband's respected position in the annals of academia, or even the baron's wealth, would open the doors that a few, properly spoken words by the right hostesses could do. And so she set about learning how to become one of them, pouring over the same books and texts and lessons that, a few weeks earlier, Beatrice had despaired of ever teaching her. As well, she worked hard to curry friendships with select individuals in the county, entertaining them at Bellehurst or accompanying them, whenever she was asked, on the afternoon promenades that were such fashionable Victorian pastimes and the current, if unspoken, criterion of a woman's success.

The baron, who at first violently opposed the sudden influx of visitors into his house, hastened to encourage it after seeing how the color bloomed in his granddaughter's cheeks as she assumed an increasingly busy schedule as hostess. Rupert, too, was quick to oblige her, holding point-to-points and field trials and organizing hunts, although normally he disliked anything smacking of the out-of-doors. Fortunately, Bellehurst's fields and forests had long been neglected by the baron, who had dismissed his last gamekeeper nearly a decade ago, and they were now overrun with foxes, woodcock, and snipe. And while the men eagerly shot, the women dawdled indoors, nibbling confections, discussing their families, and passing along the latest scandals from Town and abroad.

"You do intend to join us in London for the holidays, don't you, Mrs. Ashford?" someone inquired during one of those frequent hunt suppers held at Bellehurst, on a dark December evening nearing Christmas.

"I'm not really sure, Mrs. Olwyn. Mr. Ashford and I haven't made any plans yet to leave Kent this winter."

There was a general murmur of disapproval, and Mrs. Olwyn's fluting voice took on an edge of disbelief. "Surely you don't mean to spend the entire Christmas season tucked away in the country?"

"Letitia's right." This from an immensely overweight matron dressed in yards of shimmering bronze bombazine who had already consumed nearly half the tea cake and was surreptitiously eyeing the last piece on the plate. "The moment the weather changes, Herbert and I will be off to London ourselves. And I want to assure you, my dear, that there will be plenty to do in London in wintertime—even for a woman in your condition."

London smiled politely and said she would consider it. Later, watching through the frosty window as the guests took themselves off into the cold December night, she was filled with relief at seeing them go.

Slowly she went back into the drawing room, where the servants were stacking the last of the dishes and rearranging tables and chairs. Watching them, she felt all at once inexplicably cross, which wasn't surprising considering how little she had been sleeping of late and how much she had been eating—not only tonight, but during the countless luncheons, dinners, soirees, teas, and courses *à la russe* over which she had presided in recent weeks.

It's for Alex's sake, she reminded herself stubbornly. Only for him and for his son was she forcing herself to remain pleasant to the likes of Lady Brunnell, that unbearably arrogant specimen of Gothic rectitude who could eat more at one sitting than an entire tribe of Tuareg warriors, and doing her best to be agreeable to the likes of all those boastful men who joined the ladies after the hunt, many of whom always happened to be self-proclaimed—and usually quite moronic—experts on the Middle East.

"Do you wish anything else, madam?" Seward, the butler, did not know what to make of young Mrs. Ashford's appearance in the drawing room. It was very late, and the rest of the family had already retired.

I'd like a stiff brandy, London was tempted to say, because she had often heard Rupert utter exactly those words whenever Bellehurst was overflowing with a noisy mix of locals and friends. But the Tuaregs who had raised her had never touched spirits and London had not, despite the baron's frequent urgings, developed a taste for them herself.

"No thank you, Seward. I'm going upstairs. Good night."

"Good night, madam."

She climbed slowly to her room, holding tiredly to the railing. Upstairs she found the lamps still lit in her sitting room, casting a soft glow on her writing desk, which was cluttered with the notes she had been making earlier for her baby's layette. Closing the door behind her, London stood for a moment looking down at them.

It was late, nearly one o'clock. Lucy was already asleep on her cot in the adjoining room, and London did not ring for her. Instead she undressed herself, struggling with some difficulty alone out of her heavy cashmere sack gown. Slipping into her long white nightdress, London did up the row of modest buttons and went to the mirror to brush out her hair. She did not know it, but pregnancy suited her, for her hair shone like minted gold in the lamplight, and once again she looked as sleek and lovely as she had appeared to Alex on the first day he had ever seen her.

Sitting down at the desk, London sifted idly through her notes. She had never realized before how many clothes and accessories an English infant needed in order to be born.

Why, at Al Betain. . . . But that was a forbidden thought, and she thrust it quickly away. And became, all at once, aware of a strange fluttering sensation within her. She held herself very still, the pen poised in her hand. Then, holding her breath, she slowly placed her palms on her barely rounded abdomen. Almost immediately the faint movement came again.

"Oh!" It was a soft gasp of wonder.

"London?"

The door to her dressing room, the one that led down the narrow corridor into her husband's room, had been left ajar. London hadn't even realized that Rupert was upstairs, but suddenly he was there in the doorway, wearing a dressing gown of dark blue brocade, his long hair untidy, looking at her with an expression of intense concern.

"The baby," she said, laughing at him. "It moved!"

Impulsively he dropped to his knees and seized her hands in his. "Oh, my dear, how wonderful! I was so afraid, hearing you call out like that—" Suddenly aware of what he was doing, he released her abruptly. Not once since their wedding night had he touched her without thought, or dared set foot uninvited inside her dressing room. Now, to cover his intense embarrassment, he looked desperately around him.

Like all Victorian bedrooms, London's had originally been grim and very austere. It was an age in which luxury in the bedroom was considered suggestive, and the ornate furnishings and lovely brass bed that had graced the room during the Regency era of Admiral Waring's youth had long been discarded.

Nevertheless, London had taken it upon herself in recent weeks to make a number of changes. Because she had never owned a real bed before, she had insisted, as her pregnancy advanced and her proportions grew, that the footmen bring down from the attic an ancient four-poster, a bed so enormous that a short flight of mahogany steps was needed in order to climb onto the mattress. It was a stunning piece of French workmanship, with carvings of lithe nymphs and patterns of flowers and fruits twining about the massive headboard.

London had replaced its moth-eaten velvet coverlet with a paisley-patterned silk duvet, which was scattered with homey bolsters and frilled pillows.

With Lucy's help she had also taken up the austere carpeting—smelling strongly of age and camphor—and put down a number of colorful throw rugs found in a downstairs parlor. The dark, uninviting oils on the walls had been replaced with bright watercolors, and the heavy drapes with lacy curtains. On the nightstand of the now cheerful bedroom were housed the prerequisite Bible and candlebox—and a lovely collection of hand-blown glass perfume bottles that, in the lamplight, seemed to capture every color and nuance of the rainbow.

Rupert's wandering gaze seized upon them in astonishment. "Why, these are lovely!" His embarrassment was forgotten as he crossed to the table to pick one of them up. It was barely the size of his hand, deep amethyst in color, and exquisitely detailed, its dainty handle carved like a scroll. "Where did you get these?"

"They belonged to my foster father. One of his ancestors made off with them during a raid in Abidjan. Somehow, over the centuries, they made their way across the Sahara to Al Betain."

"From Abidjan? But I'd say these were Roman. Perhaps blown several centuries before the time of Christ."

London watched him, how his long fingers touched the glass almost reverently, his scholarly mind clearly piqued by the mystery of its origins. "I suppose we'll never know how they got from Rome to Abidjan," she said regretfully.

"No. Nothing much is known about Abidjan before the fifteenth century. I find it doubtful that the Romans brought them there, unless they came by way of Caesar's army, which was traveling north to conquer Europe. But I'd still say that they fell into a number of hands before turning up in Abidjan." Rupert looked at her. "You say they're yours?"

"Yes. Ali Wad Zarim gave them to me after I'd completed my studies."

"Studies? Of what? The Koran? Are you telling me you're a Koranic scholar?"

London smiled. "I wouldn't call myself a scholar exactly. But I did spend a number of years learning Arabic and reading the suras. You needn't look surprised. The Tuareg aren't Arabs. That means they don't follow the more literal interpretation of the Koran, which withholds the right of education from the daughters of the tribe. In some respects I believe that makes the Tuareg far more enlightened."

"In the treatment of their women, you mean."

"Yes."

Rupert put down the amethyst bottle and lifted another, this one of a murky aquamarine, much larger than the first and quite beautiful in the lamplight. Across the room his eyes met hers. "I realize suddenly how very little I know about you."

London's gaze dropped. She had no idea whether this remark implied criticism or not. There was still so much she did not understand about Rupert or his world. And she was suddenly made aware once again of the vast difference between Rupert and Alex—Alex, who had come to know her so intimately in such a very short time and who had instinctively understood the workings of her heart. . . .

But Rupert now looked at her with an interest he had never shown before, and the silence that had fallen between them was not as awkward as that which usually surrounded them whenever they were alone, which was rarely, because Rupert spent long hours every day locked away in the baron's musty library. But the presence of these beautiful glass objets d'art and the sudden discovery that his wife possessed, if anything, a fantastically unusual intellect, seemed abruptly to have done away with Rupert's shyness. For once, in her presence, he found himself on familiar ground.

"May I sit down?"

"Please."

He lowered himself into a wide-lapped chair facing her. After a moment's hesitation he began to talk. He wished to know the extent of her familiarity with the Koran, her thoughts on Islam as a whole, her judgment of the Blue Men of the desert and their Bedouin counterparts to the south. Did she have any evidence to support a recent theory that ancient Canaanites had once conquered Al-Djezair, the white isle from which Algiers had gotten its name?

They talked long into the night, companionably, like old friends. London answered his questions as best she could and told him something about her childhood, her Tuareg family, and the ancient tales the elders had shared with her around the fire. She described her journeys to the salt mines of Bilfha and the mystical world of the Blue Men themselves, as far removed and incomprehensible to Rupert as the green hills of Kent had at first seemed to her.

London's face grew softer as she spoke, losing, for the first time, the haunted look it had worn since her arrival. Unawares, she wrapped the warmth of those memories around her, because just talking about them made Alex seem real once again and, for a brief moment stolen out of time, brought him within reach.

The oil lamps burned low and the dying embers popped in the grate, before she fell silent at last. The great clock in the hall downstairs chimed loudly in the sudden stillness. Three muted booms. Her eyes met Rupert's across the darkened room.

"It's very late," Rupert observed.

"Yes."

"You'd better go to bed. I've kept you up far too long."

"I've enjoyed it," London said honestly.

Rupert smiled. "So have I." He rose and came to stand before her, offering his hand. London lifted her face to him and waited. They did not kiss. They never kissed. But there was a newfound confidence in the way he helped her to her feet and led her to the bed. There he hesitated, his hand beneath her elbow. She stood silently at his side, not looking at him. After a moment Rupert sighed and his hand dropped away. In the doorway he turned, his expression one of intense regret. "I wish I were younger. And a more interesting man. I'm sorry."

London's face was lost amid the shadows of the canopied bed. Only its sweet shape showed clearly. "It doesn't matter. I like you just the way you are."

"Oh." Then, more confidently, "Oh."
The door closed softly behind him.

The following morning at breakfast, the usual stack of
invitations lay beside London's plate. She leafed through
them without interest, then paused to turn over one bearing
an unfamiliar seal. She broke it open and unfolded it. "What's
a fancy-dress ball?"

Rupert and Emily looked at her.

"It means you're to come in costume," Rupert explained.
"Disguised as someone else, like Cleopatra or Diana, goddess of the hunt."

Emily, who had returned home from London just the week
before, smiled at a sudden memory. "I remember your grandfather once appearing at the duke of Marlborough's fancy-
dress ball disguised as Zeus. Actually he looked like a half-
naked savage, wrapped in musty-smelling badger skins with
a laurel wreath on his head and wearing a pair of your grandmother's golden clips in his ears. I can't imagine where he
got the idea. Your grandmother was positively scandalized."

Rupert roared with laughter. "As was the rest of the assem-
bly, I'm sure."

London tried hard to imagine her grandfather attending a
formal party wearing earrings and animal furs and found that
she could not.

"Who's it from?"

She handed the invitation to Rupert. "Someone named
Siddons."

Emily looked at Rupert. He looked back at her. The serving
girl was laying fresh cream and marmalade and a platter of
fried kidneys on the table. After she had withdrawn, the
sitting room remained silent but for the patter of rain against
the long windows.

"It's out of the question," Rupert said unexpectedly. He
sounded annoyed.

"Why? Wouldn't it be the perfect opportunity? Just the
right touch of fantasy, gay costumes, frivolous people, nothing formal or in any way demanding."

London laid down her fork. She looked at Rupert's set face,

then her aunt's, which was, for once, unusually animated. A nagging suspicion filled her mind that they had had similar arguments before. "You'd like to use the costume ball as a means of—what do you call it?—launching me, wouldn't you?"

They looked at her guiltily, unable to guess what lay behind that calm voice, the impassive face.

"It would be so much easier than a conventional debut," Emily explained quickly. "For you, I mean. Anything else would doubtless be far too overwhelming." Not to mention inappropriate, considering that London was married and expecting a baby.

"We're going to have to launch you sooner or later," Rupert agreed with a half-hearted smile. "We can't always hide you away from the rest of the world, can we?"

London considered this in silence while Rupert and Emily watched her anxiously. Finally, unexpectedly, she looked up and arched her eyebrows at them. "What do you think I should wear?"

For a moment they stared at her. Then they both began talking at once.

"Would you really consent to go?"

"Are you sure you want to do this?"

"Why not?"

"How very brave of you!"

London shrugged. "Who shall I be?"

"You'd look splendid as Daphne."

"No, Emily. It has to be royalty. Perhaps a Persian queen or a Slavic princess?"

"So long as the costume is flowing."

"And not too eye-catching."

"So no one will notice the baby, you mean." London had already learned—to her infinite astonishment—that a woman's pregnancy was considered an embarrassment in England, something one never acknowledged in public, least of all whenever gentlemen were present. "Insufferable prudery," she murmured now, once again annoyed at the thought.

"Not at all! You'd look charming as Calliope. Wouldn't she, Rupert?"

"I'm not sure. How about Helen of Troy? Or Mary, Queen of Scots?"

"But she was beheaded!"

"Why on earth should that matter? Perhaps Aphrodite—"

"No," said London calmly. "I've no intention of passing myself off as some silly character in a book. I'm going to go as me. Is my *gondurah* still in the attic?"

They looked at her, neither one knowing quite what to say. She laughed suddenly, a gay laugh of the sort she had rarely uttered since leaving Algiers. For a moment her pretty, pointed face glowed with it, bringing the sparkle to her eyes and leaving Rupert and Emily staring in astonishment.

A costume ball. Once again London considered the idea. It might actually be fun, and God knows she had been starved of fun far too long. Besides, there would be soldiers in London. The baron had told her so.

Ever since the ending of the Zulu war and the beginning of another, equally unpopular conflict on the African frontier, the British Cabinet had been criticized for the state of British preparedness in South Africa. To that end, the government was considering raising tax revenues for the military, and although London understood little about wars and taxes, she remembered a great deal about military policy from her childhood in Lucknow. Well, maybe not all that much, but enough, at any rate, to know that the Ministry was incapable of making any decisions without first summoning a number of military advisers from overseas and interviewing them at length. Which meant that the city ought to be full of them by now and that every self-respecting society hostess would be vying fiercely for the honor of parading them through her drawing room.

And perhaps, just perhaps, London might run into one of them at the Siddons's ball: an officer who had recently returned from India and could give her news of the Bengal Lancers. Or even—where was the harm in dreaming a little?—actually meeting someone of sufficient rank to have recently been briefed, entirely coincidentally, on the newly elected British Resident of a small Rajput kingdom known as Jhulapore.

Chapter
Twelve

Arthur and Anne Marie, Lord and Lady Siddons, resided on upper Audley Street in a magnificent mansion where the Prince of Wales could occasionally be found holding court in an atmosphere described by one visitor as a miniature Versailles. Lord Siddons's fortune, like that of his neighbors the Rothschilds and Sassoons, had been amassed over the years by shrewd financial dealings and investments. Because his wife enjoyed spending money equally as much as he enjoyed making it, the couple entertained often and lavishly.

Popular and ambitious, Anne Marie Siddons disliked being outshone, and her fancy-dress ball—while not on the grand scale of the fourteen hundred guests recently invited to Marlborough House for a similar engagement given by the Prince and Princess of Wales—promised to be an affair of unparalleled magnificence. And so it was. There was a considerable crush merely to get inside the house, and Audley Street was jammed with cabs, carriages, sedan chairs, and a veritable mob of spectators lining the curb to watch the privileged move in a glittering line up the wide steps to the front door. The January night was frosty, but no one seemed to care.

Beatrice, George, and the Ashfords had arrived in a cab because Rupert had refused to allow London to walk. George, who was dressed in the tartan regalia of some obscure Scottish clan, was shivering violently because his kilt exposed his bare, knobby legs to the icy air.

Beatrice, standing haughtily beside him, looked extraordinary herself in blood-red silk trimmed with gold embroideries, and with numerous tartan ribbons fluttering from an enormous turquoise turban set upon her head. She was dressed, she had explained to her bemused family, as her clan chieftain's patriotic Jacobite wife.

Unmindful of the stares, she swept up the steps with the others behind her and, nodding coldly to the servants, proceeded through the wide-standing doors. Inside the hall, she concluded at once, in a very loud voice, that the man in the scarlet uniform ahead of her was none other than the prime minister.

"Disraeli is at Hughenden, ailing," Rupert whispered uncomfortably.

"Nonsense. He wouldn't dare leave Downing Street until the dissolution of Parliament. Oh, do go speak to him, George!"

"I'll do no such thing. Here, Ashford, see to your wife's cloak, will you?"

London smiled gratefully at both of them. Poor Rupert. Fancy-dress balls were not meant for him, and obviously he felt—and, regrettably, looked—rather ridiculous as Marcus Aurelius in a frock coat of white tarlatan with a crown of artificial laurel leaves set upon his head. He was carrying a scroll with *Meditations* penned upon it in Greek, which he had begun shredding with long, nervous fingers the moment they had entered the tightly packed foyer.

Looking about her, London, who was by now well accustomed to the shabby, faded elegance of Bellehurst, was all but overwhelmed by what she saw. Lord Siddons had built his home in the Italian Renaissance style, and London's incredulous gaze was drawn upward to the vast, open galleries soaring four stories or more above her toward a vaulted ceiling painted with the most fantastic scenes. Twining flowers, lolling goddesses, and sleek, allegorical animals were framed by elaborate carvings picked out in gilt that would have been lost in the gloom but for the enormous chandeliers blazing in numerous arches between the marble columns running the entire length of each gallery.

"I understand it was inspired by the Palazzo Tranti in Rome," Rupert said, sounding similarly awed.

"Hush," hissed Beatrice. "People will think you've never been here before."

Rupert frowned at her. "Well, I haven't."

"Please," said George a trifle impatiently, "let's go inside."

Crossing the hall, they stepped into the magnificent ballroom. Here, amid stunning works of art and carvings of exquisite Carrara marble, servants and guests moved in a surging tide of motion and color. The costumes were fantastic; an unbelievable array of crinolined royalty, ravishing goddesses, lithe nymphs, handsome Greek heroes, and ancient Saxon kings.

In a loud voice Beatrice began pointing out the people she claimed to recognize. The crowd pressed close, everyone talking at once. Someone was tugging at London's sleeve. She turned to find a Harlequin fool with tinkling bells in his cap bowing to her. "Mrs. Ashford? Lady Siddons has been asking for you. The Prince of Wales wishes to meet you."

"I knew it! I knew it!" Beatrice shrieked. "Go on, London, go! George, is my turban straight?"

The Prince and Princess of Wales were standing in the far corner of the ballroom surrounded by a crush of well-wishers come to make their curtsies and bows. The prince was dressed in a satin uniform glittering with medals and orders. A wide blue sash covered his chest and an ornamental sword was strapped about his ample waist. His bearded, pleasant face lit with interest at the sight of London being pushed toward him by an overweight creature wearing an enormous turquoise turban. Grinning, he said something into the ear of the dark-haired Princess Alexandra.

Why, he isn't wearing a costume at all, London thought, surprised. A moment later she blushed at her ignorance when the prince, kissing her hand, inquired mischievously if she had recognized him as Peter the Great. Thankfully he did not await an answer but insisted instead upon meeting Rupert. Shyly, London presented him, finding herself warming to the prince. He was not, as she had imagined, aloof and unapproachable. Why Lady Siddons, dressed as the goddess Hebe in clinging white, hung on his arm and giggled up into his

face. Whenever she did so, the prince winked at her while
Princess Alexandra looked tolerantly on. Around them surged
the costumed crowd, curious and admiring, and of course
there were countless interruptions, which the prince accepted
good-naturedly.

"I'm afraid this isn't a good place for becoming better
acquainted, Mrs. Ashford," he remarked with a smile when
the music began at last and the guests drifted in a glittering
procession onto the dance floor.

"How long will you be staying?" Alexandra inquired.
"Perhaps your husband could escort you to Marlborough
House this week? We keep an open house most evenings."

London hesitated. Rupert had wanted to take her back to
Bellehurst as soon as possible, but was it polite to mention
her pregnancy to the future king and queen?

"We plan to leave for Kent on Thursday," Rupert volunteered.

"Oh, but that leaves plenty of time," Alexandra insisted.
"I'll send a card round tomorrow."

With the matter satisfactorily settled, the prince excused
himself, explaining that others were waiting to see him. Alexandra followed, smiling and saying it was only the gaming
tables demanding his attention. The moment they were gone,
others moved in to take their place—people who seemed to
know either Beatrice or George but who were mainly interested in meeting London. Not only the mystique of her origins, but her golden hair, her fine features, and the deep blue
of her robes and eyes could not help but attract numerous
admirers.

London answered their many questions as best as she could,
although she soon found herself growing tired and hot. She
had also begun wishing, unexpectedly and almost without
conscious thought, that she hadn't chosen to wear her *gondurah* tonight. Somehow it seemed indecent to flaunt such
noble Tuareg attire in the company of grown men and women
disguised as opera singers, Egyptians, buffoons, and even,
unbelievably, fur-bearing animals and pieces of fruit.

Eventually her head began to ache, and London turned to
Rupert in a silent appeal for help. But Rupert had been trapped

by the stout Queen of Palmyra, looking terribly out of place himself because the laurel wreath he wore kept slipping into his eyes. Beatrice and George were nowhere in sight, but London thought she caught a glimpse of Beatrice's turquoise turban bobbing on the dance floor.

I should never have come, she thought, and was annoyed that this snippet of wisdom hadn't occurred to her earlier. Thankfully, Aunt Emily had been right about one thing: there were countless other distractions to divert the guests here tonight. Even London's most smitten admirers had shown themselves largely uninterested in the history of the Tuareg tribe and had eventually drifted away from her. After all, there was better sport to be had in trying to guess who the other guests were supposed to be or in shredding, with gleeful malice, the reputations of those whose costumes were judged neither flattering nor clever, or—worst of all— had been duplicated with far greater success by somebody else.

Looking about her, London suddenly realized that she was bored. Without another word to Rupert, she slipped outside alone and wandered for a time down the marble-columned gallery studying the magnificent works of Velázquez, Murillo, Van Dyck, and Cuyp hanging on the brocaded walls. Rather regretfully she had to conclude that their subject matter, like the costumes of the people dancing in the ballroom behind her, were largely incomprehensible to her and therefore quite dull.

Sighing, she passed through a pair of double doors set beneath a stunning gold arabesque and found herself all at once in a sumptuous drawing room filled with a number of gilded tables and chairs. Which were, London was startled to see, occupied wholly by costumed gentlemen. Some were playing cards or dice while others conducted discreet conversations in intimate groups of two or three. In one corner, Charles I was holding forth on last year's retreat at Rorke's Drift while his interested audience—two dashing chevaliers, one armored crusader, and a tall, Byronic fellow with a high Regency collar—listened attentively as they puffed their cigars. Elsewhere, newspapers rustled and footmen moved about with serving trays and matchboxes. No one took the slightest notice of her.

Cheeks burning, London retreated. More cautiously, she opened another door at the far end of the corridor. Half expecting to find it similarly occupied, she peeked hesitantly inside. "Oh—!" It was a drawn-out breath of wonder.

Before her lay a long, narrow room with walls of sheer white marble, the colonnades richly carved in the Italian Renaissance manner and picked out here and there in gold. Windows with heavy velvet drapes were set within their flowing arches, and these in turn were flanked by lovely statues on podiums of deep green marble. Priceless carpets ran the length of the vast floor, interspersed by richly colored porcelain cachepots containing miniature orange trees and feathery palms. Ferns and flowering vines drooped gracefully from planters affixed to the ceiling, and somewhere in the distance a fountain gurgled. The effect was one of cool, restful beauty.

"I should love to have a room like this!" London exclaimed aloud. Indeed, it seemed the perfect place to escape the noisy crush in the ballroom, and so she wandered slowly down the length of it, pausing now and again to touch the petals of some exotic bloom.

"But I would have done things differently," she decided at last. Made it less formal somehow, with lots of windows to let in the sunshine and no statues or chandeliers to clutter the floor and compete with the natural beauty of the plants and potted trees. Only a few chairs for sitting and reading, or for doing nothing at all. And flowers. Lots of them, growing everywhere, with no dour old Mr. Bozman to keep them locked away from the world. The thought made London smile.

Eventually, reluctantly, she went back outside. The baby chose just then to move restlessly within her, and London leaned for a moment against the wall, breathing slowly and deeply until, mercifully, the tightness in her throat receded. Lately, she had been weeping over the silliest, most trivial things, and she would never forgive herself if she shed tears at Lady Siddons's fancy-dress ball simply because Alex's unborn son was suddenly making his presence known.

Tiredly, London straightened and opened her eyes. Ahead of her, a door in the corridor opened and two men emerged. One of them was elderly, with yellowed, drooping whiskers, wearing the age-stained uniform of a regiment London recognized instantly although it was rarely seen outside India: the canary yellow of Skinner's Horse. The other man was considerably younger and was dressed in the more familiar scarlet uniform of the India Infantry. He was speaking loudly to the older man, who was obviously deaf, and London had no trouble understanding him. He was talking about India.

All at once the weariness seemed to leave her and her heart gave a great, bounding leap. Brushing the hair from her eyes she stepped eagerly into the light. Both men stopped. The older man stared at her, at her dark blue robes which, because of her growing belly, London had not belted that night but had allowed to flow freely in the manner of Tuareg men.

Their eyes met. She cleared her throat. "Excuse me—"

"Good God!" His voice was as thin and raspy as dried leaves. "Will you look at that, Harry! Bloody fellow has the nerve to dress like a wog! Never seen anything like it in all my years, have you?"

"No, sir," admitted the other.

"Eh? Eh?"

In louder tones: "Can't say as I have, sir!"

"Well, it's bloody inexcusable, I say! Shouldn't be allowed! What next? Inja niggers in British uniforms? Blackies in court attire?"

"*Yeh-log!*" The contemptuous Hindu word rose suddenly, furiously, to London's lips. Both men stared at her. She bore down on them, shaking with anger. "You! How dare you call them that? You, who probably weren't even fit to taste the salt of the Indian *sirdars* who served you!"

The old man's face had turned a deep, mottled purple. "Outrage! Outrage!" Spittle flew from his lips. "Here, Harry, where's m'whip? I'll cane the young beggar myself! Unbelievable impertinence! Ought to take it up with the Master General of the Ordnance! And I will, by God, I will!"

"Never mind, Sir Frederick! There's no need to excite yourself! You there!"

But London had brushed past them and was running down the corridor, blinded by rage and scalding tears. Rounding the corner she bumped squarely into someone, a tall man in a frock coat with a thin, kindly face. She gasped out his name and he caught her by the shoulders, gripping them hard.

"London, are you all right? The baby—"

"Take me home," she choked. "Please."

"I'll call a cab—"

"No! I want to go home. Home to Al Betain."

Rupert's mouth twisted. "How can you? You belong in England now."

"And whose fault is that?" London flared at him.

She regretted the words the moment she said them. But they were out, and now they quivered between them, bitter, unfair, and irrevocable.

Rupert's hands fell abruptly from her shoulders. "Come," he said woodenly, "I'll take you home. But not to Al Betain. To Bellehurst."

She followed him, her head bowed, and they went silently out into the cold night together.

Chapter Thirteen

London's baby was due at the end of July, unless it fooled everyone by arriving early, which Dr. Carne thought might be entirely possible. Mrs. Ashford was carrying unusually low for the seventh month, but with first babies one never knew for sure. Not that he was the least bit concerned by the likelihood of an early delivery. On the contrary, he pronounced himself more than satisfied with his patient's progress. She was a quiet thing—calmly accepting of the situation

and in excellent health, the way all expectant mothers ought
to be and so seldom were.

It was May now, and the countryside was groggy with
spring. In the orchards, the pear and cherry trees were
drenched in pink and white. Forsythias flamed along the roadsides, and the fields were a carpet of wild mint and flowers.
Seemingly overnight Bellehurst's gardens had come alive
with the warbling of thrushes and the drunken humming of
bees.

Mr. Bozman, more dour than ever, guarded his young
flowers with a hostility that even London no longer cared to
challenge. At any rate she had decided that he no longer
mattered. She had made up her mind that Bellehurst was
going to have a conservatory like Anne Marie Siddons's one
day, a conservatory lorded over by an entirely new gardener
so thoroughly in love with his work that he couldn't help
sharing the fruits of his labor with the rest of the world.

But that wasn't the only reason she had given up doing
battle with Mr. Bozman. She simply didn't have the time
anymore, and that was because, with the coming of spring,
she had suddenly discovered the incomparable delights of
the awakening countryside that sprawled beyond Bellehurst's
carefully tended gardens. The brilliant green of young leaves,
the fragrant carpet of new grass, the stirring, humming, and
rustling of tiny animals and birds amid the unfurling shoots
enchanted London after the gray stillness of the winter, which
she had sometimes despaired of dragging on forever.

Only one problem arose to mar her newfound pleasure in
the out-of-doors these days: the larger and more ungainly
London grew, the more the baron forbade her to do. Indeed,
he would have preferred confining her indoors altogether until
the baby was born, but when London calmly threatened to
climb out the second-story window to avoid such ridiculous
house arrest, he relented. Reluctant orders were given to bring
the dogcart out from storage, and London soon became a
familiar sight to the locals, trundling along the sun-dappled
lanes through Millham Cross and past the sleepy farms beyond.

Regrettably, those excursions ended abruptly when the normally placid mare that pulled London's cart was spooked by the clanking pots dangling from a passing tinker's wagon. London had come very close to being thrown from the vehicle, and the baron, infuriated, refused to allow her to drive again.

But much to the collective household's surprise, London appeared not to mind. And that was because she had stumbled in turn upon a new diversion she found even more pleasurable than driving: walking. Oh, not the sort of walking one did when promenading through stately Italian gardens with other society ladies and conducting subdued—and quite boring— tête-à-têtes, or strolling ever so slowly down to the bower of an evening with the baron leaning heavily on his cane, to look in on his doves. Nor was it anything like the walking London had done in Al Betain, where she had crossed great distances of thorny brush on foot every morning to round up Ali Wad Zarim's hobbled camels or fetch water from the distant wells.

This was an entirely different sort of activity, a quiet luxury with no specific destination in mind, a chance to indulge in nothing more arduous than aimlessly following the narrow lanes threading between grassy hedges studded with wildflowers, and to sit and rest, when she became tired, on the fragrant turf with her face turned toward the sun. Sometimes Rupert or Aunt Emily accompanied her, but more often than not London went alone, until she grew so enormous that Emily began fearing for her safety and arranged for someone to accompany her every time she left the house.

This, too, London accepted without protest. By now she had become friendly with nearly everyone on the estate, and if Rupert and Emily were otherwise occupied, there was never any lack of volunteers willing to abandon their chores in order to accompany young Mrs. Ashford on an amiable ramble.

Above all, London preferred slipping away from everyone altogether and following the footpath the short distance down to the lodge-keeper's house, a little thatched cottage standing in the midst of a sea of murmuring grass. It had about it a sense of tranquil slumbering that had enchanted her the first moment she saw it. At the back of the cottage stood a sagging shed where all manner of curious things were stored, and which could be reached by way of a tiny cobbled yard overrun with chickens and a tangle of lines where Mrs. Skelton pegged out her wash. The cottage had its own garden, small and impossibly wild, surrounded by a crumbling wall that was bosky with trailing roses. Unlike Bellehurst's own gardens, it had no trimmed box hedges or embroidery-neat plots, only a disorganized explosion of fragrance and color.

Now, with the advent of spring, its borders were groaning with blooms spilling untidily over the walks. Clumps of spiky hostas and lovely primroses fought for space amid wild cowslips, lupines, and fragrant scilla. London, quite naturally, loved it. The moment she closed the creaking gate behind her she felt as if she had shut herself away from the rest of the world and was enveloped by a tranquil sense of timelessness that was only enhanced by the kind, accepting presence of Mr. and Mrs. Skelton themselves.

There was, as well, a horde of babies, but their noisy and seemingly inexhaustible ac:.:ity had a strangely soothing effect upon London. She supposed it was because they reminded her so much of life at Al Betain. There had always been babies at Al Betain, lots of them, slung upon the hips of mothers, sisters, and aunts, or wrapped in lengths of muslin and left playing with beads outside the tents while bread was baked and coffee beans ground, or tottering with naked bottoms around the wells while the women chattered and did the wash.

The Skelton offspring, too, ran about in much the same wild state of undress. They were not at all like the other children London had seen in England so far: pale, silent creatures she had glimpsed on occasion when she and Rupert visited the homes of acquaintances in the area, or who were brought downstairs to be introduced, invariably shy or bored and fidgeting, before being whisked away by their sternlipped nannies as though their very presence might cause offense.

I shall never allow my children to be treated that way, London had decided fiercely. To that end she had already made certain that the cold, uninviting upper rooms at

Bellehurst had been converted into a lovely nursery suite. The work had been initiated a month ago or more, when a strange sort of boundless energy had come over her, and she had personally overseen the stripping of the stained William Morris paper, the taking up of uneven flooring, and the removal of untold pieces of ugly, outmoded furniture. Without consulting either her husband or her grandfather, she had even arranged for day laborers to come down from London to install a bright new bath, plaster over the sooty stone fireplaces, install modern stoves, and replace the tiny, leaded windows with long casements through which the sunshine could pour inside.

After considerable grumbling, the baron had provided the necessary funds, and Rupert had appeared occasionally from the musty confines of his library to take stock of, and praise, her efforts. Most gratifying of all was Aunt Emily, who unexpectedly shook herself out of her lethargy long enough to rally Mrs. Gray and the housemaids into sewing and laundering new slipcovers, bedclothes, and curtains. Under her direction a bassinet and trundle bed were brought down from the attic, and a pair of footmen set to work painting and repairing them.

London was touched by these good-natured efforts on her baby's behalf. But by the time the nursery was decorated, scrubbed, and smelling sweetly in anticipation of the baby's arrival, she found her energy abruptly gone and time once again hanging heavily on her hands. Rupert returned to his books and the baron to his bed, complaining of his aching bones and bothersome digestion to anyone who would listen. Aunt Emily too lapsed into her perpetual, silent mourning for her son, and life at Bellehurst went on very much as it always had.

Things were entirely different at the lodge-keeper's house. Plump, blowsy, and wonderfully maternal, Mrs. Skelton was forever to be found in the kitchen preparing mouth-watering roasts, hams, jellies, and Cornish pastries, or putting the finishing touches on a half-dozen mincemeat pies, while cheerfully dodging the crawling, cooing babies that were always underfoot. Some crisis or another was forever crop-

ping up without warning: perhaps Herbert, at seven years the
oldest of her children, had gotten into the unripened gooseber-
ries and been sick all over his father's Sunday shoes, or the
cat was having a litter of kittens under Louisa's crib, or
Piggle, the enormous pink sow that lived beneath the tin roof
at the back of the sagging shed had eaten her way through
the pen and was wallowing in the washtub with Alfred, aged
three.

Mrs. Skelton invariably handled these emergencies with
enviable calm. Efficient, bustling, tireless, she would brew
London tea and cut London a slab of crusty oat bread while
dealing simultaneously with myriad disasters such as chasing
a mouse from the larder while shoving a shoulder of lamb
into the fire—all of this while scarcely pausing for breath in
what she liked to call her little chin-wags with the missus.

She had been born in Millham Cross and never been farther
afield than Chiddingstone in her life, but she knew everything
there was to know about things that really mattered: trimming
candles, brewing fever cordials, laundering yellowed sheets
to make them crisp and white again, fermenting cider, stretching the food stores in the larder to feed her ravenous brood,
and, best of all, raising babies. And she was not at all averse
to discussing them, quite openly, with London.

"You'll find no prunes-and-prisms manners round 'ere,
lovey," she liked to say. And it was true. The insufferable
prudery of the age, which made even Emily blush whenever
London asked her the most innocent of questions, seemed not
to extend beyond the Skeltons' cottage door. With Ida Skelton, London found that she could talk about everything and
anything: her aching back, her swollen belly, the heavy
breasts that had begun in recent weeks to leak a little milk,
and especially the wondrous miracle of feeling the baby move
within her while she tried to determine if the little lump
jabbing her so lustily in the belly was an elbow or a foot.

London had never doubted for a moment that Alex's baby
was going to be a son, and neither did Ida Skelton. "You'd
best be ready to meet 'im soon, lovey," Ida had begun adding
in recent weeks. "Real soon. July, Dr. Carne says. In a pig's
ear, says I!"

The first time she had uttered those words London had grown quite still. Across the warm, drowsy kitchen their eyes had met. It would be, London had known in that instant, ridiculously easy to confide in the practical, uncensuring Ida. But she had not. Because the empty place that Alex had left within her heart was still too battered and raw. And while she had been truly grateful to find that she possessed the strength to go on with the daily routine of her new life without him, to shut her mind to the pain and longing, and now and again even find pleasure in simple things—like the beauty of Kent in the springtime—she could not yet speak of Alex to anyone. Not even to Ida.

But Ida must have guessed, or at least drawn some sort of conclusion of her own; but whatever it was and whatever she thought, the two of them never spoke of it. But as the month of May ripened and London's baby grew heavier within her, Ida began insisting that London no longer walk the short distance from the manor house to the cottage alone, which was something the baron—assured that the birth remained eight weeks or more away—continued to permit.

Ida always made certain to send along Tom, or her oldest boy Herbert, or sometimes, if her own chores were miraculously finished, she would come herself, puffing up the drive at London's side with six-month-old Louisa clinging to her ample hip. Refusing an invitation to rest and fortify herself with a cup of buttermilk or tea, she would linger only long enough at the bottom of the lawn to watch London vanish, waving, into the house, before going home herself.

With so much vigilance on all sides, it was perhaps surprising that London should have been outdoors alone at all when her labor pains began. But she was, and in a way it was something of her own fault. She had told Emily that she would be spending the morning at the Skeltons but had gone instead on a forbidden ramble down to the river. Not that she had been deliberately untruthful to her aunt, for it really had been her intention to pay a visit to the lodge-keeper's cottage. But crossing the lawn toward the bottom of the park, she was distracted suddenly by the beauty of the flower-speckled meadows unfolding beneath her, and the river, glittering with

golden sun-coins, flowing beyond. Changing her mind, she
had gone back to the stables, quietly, so as not to alert Mr.
Bozman, who was scratching at a nearby border with his
rake.

Inside the dark shed, which smelled sweetly of hay, saddle
soap, and linseed oil, she fetched down from the tack-room
shelf a man's wide-brimmed straw hat and a pair of heavy
work boots. These were difficult to put on because her huge
belly kept getting in the way, but eventually she had managed
to wriggle into them, and paused for a moment to admire
their clumsy black tips protruding from beneath the hem of
her dainty sack gown. How Cousin Beatrice would have
swooned at the sight!

Smothering unexpected laughter, London jammed the hat
onto her head and took down the shotgun from its peg high
on the wall. Normally all of the guns at Bellehurst were kept
locked away in a walnut cabinet in the back hall, but Mr.
Bozman always kept an old shotgun at the ready in the event
his precious flowers were invaded by rodents.

Last autumn, when London had first arrived from Algiers
and everything she had said and done had seemed so utterly
foreign to her family, nothing had shocked them more than
her casual use of firearms. She had tried explaining to them
that this was not an unusual practice in Algeria; that it was
considered downright foolish to go anywhere without one,
but she had merely ended up wasting her breath. There was,
as Beatrice had so frostily pointed out, no need to roam the
countryside armed to the teeth, since no poisonous snakes or
dangerous animals lurked in the fields of Kent, and it was
further unlikely that Millham Cross would ever be overrun
by bandits intent on raiding one's camels or stealing water
from one's wells.

Emily, too, had been horrified, and Rupert had expressly
forbidden London to touch the firearms again. As had the
baron—until he had witnessed at his own request a single,
secret, and quite impressive demonstration of his granddaughter's marksmanship one morning when the rest of the family
was by chance away from home. Afterward he had become
less vehement on the subject and had been heard to remark

from time to time what a bloody shame it was that they didn't allow females to compete for the Squire's Cup at the local sporting match every year.

London had, as usual, paid none of this any mind. The only thing that mattered to her was the fact that she felt uncomfortable going out into the countryside without a gun in hand, and so she simply ended up taking one along, whether it caused a row at home or not. Today was no exception. Almost without thought she slipped the weapon familiarly into the crook of her arm and set off down the path, the wet grass squelching beneath her boots.

All things are in the hands of God, as Ali Wad Zarim would have said. And to hell with the consequences, London decided with a grin.

Because she was much too large and ungainly by now to climb the stile, she followed the old bridle path downhill. The path was flanked by mossy ditches and hawthorn hedges just coming into flower. Eventually she reached the gate and, opening it, strolled slowly toward the river. Here, the tall grass was still wet with dew, and so she seated herself on the roots of an ancient beech, where she wriggled about until she was comfortable. With the shotgun laid across her knees and the hat brim pulled low over her eyes, she leaned back against the trunk and allowed her mind to wander.

Unparalleled luxury. That was the first thing that came to her mind. When had she ever known the luxury of sitting in a meadow as lush and sweetly scented as this one? She remembered the long, hot afternoons at Al Betain when, her work finished at last, she had slipped away from the tents to sit just so, listening to the stillness of the desert and thinking about nothing at all. Though perhaps that was a ridiculous comparison, considering that sitting on the rust-colored banks of an arid wadi in northern Africa was not in the least bit like daydreaming alongside the flower-dusted banks of an English stream. Alex had been right when he had once remarked that—

But it was not the forbidden thought of Alex that made London catch her breath and sit up, the gun sliding unnoticed into the grass. It was the bellowing of a cow, curiously insistent and very clear in the drowsy morning air, that had startled her from her reverie. London looked around quickly and spotted the animal almost at once galloping toward her from a distant stand of trees. It was an enormous red thing with a sloping neck and muscular chest, and it had lowered its head in a manner that could only be interpreted as hostile.

London was puzzled but not frightened as yet, because she knew that her grandfather's cows were usually quite timid and could easily be shooed away by waving one's arms and calling "Cush! Cush!" For that reason she stood up without haste, collected her gun, and then turned around to take one more look.

It was then that she noticed for the first time that the enormous red beast thundering toward her possessed a disconcertingly large set of masculine reproductive organs. Recognition dawned instantly. Grandfather's bull, a prize Devon with a temperament so unusually fierce for his breed that Justin McTyne, Bellehurst's Scottish-born cowman, had nicknamed him Auld Nasty. What on earth was he doing running loose in the pasture?

Auld Nasty, whose registered name was Medway's Arran Rob, seemed to be wondering exactly the same thing about her. And he had obviously decided that, regardless of her identity, she was a creature who must be dealt with quickly, in the manner of all intruders. Head down, he came on with his charge, and suddenly there was no doubt in London's mind as to his intent.

Tossing aside her hat, she cocked the gun and lifted it quickly to her shoulder. She knew enough about the bull's reputation to realize that there was no other way of deterring him. Taking careful aim, she smoothly squeezed the trigger.

The explosion was deafening, the recoil unexpectedly bruising her shoulder. Ignoring the pain, London reloaded, but there was no need. Auld Nasty had stopped dead in his tracks. He seemed confused, and stood shaking his head as though trying to clear it. But he had not retreated, and London's hands shook a little as she snapped the barrel shut. She had meant to scare him off, but obviously the ratshot Mr. Bozman favored for rodents was not effective enough for a fully grown bull. Supposing he were to charge again and she was unable to turn him? She was far too fat and ungainly in her last month of pregnancy to beat him to the fence.

Fortunately, Auld Nasty had not mistaken the soft, decisive click of the closing gun barrel. Bleeding and snorting, he turned without warning and tottered back toward the herd, which stood milling uneasily on the slope beneath him. For a frozen moment London watched him go, then ran as quickly as she could toward the fence, her heavy boots clumping through the grass. Tossing the gun over the top, she hauled herself up and after it to land, clumsy, fat, and altogether undignified, in the soft grass on the other side.

It was when she rolled over, laughing a little with breathless relief, that she felt a sudden warmth soaking her undergarments from a rush of water between her legs. She fell back on her elbows, instantly aware of what was happening. Hatless, she turned her face to the vivid blue of the sky.

"Oh, God," she said. "What on earth do I do now?"

Chapter Fourteen

"Well? What happened then?"

"Not much, sir, really. One of the stableboys finally found her in t'west pasture. Raised the alarm like we'd all agreed. Then the rest of us brought t'cart and fetched her home."

"Who's with her now?"

"The housekeeper."

"And the doctor?"

"Hasna come yet, sir."

"Very well. You can go back to your duties, Mr. McTyne. Please extend my thanks to everyone who helped."

"Na need for it, Mr. Ashford. We was all glad tae do't."
The Scotsman tipped his battered cap and went back to the
stables while Rupert clattered up the terrace steps and into
the house. His mind was racing. London, he recalled, had
left for the lodge-keeper's house hours ago. It had been long
enough for the sun to climb upward into a sky more impossibly blue than any he could remember, before beginning its
slow descent toward the farms and orchards and sleepy rooftops of Millham Cross. While Rupert, oblivious, trundled
slowly homeward in the dogcart from Beckwith Manor.

He remembered, with something of a guilty pang, how he
had been humming to himself as he drove, quite in ignorance
of the dramatic events transpiring at home, but aware for
once, as he so rarely was, of the soft, compelling beauty of
the countryside. Rupert had been born in the industrial north
and raised, along with a younger brother and sister, by parents
who shared a passionate urgency and an inexhaustible need
for productivity—whether it was domestic or charitable as in
the case of his mother, or in the long grind of hours his father
put in at the family's small manufacturing firm in Leeds.
Neither of them, quite obviously, had ever spared time for
the contemplation of nature, and could therefore not have
been expected to instill a similar sense of appreciation for the
out-of-doors in their daughter and sons.

"Perhaps I shall ask London to take tea with me on the
terrace this afternoon," Rupert thought as he drove. And was
instantly struck by another thought, one that was equally
pleasant: the gratifying success of his visit with Squire Beckwith. He had gone to Beckwith Manor seeking permission to
inspect the letters of a certain Beckwith ancestor who had
spent many years in diplomatic service in Italy and had thus,
so Rupert fervently hoped, paid a number of official calls on
the Doge's Palace in Venice. Surely his memoirs would contain a number of references to those occasions?

To Rupert's horror, the squire had sheepishly confessed to
burning the papers when the manor library had been remodeled several years ago after Lady Beckwith had been seized
with the sudden urge to knock down walls and shift furnishings in order to obtain for herself a large and very formal

withdrawing room. But after a hasty conference with the butler—prompted, no doubt, by the look of disbelieving horror on Rupert's face—and several trips to the attics by a pair of grumbling footmen, the papers, bound in mildewed tan morocco, had been happily located at last, and these were now safely stowed in the back of the dogcart.

Although Rupert was reluctant to admit it, there was a great deal of importance riding on those musty-smelling tomes, because his research had, in recent weeks, reached an unexpected and thoroughly frustrating impasse. As a matter of fact, if the Beckwith papers did not reveal anything noteworthy or new about his latest subject, a text cataloging the antiquities and marvels of medieval Venice, then—

But Rupert deliberately thrust away this unthinkable notion. Briskly he turned the mare down the long avenue of trees leading into Bellehurst's park—only to be met in the stable yard by Justin McTyne with the shocking news of Mrs. Ashford's encounter with the baron's bull and the part Auld Nasty had played in precipitating the untimely arrival of the baby.

Now, sweating profusely, Rupert burst indoors. Apparently they had been watching for him, because he was met immediately in the hall by Emily, gray-faced with anxiety.

"Oh, Rupert, I'm so glad—"

She was interrupted by the baron's furious voice calling from the parlor. Rupert looked up, wincing. This, more than anything, was an alarming indication of the way things stood, because nothing had induced the baron to leave his rooms for a month or more.

He turned back to Emily. "London?" he demanded.

Emily laced her fingers together in a visible effort to stop their shaking. "She's been taken upstairs."

"And the baby?"

"I'm sorry. It's much too early to tell yet." And she promptly burst into tears.

"Oh, for heaven's sake." Whipping out his handkerchief, Rupert dried Emily's eyes and tried to calm her as best he could. Turning his head, he gave curt orders to the servants milling in the doorway to get back to work. Then, striding into the parlor, he confronted the baron. Was it true, he demanded in a voice no one had ever heard him use before, that Dr. Carne had not as yet arrived? Why in bloody hell hadn't he been sent for?

"How stupid d'ye think I am?" Powney shouted in turn, thumping his cane on the floor for emphasis, his bony face splotchy with agitation. "It's been done! Hours ago! But his housekeeper says he's gone off God knows where to sign the death certificate of some bleedin' sod what has no further need of him! While my own granddaughter—"

Rupert spun away without comment. "Emily. I was told Mrs. Gray is upstairs with London now."

"Yes. Along with Mrs. Skelton from down the hill. I was just fetching them tea when you came. It's—it's tiring work, you understand. Not so much for us as it is for her."

Rupert said nothing. Emily looked up at him, her face pale and frightened. The baron, cadaverous in black, sat propped up by pillows on the sofa, watching him as well. "You'd better see to the tea, Emily," Rupert said curtly.

"Oh. Yes, yes, of course. I'd forgotten."

The room was silent after she hurried out, so silent that the buzzing of a bluebottle against the windowpane seemed unnaturally loud. But not for long.

"Goddamn it!" Rupert exploded. "Whose idea was it to send for that woman, that lodge-keeper's wife? I thought we'd agreed that if anything were to happen to London while Dr. Carne was away we'd send to Temple Lynn for the midwife!"

The baron's eyes bulged and his face turned so red that one would have thought his high collar was choking him. "It was my idea!" he snapped, the cane thumping loudly on the floor once again. "What else would you have me do, eh? It was hours before anyone even realized the stupid girl had disappeared, and hours after that before we found her! The Skelton woman's only just now arrived, but I can tell you she'll be a damned sight more helpful than Emily or Mrs. Gray!"

"Better than the midwife? How can that be? She's had no formal training at Bart's!"

"What in hell does that matter? Neither has anyone else

around here! And until Carne arrives she's the best we've got. Six children of her own and not a one of 'em stillborn. Can Mrs. Gray—the *Mrs.* you'll recall is merely courtesy— boast that kind of experience? Can Emily? Or you, for that matter? Now sit down! You're like an untried hack waiting to bolt upstairs!''

It was the longest, most coherent speech the old man had made in quite some time, and it was not without a measure of common sense. Jaw working, Rupert strode to the window, where he thrust his hands deeply into his pockets. Silence fell between the two of them, stretching interminably, broken only by the loud ticking of the cherrywood clock. And then, unexpectedly, there came a muffled cry from upstairs, a sound of agonized pain that seemed to have been drawn unwillingly from between clenched teeth. The baron, who had been dozing on the sofa, looked up, wincing, while Rupert spun away from the window as though he had been struck a physical blow.

"Oh, God, I can't bear it! I'm going to her!"

"What the devil for?" The baron's tone was withering. "To pull the babe out by yourself? You'll only terrify her charging up there like some maddened bull! Now do as I say and sit down!''

Groaning, Rupert sank into a nearby armchair, his head in his hands. His uncle watched him for a moment or two in wheezing silence, then observed unkindly, "I could almost believe you're in love with the girl yourself, the way you're carrying on.''

Rupert's lips thinned but he made no reply. At that moment the door opened. Both men looked up. It was Mrs. Gray, wearing a white flannel apron over her sensible working dress and looking as calm and unruffled as always. Rupert leaped to his feet. "My wife—"

"Nothing to report as yet, Mr. Ashford. I just came down to fetch a few things and thought I'd look in on you. Mrs. Ashford has been told you've returned. That will help her, I expect.''

"Dear God! How much longer?"

"Quite some time, Mrs. Skelton thinks. First ones are

always difficult. But you needn't worry about either of them. They'll be fine." Apparently this was all she thought fit to tell them, because she smoothly interrupted Rupert's next question by curtsying and retreating.

"Bloody frigate," the baron muttered.

Half an hour later, mercifully, Dr. Carne arrived in his battered carriage with the midwife seated beside him carrying a huge leather satchel on her lap. "Nothing to worry about, Mr. Ashford," he called to Rupert as he pounded up the stairs. "We'll let you know the moment it's done."

The next person to appear, some time later, was Ida Skelton. The drowsy afternoon had long since faded, and dusky twilight shadows were beginning to fall across the Kidderminster carpet in the parlor where Rupert and his uncle waited. Once again the baron had fallen asleep on the sofa, and Rupert rose quickly to speak with Mrs. Skelton in the doorway.

"Wasn't much left for me to do," she said in a whisper, "now the doctor's here. I'm off to look after me own little ones."

"You've been very kind."

"It's a long, hard business for the poor dear. Never hurts to have a friend."

"At the moment," Rupert said emotionally, "I believe you're the best friend my wife ever had."

Embarrassed, Mrs. Skelton patted his hand. "Taking it well, she is. Not an easy confinement. Not easy at all, I'll tell you. But she knows more'n most about birthin'—what the babe's doin' and how it's supposed to get out. Comes from her life with them Arabs, I'll expect. Good thing, says I. Takes away the mystery and, with that, the fear. And that's half the battle, I've always thought."

Now it was Rupert's turn to be embarrassed by such baldly uttered remarks, but Mrs. Skelton, rosily sentimental, rambled on unawares. "Keeps askin' what's keeping Alex. Won't be much longer, I told her. Another hour, maybe two. Lovely name, that. Have you thought up another, in case it's a girl?"

"No," said Rupert slowly. "No, we haven't."

Mrs. Skelton nodded. "Waste of time, I agree. Never doubted it'd be a boy. Well, then, I'll be off. My Tom'll be wonderin' what's become of me. Best of luck to you, sir."

"Yes," said Rupert vaguely. "Good-bye." And he stood there for some time without moving, after she had gone.

It was nearly nine o'clock before Dr. Carne finally made his first appearance downstairs. The baron had long since been carried, protesting, to his own bed, while Rupert had continued to wait alone in the chilly, unlit parlor.

"Well, that's finally done," Dr. Carne said triumphantly, "though I'll own it wasn't easy. Not for either of them. But Mrs. Ashford's doing fine. The baby's small but seems to be holding its own. I suppose that's all that matters."

"Is it—"

"Oh, sorry. A boy, Mr. Ashford. A fine boy."

Jubilant, Rupert shook the doctor's outstretched hand. "What can I offer you? Champagne? Brandy?"

"Actually, I'd prefer something hot to eat, if you don't mind."

"Of course not. I'll have Mrs. Gray—"

"No need to bother, young man. I'll speak to Mrs. Gray myself. You go up and see your wife and son."

London was lying in the big French bed looking so tired and worn that Rupert's heart contracted. Stepping inside, he paused for a moment to admire the infant lying in its bassinet by the far wall, then seated himself at the edge of the bed and took her cold, pale hand in his.

"We have a son," London whispered hoarsely. Her eyes shone, dark and lustrous, despite her exhaustion. "Don't you think he's beautiful?"

Rupert said abruptly, "Why did you name him Alex?"

London looked at him, startled. "What?"

"That's what you decided to call him, isn't it? Mrs. Skelton told me you'd mentioned the name several times. Alex. Why Alex?"

London gasped and looked away, and all at once a frustrated anger shook Rupert. "I thought we agreed that he'd be named after me."

London's face remained averted. Her pale lips quivered as though she meant to speak—or weep—but she made no sound.

Rupert's despair deepened. His voice became clipped and cold. "Can you give me a single reason why he shouldn't be named after his father?"

"His father? His father! A fine one you are! Aren't you the man who married me for my grandfather's library?"

"Oh, for God's sake, London! That isn't fair!"

"Isn't it?"

"No, damn it! I admit I was eager to get my hands on your grandfather's manuscripts, but that isn't really why I agreed to marry you!"

"Then why did you?" she demanded.

Rupert rose from the bed and turned his back to her, unable to bear the coldness in her eyes, her voice. They had never quarreled before, but now hurt lay like a yawning rift between them, worse than it had been on the night they had returned from the Siddons's fancy-dress ball. Finally, he said, "It was mainly because of your mother."

"My *mother*? What do you mean? Did you know her?"

"Not very well. My family didn't come to Bellehurst much, even though your grandparents entertained often in those days. She was considerably older than I was and of course never took any notice of me."

"You were in love with her," London said, her voice filled with wonder.

Rupert smiled faintly. "It was more a matter of worship. She was extraordinarily beautiful. Ethereal. Golden-haired and gay, always filled with laughter. Bellehurst was never the same when she left."

"I never knew," London said softly.

Both of them fell silent. Then Rupert shrugged. "I suppose it doesn't matter anymore. It was years and years ago. Before you were even born." Restlessly, he crossed to the bassinet and peered inside. The baby lay sleeping, wrapped in a soft flannel blanket, his crumpled face sweet in repose. The lamp on the nightstand lent a soft glow to the room, illuminating the fuzzy down on his head. His mother's hair, Rupert saw, just as blond and fine, but with a reddish tint that was all his own. Alexander. Such a big name for so small a scrap of humanity. Rupert's heart contracted. He said, "We could always give him a nickname."

London turned slowly to look at him. "What?"

"I said we could always call him something else. Give him a nickname. But he'll be christened Alexander if that's what you wish."

London uttered a low sob, mastered it, and said huskily, "That's very kind of you. More than kind. If you'd rather we named him Rupert—"

"No. Alexander suits him. It just took me a while to realize it." Rupert came back to her, smiling tentatively and offering his hand. London took it between both of hers, swallowing the hot lump burning in her throat. She found it hard to believe that shy, silent Rupert could be so kind in the face of the truth he must surely suspect.

That he, too, had known the awful ache of forbidden love was something London had never realized. Somehow, it endeared him to her all the more.

From the baby's crib came a sudden, thin, but insistent wail. Alex's son. Crying because he was hungry. Because he wanted his mother.

"Give him to me," London said softly. Rupert stooped and awkwardly lifted the infant from the bassinet. Tenderly he laid it into London's arms. Above the downy head his eyes met hers.

"Truce?" he whispered gently.

Smiling, London nodded.

FOUR
Echoes

Come back in tears,
O memory, hope, love of finished years.

Christina Rossetti

Chapter Fifteen

"Your father was christened Alexander Powney Rupert in the church at Millham Cross," London said softly, "and before the week was out everyone had forgotten that he ever possessed such a ponderous name. We all called him Sandy."

"Which was probably just as well," Sara remarked, "because he was fair-haired all his life, wasn't he?"

"Yes. 'My sunshine boy,' his great-grandfather used to say, and it was true. Nothing but sweetness and laughter in him. He was everyone's favorite, you know, and I suppose it was a measure of your father's character that he turned out so well after being so thoroughly spoilt by the lot of us."

"It must have hurt very much, losing him."

"Oh, Sara. It happened so long ago."

"I've always been sorry I never met him."

"So am I."

"Mother rarely mentioned him, even when I was growing up. Now, I think she's forgotten him completely."

"Time has a way of devouring everything, my darling.

Even those memories we arrogantly believe we can hold
forever and thus make immortal.''

"Yes," said Sara. Her voice sounded rather strange, but
when London looked at her sharply, she saw only the sweet
innocence of her granddaughter's face.

She felt enormously tired all at once, and, as well, very
sad. She knew that she had not been totally honest with
Sara. The girl did not know—had never known—who her
grandfather really was, and London was painfully aware that
she was growing far too old for confessions. There was safety
in silence, and the comfort of knowing that, by keeping her
silence, she was making sure that Rupert's role in his granddaughter's life would never be diminished.

London sighed. There seemed little sense in worrying. On
the table behind them lay the cluttered remains of breakfast.
Bleak morning light filtered through the French windows,
filling the cozy room with a haze that, earlier, had seemed
almost alive with the whispering shadows of very real memories. London looked once more at Sara and saw the clean cut
of the girl's features as she sprawled, long-limbed and relaxed, in a worn Victorian armchair. London half expected
to feel a pang at the sight of her, but already the memories
that had filled her mind like a brilliant dream with the telling
of Sandy's birth were fading, slipping back into the past
where, of course, they belonged.

She knew that she had not answered Sara's earlier question
truthfully either. She had merely evaded it. Because, although
Sandy had been dead for a great many years, she had never—
would never—get over the loss of him. And that was because
Sandy had always been the gift, the wondrous anodyne, sent
her by God to heal over Alex. And though she had loved both
of her daughters equally when they, in turn, had been born,
they had not been a part of Alex, and so had never, like
Sandy, been special to her in that way.

But I never loved them any less, London told herself
fiercely. Never.

But her heart still ached at the thought. She knew that she
had not been equally fair when it came to the question of her

grandchildren. She had made the dismaying discovery long ago that she would never cherish Victoria's offspring as much as she did this strong-minded girl who was Alex's granddaughter and who was so like him in so many ways. Sadly, Victoria knew, or at least suspected, that her mother harbored preferences, and she had made reproachful—and quite justified—noises to that effect in the past.

With Eugenia, on the other hand, things had been entirely different. It had never been Eugenia's nature to be jealous of anyone, and London had often thought it a shame that Eugenia hadn't been born with the same strong, motherly instincts as Victoria. Then, too, Eugenia's children would probably never have been as disappointing as William Warburton's, which meant that London would never have found herself in the difficult and unwanted position of playing favorites to begin with.

At least in her own defense she could say, quite honestly, that she had always treated Victoria's children fairly and lovingly and denied them nothing they asked for. So it wasn't really as if Victoria had any right to complain.

The telephone rang. Sara motioned her grandmother to remain seated and, rising, picked up in the hall. "Rose Cottage."

Nora's voice boomed cheerfully across the wire. "Good morning! Vile weather, isn't it?" The morning had dawned with a drenching downpour that had roared through the trees and scattered leaves and flower petals across the garden path. "Let's forget about tennis and go shopping instead."

Sara thought of the few, modest businesses in the village. A greengrocer, a chemist's, the butcher, and a musty shop next door to the Paxton Hotel crammed with antiques and secondhand furniture. "Shopping? Where?"

"Mummy says we can use the car, and Francis has agreed to take us to London. If you like, we could meet Daddy for lunch."

Sara considered this. She remembered the narrow, twisting road that led into the city, and the bus that had brought her to Millham Cross, swaying and crashing its ancient gears as it careened around the curves with impatient Jaguars and Austins honking behind it. She shuddered. "Would you mind very much if we didn't?"

"Not really. To be honest, it's no fun fighting the crowds when the weather's like this. We'd get drenched. But we have to do something. Got any ideas?"

Nora's voice had taken on a pleading tone, although she probably didn't realize it. It occurred to Sara that life must be terribly dull for Nora with no brothers or sisters at home and all her chums from the public school she attended living scattered across the countryside and therefore not easily accessible. And today it was raining, so of course she couldn't ride, and the prospect of playing records for hours on end had undoubtedly filled her with gloom.

"You could take me to lunch," Sara suggested.

"Lunch? Where?"

"Don't sound so skeptical. I'm sure there are loads of new restaurants around here. Hard to imagine that your wealthy neighbors and those Bored Young Things making the daily commuter grind to London don't have anywhere chic to dine locally."

"Oh, Sara." Nora sounded doubtful. "We've dozens now, but I've never been. Mum and Daddy don't usually go out when they're here, especially not with me. Umm, I suppose we could try the Mayfair in Temple Lynn. It's the closest one, and I've heard it's wonderfully chichi, but—" She broke off, considered, then warmed to the idea. "Oh, why not? I'll ask. I'm sure Mummy won't mind. And it isn't too far, so Francis can't grumble about driving us. Will Gran want to come, do you think?"

Sara considered. "I think she'd very much prefer a day alone."

"Then I'll see you in a bit."

Despite its name, the Mayfair was a very modern establishment located next to the cinema in the cobbled center of the medieval village of Temple Lynn. Outside there was a brightly painted signboard swinging above brass-plated doors, and fat clumps of geraniums blooming on the sills.

The interior was filled with round tables of pickled wood, curving banquettes, and whitewashed walls hung with contemporary art. The central heating was turned up to a comfortable degree, and because it was midweek only a handful of businessmen were lined up at the bar, while one or two tables were taken by ladies in smart suits and ribboned hats. Sara and Nora were given a small booth in the back and left to cope with the enormous menus on their own.

Nora, fresh-faced and dressed in a blue frock with white piping, looked exactly like the schoolgirl that she was. She had said little in the car on the way down, no doubt intimidated by the chauffeur's unenthusiastic responses to Sara's attempted conversation. Here, however, she seemed overcome by sudden excitement and could hardly keep still.

Before the waiter had returned for their orders she had already divulged to Sara that she would not be going to Switzerland to finish her schooling because of the situation heating up in Germany, but that her father had promised to make it up to her with a trip to Boston, in America, later that summer. She confessed that Amabel Leavenham, her dearest friend from school, had actually become engaged without her parents' knowledge; that Daddy was thinking of tearing down Granny Ashford's conservatory because it was terribly old-fashioned and cost too much to heat—only Sara must swear not to say a word to Gran until Daddy told her himself; that Mum and Daddy had had a ripping argument several nights earlier about trading in the Daimler for a new car; that Madrigal was to be shod tomorrow and that one of the dogs had gotten sick all over the rug in the drawing room last night.

"Madrigal means a lot to you, doesn't he?" Sara asked.

Unexpectedly, Nora's eyes filled with tears. "Daddy wants to sell him." There was nothing theatrical about this whispered confession, and Sara felt a rush of sympathy for her cousin.

"Why?"

"He says we can't afford him. That it costs too much to feed him and van him to the shows, and Daddy says it's silly keeping a stableman on staff just to muck out a single stall."

Sara thought about this. Apparently economic gloom had

settled over Bellehurst just as elsewhere in the country. And Uncle William was obviously trying to tighten the family belt, as it were, by tearing down the conservatory and selling his daughter's much-loved horse. But apparently that did not stop him from thinking twice about buying another car or entertaining dozens of people at lavish parties every weekend. The thought angered Sara. "Have you ever told him how you feel?"

Nora shook her head. The waiter arrived with their soup, and she kept her head bowed until he was gone. Then she looked up, sniffling a little. "Do you think it would help?"

"I've no idea. But you really ought to try. Perhaps you could suggest ways of cutting the costs. Maybe you could clean Madrigal's stall yourself?"

Nora shrank from the thought of performing this loathsome task. She loved her pony, truly she did, but to do the sort of work the stableman did. . . . She forked a piece of salad into her mouth. "Funny to think we're cousins, isn't it, when you're nearly old enough to be my mother?"

Thoughtless, and so typical of someone barely sixteen. Sara took no offense. To Nora, she supposed she seemed very old indeed. She was exactly the same age Wallis Simpson had been when she made off with England's king the previous year, in what had certainly been the most scandalous love affair of the century. It was also the time of life in which most of Sara's girlhood friends found themselves married ten years or more and, finished with childbearing, were settling down for that long, comfortable stretch of middle age.

"Why haven't you gotten married yet? Mummy thinks it's very odd. I suppose if you were unattractive or crashingly dull it would make more sense, wouldn't it?"

Sara burst into laughter. There was no doubt that what she was hearing was a parroting of Aunt Victoria's old-fashioned views. "Would you mind telling me why someone who is attractive and pleasant—thanks for the compliment—can't be single? Or that dull, unattractive people never get married? They do. All the time. In my case I suppose it's because I haven't said yes to anyone yet."

"But you've got heaps of admirers, haven't you?"

"Maybe. Let's just say that right now I prefer working to being married."

This was such an alien concept to Nora that she considered it in silence for a long moment. None of the women she knew had ever worked, unless one counted their efforts at charity bazaars and church fetes, or at organizing musicals and May Day celebrations. They did not drive off to London for the week, the way Daddy did, to sit in an office or a bank and make important decisions before coming home at weekend grumpy and complaining about the appalling traffic. She decided suddenly that she wouldn't ever want to do that either.

She stole a swift glance at her cousin. Tall, leggy, and wearing just enough makeup to enhance her sculpted features, Sara looked very pretty in a gray woolen dress, although it was admittedly ordinary compared to the Parisian creations splashed across the glossy pages of the magazines Nora devoured. Hard to believe that someone as pretty as Sara wasn't interested in marriage and that she preferred having a career over an adoring husband and a beautiful home filled with babies.

Why was that, Nora wondered? Certainly not because Sara needed money. Sara's mother, Nora knew, had married a wealthy American years ago with whom Sara had been on excellent terms until he died. Why, then?

She leaned forward, curious. "What is it that you do? Your work, I mean?"

"Patent medicines."

"I've never heard of them. What are they?"

"It's really very simple. I work in a research laboratory developing new medicines for a large chemical company in New York." Sara knew better than to bore Nora with the details. "At first I wanted to be a doctor."

Nora's nose wrinkled. "A *woman* doctor?"

Sara laughed. "That's what everyone else always says. But I could have gone to medical school if I'd really wanted to. Archer Lloyd, my stepfather, endowed a chair of medicine at New York University, so it wouldn't have been difficult to wheedle my way in."

"What made you change your mind?"

"I suppose it was the nursing I did at a halfway house back home in New Jersey. Working with the doctors there made me realize that I was much more interested in the medicines they used than in the actual healing they did. And when my stepfather found out that I was drawn in that direction he arranged for me to meet with his neighbor, Mr. Humphries, who'd founded the Homeopathic Medicine Company in Brooklyn. I went to work for him when I turned twenty-one, and I've been there ever since."

"You must have been very sad when your stepfather died."

"Yes," Sara said, but did not elaborate.

Nora accepted this. With a sigh she laid aside her fork, sated from cleaning up the remains of an enormous serving of veal escalope smothered in mushroom sauce. Leaning back against the banquette she wondered if Sara would object were she to light up a cigarette. No one at home knew that she smoked, and Mummy would probably have a rugger of a fit if she ever found out, but Sara didn't seem the type to tell.

"Oh, no," she said suddenly, looking past Sara's shoulder toward the door. "I can't believe it. It's Colonel Packer. What rotten luck! Would you mind terribly if we left?"

Sara turned around. "Why? He doesn't look particularly dangerous."

"Well, he is. He happens to be the loopiest old thing you'll ever meet and a crashing bore as well. He's been half in love with Gran for years, and we'll never get out of here once he sees us. He'll pump us for every detail of her life since he saw her last, how her garden is getting on and how her cows are doing and if she intends to make the flower show at Ealham this year."

"I've never heard of him. But where's the harm in being interested in Grandmama? Grandmama has always had admirers."

"This is different." Nora lowered her voice to a conspiratorial whisper. "Colonel Packer considers himself her suitor."

This shed an entirely different light upon the ruddy-faced old man. Deeply interested, Sara turned her head and watched as he crossed to the bar to greet the few gentlemen gathered there. He was out of uniform—probably had been for years—but there was no mistaking that hidebound expression or rigid military posture. His face, tanned to leather after years in the cruel Indian sun, was nevertheless pleasant, and Sara was suddenly delighted by the thought of Grandmama having a serious admirer. No doubt he drove her utterly mad.

"Do you really think he means to offer for her?"

"Oh, yes," Nora whispered back. "He joined the Millham Music Society after his wife died just to be near her, even though everyone knows he only abides military marches."

Sara was amused. "Persistent fellow, isn't he? Well, if he's really as awful as you say, then I suppose we'd better escape now, while he's over at the bar."

They managed to signal the waiter, pay their bill, and slip away without attracting the colonel's attention. Outside the rain had stopped, and the air was cool and fresh. Francis was waiting for them in the car, which was parked beneath a dripping canopy of oaks, and they ran to him, their shoes crunching across the wet stones.

Rigid with disapproval at this breach of etiquette, Francis opened the back door for them. Sara scooted in, Nora behind her giggling breathlessly. The Daimler purred to life, swung around, then halted at the exit to await oncoming traffic. As it did so, a vintage Austin shot into view from around the bend, its green paint badly faded, the windshield covered with a network of tiny cracks. At the sight of the Daimler's sleek bonnet angling out into the roadway, it braked sharply and set up a wild honking.

Francis stared after it, incredulous. The Daimler was not, by any means, blocking the Austin's passage, but apparently the other driver seemed to think so, because abruptly he pulled off into the grass and killed the engine.

"I don't believe this!" Francis was fairly spluttering with indignation. "What in bloody hell does he think he's doing? Just a moment, Miss Nora. I'll see what's eating the bloke."

Tires screeching in a manner that would have horrified his employer, Francis backed up and, bristling with self-righteousness, got out to confront the other driver. They saw

now that it was a middle-aged woman of undistinguishable
proportions wearing knee-length rubber boots, a rain bonnet,
and an oversized, army-green mackintosh. Nora and Sara
watched expectantly as she bore down upon the bravely
poised Francis brandishing her umbrella.

"Oh, my God," said Nora all at once. "It's Aunt Eugenia."

Apparently Francis had also made this startling discovery,
because suddenly he snapped to attention, his boot heels
clicking. "Miss—Miss Ashford! We had no idea—!"

"Hullo, Francis. Did I frighten you? Sorry. I couldn't help
it once I recognized the car. Not another like it in all the
county, I'll wager." Eugenia craned her neck to peer inside.
"Who's that with you? My sister? No, impossible. Vicky
would never allow herself the pleasure of lunching at the
Mayfair with William away at work."

"Auntie, it's me!" Nora had rolled down the window and
was waving madly to attract Eugenia's attention. "Were you
on your way to Millham? Have you come early, then? Won't
Mummy go all horse-leechy when she sees you! You're not
expected until Saturday, you know, and now you've gone
and done the same, naughty thing as Sara."

"Sara? Is she here in England then?"

Nora giggled. "Even better. She's right here in the car."
Eugenia whirled to look, and Sara obligingly got out.

"My dearest girl!" Eugenia opened her arms wide to offer
a hugely warm embrace, her rubber raincoat flapping madly.
No one could have guessed from her joyous expression how
shocked she had been to see the resemblance to her brother
Sandy in Sara's young face, a brother she had loved and
revered all her life.

"You'll drive back with me," Eugenia said firmly once
hugs and kisses had been dispensed with and the usual questions asked and obligingly answered. "And I'll tolerate no
protests from you, Nora. You've had her long enough."

Nora laughed. "Oh, I wasn't going to complain. I just felt
it my duty to warn Sara about your frightful driving."

"There's nothing wrong with my driving, you wretched
girl. It's simply the car. Bit of a groggy heart, it has—"

"And no brakes or steering to speak of. Just ask Francis, Sara, he'll tell you. But it's your funeral, as the saying goes."

Sara smiled at her aunt, warming to her because she looked so much like Grandmama had when Sara was young. "I suppose I'll have to risk it."

Nora shook her head pityingly. "Don't say I didn't warn you."

"Cheeky thing," Eugenia shot back.

It took less than a minute for Eugenia's little Austin to leave the Daimler behind on the winding, dipping road and for Sara to realize that perhaps she ought to have driven back with Nora after all. Never mind that the tiny vehicle clanked and screeched and groaned uphill and down and seemed on the verge of collapsing. Eugenia did not appear to notice and adamantly refused to abandon the killing pace she had set. Furthermore, it was raining again, and of course the wiper didn't work, so Eugenia was forced to drive with her head out the window, her rain bonnet slapping madly against her forehead and cheeks.

"How's Mother?" she shouted above the roar.

"Very well," Sara shouted back. "A little tired today, but looking much more wonderful than I expected."

"I haven't seen her since she moved into that ancient lodge-keeper's place. What do you think of it?"

"Cozy and charming, just like Grandmama. She seems very happy there."

"As well she should be. That creaky old house of Papa's—nothing good to be said about it. I never did like it myself, you know. Too shabby and Gothic for my taste. In my opinion, Vicky's remodeling didn't help much either. They should have gutted it and started over entirely, leaving the conservatory, of course."

Sara wondered if she should tell her aunt that Nora's father was planning to raze the conservatory, then decided it was better not to. "Will you be staying at Bellehurst until the party?"

"If Vicky doesn't object. Lord above. From what Nora said I gather she wasn't too happy when you showed up early?"

"No. And she didn't like it either when Grandmama insisted that I stay with her at Rose Cottage."

Eugenia snorted. "My dear sister, I'm sorry to say, has suffered from storm in the brain all of her life. There's no telling what she'd do without the high drama of misfortune and martyrdom to fill her days."

The little Austin hurled over the top of a hill as she spoke, then went airborne for a second or two before crashing back onto the tarmac with a bone-jarring jolt. Below them, Millham Cross appeared amid the green folds of hills, the gray stone houses slumbering beneath a pewter sky. Far in the distance they could see the church spire rising above the ancient yews and beyond it, in the terraced fields, the shaggy dots of grazing sheep. Beyond the village and the outlying farms, the road narrowed sharply before beginning its final, tortured climb toward Bellehurst estate.

"Beautiful, isn't it?" Eugenia sighed. Mercifully, she had slowed the Austin to make the sharp turn past the Paxton Hotel before clattering across the rough cobbles of the market square. "Nothing could ever induce me to return, but sometimes I think city life makes one forget how blessed we English are with extraordinary countryside. How green and utterly peaceful it is. Top-hole, as your cousin Nelson would say."

"I haven't met him yet. He's away at school."

"Is he?" Eugenia laughed. "Then I wonder why he showed up at my flat Sunday night begging a large sum of cash? There wouldn't be any need for it were he dutifully attending classes. His allowance is certainly generous enough. Lousy little beggar. I'll bet he's cut out for Paris with those Bolsheviks he hangs around with. What about you, Sara?"

"Me? Why, I don't belong to any political—"

"Sorry. I meant, what have you seen of the countryside so far? Has Vicky taken you on any day trips? Leeds Castle, Windsor, that sort of thing?"

"Actually, I've only seen Victoria once. She's been so busy planning the party. I'm spending most of my time with Grandmama."

"Talking scandal and laughing yourself ill over your childhood naughtiness, no doubt. And I'll wager she's dragged you to all the neighbors to show you off, with poor, fat Jessamine huffing and puffing in front of that silly pony cart."

This was such an accurate description of her visit so far that Sara could not help laughing. Eugenia joined in, and by the time their mirth subsided, the Austin had started up the hedge-flanked lane toward Bellehurst's front gate. The long avenue leading into the park was like a brilliant green tunnel, and the ivy-covered walls of Rose Cottage showed comfortingly between the dark, upright tree trunks.

Eugenia halted against the brick-edged curb. "Will she be sleeping, do you think?"

"I doubt it. It's nearly time for tea. Why don't you come in and say hello before you go up to the house?"

But Eugenia was suddenly reluctant. She hadn't seen her mother in a number of months, and they had not, she was a little ashamed to admit, parted on the best of terms the last time. The crux of their disagreement had been Mama's move to the lodge-keeper's cottage. While Eugenia disliked the big, rambling old house, she suspected her mother's decision had been prompted by some underhanded scheming on the part of William, her brother-in-law, whom she detested.

London had dismissed this accusation with alacrity, but the exchange between mother and daughter had not been a pleasant one considering that the two of them never had rows. Later, over the phone, they had of course made up, but Eugenia was still not convinced that her mother was truly happy with the decision she had made.

The moment she followed Sara into Rose Cottage's hall, however, Eugenia saw at once how wrong she had been. The newly papered walls and colorful scatter rugs gave the raftered corridor a homey air made all the more pleasing by the mixed aromas of freshly picked flowers, mouth-watering pastry, and steeping tea scenting the air. A charming first impression, heightened all the more by London herself as she came out of the kitchen to meet them, drying her hands on her apron. Her fair hair was pinned in a tidy knot at the nape of her neck, and she looked happy and well-rested and, to Eugenia, as tall and regal as a queen.

"My darling." They embraced. "I thought I recognized that frightful car of yours clanking up the hill. Didn't we agree that you'd spend some of your Uncle Charles's inheritance on a new one?"

"We did, but I changed my mind. Now don't say a word. You'll be glad to know I invested most of it quite prudently with Papa's firm and used the rest for a grand fling. The Adriatic, Budapest, and Brac. Didn't you get the cards I sent?"

"I cherished every one. You always were a bewildering mix of prudence and extravagance, Eugenia. Nothing, it seems, ever changes. Come, take off your wet things. Wherever did you get that dreadful coat? It reminds me of something Mr. Brockman would wear."

"That's exactly what I thought when I saw it. Somber military colors were always his passion, so of course I had to buy it. Sara, do you remember how we used to devour the Army and Navy catalog together when you were small?"

Of course Sara remembered. The big red catalog, as bulky as a copy of *Burke's Landed Gentry*, had arrived once a year in the mail, an event as eagerly anticipated as any holiday. Laughing, the two of them discussed the memory as they trooped into the parlor, where London had already prepared tea and where a third setting was quickly laid out for Eugenia.

Prodded by her mother, Eugenia talked briefly about her trip, describing the sights she had seen and touching on the political turmoil unfolding in central Europe. London asked numerous questions, clearly disturbed by the growing threat of Fascism and the fact that German warplanes had recently dropped bombs on the Spanish town of Guernica.

Sara listened quietly, her eyes on Eugenia's strong, animated face. She liked the way Eugenia talked with Grandmama and how they laughed together once the conversation took a more lighthearted turn, as if they were best friends who had only been apart for a matter of hours rather than months. Sara tried to imagine having a similar relationship with her own mother, and failed.

"Perhaps it's because we spent so many years apart," she thought. After all, she had been fourteen and nearly grown up when she left England and went to live with her mother in America. A silent, miserable adolescent horribly homesick for England, just the way Grandmama had been when she'd first arrived at Bellehurst after leaving Algiers. Fortunately Grandmama had understood what lay ahead of her and had prepared Sara as best she knew how, telling her what to expect and promising her that things would get better if only Sara would let them and not look back too often on what she'd left behind.

Sound advice, as it had turned out, and Sara had clung to it during the difficult months of adjustment that had followed. But even though she had grown to like New Jersey and was genuinely fond of her mother and stepfather, she had never managed to recapture the magic of her childhood while living with them. But then, how could she? Growing up in the big, dilapidated manor house of Bellehurst had been a singularly magical time—an enchanting interlude filled with the sort of love and laughter that came so rarely, if ever, to anyone's life.

And she would always be so grateful for it, Sara thought, looking up into her grandmother's elderly but still beautiful face, her throat closing with emotion. She wished there was some way to tell her, to make her aware of how terribly important she had always been to Sara, and how bitterly Sara regretted the long years without her. Had Grandmama felt the same? She seemed so happy nowadays, as though she had come to terms with her life and no longer regretted anything.

Sara couldn't help but wonder what she had been like when her father had been alive. She knew that those had been good years, because of the way Grandmama's face changed whenever she talked about them. Sara tried to imagine Bellehurst when her grandparents had been young: prosperous years when England itself had been at the height of empire and the Ashfords had been blessed with a strong, handsome son and two lovely daughters, and life must have seemed so rich and easy.

Once, just once, Sara thought, I would like to have seen

them then. To have known them at the peak of their prime: Lord and Lady Ladbroke, popular and privileged, her father, Sandy, young and dashing before he was killed and the economy had crashed and sorrow had, for the first time, brushed like a shadowy wing across their lives.

Chapter Sixteen

**1882
London**

London Ashford sat in the shade of a gnarled oak in the small, terraced garden of the Ladbroke town house, insulated from the noise and bustle of the London streets by a high, brick wall and hedges of brilliant hawthorn. It was an unseasonably warm October afternoon. The sky was a dazzling blue, and sunlight glistened on the lawn and on the fat hips that were all that remained of the summer's roses. Along the borders and in the big ceramic pots lining the terrace bloomed autumn asters in splashes of yellow, bronze, and white. Beyond the garden wall, the muted sounds of city traffic came to her on the crisp air. London was staying with Emily and Beatrice, who had been living in the town house ever since the baron's death earlier that spring.

It had been a year of mourning. Not just for the baron, but for Beatrice's fiancé, George Warburton, who had been stricken less than a month before their wedding while returning from an evening engagement at the Duke and Duchess of Devonshire's. The end had come quickly, without warning; pulling up in front of Augusta Warburton's house, the coachman had discovered George slumped over in the carriage seat.

The doctor, hastily summoned, had suspected his heart. A similar attack had overcome the baron barely two months later, but this time no one doubted it had been old age. Except perhaps Mrs. Garroway, who was heard to say that the baron had finally died from pure meanness.

Rupert had spent a number of months settling Bellehurst's affairs and grumbling at being named his uncle's heir, because it meant spending too much time away from his books. London did her best to help him, but she was busy herself dealing with the family. Beatrice had not taken George's death lightly. Her future as a comfortably married woman was now shattered, and there seemed no acceptable alternative beyond spinsterhood. Dressed in deepest mourning, she had begun haunting Bellehurst like a specter, unnerving the servants, annoying London, and worrying her mother to distraction.

When she could stand no more, London suggested discreetly to Emily that she and Beatrice move into Amanda Waring's Saint Marylebone home, which the baron had left to Emily when he died. Beatrice, London felt certain, would benefit enormously from this change of scene.

Emily had seized upon the suggestion with alacrity. The house, a lovely, three-story Georgian, lay in the heart of the West End, within comfortable walking distance of Hyde Park and the zoo. Because it had not been used since Amanda's time, it was, of course, badly in need of attention, but the prospect of refurbishing it had unexpectedly brought a little of the old, domestic gleam back to Beatrice's eyes.

They had left shortly after Sandy's second birthday and never returned. City life had appealed to them, and they had made the decision to remain. Once the shock of George's death began wearing off, Beatrice found that she enjoyed the never-ending social season considerably more than the quiet isolation of Kent. Although she and Emily were still in mourning and so avoided evening balls and receptions, they had recently begun attending some quiet teas and dinners and entertaining modestly themselves.

Now Emily came up the neatly trimmed garden path and settled herself at London's side. "How do you feel, dear? Is the baby giving you trouble?"

Smiling, London shook her head. Bars of golden sunlight dappled her gray cashmere gown and revealed the swelling of her belly beneath the flowing skirts. She was eight months pregnant with her second child. "Believe it or not, he's being quiet for once." And she patted her swollen stomach with maternal pride.

"How do you know 'he' won't be a she?" asked Emily.

London's smile deepened. "Let's hope not. Sandy was very clear about wanting a brother."

"Well, I shall welcome the baby gladly, whatever it is. I do so love them," Emily confessed, glancing rather wistfully over her shoulder at Beatrice, who was strolling down the garden path with Augusta Warburton and her daughter Clarissa, both of whom had been invited to tea. Despite the warmth of the afternoon, the three women were dressed in heavy mourning. As they walked, they spoke softly together, their heads bowed, drawn closer in recent months because of their mutual grief over George.

"She'll marry eventually," London said now, following her aunt's worried gaze.

"Do you think so?"

"Why not? She's only twenty-three."

"A spinster—"

"Nonsense. She's spent a lifetime learning to become the perfect wife and helpmeet. Sooner or later she'll come across a man who values that."

Emily sighed. More than anything she longed to have grandchildren like dear little Sandy. A woman needed the deliciousness of babies when she began to grow old, and her one regret about moving away from Bellehurst was leaving Sandy behind. She looked again at London, who had closed her eyes and was leaning back against the padded cushions of her chair.

"You look tired," Emily said with sudden concern. "Didn't you sleep well last night?"

London smiled without opening her eyes and patted her enormous belly. "I'm afraid I didn't sleep a wink. How can I, when I'm as fat as this?"

"You should ask the doctor for some laudanum to help

you rest. It's important to conserve your strength for the confinement."

"Oh, Em, don't be silly. The second one is supposed to be much easier."

"Then why, if you'll forgive my asking, don't you act as though you believe it? You've been so quiet these past few weeks. It's not like you at all. Are you sure you're not worried about the lying-in?"

"No, I'm not, honestly," London assured her quickly. She opened her eyes and smiled reassuringly, and was glad that Emily appeared relieved. She did not want Emily to guess the truth; that she had been plagued in the last few months by a sense of foreboding, even fear, and it was all because of Alex.

Alex was no longer in India. He was poised on the field of war in faraway Egypt. He had told her so himself in a letter London had received early that spring; it had been the only correspondence she'd ever had from him. A politely worded missive it offered his condolences on the loss of London's grandfather, whose obituary had appeared in a Cairo newspaper.

Undoubtedly aware that his words might be read by others, Alex had taken care to briefly and dispassionately relate his reasons for being there: that Egypt's bankrupted government had recently fallen into the hands of a nationalist calling himself Arabi Pasha, a renegade who had scandalized the British government by halting all debt payments to European bondholders (most of whom were English) and demanding the immediate expulsion of all foreigners from the country.

Infuriated, the British government had refused to recognize him, and the situation had quickly heated up. No sooner had Arabi Pasha's army mounted guns along the harbor of Alexandria than a joint Anglo-French squadron was dispatched to Egypt. Riots had broken out in the city and a number of Europeans had been killed. In return, the British fleet had bombarded Colonel Arabi's shore batteries while the French prime minister, fearing retribution, had promptly withdrawn his squadrons and left the British to fend for themselves.

Alex went on to say that he was glad to be gone from India at last, because he had long ago discovered that the duties of the guard commander of a peaceful, backwater kingdom like Jhulapore consisted mainly of paperwork and a regiment so routinely dull as to leave far too much time on his hands. London, who knew him well, had not failed to read between the lines, and she understood that Alex welcomed the forthcoming diversion of hard labor, hard fighting, and long hours in the saddle.

She had never shown the letter to her family or discussed its contents with anyone. Brief as it had been, she knew it was Alex's way of telling her where he was, and that he welcomed this campaign. But London, who was afraid, could not share his enthusiasm. Secretly, she began scrutinizing the newspapers for more information and, in July, read that Alex's regiment had been dispatched into the desert to reconnoiter the terrain surrounding Fort Tel-el-Kebir, which was the stronghold of Arabi Pasha's rebel army. There, within clear sight of the enemy's guns, troop movements were logged, supply trains counted, Sudanese guards waylaid or kidnapped or bribed, so that, by the end of August, the *Times* could report with certainty that the number of rebel troops entrenched at Tel-el-Kebir was estimated at twenty-five thousand.

London shivered now, recalling the fear that had tightened her throat when she had read accounts of the attack of September 13, when the British guns—the newest made by Krupp—had finally delivered their awesome cannonade against the Egyptian fort. In a matter of hours, it seemed, the ragtag army of Colonel Arabi had been completely routed; a stunning success that the British newspapers had crowed over for weeks, their headlines blaring (to London's intense relief) that the entire Egyptian army of twenty-five thousand had been effectively smashed with fewer than fifty English lives lost.

But that had been in September, and it was nearly November now. Surely Alex would have written to let her know he was safe? Or would he? Alex had been every bit the gentleman over the years; there was no reason for him to change now.

London gave a low exclamation of pain at the thought and instantly felt Emily's hand on her sleeve.

"London, what is it?"

She looked up and smiled. "Nothing. I was just thinking about Sandy. I miss him so much. We've never been apart, you know."

The little boy was back at Bellehurst in the care of his nanny, a young and energetic Scottish girl London had engaged not long after his birth. Nannie, as everyone called her, was dependable and experienced, and London had suffered no qualms about leaving the boy in her care. Nevertheless, she missed him unbearably—and Rupert as well. She had been surprised to realize how much she had come to miss his calm presence once she had left him, at his insistence, to take up residence with Emily and Beatrice and so place herself in the capable hands of Dr. Sir Charles Locock, whose attendance on Queen Victoria during her numerous lyings-in had made him one of the most fashionable obstetricians of the day. At first London had refused, but Rupert had been adamant. He was not, he had firmly maintained, about to risk repeating the nightmare surrounding Sandy's birth.

"It will be over before you know it," soothed Emily now, casting a sidelong glance at her niece. She did not say so, but she was concerned by London's appearance. Though the girl still looked beautiful, despite the pregnancy that distorted her slim body, the lovely color had faded in recent months from her cheeks, and there was a listlessness about her that Emily found disturbing.

"Come," she said, taking London's arm, her voice sharpened with an anxiety that she couldn't quite conceal. "You've been outside long enough. Let's go in. You can rest in the sitting room, and I'll bring you tea and the newspapers."

London laughed. "Darling Aunt Emily, you'll spoil me."

Emily smiled, and with it her plain face was transformed so that for a moment she looked almost beautiful. "I'm only following Rupert's orders, dear."

The sitting room was done up all in gold and blue. Heavy blue drapes fell in swags and folds from the tall windows.

The sofas and cozy armchairs were picked out in matching gilt, and over a lovely rosewood sideboard hung a collection of blue-and-white porcelain plates. There were fresh flowers on the top of the sideboard, and another vase on the small corner table where London lowered herself, with considerable difficulty, into the largest of the armchairs.

"I won't be a moment," promised Emily.

Alone, London leaned her head against the plump cushions and closed her eyes. It was a relief to be off her feet. The baby moved restlessly and she patted her bulging abdomen almost without thought. Sunlight streamed through the windows and laid a sharp-edged pattern of shadows across the colorful rugs. The room was all Emily: peaceful, cozy, and very unassuming.

Her thoughts, unfettered, moved back to Emily's concern about Beatrice. Once again London found herself wishing that she could assure Emily everything was going to be all right. Because London was aware, as her aunt was not, that Beatrice was already intending to get married. Not until the traditional mourning period was over, of course, but because Beatrice had only been engaged to George, not actually married to him, it wouldn't last much longer.

London had been rather taken aback when Beatrice had revealed her plans to her, for their relationship had not warmed appreciably over the last few years. But now, apparently, Beatrice had discovered that she needed someone to talk to, and for reasons known only to herself, she had chosen London. Beatrice, it would seem, was in love again—this time with Edmund Warburton, a distant cousin of Augusta's whom she had met at George's funeral.

London had been shocked at first considering that Edmund Warburton was well over forty, very untidy in his personal appearance, and, more disturbingly, given to recurring bouts of depression. He was pudgy and balding and, as well, had been married before; he was now a widower with a five-year-old son named William.

London had suggested that Beatrice take a little more time considering Edmund's offer, but Beatrice could see no reason why she should refuse him. At their first meeting she had been greatly moved by his resemblance to George, and what other people were inclined to see as slovenly habits and a predilection for drinking and avoiding work, Beatrice considered the understandable behavior of a lonely and disoriented widower. She had decided at once that she would set about reforming him, take over his life, manage his household, and make friends with the sullen little boy who was going to be her stepson.

Edmund, in turn, seemed to have found in the fading, unhappy Beatrice a dependable, efficient helpmeet willing to tolerate his occasional black moods; someone to love and lean on in the waning of his youth and who was obviously skilled enough to keep his disorganized household running smoothly.

"Promise you won't tell Mama," Beatrice had begged of London, and London frowned now, thinking how unfair she was being to Emily in keeping that promise.

"There," said Emily now, entering the sitting room.

London opened her eyes and pushed her troubled thoughts away. A servant brought tea, a milk jug, and honey, and a plate of lemon cookies dusted with sugar. Emily produced the *Times*, which she gave to London after making sure she was comfortable.

"You're not joining me?" London asked, seeing that there was only one cup.

"Augusta and Clarissa prefer to take their tea outside. I hope you don't mind staying alone, or would you rather I brought you back to them?"

"No, this is fine. You're ever so good to me."

They smiled at one another. Left alone, London stirred honey into her tea and, reaching for a cookie, unfolded the paper. She had become a voracious reader during the last three years, devouring everything that Rupert recommended from Bellehurst's small but well-stocked library.

Last winter she had plowed through the whole of Horace, Pliny, the *Iliad*, and a good deal of Shakespeare and Dickens and most of the essays of Froude. Those works had been a turning point in her life because they had opened up for her the vast realms of history that had been closed to her for so long in the isolated world of the Tuaregs. She was certainly no longer the innocent she had been at seventeen, but sometimes she was saddened by the thought of how English she had become. The East, and the girl who had lived in that fantastic, foreign world, seemed as far away to her nowadays as the mountains of the moon. While Alex . . .

Without her realizing it, London's expression became anxious. Despite everything, she loved him still, with all her heart, and longed for him in the same manner that she longed for his son when Sandy was not with her. She wondered if Alex still thought of her, too, and if he ever imagined what the last three years had done to her. What did he look like? Had the long, hot seasons in Jhulapore and the difficult Egyptian campaign changed him at all? Where was he now? Still in Alexandria or on his way home to Calcutta?

"Some day, one day," London said aloud, then stopped, because she had no idea what she had meant to say. She thought of the baby growing inside her, and of the shy and tender lover Rupert had been the night she had conceived it, and then, almost unwillingly, she remembered Alex's kisses and his lean hands roving her body.

With a painful exclamation she snapped open the paper. Her eyes fell at once on the large type heading of the Court Circular and her heart leaped: HER MAJESTY TO REVIEW EGYPTIAN TROOPS IN ST. JAMES'S PARK.

Over three hundred returning soldiers, London read, including Prince Leopold, the Duke of Connaught, were to parade before the queen early in November in order to receive Egyptian Campaign medals for their valor in the taking of Tel-el-Kebir. Others among them were to be awarded the Victoria Cross or, for a coveted few, the Order of the Bath, Military Division. The newspaper, in a fit of patriotic fervor, had even published a complete listing of names, adding tiny crosses in front of those unfortunate men who were to receive their campaign medals posthumously. London idly scanned the list.

†*MacLaughlin, Alexander, First Lieutenant*

She sat quite still. She heard Emily calling to her from the hallway but did not answer. The room seemed all at once to be pressing in on her, and she shook her head as though to clear it of the terrible weight and the blurred colors spinning before her eyes. She must have made some sound, because suddenly there was a rustle of skirts in the doorway and Emily appeared, her face white and frightened.

"London, what is it?"

London rose slowly, shaking her head. She tried to speak but her lips were stiff and no words would come out. Emily started toward her, hands outstretched, but London whirled and ran past her, out of the room and across the flagstone hall.

"London!"

She tugged frantically at the front door. She had to get out. Go somewhere. Anywhere. Emily was kind, but she did not understand. She did not know that Alex was dead.

"London, what *is* it?"

Emily's voice, shrill now with fear. The door finally opened and London stumbled down the short flight of steps, across the brick walk, and through the front gate. She heard Emily's running footsteps behind her and glanced over her shoulder. As she did so, she tripped over the curbstone. Emily screamed as London lost her footing and tumbled into the busy street.

"How long has she been like this?" whispered Rupert.

"Days," said Emily brokenly. "Ever since the baby was born. Oh, Rupert. I'm so glad you're here."

"I came as fast as I could."

"It—it was horrid. Unbelievable. I can't imagine why she did it—throwing herself in front of a carriage that way. The coachman was distraught, but of course it wasn't his fault."

Rupert reached down with an unsteady hand to stroke his wife's matted hair. London lay oblivious in a heavy chloroform coma. She had been bound from waist to ankle in thick strips of bandages that would keep her immobile while her body knitted from the birth of her child.

Earlier, the doctor had stopped in to make another examination and instruct them to tuck padded quilts around her when the fever mounted in her bruised and broken body. Then Emily had laid the newborn child, a tiny scrap of a girl with her father's dark hair, in the bassinet beside London's bed. The baby whimpered but London never stirred.

"What have you decided to call her?" Emily asked now.

"Eugenia," said Rupert. "After my mother."

"How lovely."

They fell silent. Outside the rain tapped against the windows. Mist lay like a veil over the trees and the garden. Earlier, Emily had asked Rupert to build a fire to drive away the chill. She said now, worried by the exhaustion on his face, "Why don't you rest? You've had a long journey. I've prepared a room for you. It's upstairs at the end of the hall."

"I'd rather stay with London, if you don't mind. I want to be here in case she awakens."

"Then I'll bring you tea."

Emily went out, shutting the door softly behind her. Alone in the small downstairs bedroom where London had been carried after her accident and where she had eventually been delivered of a healthy baby girl, Rupert stood anxiously beside the makeshift bed, taking stock, trying to maintain the rigid calm he had displayed for Emily. His darling girl. Disastrously involved once again in impulsive behavior of the sort that had, once before, nearly cost her her life and the life of their child.

But this time it was worse, much worse. There were broken bones, the doctor had said, and perhaps some internal damage because the off-side carriage horse had stepped on top of her after knocking her down. She could easily have died—

Oh, God. Anguished, Rupert stared down into the still, white face. *What were you running from? Whatever was wrong?*

Bereft of answers, he ran his hands through his graying hair. He looked, and felt, like a man who had been dealt a staggering blow from which he had yet to recover. The shock of Emily's cable, his own disbelief and denial, the whirlwind trip to London's side, and now this: the sight of her ghostly face with the bruise on one cheek and a cut on the chin, and her skin so translucent that Rupert was afraid; more afraid than he had ever been in his life.

Please, London, please. Won't you wake up and tell me what happened?

At first it was like swimming through murky darkness in which nothing existed but pain. Later, much later, when the pain mercifully receded, there was finally room for cognitive thought—and the first, agonizing stab of grief. For Alex, who was gone. Forever.

The thought made her moan aloud. Had it been fast or slow? Inside the fort or out in the desert, alone, bleeding into the sand? Lying there, waiting for death, had his final thoughts perhaps been of her? Intolerable thought. But it did not matter. Not anymore. Nothing mattered but the fact that he was gone. Somewhere. She did not know where. She only prayed that it had been instantly.

Tears trickled from between her closed lids, down her cheeks, to wet the pillow on which she lay.

"There, there." Rupert's hand, soothing and familiar, brushing the tears away. He leaned closer and spoke softly in her ear. "London? London, can you hear me?"

She could, but it was too much of an effort to open her eyes. She had no wish to drag herself out of the darkness that buoyed her. To open them now would be to acknowledge that she was alive; that her body, torn by childbirth and the crushing weight of the carriage horse that had trampled her, would heal. She did not want it to heal.

"London, look." Rupert was still speaking in a whisper, but now there was a compelling urgency in his tone. "We have a daughter. A beautiful daughter."

Something warm and squirming was laid against her side. London struggled violently against it. She did not wish to see it. Couldn't Rupert understand that?

But the baby, with the innate drive for survival possessed by every newborn, had already sensed its mother's nearness. With a soft mewling sound, it began rooting for the breast.

Slowly, against her will, London turned her head and opened her eyes. She saw that it was evening and that the lamps had been lit. Against the soft light she could see the outline of her daughter's fuzzy head on the pillow beside her. Unable to help herself she stirred and, with her finger, pushed aside a corner of the blanket. She saw the rosebud mouth, the dimpled cheeks, the deep blue of the unfocused eyes. And all at once a savage pain stabbed through the numbness in her heart; the inevitable grief, though mercifully tempered by the quickening of motherly love.

In'shallah. What is written, is written.

London looked up into Rupert's anxious face. She saw the joy and the relief there as her eyes met his, and she wondered why she had never realized before how much he loved her. She looked again at her tiny daughter, then reached out to caress the infant's silken hair. As she did so, Rupert took her other hand in both of his and held it to his unshaven cheek.

It was all in the hands of Allah, as Ali Wad Zarim would have said, London thought. And it seemed as good a reason as any to go on with the rest of her life.

Chapter Seventeen

Sometimes it seemed to London that looking back over the years following Eugenia's birth was not unlike stumbling across an old photograph, long forgotten, in the bottom of a drawer. Faded now, the once-sharp images were blurred to sepia-toned softness, but still one could remember, with a stirring sense of nostalgia, what it had felt like when those dear faces had been eager and young: London returning home to Bellehurst at last, her injuries and emotions mended and Eugenia asleep in her arms; Sandy storming through the front door to throw his little arms about her neck, talking twenty words to the dozen and standing half a head taller, or so it had seemed to her, than when she had left him.

Then Rupert, beaming with anticipation, had led her into the new conservatory just off the main drawing room. He had had it built for her during her absence. London had never forgotten the wonder of stepping into it for the very first time: the warm, loamy smell of the soil, the brilliance of the flowers that the new gardener—a considerably younger, less dour version of Mr. Bozman—had begun forcing in the neat rows of frames. Harsh winter sunlight had poured through the tall glass windows, illuminating the lovely wrought-iron benches and the burbling fountain frothing away between the flagstones to aerate a small goldfish pond.

It seemed as though the years passed so quickly after that. Sandy and Eugenia grew taller, sturdier, far more independent. Victoria arrived not long afterward like a lovely bloom, the last of London's children and, as well, the easiest and most painless to bear, having entered the world under far less shocking circumstances than either of her siblings. Life at Bellehurst had hummed in those years with house parties, dances, teas, and shoots because Sandy, unlike Rupert, had been born with a passion for hunting. There had been picnics in the fields in summer and harvest fetes and balls in the winter, and, whenever Rupert could be persuaded to leave his research behind, visits to Emily and Beatrice and the whirlwind gaiety of a London season.

Then, subtly, their fortunes had changed. A lengthy agricultural depression and the increase of death duties and taxes left the family coffers sadly diminished. Rupert did what he could, but he quickly proved hopelessly impractical once out of the study. London did not care. She knew perfectly well that the Ashfords were far more fortunate than many of their neighbors, who had been forced to sell their properties at ridiculously deflated prices or to simply board up their grand houses and move back to Town.

Then there was the horror of the war in South Africa, where native Dutch Boers were waging a bloody struggle against British colonials. Political unrest flourished as well, and Parliament charged that Germany was stretching too far as a colonial power and unnecessarily increasing the size of her navy. No one trusted the German emperor, Wilhelm, the intensely disliked grandson of Britain's own queen, while Victoria herself was nearing eighty, and her health and eyesight were reportedly failing.

Into this rather morose period pierced one ray of unexpected sunshine: in June 1900, Millham Cross's vicar departed on a lengthy visit to his daughters, who were attending boarding school in Switzerland, and let out his vicerage to a family of charming Americans.

"I'm afraid I don't understand you at all, Lawrence," said Mrs. Adeline Parker for perhaps the twentieth time that morning. "I thought you wanted our Gwen to make a good marriage?"

With a weary sigh, Mr. Parker turned from his correspondence in the small upstairs room that served as his office in the Parkers' rented town house just off Marylebone Road. Normally he was a patient man, even when his equanimity was tried beyond endurance by the pestering of his wife. Today, however, he found Adeline's inability to drop the subject of Gwendolyn's nuptials vexing in the extreme.

Perhaps that was because there weren't any marriage plans as far as he could see. Even after nearly six months abroad and considering the tireless manipulations of her ever-doting mama, eighteen-year-old Gwendolyn had failed to make what her mother termed a brilliant match. Oh, there were admirers aplenty, but none of them good enough or rich enough for Adeline, whose frosty and quite blatant disapproval always sent them scurrying after more receptive game.

"I simply don't see why we can't spend a few months in the Riviera," Adeline continued, taking her husband's silence as a sign that he was, at last, growing more receptive to the idea. "I've already told you that the Prince and Princess of Wales will be there. And Caroline Houston told me that wherever they go, the cream of Debrett's is bound to follow."

Mr. Parker made a strangled sound and put his head in his hands. If not for Adeline's obsession with their daughter's marriage, he could truly claim to be enjoying their overseas stay. After years spent dutifully ensconced in the offices of his photography business back home in New Jersey, he had at first been violently opposed to Adeline's madcap suggestion that they spend a year abroad.

First off, he was a retiring sort of fellow who thoroughly disliked change, and second, and most important, the Parkers could not, at present, afford it. Gwen's private schooling in Philadelphia had cost him dearly, and the Parkers were not the exceptionally moneyed people that Adeline liked pretending they were. Furthermore, Mr. Parker knew perfectly well that Adeline was not so much interested in soaking up foreign landscape and culture as she was in finding the right sort of husband for their only daughter—preferably one with a marquisate, a country house, and an income of thirty thousand pounds a year.

Not that Adeline hadn't admitted her motives right from the outset. She had, in fact, been embarrassingly direct about them. The moment she had heard that Alva Vanderbilt had married her daughter, Consuelo, off to the English duke of Marlborough, Adeline had instantly become one of the most vocal supporters of American mothers' mad stampedes abroad.

The only problem as far as Lawrence could see was the fact that all her plans were doomed to fail, simply and solely because Gwen was not an exceptional heiress. While the Parkers could consider themselves comfortably well off, they were by no means as wealthy as their millionaire New Jersey neighbors, who lived in luxurious mansions in the green hills surrounding Madison, the town in which Lawrence and Adeline made their permanent home. And surely Adeline must be well aware that the British nobility, whose wealth had been sadly diminished in recent years by economic slump, death duties, and taxes, were anxious to avail themselves only of the greatest sums of American dollars.

Regrettably, none of this had made the least impression on Adeline, and Mr. Parker, worn down at last by her pleading and his daughter's shy insistence that she would like to see something of the world, had given in. He had never been able to stand up to the combined insistence of his womenfolk, and, to be fair, he could not consider himself displeased with the cozy life they had made for themselves in London thus far.

Nevertheless, he remained adamant on the score of removing to Cannes for the summer. Indeed, the whole affair was out of the question, and when this sad fact finally dawned upon Adeline, she withdrew from the study with such an air of wounded dignity that Mr. Parker became alarmed. Tears and recriminations were more in Addie's line. What on earth was he to make of this?

Later, returning home from a lengthy gentleman's supper given by the American consul, a distant relation of Adeline's mother, Lawrence found Adeline dressing to go out. Not entirely certain of his reception, he hesitated in the doorway, watching as the housemaid crimped his wife's glossy chestnut curls *à la reine*. Plucking up his courage at last, he strolled casually inside. "I assume you're not dining here tonight?"

"No. Gwen and I are joining the Lavenhams over at the Trocadero. I didn't expect you back so early. Why don't you join us?"

"I'd rather not, if you don't mind. But I've some news for you."

Adeline, glowing, sprang to her feet. "Oh, Lawrence, you've changed your mind! I just knew you would! When can we leave? How long can we stay? Do you suppose we could—"

Mr. Parker detached himself quite firmly from her eager grasp. "No, Addie, I'm afraid you've got it all wrong. I haven't changed my mind about France. Still think it's a darned silly idea and I wish you'd see it, too. But we're off for the summer, you and Gwennie and I. To Kent."

"Kent?" He might just as well have suggested that they were shoving off in the dank steerage of a freighter bound for the Congo. "You can't be serious! Don't tell me you've accepted an invitation to spend a few weeks in the *country*?"

"Er . . . well, yes. I thought it might cheer you up. Put that nonsense about France out of your head. See something more of England than the inside of restaurants and shops and other people's drawing rooms."

Adeline stared at him, her bosom quivering with indignation. "Lawrence Parker, sometimes I think you must be the most obtuse man I've ever met! Where, for heaven's sake, are we going in Kent? Whatever will we *do* there?"

"I—well—I've let a vicarage for the summer. The parish padré plans to spend three months in Switzerland visiting his daughters at the convent school they're attending. He was only too happy to give us the place. I understand it's got several bedrooms, adequate plumbing, even a housekeeper and a gardener."

Adeline's handsome face had sagged considerably as he spoke. Now she collected herself with a visible effort. "Lawrence. I insist you go at once to see this minister person, or his agent or whoever he is, and tell him we've no intention of accepting. In fact, I don't care what you tell him so long as you make it clear—"

"All right, Addie." Mr. Parker spoke wearily. "I'll tell Ladbroke something's come up. That you're ill. That Gwen has already accepted an invitation to spend the summer elsewhere."

"Ladbroke? Who in the world is Ladbroke? The minister?"

"Really, Adeline, now who's being obtuse? How many Ladbrokes do you know?"

"You don't mean the *baron*, Lord Ladbroke, do you?"

"As a matter of fact, I do. Saw him at the consulate earlier today. The parish is on Ashford land, and I guess he feels sort of responsible for the preacher. He's the one who suggested we take the vicarage when I mentioned you were wanting out of London for the summer."

"I wasn't even aware you knew him. Not personally."

"That's silly, Addie. We've met a number of times at the coffeehouse in Temple Bar. He's a regular there whenever he's in town. And you'll remember his brother Charles sat across from us at the Woolfords' jubilee in April—"

"—An older man with side whiskers and a big, hooked nose? Who talked about chemicals or petrol or some such boredom all night?"

"Distillates. He's founded a company called Merrick Distillates. That was him, all right. And Charles's older brother is Rupert Ashford, who suggested we let the Millham vicarage for the summer. But now I suppose I'll have to tell him—''

''—That we'd be absolutely delighted to accept.''

Lawrence stared. ''We—would?''

''Yes, of course. I think it's the most wonderful idea you've ever had!'' Standing on tiptoe, Adeline kissed her bemused spouse heartily on the cheek. ''How soon can we leave?''

If Mr. Parker was understandably mystified by his wife's sudden eagerness to spend the summer in the country, his daughter, Gwendolyn, most certainly was not. Gwen had no illusions as to why her mother had changed her mind, because she was well aware of the fact that the Ladbroke name was included among numerous others on a lengthy list Adeline kept locked in her escritoire—a list consisting of eligible young men who, in Adeline's opinion, would someday inherit sufficient wealth and rank to qualify as serious suitors for her daughter's hand.

Now, riding with her parents in the hot compartment of the train that was chuffing south from London through the unfolding countryside, Gwendolyn mentally reviewed the information on her mother's list with an antagonism that would have shocked and dismayed her unsuspecting parent.

Alexander Powney Rupert, aged twenty. Only son and presumable heir of Rupert and London Ashford, styled Lord and Lady Ladbroke of Bellehurst, Millham Cross, Kent.

The baron was also the only living male relation of one Charles Merrick Ashford (so Adeline had scribbled in a recent footnote), the founder of Merrick Distillates Company, a small but apparently thriving business in Leeds which had recently opened offices in London.

Adeline, who kept her ears open to every rumor, no matter how insignificant or unlikely, had also heard that Charles Ashford was being considered for a peerage. Whether Rupert, and presumably his son in turn, would inherit either the business or the title when Charles died remained to be seen; ergo Adeline's thoughtfully included question marks.

"Well, I don't care if he inherits it or not," Gwendolyn thought now, her pink mouth puckered mulishly. She had already made up her mind that she was going to dislike everything about Alexander Ashford, just as she had come to dislike the countless other eligible men, young and not so young, that her mother had been flinging at her with unflagging enthusiasm all season long.

Gwen was a pretty girl, small, slim, and red-haired, with lustrous brown eyes and a subdued manner that most men found appealing. She was, as well, painfully shy, and for this reason quailed with embarrassment at the thought of enduring still another round of her mother's tireless matchmaking. Surely the Ashfords would prove intelligent enough to see at once how shameless was her scheming?

The thought made Gwen shift restlessly on the hard wooden seat. At eighteen, still innocent and remarkably unworldly, she had no intention of marrying anyone. Least of all an Englishman, considering that every one of them she had met thus far had been so terribly polite and formal with her that she had felt miserably gauche and tongue-tied in their presence.

But at least she could take heart in the passing scenery, which was remarkably like the pastoral hills of her beloved New Jersey, only much more green and intensively farmed. There was a novel charm, too, in the oasthouses, whitewashed pubs, and thatched cottages clustered around the cobbled streets of the picturesque villages they passed. Gwen's spirits could not help but rise a little as the train plunged deeper into the jewel green of the countryside. She thought of the long walks she could take through the woods, and the picnics she and her parents would have in the meadows surrounding the vicarage. Perhaps the next few months wouldn't prove such an unqualified disaster after all.

Two hours later the Parkers disembarked from their train, not in Millham Cross, which had no railway station of its own, but in the larger settlement of Temple Lynn, an industrious town of neat houses and smartly kept shops surrounded by an ancient stone wall from which trailing wisteria showered the walkways with fragrant purple blossoms. A carriage and a baggage cart were waiting for them in the golden dusk, and it was fortunate that Lawrence had had the foresight to order them since Adeline had brought along considerably more luggage than was warranted for a summer in the country.

"I really haven't any idea what we're going to need," she had informed her husband tartly when he first taxed her with this. "It could rain the entire time and be awfully cold and wet, which will mean entirely different clothing than if it doesn't rain at all and ends up being dry and hot. You wouldn't want Gwen to be without adequate attire, would you?"

"No," Mr. Parker had allowed, although he found it both shortsighted and silly of his wife to pack endless trunks of balldresses and tea gowns in lieu of more sensible skirts, walking shoes, and woolen shawls.

Because it was a warm, overcast evening, the baggage handler was sweating profusely by the time he had humped the last of the Parkers' trunks, valises, and hat boxes into the cart. With a rather rude toss of the head he indicated that the family was to ascend into the carriage. Lawrence, seeing the affronted quivering of Adeline's lips, mopped at his own brow with a crumpled square of handkerchief. He could only hope that the fellow's churlish behavior was not the first indication that their vacation was going to end in disaster.

Fortunately the vicarage turned out to be far more pleasant than even Mr. Parker had anticipated. Knowing his Addie would never tolerate primitive living conditions, he had been worrying secretly about the validity of Lord Ladbroke's claim that the place was "charming" and "well lived in." Such recommendations usually left room for a number of interpretations, but even Adeline could not fault the cozy stone house in front of which the carriage halted after trundling down a shaded lane past a lovely Norman church with lichen-covered walls and leaning tombstones.

The cottage was made of native gray stone, snuggly gabled and very picturesque. The planting beds and borders, which the vicar had lovingly weeded before his departure for Switzerland, were bursting with old-fashioned English blooms:

tall hollyhocks, multicolored phlox, and deep scarlet poppies. Bees hummed drunkenly amid sweet blue cornflowers, bright orange marigolds, and tangled masses of anemone japonica and forget-me-nots. Dainty white roses nodded on the trellis above the door, and inside it was cool and bright and very clean. The raftered ceilings were hung with great bunches of dried wildflowers, and the cozy, countrified feeling was especially in evidence in the kitchen, with its flagstone floor and great, arching hearth of brick. The sink was surrounded by a backsplash of lovely blue-and-white tiles, and there was, to Lawrence's infinite relief, a working water closet just off the hall.

The housekeeper, large and kindly, welcomed them inside and showed them the bedrooms and the brass bedsteads with their fresh casings of crisp linen. The windows stood open, and the heady scent of lilac and meadowsweet wafted inside.

Adeline was enchanted, and even Gwen forgot her earlier misgivings, sensing that here she would find the peace and the privacy that had eluded her until now in the hustle and bustle of London. Wandering outside, she breathed deeply of the pine-scented air while her mother and the housekeeper completed their inspection and Lawrence paid the carriage drivers and sent them on their way.

The vicarage lay nestled at the bottom of a small valley, surrounded by the thick foliage of elm and ash and beech. Behind the house a silvery stream wound its way across smooth gravel and moss-grown stones before plunging away beneath an arching bridge that presumably led the villagers to church on Sundays. Beyond the bridge the hills rose higher, toward cultivated fields and neatly tended farms. To the west, amid a stand of stately trees, Gwen could make out the steeply gabled roofline of a manor house with ivy-covered walls and an air of timeworn grandeur.

Bellehurst, she thought, and instantly the golden evening lost most of its charm. The Ladbrokes' ancestral home looked every bit as imposing as she had feared. To her, such houses always bespoke of old money, traditional values, and the overwhelming stuffiness of the British upper class that had intimidated poor Gwen from the very first.

No doubt the Ashfords would waste little time in extending an invitation to meet the Parker family. Gwen dreaded this, aware from past experience that her mother would behave in a very embarrassing manner, bombarding everyone with baldly transparent remarks about the obvious suitability of her daughter and the Ashford son. Why, oh why couldn't they have stayed home in America?

The dreaded summons came barely three days later. To Gwen's horror it was not just an informal "at home" intended to officially welcome the Parker ladies, but a formal tea, at four o'clock on Tuesday afternoon, with all the family in attendance. Gwen's heart seemed to sink into her shoes, while Adeline could scarcely contain her delight.

The furious activity that erupted on Tuesday morning in preparation for the tea was, of course, a familiar and by now thoroughly loathed ritual for Gwen. She wished that she had the courage, just this once, to stand up to her mother and simply refuse to go. But she knew that she did not, and that Adeline would only shrug off any hint of rebellion as nerves.

Awash in misery, Gwen sat stiffly between her parents, her red hair fashionably crimped, her high-collared dress far too hot and uncomfortable, as the vicarage carriage rolled down the long, tree-shaded drive toward the Ladbroke home. They were let through the gate by a smiling keeper and admitted into the house by a formidable butler in proper tails and white gloves—just as Gwen had feared they would be. She already knew, too, without having to look, exactly what the entrance hall would look like, because she had seen plenty of stately homes in London: glittering with gilt and marble columns, the overpowering Renaissance architecture would doubtless be complemented by graceful statues and countless other priceless works of art. In other words, a gloomy museum.

"Please," said the butler with a bow, holding the door aside.

"Oh—!"

Gwen's exclamation of wonder was purely involuntary. She had been expecting any number of things, but not this. Never this. A great hall with a double staircase paneled in rich wood and hung with a number of hunting prints and colorful landscape oils. A huge brass bowl filled with sweetly scented wildflowers on the mahogany refectory table, and more flowers in other pots and vases scattered throughout the large but welcoming room. The timbered rafters, the twin fireplaces, the worn but very comfortable-looking settee beneath the long window at the far end of the hall—all served to give the impression of lived-in comfort, a place where visitors could feel instantly at home.

They were courteously ushered through a drawing room which, though somewhat more formal than the hall, also gave the impression of being regularly and enjoyably used. There were books and well-thumbed stacks of *Country Life* on the tables, and a hand-knitted and obviously much-loved shawl draped comfortably over one of the wide-lapped chairs.

Then the conservatory and its brilliance of color and wonderful smells. Sunlight poured through the countless windows and danced across the fountain and the ornamental pond before sparking off the crystal and silverware set on a table that had been charmingly arranged for tea between a grouping of lovely potted orange trees and palms.

The butler said: "Mr. and Mrs. Lawrence Parker and Miss Gwendolyn Parker, my lady."

A woman rose gracefully from a wicker armchair tucked in a sunny corner of the room and came toward them, smiling. She was much younger than Gwen had expected, and very striking, with thickly lashed blue eyes and ash-blond hair artfully arranged in an aureole about her small head. Her gored skirt of stiff blue broadcloth revealed the slender shape of a younger woman, one who could not possibly have a grownup son and two daughters.

"It's so lovely to meet you at last," the baroness said. Her voice was low and musical, and sounded as though she meant it. She smiled again, and this time, fine lines fanned out from the tilted corners of her remarkable eyes, which alone served to betray her age. "May I present my husband, Rupert?"

From around the potted palm came an older man, tall and not unhandsome, with graying hair and the grave, courteous manners of a former day and age. As soon as introductions had been dispensed with, Lady Ladbroke apologized for the tardy appearance of her children.

"They should be down any moment." She turned to Gwen, her slimly elegant hand outstretched. "You look about the same age as my oldest daughter, Miss Parker. Do you play tennis?"

Gwen nodded and smiled, warming to the baroness. It was impossible not to like her.

"Oh, good. Eugenia will be delighted. Ah, here they are." She turned toward the doorway and beckoned. "This is my son, Alexander."

Adeline stepped forward quickly. "My daughter, Gwendolyn—"

"A pleasure, Miss Parker."

Blinking, Gwen looked across the cool, sun-drenched length of the conservatory and saw before her a tall young man with blond hair who was smiling down at her. Tiny laugh lines crinkled at the corners of his eyes—which were as brightly blue as his mother's—in a manner that suggested he laughed often and heartily. His features were roughly hewn, and his tailored gray suit revealed a slimly athletic form possessing an almost animal grace.

"If you're keen on tennis then I insist you play me, Miss Parker, not my sister. I've been hoping for the appearance of an adequate rival. Eugenia, I fear, is far too clumsy on the courts."

"You prawn," came the teasing voice of a young girl from behind him, but Gwen didn't notice. She hadn't even heard. She was staring at Sandy, her eyes wide with wonder. How sweet his smile was! How warm and kind the expression on his face! All her miserable preconceptions about him promptly flew from her head. A rush of some odd, new emotion shook her. It was too much, too sudden. Her brown eyes filled with confused tears.

"Come, introduce me to your parents, Miss Parker."

The lightness had vanished from Sandy's tone. Now it was steady and reassuring, as though he was aware of her confusion and wished to help her find her way back to calmness.

Gwen took a deep breath. She had the sudden, warm sense of being drawn into his protection. She stood beside him as he shook hands with her father and bowed to her mother. The top of her head barely reached his shoulder. As they moved toward the tea table, she searched her mind desperately for something clever to say that would make him talk to her again.

There was no need. Sandy's questions and his genuine interest in her drew Gwen out of herself and made her feel, for the first time in her life, that she was not some shy, shrinking violet. In his presence she seemed to bloom, all softness and sweetness, like an unfurling flower. She had no idea that Sandy was equally charmed, accustomed as he was to his boisterous sisters, his strong-willed mother, and the very determined young ladies of the county who were constantly throwing themselves at his eligible head.

The luncheon proceeded amiably. Over the years, London had become quite skilled at making small talk, while Adeline could be charming when she chose. Lawrence and Lord Ladbroke had already discovered that they shared similar views on politics and business, and this kept them occupied throughout the meal. In the meantime, Sandy squabbled good-naturedly with Eugenia, teased his younger sister Victoria into fits of girlish giggles, and left Gwen—an only child herself—dazed with wonder at the noisy confusion provided by this obviously happy family.

After luncheon, Rupert led Lawrence into the house for a look at his library while London and Adeline strolled out into the garden. Victoria, pouting, was whisked away by Nannie to change her party dress and wash the crumbs from her mouth and fingers. Eugenia, filled as always with restless energy, vanished in the direction of the stables so that, quite by accident, Sandy and Gwen found themselves alone.

The conservatory was filled with a warm, cozy silence and Gwen, somewhat intimidated by this, lowered her eyes to her lap. She had never been very good at conversation, and she was painfully aware of Sandy's gaze upon her as he lounged negligently in the chair across the table. After a moment, however, he smiled at her, his father's rare smile. "I'm much too full to play tennis. How about you?"

Gwen nodded.

"We could always play tomorrow."

Her heart sang. "I'd like that."

"What shall we do in the meantime? Join Eugenia in the barn?"

Gwen hesitated. She was ashamed to admit that she was afraid of horses. "I—I suppose we could."

"I've a better idea." The chair scraped on the stone floor as Sandy came to his feet. "I'll take you down to the Skeltons'. They've a new litter of puppies born only two days ago. Their eyes haven't even opened yet. Would you like to see them?"

"Oh, yes!" This time it was Gwen who dazzled him with her smile, reminding him of some wild woodland creature coming to life beneath the caress of a trusted hand.

As they walked, Sandy told her a little about his family and the richness of life on Bellehurst estate. Gwen's admiration and sense of wonder grew, for her own, sheltered existence in New Jersey seemed mundane by comparison. When she told him this, ruefully admitting that she must seem an utter bore to him, Sandy tipped back his head and laughed. Nothing could have disarmed him more than such an honest, though inaccurate, confession.

When they said good-bye, later that afternoon, he knew that he wanted to see her again.

And so he did. It proved a warm, lazy, seductive summer, with endless sunshine and soft breezes. More often than not, the Parkers could be found at Bellehurst, picnicking on the lawn with their hosts or relaxing, in the cool of twilight, on the terrace. Eugenia, who had never really displayed much patience with her own sex, discovered Gwen to be a surprisingly good tennis player, and the two of them met on the court nearly every morning. Occasionally they were joined by Sandy, but as June slid by and the days became sultry, the three of them abandoned the game to spend their afternoons boating on the nearby river or swimming at the Beckwiths, who had recently installed a lovely artificial pool.

Once, Sandy took Gwen bicycling down the drowsy lanes to Millham Cross, and after stopping for ice cream at the greengrocer's they pedaled home again. And it was in the cool green tunnel of trees lining Bellehurst's front drive that he kissed her for the first time. Taken totally by surprise, Gwen blushed prettily, and in response there awoke within Sandy's heart the desire to make her blush like that often, and to cherish and protect her.

Not long afterward, at a country dance hosted by the Olwyns, he asked her to marry him, and Gwen, happier than she had ever been in her life, accepted.

Chapter Eighteen

There were bound to be complications, of course. It was impossible not to have them, considering the many wishes and conditions on both sides. Adeline, for one, was adamant that the wedding take place in Saint Margaret's, with numerous bridesmaids to attend the bride and a flower-festooned carriage to drive the young couple away. Rupert, horrified by the idea of such a public spectacle, campaigned vigorously for an uncomplicated ceremony in the local church, until London pointed out that this was impossible considering that the vicar was away.

Neither Sandy nor Gwen were in the least bit cooperative themselves, considering that neither of them had any specific wishes about where or how they married, just provided it was soon. There was, in fact, a certain element of urgency about the entire situation because Sandy was going away. To war.

It had all started back in October, shortly after the Boers had besieged the South African frontier town of Mafeking and reduced the British garrison there to nearly nothing with heavy shelling and forced starvation. Then, in December, came "Black Week," seven long days of bloody defeats and enormous casualties for the British army at the hands of the well-supplied and skillful enemy. Back in England, patriotism rose to hysterical heights, and Lord Roberts was promptly dispatched overseas to head the British forces. Anxious to relieve their beleaguered countrymen in Mafeking and elsewhere, thousands rallied to join him in service. Among them, grimly determined, was young Alexander Ashford.

He had told his mother first. Alone, in the conservatory at Bellehurst, surrounded by the brilliance of hothouse roses, the tinkling fountain, and the drowsy warmth of the rising sun, while outside the naked tree branches lifted into the cold spring sky. Explaining softly what he had done and what had compelled him to do it, though perhaps his words were somewhat hesitant because he scarcely understood it himself.

But, oh, the look on her face when he told her! She had never looked at him that way before. Never. All her life, his mother's beautiful eyes had shone with love and pride for him, had warmed him, comforted him, made him feel as though he could do no wrong. In despair, he tried once again to explain, but London's cold voice interrupted him.

"You're just like your father." Tonelessly, the dying eyes looking past him now at something Sandy could not see.

"Like Father?" He was genuinely puzzled. "How can that be? If I were anything like Father I'd live with my head in a book."

Watching her, he could see the struggle going on inside her and for a terrible moment thought that she would weep. He had never made her cry before. "Mum—"

But the struggle had not been against the tears, though they ached unshed in London's throat. Oh, God, the anger, the frustration, the terrible despair that shook her at being shown that this was Alex's son, not hers, but Alex's. The one man she had loved above all others, the man who had left her to chase a dream that she had never—would never—understand. A dream that Sandy now seemed ready to share.

"Mum, I have to go. Please try to understand that."

She turned her head and looked into Sandy's eyes. And saw in them the same desire that had burned in Alex's eyes long ago when they had talked until dawn in the tent at the Faraji oasis and he had tried to explain to her what it was that compelled a man to turn his back on love and family and pick up a sword for queen and empire. At the time, her heart aching, London had realized that there were certain things in the souls of men that a woman could never hope to understand.

But I do, London thought suddenly. *I do understand.* Alex and she had both made him. He was a part of each of them. And that which she had taken away from Alex twenty years ago she must now give back.

But Alex was dead.

A sudden stab of maternal fear took possession of her heart. She caught Sandy's shoulders, the pressure of her fingers hurting him. "You won't let yourself be killed."

It was not a question, but he answered it anyway. "No, Mum, of course not."

And he smiled at her, and it was Alex's smile, so charming and full of life that her heart twisted. An old Arabic saying, long forgotten, sprang suddenly to her mind. *Allah, in his infinite wisdom, gives walnuts to the toothless. . . .*

"Oh, God," she said, and now she was laughing and crying at the same time, "I suppose Beatrice's husband can arrange a commission for you in the family regiment. Your father can write—"

"There's no need. I've already written. Not to Uncle Edmund, because I've no interest in the infantry." Sandy's eyes shone. "I've joined the cavalry, Mother. The twenty-third Lancers. We leave for Cape Town in August."

Gwendolyn, radiant in white, was duly married at Bellehurst on the fifteenth of July. There had been no time for an elaborate wedding since the bridegroom was due to join his troop ship in Gravesend at the end of next month, but given the circumstances, those who attended could find no fault with the ceremony. There was no talk of scandal, as Adeline had feared—the sort of speculation that invariably arises whenever a young couple is forced to marry in haste.

Instead, it was a decision applauded by all, with the possible exception of a few hard-nosed mamas who had hoped to bring their own daughters to the altar as Alexander Ashford's bride.

Nevertheless, the vast majority of assembled guests grew misty-eyed over the thought of young Sandy marrying a girl he had fallen in love with at first sight, and practically on the eve of his departure for war. It was so romantic and heroic, everyone said, and, that summer, the county could talk of little else.

After a brief honeymoon in Italy, Gwen and Sandy returned to Bellehurst. August came with its drowsy heat lying over the hills and forests and ripening corn. The harvest began, and great, horse-drawn wagons rumbled daily among the sheaves. Asters, zinnias, and tangled masses of stocks and lilac-tinted mint took over the roadsides and gardens, displacing the last of the midsummer flowers. A hint of autumn lay in the air, and skeins of wildfowl could be seen unwinding through the enormous blue of the sky.

By the end of the month Sandy was gone, but life went on very much as it always had without him. Ida Skelton's daughter, Louisa, presented her parents with their first grandchild, a great, gawky, redfaced girl proudly named Mirabelle. The Millham Amateur Dramatic Society staged a summer theatrical in the village schoolroom and scandalized everyone by charging the outrageous sum of three pence admission. At Bellehurst, preliminary plans were drawn up for Victoria Ashford's eleventh birthday party, which would be, according to her wishes, held in London that fall. And eighteen-year-old Eugenia, who had borne her brother's hasty courtship, marriage, and departure for South Africa with a thundercloud mien, stunned everyone by announcing her intention of leaving home for good and moving in with her great-aunt Emily.

It was, in all, a dreadfully fatiguing time. Although London secretly sympathized with her willful older daughter, she had no choice but to smooth over the situation, which Rupert had understandably taken very badly. Eugenia had made a brilliant debut the previous year, for she was not only tall and beautiful, but refreshingly intelligent and, as well, the daughter of a baron. Older men found her both attractive and stimulating; younger men, while more cautious of her intellect, were equally admiring. There was no reason, Rupert argued, that Eugenia shouldn't marry well and settle down. Which was something that Eugenia, it seemed, had no intention of doing.

The Parkers, too, were planning to depart in September, and here arose another crisis to bedevil those endless summer days: Adeline was adamant on the score of taking Gwen home to America to live.

The prospect of being deprived of her daughter-in-law filled London with unreasoning anger. She had grown fond of Sandy's quiet, dainty wife over the last few months, but even more than that she resented Adeline's proprietary attitude. The girl was an Ashford now. Bellehurst was her home and it was here that she should remain to wait out the war. Supposing Sandy were to be sent home from Africa and not find her here?

Adeline, who was normally intimidated by anything the energetic and outspoken baroness said or did, for once dug in her heels and refused to relent. New Jersey, she calmly pointed out, was not that far removed from England nowadays, considering that the German steamer *Deutschland* had recently made the Atlantic crossing in under seven days. Furthermore, the British War Office would undoubtedly give them ample notice before sending troops back home, which served to bring up another point. Why did Lady Ladbroke assume that the newly wedded couple would wish to remain *in England* once reunited? Perhaps they would prefer setting up their own establishment in America until such a time— Adeline hoped she was putting this delicately enough—that Alexander inherited his father's estate.

"She's a horrid old besom," London stated unkindly, sitting at her dressing table one warm summer night unpinning and brushing out her hair. It was nearly eleven o'clock and Bellehurst's day was done. Seward, the butler, was downstairs closing up for the night, and the Parkers had returned to the vicarage more than an hour ago. Daylight lingered in the heavens far to the west, but the windows of London's bedroom, overlooking the eastern side of the park, opened onto a velvety blackness. Somewhere in that darkness an owl hooted.

"She doesn't like the idea of losing her daughter," Rupert said. He was sitting on the edge of London's bed, watching the brush glide through the silky length of his wife's hair.

"She should have thought of that sooner. Or found a son-in-law closer to home."

"London—"

In the mirror, their glances met. Slowly, London laid the brush aside and turned to face him. "I'm being very churlish, aren't I?"

"It's understandable. Our son is fighting a war in South Africa and neither of us want to admit how worried we are about him. But anxiety has a way of cropping up anyway, doesn't it?"

London drew a shaky breath and turned back to the mirror. On the dresser before her stood a silver frame with a photograph that Sandy had sent her shortly before his departure. In it he was wearing his khaki uniform and gaiters. The hilt and scabbard of his sword had already been painted khaki for active duty. Beneath the tall helmet his smiling face looked especially eager and young. A handsome man, with all the world laid before his feet. London quickly averted her eyes.

Behind her, Rupert said gently, "Adeline doesn't want to lose her daughter any more than we wish to lose our son. And beneath that gushing exterior of hers beats a very determined heart."

"Then you don't think she'll give in?"

"No more than you will."

"If only Gwen could decide one way or another! It would make things so much easier."

"Poor little Gwen. I don't think she knows how to make up her own mind."

"No," London agreed. "That's probably what attracted Sandy to her in the first place. He's been surrounded all his life by willful women. She must have seemed a sweet, refreshing change after Beatrice and myself."

"And Eugenia," Rupert added glumly.

London rose and went to him, slipping her arms about his

neck and bending to kiss his cheek. She knew that he was still deeply hurt by Eugenia's departure and puzzled by what he saw as her defection from the family. London, who understood her older daughter far better than Rupert, had accepted it more magnanimously.

"In a few weeks we'll be taking Vicky to London ourselves," she reminded him. "Then we'll all be together again. Besides, Emily promised to look after her, and you know she can be trusted to keep her word. Why don't you look on the bright side?"

"Is there one?"

London smiled. "Yes, of course. It's entirely possible that Emily will finally contrive to introduce Eugenia to a man attracted to her outspoken ways."

"I'm afraid you're dreaming, my darling."

"No. No, I'm not. Times have changed, Rupert. Women are growing dissatisfied with the roles they've been forced to play. They're tired of being quiet, unassuming wives whose only duty in life involves nurturing a shadowlike devotion for their husbands."

Rupert snorted. "Now you sound exactly like Eugenia."

"Our daughter has far more sense than you give her credit for!"

"Maybe so, but she's still unbearably brash. It's no wonder she's scared off half the admirers she attracted at her debut. Who in his right mind would marry a stubborn, disobedient creature like that?"

"You did."

Instantly the harsh lines eased from Rupert's face. He looked much younger when he smiled. Putting his arms about his wife's waist, he drew her down beside him. For a moment they looked into each other's eyes. Two decades of marriage had invariably forged between them the affection and understanding that were the touchstones of any satisfying relationship. Words were often unnecessary. Especially now. London knew that Rupert was pacified for the time being about the fate of his unruly daughter. And somehow she herself had managed for the moment to bury her ache for Sandy. But there was still the matter of Gwen.

Rupert said, "We'll talk to the Parkers tomorrow. And to Gwen, too. Calmly and reasonably. It's time we were finished with all this nonsense."

"Yes, you're right. As always." Kissing him, London slipped out of his grasp and bent to douse the light on her nightstand. The room went dark. From the open window came the chirping of crickets. The air, cool and fresh with the first hint of autumn, wafted inside, flowing softly over London's bare shoulders as she drew off her wrap, making her shiver a little.

"Rupert?"

"Umm?"

"Will you—would you stay here the night, please?"

She heard him chuckle in the dark. "I thought I'd grown too old for that."

But he came to her nonetheless after he'd undressed in his own room, slipped into his nightshirt, cleaned his teeth, and washed his face and hands. London was lying on her side with her head on her arm, but she turned to him gratefully when he got in beside her. Rupert gathered her to him and they lay together, London with her head on his shoulder, Rupert with his arms about her. Silence fell between them. Both were preoccupied with their own thoughts—London anxious about Sandy, Rupert thinking of Eugenia—although both knew better than to say as much out loud. Still, it was easier to face one's own private fears while drawing comfort from one another this way. Gradually, gratefully, they drifted off to sleep.

It was meek little Gwen, surprisingly enough, who settled the matter of her departure for everyone. On the following morning, she drove away alone in the vicar's little cart, refusing to tell her mother where she was going or when she would return. This uncharacteristic behavior would normally have disturbed Adeline, but because she was presently embroiled in an argument with the housekeeper concerning the proper airing of the vicarage linens, she scarcely noticed her daughter's departure.

An hour later Gwen returned with the calm announcement

that she had been to see Dr. Carne and that he was reasonably certain she was going to have a child.

Adeline's jaw dropped. She gasped. "Oh, my dear, I don't know what to say!"

"Then please don't say anything, Mama." Gwen's dark eyes glowed with a quiet contentment. "Especially when I tell you that I'm going to stay here in England until I have it."

Adeline's voice sharpened. "Did the doctor tell you you couldn't travel?"

"No." In fact, he had merely cautioned Gwen about avoiding strenuous exercise, eating properly and maintaining adequate weight. But while he had also assured her that there was no real danger in attempting a transatlantic crossing so early in her pregnancy, Gwen refused to consider it.

"You can't really expect me to spend a week on board a stuffy, tossing ship with no means of getting off and no doctor around should I happen to need one!" she told her mother now. "Thank you very much, but I'm going to stay right here at Bellehurst until Sandy comes home." She smiled dreamily. "If they'll have me, that is."

The war dragged inexorably on. Thankfully, the tides of fortune had shifted in recent weeks to favor the British at last. By the end of the summer, the combined troops of Lord Roberts and General Buller had managed to disperse the Boers at Vlakfontein and defeat them soundly at Bergendal. Not long afterward, the Transvaal and the Orange Free State were annexed, forcing the Boer leader, Paul Kruger, to flee to Mozambique. Lord Roberts declared that the war was over at last.

At Bellehurst, a telegram from Sandy arrived shortly before Christmas informing the family that they could expect him home in a month or two—as soon as his regiment finished dealing with the few rebel Boers remaining at large.

In January 1901, Queen Victoria died and, with her, one of the most remarkable eras the world had ever seen came to an end. She had risen to the British monarchy at a time when stage coaches rumbled across the rutted English roads and the country itself was little more than a wet, gloomy island isolated from the rest of the world. By the century's turn, Victoria left behind a sprawling empire of unbelievable popularity and prestige, as well as fifty years' worth of turbulent expansion that included the establishment of a huge network of railroads and telegraph lines, and the introduction of electricity, photography, and moving pictures. The nation deeply mourned her death. Fat, vulgar Edward was now king.

In late February, Gwendolyn Ashford was brought to bed of a girl. Although the baby was born several weeks too early following a night of what had been, for Gwen, an agonizing labor, she was a lusty little thing with a voracious appetite and a very insistent way of letting the adults in her life know what she wanted. As well, she was an exceptionally pretty baby, with milk-white skin and a downy layer of reddish-gold hair.

It's the color of desert sand, according to your mother, Rupert wrote to his son on the evening after his granddaughter's birth. *Neither yellow nor red, but a seeming mixture of both.* He went on to say that mother and daughter were doing well, and that the only thing lacking was a name for the mite.

Sandy, who had remained in Cape Town fighting what was turning out to be a lengthy guerilla war against the regrouped Boers, cabled back a single word: *"Sahra."*

"Whatever does it mean?" demanded Gwen, mystified. "Surely he's not suggesting we name her that?"

"It's Arabic," London told her. "The word means red. I'm surprised Sandy remembers."

"I don't think it particularly attractive," Gwen persisted. *"Sahra . . . Sahara.* No, I don't like the sound of it at all."

"We could always change it a little," Rupert suggested.

"What do you mean?"

"We could drop the h."

"To Sara?" Gwen said, surprised. "I—I don't know. I'm not sure I like it. Let me think about it, please."

"Take as long as you need, dear," London said soothingly. "We've all the time in the world."

Chapter
Nineteen

Two weeks later word arrived at Bellehurst that Sandy was dead. The War Office could supply only scant details: the Boers, whom Lord Roberts had mistakenly declared defeated in December, had regrouped and launched an aggressive assault on the British settlement at Cape Town. Sandy's regiment, the Twenty-third Lancers, had been ordered to blow up all extra munitions to keep them out of enemy hands.

According to the War Office report, something had gone wrong. Several soldiers—Sandy among them—had been accidentally killed. It was a bitter blow and all the more brutal considering how senseless his death had been. The agony of trying to accept that it had happened—and only a scant two weeks before Sandy's discharge—was unbearable.

For the people at Bellehurst, it proved a long, frigid, unEnglish winter. The snow fell and fell, blanketing the trees in the park and burying the front drive so that Tom Skelton was hard-pressed to keep it cleared for the carriages that kept coming through. There were many visitors: mourners come to pay their respects to the family and, later, guests invited to the quiet ceremony that was the christening of Lord and Lady Ladbroke's infant granddaughter.

Gwen was not present on either occasion. Her labor had been both difficult and protracted, and the doctor had ordered her to remain in bed until her body knitted and her strength returned. Rupert arranged for a private nurse to look after her, although the cost was dear, but Gwen's condition remained tenuous. She showed little interest in her daughter, and preferred to lie unmoving on her bed for hour upon dragging hour, with the heavy drapes drawn across the windows and the tears trickling down her cheeks.

Sandy was dead. Even now she could scarcely comprehend it. In the short time they had been together he had made her feel so cherished, so safe. There would never be another like him, never. She quailed at the empty future that yawned without him.

I want to go home, she thought desperately. *Away from this echoing old house and the people who knew and loved him too.* She didn't think she could bear another moment of their silent grief, which had so aged them in the last few weeks. But she shrank away from the difficult voyage that stood before her because, if the truth must be told, she had no desire to be alone with her baby without London or Nannie there to help her with it.

Oh, she had tried. Really she had. She dutifully changed, fed and held the baby, but it hadn't helped. None of those wonderful, surging emotions that a new mother was supposed to feel had assailed Gwen whenever she stroked her daughter's downy head or watched her lying on her back in the bassinet, waving tiny fists in the air. She was only too relieved to hand the infant back to its nurse.

I must be dead, Gwen thought. Dead inside.

The birth of her child and her new status as both a mother and a widow were difficult adjustments for any woman to make, and even more so for one with Gwen's delicate constitution. Had she given herself time, allowed herself to grieve and to learn to love her daughter as, invariably, all mothers do, then perhaps things might have turned out differently.

But Gwen was impatient as well as heartbroken. She wanted, most of all, to be held and caressed herself, and since her husband was no longer capable of giving her such comfort, she wanted her own mother to hold her and tell her all would be well. But Adeline was in America.

There was only one thing to do. She must go home. What reason did she have for staying here, in this lonely old house where she had known only a few blissful weeks of married life? So she wrote to her mother, a long, pleading letter revealing her loneliness as well as the shameful confession that her infant daughter was nothing more to her than a wearying emotional burden.

Adeline's reply arrived promptly by return mail, and its brisk tone served as a healthful tonic for poor Gwen. Certainly Gwen must come home, Adeline wrote. Where else could her darling girl possibly hope to recover from her recent, horrifying ordeals? As for the child, why, it was only natural for a new mother to feel resentful toward a demanding, colicky infant, and Gwen should by no means feel guilty about it. As for the baby being a burden, surely the Ashfords would agree to look after it until such a time that Gwen felt sufficiently recovered to return to England and claim it?

Gwen read through the letter with a growing sense of relief. Leaning back against the cushions of her daybed, she laid the letter aside and stared thoughtfully out across the barren treetops of the park. Sleet was falling, and the air was damp and cold. Shivering, Gwen sat up and reached for her shawl. It was nearly time for tea, and the Ladbrokes would be waiting for her in the parlor.

Descending slowly downstairs, she wondered how best to approach the subject of her leaving them. She was not so self-absorbed in her own grief that she was unaware of the hurt she would be causing them by returning home. Still, she had no intention of remaining at Bellehurst. Not any longer. The only thing lacking was the courage to tell them so.

She found the parlor cozily warm and still. Rupert was reading while London embroidered in an armchair beneath the window. She had taken up needlework in recent weeks, and now regularly produced exquisite pinafores, bibs, bonnets, and blankets for baby Sara. Presently she was stitching a fine piece of white lawn, her slim, youthful hands working busily. But her expression was distracted, and the bleak daylight falling through the window behind her revealed the sharp hollows of her cheeks. She had lost considerable weight since Sandy's death.

"There you are." The newspaper rustled as Rupert laid it aside. "Ready for tea? Vicky's gone ahead. Said she was too hungry to wait . . . Why, what is it, my dear? Is something wrong?"

Gwen laced her fingers together. "I want to go home."

Silence fell. Outside, the sleet tapped against the panes. Rupert slowly removed his spectacles. "Home? Do you mean to America?"

"Yes."

"When?" London managed.

"As soon as possible." Gwen looked imploringly at Rupert. "You could make the arrangements for me, couldn't you?"

Rupert pursed his lips and hesitated. "I suppose I could, though it'll mean a trip to London. Perhaps when the weather clears—"

Gwen's mouth twisted. "But that could take forever!"

London said slowly, "Couldn't you wait until spring, Gwen? When the crossing won't be so difficult? Besides, Sara isn't really old enough yet."

Gwen cleared her throat. "Yes, well, that's what I wanted to talk to you about. You see—" She broke off as the door opened unexpectedly behind her. The three of them turned. It was Nannie, an older, plumper version of the charming, ruddy-faced Scottish girl who had looked after Sandy and his sisters when they had been young.

"There ye be, ma'am," she exclaimed in relief, her eyes going to the armchair where London sat. "Will ye come upstairs? The wee bairn doesna seem well."

In the nursery Sara lay in the crib crying feebly. Her little face was blotchy and red. London leaned down and laid her cheek against the infant's hot little head. Her frightened eyes sought Rupert's. "Nannie's right. She's got a fever."

"I'll go at once for Dr. Carne."

The wait seemed an interminable one. London and Gwen remained with Sara in the nursery while the servants crept around the house avoiding each other's eyes. There had recently been news in the village that scarlet fever was once again stalking victims in London.

No! thought London, agonized. *Not this*. Not for Sandy's daughter.

But it was not scarlet fever. Dr. Carne, hurrying over from Temple Lynn, was reasonably certain of that. Sara's fever was high, it was true, but more likely than not some common childhood ailment was responsible. He felt reasonably certain that she would recover quickly, given adequate rest, fed warmed milk whenever she was hungry, and, above all, kept well protected from the damp, killing air.

Rupert, London, and Gwen stood around the crib after the doctor had gone. None of them spoke. Sara had fallen into a light sleep, but her breathing remained labored and uneven. Now and then she whimpered, and her tiny limbs jerked restlessly.

Watching her, Gwen felt a sudden, helpless anger rise in the back of her throat. It wasn't fair! Now she'd have to delay her departure until Sara was well, and that might take weeks! Unless . . . She looked up unexpectedly and caught the eye of her mother-in-law, who was standing on the far side of the crib watching her. A flush stole across Gwen's cheeks; she suspected that London had been able to read her thoughts as clearly as though she had spoken them aloud. But, surprisingly, there was no blame in that steady gaze, only kindness and a measure of understanding. It occurred to Gwen suddenly that there had never been anything save love and understanding in that gaze for her, even after Sandy had died.

"You don't suppose—" Gwen's voice faltered. Clearing her throat, she tried again. "You don't suppose I could leave her here? Just for a little bit. Until I'm settled in back home. It wouldn't be fair taking her while she's ill, and I don't want to wait any longer. You could always bring her to me later, perhaps in the spring. Would you do that for her? For Sara?"

A trace of color stole into London's pale cheeks. Rupert came up behind her and gave her shoulder a reassuring squeeze. Slowly, not trusting herself to speak, she nodded.

"Thank you," Gwen said emotionally and looked down at her sleeping daughter through a haze of happy tears. *It won't be long*, she vowed. *I'll send for you as soon as I can. I promise.*

She did not know then that she would not see her daughter again for thirteen long years.

FIVE
Days of Wine and Roses

They are not long, the days of wine and roses:
Out of a misty dream
Our path emerges for a while, then closes

Ernest Dowson

Chapter
Twenty

December 1913

"Sara!"

"Oh, bother."

"Miss Sara, where are you?"

Closing the door quietly so that the latch wouldn't click, Sara tiptoed across the bare floorboards toward the attic steps. Minnie, she knew, was afraid of spiders, and since the attic housed a number of particularly loathsome arachnids, Minnie wouldn"t dare venture farther than the upper hall in search of her.

Climbing into the musty gloom of the attic and brushing aside the cobwebs, Sara sat down on a mildewed trunk, shivering with the cold. Snow was falling in the park outside, and the bitter wind blew through the rafters of the roof. But she knew that she would be safe here, at least until dinner. No one would miss her once the flurry of greetings, the hugs and kisses, the inevitable questions and answers had all been dispensed with. The Ashfords and the Warburtons had arrived en masse to celebrate Christmas, just as they had every one of Sara's twelve years.

At the moment, Sara felt she could do very well without them. She was ashamed to admit that she was a little bit afraid of her Great-aunt Beatrice; that she could make no sense out of the rambling scientific conversations of her Great-uncle Charles—and of course she had no use at all for Henry and Wallace Stours, the extremely ill-mannered sons of Clarissa Warburton Stours. Oh, and then there was Aunt Victoria's daughter Louisa, aged three-and-a-half, who delighted in breaking things and shrieking herself hoarse whenever she was reprimanded. Four cousins in all—counting the new baby—and Sara could not own to caring for a single one of them.

Unlike other girls her age, Sara had no patience with babies. She resented the fact that Louisa's crib had been moved into her bedroom for the holidays so that Aunt Victoria's newest arrival, six-month-old Charlotte, could have the nursery all to herself. She didn't think she was the only one who felt that way, either. Earlier, at breakfast, Sara had overheard Mrs. Gray and Minnie trading heated words over the number of settings of blue Worcester to take down for Christmas dinner. Minnie feared that they'd be broken in the clumsy hands of Henry and Wallace, while Mrs. Gray had responded tartly that it wasn't her place to be making those decisions and she'd not be the one to insult the baroness by laying out less than the best bone for Christmas dinner.

Aunt Victoria's husband, William, had also seemed in a foul mood ever since his arrival, because, although the footmen had been toiling since daybreak keeping the great fires lit, the house was icy cold. Sara had overheard him muttering about the lack of modern heating at Bellehurst and intimating that Grandmama and Grandpapa were somehow to blame. Which had immediately served to make him an enemy in Sara's loyal eyes.

Now the wind moaned, rattling the attic panes, and Sara was glad for the thick woolen stockings she wore beneath her button-down boots, although earlier she had fought Minnie like a small savage when ordered to put them on. Lifting her head, she listened attentively to the sudden approach of voices in the downstairs hall. Was it possible that Minnie had been clever enough to send one of the footmen to fetch her?

Sara was about to scramble behind the trunk when she recognized the voices as those of her cousins, Henry and Wallace. She knew a flash of irritation because she disliked them so intensely. They were forever getting into trouble by fighting with the bootblacks and the village boys, disrupting Grandpapa's library, throwing soap in the goldfish pond, or hiding in the dumbwaiter hoping to scare the kitchen maid half to death.

But the young male voices passed the attic stairs without pausing, and then Sara heard the far-off slamming of the schoolroom door. Her sigh of relief was not even half expelled, however, before it changed to a gasp of dismay. Scrambling swiftly down the uneven steps, she tried to remember whether or not she had taken the precaution of locking up the kittens the night before. Oh, surely she couldn't have been so stupid!

Regrettably, she had. Even as she hurried across the landing she could already hear the gleeful whooping of her cousins and the pitiful mewling of the kittens.

"Stop it!" she shouted, breaking into a run.

"Oh, lord—" squeaked Wallace as the door crashed open.

Henry, the oldest at fifteen, whipped about, nearly dropping the struggling fluff he held by the neck. Then he grinned, seeing Sara standing breathlessly on the threshold. "Give over, Wallace," he said mildly. "It's only Sara." Calmly, he resumed swinging his helpless burden to and fro.

Emitting a shout of rage, Sara lunged at him, her hands balled into fists. Henry, who had a bully's dislike of all girls and of his cousin Sara in particular, responded swiftly, grabbing one of her long, swinging braids and giving it a savage yank. But Sara had been prepared for that, and now she stooped quickly to grab hold of a cricket bat lying nearby.

The first blow caught Henry square on the shoulder and sent him staggering. Dropping the kitten, he threw up his arms and yelled for mercy, but Sara swung anyway, ruthless. There was a dull crack and a pained grunt as the blow hit home.

Henry looked up, blinking stupidly, unable to believe that he had been spared. The three of them stared in shocked silence at the strange boy who had burst in unnoticed from the hall and who was now bleeding copiously from a cut across his nose. Henry, never one to maintain his courage under debatable odds, turned and fled, with Wallace following swiftly behind.

Left alone, Sara dropped the bat with a clatter. "Your nose!" she gasped. "Is it broken?"

"Very nearly. Who the devil are you?"

"I-I'm Sara."

"And the others?"

"My cousins, Henry and Wallace Stours."

Taking out a handkerchief, he wiped away the blood and then, unexpectedly, he grinned at her. "With an arm like that you'd beat the best striker on my eleven."

Grimacing, Sara looked down at the bat, then back up at him. "Who are you?"

"Nicholas Warburton."

Sara fell silent, considering this. She had never seen him before, or, for that matter, heard his name mentioned at Bellehurst. Being a Warburton meant that he had to be family, of course, but Grandmama had said nothing whatsoever about his coming.

"I know!" Sara said suddenly. "You're the one who lives in Scotland, aren't you? Your mother and my grandmother are friends. Grandmama told me you might be coming but she wasn't certain—" She broke off, seeing that Nicholas wasn't listening. He had picked up one of the kittens, which mewled weakly, and was examining it with great care. "Will it die?" she asked anxiously, kneeling beside him.

"What did they do to it?"

"I'm not sure. Henry was swinging it around by the neck when I came in."

"Do you have a box for them? They ought to be kept warm."

"In the cupboard. That's where I've been hiding them. Francis ran over their mother with Uncle William's car. He was all for drowning them in the spinney pond, but I wouldn't let him. Nannie doesn't know they're here. Nobody does.'' Sara's eyes were wide, uncertain of the wisdom of revealing such an enormous secret.

Nicholas said nothing. Instead he gathered up the three tiny creatures and transferred them to the box, carefully tucking them in amid the strips of newsprint Sara had provided for bedding. She watched him admiringly. He was older than Henry and by far the darkest Warburton she had ever seen with his shock of black hair and deep green eyes. His face was thin, his cheekbones high and very pronounced, but it was a handsome face nonetheless, if not a bit too grave for Sara's liking.

"I'd feed them something as soon as possible,'' he told her. "Are they eating solids yet?''

"A little porridge, and sometimes cream, if I can nip it from the kitchen.''

"Hmm.''

Sara wasn't sure if this conveyed approval or not. "I wish Henry hadn't found out about them,'' she added anxiously. "He's ever so mean to animals. Last Christmas he got the pigs drunk with Grandpapa's brandy. But at least he got caned for that.''

"Apparently not hard enough.''

Sara was awed by this casual remark. How grown up he sounded, and how heroic! Worshipfully, she followed him to the basin, where he dipped his handkerchief and gingerly washed his face. A purple bruise was beginning to darken the bridge of his nose, but at least the bleeding had stopped.

"I'm sorry I hit you,'' she said remorsefully.

"Believe me, if I'd known you were going to defend yourself with a cricket bat I'd not have interfered,'' Nicholas assured her.

"It was nice of you to help me.''

"Actually I came because of the kittens. I heard them crying on my way up the stairs. I thought they could use a friend. You, on the other hand, don't seem to have any sort of trouble taking care of yourself.'' His green eyes looked her up and down, taking note of her rumpled dress, her torn stocking, and untidy red hair. "I think.''

"When did you arrive?"

"Only just. My mother's still downstairs with your grand-mother."

"Then you know who I am?"

"Sure. You're the Ashford cousin whose mother went back to America to live. Why didn't she ever send for you?"

"I suppose because she was too busy. She got married again."

"Your stepfather didn't want you?"

"I don't think either of them did."

"Doesn't that make you feel the least bit angry?"

"No," Sara said, annoyed, "it doesn't." Which was per-fectly true, because she would much, much rather live here at Bellehurst with her grandparents than anywhere else in the world. Only, it was none of Nicholas Warburton's business.

Apparently he must have sensed her thoughts, because he tucked the handkerchief back into his pocket without another word and then grinned at her, which made him look much less harsh and grown up. "I'll come back tonight and have another look at the kittens, if you like. But don't for God's sake tell anyone what happened. Let me take care of it, will you?"

Sara nodded, her anger fading into a warm feeling of grati-tude. The secret of her kittens was safe, and Nicholas obvi-ously intended to see that Henry paid for his cruelty. She had never before met anyone willing to keep a confidence that could end up getting both of them into trouble. If Nannie or Great-aunt Beatrice should find out she was keeping cats in the house. . . .

Sara gave a little shiver of terror at the thought, then told herself there was nothing to fear. Not after Nicholas had promised to take care of them, because she sensed instinct-ively that he was not the sort to go back on his word. The thought gave her a great deal of comfort, and she began to love him a little, in her secret heart of hearts.

By evening the snow had turned to a frozen rain that rattled the panes and heralded a dreary commencement to the holiday season. The grownups of the family had gathered in the parlor, which had recently been redecorated with friendly rose-wood furniture and bright chintz fabrics, to discuss the situation in Persia and complain about England's reawakened industrial gloom over hors d'oeuvres and drinks. Until recently, the country had been enjoying a gratifying burst of prosperity, fueled in part by the ending of the Boer War. Most of the benefits had been gleaned by the landed gentry, whose rents had recovered rapidly as land values soared. Bellehurst itself, with several hundred acres under cultivation, had been able to hire back a number of servants and undergo some much-needed repairs as well as the introduction of electricity in the kitchen and family rooms.

Rupert, however, had balked at installing further amenities such as modernized plumbing and central heating, and had also refused, despite Victoria's pleading, to purchase the family a motorcar. Both he and London preferred driving in the carriage or riding their bicycles when the weather was fine, and they had made the decision to leave the ownership of those noisy, smoking vehicles to the likes of Beatrice's brash stepson William, who had married their own Victoria four years ago.

Neither Rupert nor London had been overjoyed by their daughter's marriage. Victoria, then barely twenty, had made a very successful debut, for she was charming and had inherited her father's dark looks, which complemented her tall, slender frame prettily enough. She could have had her choice of any eager young man but had, to her parents' secret dismay, settled on the rather morose and simple-minded William, her first cousin by marriage if not by blood.

The young couple had set up an establishment of their own on the ground floor of Beatrice's sprawling London town house, where Victoria had, in rapid succession, presented her husband with a pair of plain and very temperamental daughters. William, who had inherited all of his father's ambition but none of his business acumen, was presently struggling to keep alive the modest mercantile firm he had inherited upon Edmund's death the previous year. The economic gloom that was casting a new pall over England had affected William badly, and he was hoping that the Christmas holidays would present him with an opportunity to broach the subject of a loan with his father-in-law.

At present, Lord and Lady Ladbroke were standing beneath the tall windows of the parlor conversing with Charles Ashford, Beatrice Warburton, and the vicar, who always took Sunday supper with the family. The vicar was now well over seventy, but time had not dimmed his fiery rhetoric or his long-standing admiration for his hostess, whose fair hair was still untouched by gray and who looked as slimly beautiful in middle age as she had when she was young. Although Rupert had aged considerably during the last few years, there was a quiet, courtly air about him that one could not ignore. His younger brother, Charles, though slightly less bent and white-whiskered, possessed the same grave courtesy.

Regrettably, the passage of time had not treated Beatrice with similar kindness: she was stout and graying, and her sour expression seemed all the worse these days because of the harsh lines scoring the sides of her nose and mouth. Dressed in a clinging, fur-trimmed gown of burgundy crepe to prove that she still considered herself attractive, she stood toying impatiently with the pearls about her neck, wishing that Charles and the vicar would take themselves off so that she could give London Ashford a healthy piece of her mind. How dare the impudent creature invite Olivia Warburton to Bellehurst while Clarissa and Ashton were here? Surely she was well aware of the bad blood between them!

William was presently standing near the fireplace doing his best to comfort his wife, whose feelings had also been deeply hurt by London's refusal to confide in her that Olivia and Nicholas were coming. Olivia, who had wed the long-dead George Warburton's charming cousin Archibald shortly after the century's turn, had been widowed earlier in the year, and for this reason London had urged her to spend Christmas at Bellehurst, a decision she had not, apparently, bothered to discuss with anyone.

"She could at least have told me," Victoria was saying now, casting a pouting glance in her mother's direction. "Doesn't she trust me?"

"Apparently not," William replied unkindly.

Victoria ignored him. "I should have suspected something the moment she said Louisa was to double up with Sara. Why couldn't she tell me the truth? Why keep it a secret from the rest of the family?"

"Victoria, really. You know perfectly well that Clarissa hasn't spoken to Olivia in years. She probably would have refused outright to come had she known the two of them would be staying under the same roof. Obviously your mother suspected the same."

"What do you think she means to do?" Victoria inquired, casting a nervous glance at the tall, imposing Clarissa, who was accepting a drink from her husband, Ashton Stours, and looking very superior in an embroidered shirtwaist and flowing green skirt.

"Nothing, of course. Not at Christmas and certainly not with the family present."

"No, I suppose not." Victoria still looked doubtful.

"I'm willing to bet your mother is trying to bring about a reconciliation."

"Between Clarissa and Olivia? Oh, William, don't dramatize! Mama would never meddle in their affairs."

"Wouldn't she? My, how you underestimate her. Just because she always acts cool and detached about everything doesn't mean she isn't interested in running the whole bloody show."

"Really, William," Victoria cried, genuinely stung, "now that is utterly disloyal of you, and I won't listen to another word! Mama took over the task of corresponding with Olivia after Great-aunt Emily died, and I think it's wonderful that she kept in touch with her over the years and that they've become such good friends! And I'm glad Olivia's come to spend the holidays with us!"

"Keep your voice down, will you?"

Turning her head, Victoria saw that Olivia Warburton had appeared in the doorway. A palpable hush fell over the room as she crossed to London, her black mourning skirts rustling across the parquet flooring.

Looking at her, William was at a loss to explain why the supposedly dashing Archie Warburton had chosen to marry

this mousy-haired creature rather than the dramatically beautiful Clarissa. Oh, she was pleasing enough in a pale, fragile
sort of way, but certainly not the striking sort of woman who
could, to William's mind, make a man lose all sense of
proportion—and a healthy dowry like Clarissa Warburton's
in the bargain.

Victoria tapped him discreetly. "We should go up and say
hello."

William smiled down at her with sudden fondness. His
darling Vicky. No one could ever fault him for having made
a similar mistake. Five thousand pounds a year annuity is
what the dear girl brought him, and although it wasn't exactly
a brilliant income, he knew that he could count on more—
considerably more—in the future. "Of course, my pet."

"I'm so glad you're here. You look lovely," London was
saying to Olivia. She spoke in her most reassuring tone,
infuriated by the fact that Beatrice had rudely stalked away
without even acknowledging Olivia's presence. As well, she
could not ignore the hostility radiating from Clarissa, who
stood with her back to them while her husband plinked nervously on the piano.

"It was kind of you to invite me," Olivia responded hesitantly. "And Nicholas too. It's lovely here, and we would
have been so dreadfully lonely in Edinburgh."

"Oh, Livvy, what liars we are," London said with a faint
smile. "I never dreamed the others would behave so badly."

Olivia's pale cheeks colored. "It's all right, truly it is. And
I didn't really come unprepared. Clarissa never wrote a single
word of condolence when Archie died. Archie always used
to say the Warburtons were aptly named." She smiled thinly.
"I see now what he meant."

In full view of everyone, London embraced Olivia fondly.
As a favor to her aunt, she had taken over corresponding with
Olivia years ago, when Emily's health had first begun failing.
Ever since then, she and Olivia had kept up a lively exchange
of letters, their correspondence lasting long after Emily's
death. They had met each other only once—at Augusta Warburton's funeral—but those few hours together had been
enough to seal their remarkable friendship.

"Come and meet the others," London said now, determined to make Olivia feel more at ease. "You know Rupert, of course, and this is his brother, Charles. I'm afraid Rupert's sister Isobelle was unable to attend this year. Her family had other committments in Leeds. This"—she beckoned—"is my daughter, Victoria, and her husband, William Warburton. Our oldest daughter, Eugenia, isn't here either."

"She rarely attends family gatherings," Rupert explained, bowing over Olivia's hand and smiling wryly. "I'm afraid she'd rather roast on a spit than succumb to the boredom of Christmas hols at home."

"Not to mention that she hasn't dared show her face since getting married to that artist fellow and running off to Paris with him," Beatrice boomed, coming up behind them in time to deliver this unexpected broadside.

"Yes, London wrote me about it," Olivia said, gazing at Beatrice with dislike. "Children do have a way of causing unending heartache, don't they?"

"Are you talking about yours?" came a clipped voice from behind them. "Because I vow my own have rarely troubled me."

"Hello, Clarissa," Olivia said uncertainly.

"Hello, Livvy. It's been ages since we've seen you. Ten years at least, not counting Mother's funeral. We were quite surprised when you attended."

"Archie was always fond of Aunt Augusta."

"I understand you're widowed now?"

London bristled. In her youth, Clarissa had fancied herself in love with Archie Warburton and had blamed Olivia for the fact that he hadn't married her. Which was utter nonsense. Emily, who had corresponded regularly with the Edinburgh Warburtons until her own, recent death, had scoffed at the notion of laying any blame before Olivia's door. Theirs had been a loving marriage, she had firmly maintained, and any interest that Archie Warburton had shown his cousin Clarissa had obviously existed in her mind only.

Nevertheless, it was an awkward moment. Olivia made no reply while Victoria, young and inexperienced, blushed and looked helplessly at her husband. It was Rupert who finally smoothed things over, although his amiable words were drowned by the slamming of the outer door in the hall.

"Oh, thank goodness," said Victoria with ill-concealed relief. "Here come the children at last."

All of them turned.

"Henry!" Clarissa shrieked. Pushing the others aside, she fell to her knees before her oldest son, who was sporting a grotesquely swollen black eye. "What happened, my darling? Who did this to you?"

Henry lowered his head. "It's nothing, Mama."

"Nothing?" Clarissa gave him a slight shake. "You look absolutely dreadful! Now, who was it?"

Henry mumbled something inaudible.

"What? I can't hear you, darling."

"I did it, Mrs. Stours."

Clarissa's disbelieving gaze flew to the bruised face of Nicholas Warburton, who stood behind Henry, his hands thrust into the pockets of his trousers. "You?" she gasped.

Rupert stepped quickly between them and laid his hands on Nicholas's shoulders. "I'm certain there's a simple explanation."

"I'm ever so sorry," Olivia added unhappily.

"As well you should be," Clarissa snapped. "How dare you turn that wild creature loose on my poor Henry?"

"Oh, this is dreadful!" wailed Victoria, who hated scenes.

"Come, now," Rupert said briskly. "There's no real harm done. Boys will be boys, as Clarissa well knows."

"But his face—"

"So long as Henry and Nicholas consider their differences settled," Rupert continued forcibly, "I don't see any reason why we can't forget about it and enjoy our supper."

"Well?" prompted Henry's father, speaking for the first time.

"Yes, sir," Nicholas said, looking Rupert squarely in the eye.

"Good. What about you, Henry?"

"Yes, sir," mumbled Henry without lifting his head.

"Then it's settled," Rupert announced. "Olivia, come sit by me. Ashton, will you see to my wife? Oh, there you are,

Seward. Will you please tell Mrs. Gray we'll be ready to start as soon as Mr. Wynstaffe has said the blessing?"

"What did you do to him?" Sara whispered to Nicholas during the lengthy invocation that followed, leaning toward him across the small children's table that had been set up in the far corner of the dining room.

"Nothing."

She scowled. "But his eye—"

"Oh, that. He did that himself. The minute he saw me coming he ran away—right into a door."

Sara smothered a giggle. Henry, at the head of the table, glared at her. She was tempted to stick out her tongue, but knew better.

"How are the kittens?" Nicholas asked.

"Fine. Truly. None of them are hurt."

"They'll be safe now, I'm thinking." Nicholas threw a meaningful glance at Henry and Wallace, who both looked quickly away.

Sara thought so too. And the smile she turned on Nicholas was radiant with gratitude.

There were fresh snowdrifts banked against the house on Christmas morning, and the longed-for stockings were hanging at the foot of each child's bed. Henry and Wallace, ignoring their mother's warning, ate all their chocolates and pink sugar mice before breakfast and suffered horrid stomach pangs as a result. Sara, as usual, carefully hoarded hers and later, while gifts were being exchanged around the fruit-and-nut-hung Christmas tree in the withdrawing room, shared her peppermint stick with Nicholas.

There were guests for dinner that evening: the Beckwiths, the Olwyns, and Colonel and Mrs. Horatio Packer. An enormous log fire had been lit in the hall, which was decked with holly and had been cleared for dancing. This time the children were not permitted to eat downstairs, but Sara greatly preferred the coziness of the nursery. Here, Nannie awaited them with tea cakes and hot milk spiced with ginger, and the cheeriness of the deep red geraniums blooming throughout the room gave the nursery a festive air that convinced even

Henry to forget his earlier grievances and share his new set of lead soldiers with the others.

Much later that evening, after the guests had gone home and little Louisa had fallen asleep on her cot, Sara tiptoed downstairs in her nightgown and woolen stockings. Though the annual servants' ball and tenantry dinner wouldn't be held until New Year's, the Ladbrokes had always permitted the staff a Christmas celebration of their own. For the past few years, Sara had been creeping downstairs to watch the stable lads and footmen join the cook and kitchen maids in lively dances and games of spoil five, backgammon, and patience.

This year the crowd was smaller than in previous years, for the Ladbrokes, like everyone else, had once again reduced the size of their staff. But the mood was festive nonetheless as frothing pints of Whitbread's were downed and the cards slapped endlessly upon the table. The air was redolent with the yeasty smell of beer and the scent of woodsmoke and pine cones, and Sara, sitting at the long table between old Mrs. Garroway and Mr. Brockman, the gardener, basked in the earthy atmosphere.

Great-aunt Beatrice would have been horrified by the girl's presence at a party where ale was being drunk and cigarettes smoked, but Sara felt quite at home in the company of these good-hearted people she had known all her life. They, in turn, had always welcomed the engaging little girl who was Master Sandy's daughter, and none of them objected when she joined them now.

Much to Sara's surprise, Nicholas Warburton was present as well, having been invited by Tom, the Bellehurst boot-black, with whom he seemed to have made fast friends. At fifteen, Nicholas was old enough to drink beer and wager money when the card games grew earnest. Sara couldn't help noticing that the younger footmen and the grooms with whom he played deferred to him whenever disputes arose concerning a particular hand. With a dark lock of hair tumbling over his brow and his thin, intelligent face illuminated by the ruddy glow of the fire, he seemed older somehow, and Sara found herself feeling strangely shy in his presence.

But when Nicholas made what she considered an imprudent

wager, Sara wasted no time in boldly drawing attention to his folly. The others laughed and jeered while Nicholas regarded her intently. "Think I'm wrong, do you?"

Her chin tipped. "Yes."

"Serious, are you?"

"Yes."

"Then prove it."

"I haven't any money," Sara reminded him haughtily.

"It's always best to keep your mouth shut when you haven't any coppers to back yourself up."

Infuriated, Sara unclasped from about her neck the gold locket her grandparents had given her on her twelfth birthday and tossed it onto the table. One of the stable hands picked it up and rubbed it carefully with a horny thumb. "Looks real enough. Be that your wager, Miss Sara?"

She nodded, her jaw stubbornly set. Grinning, Nicholas reached into his pocket and withdrew a silver-plated watch engraved with an elaborate hunting scene. This was added to the pile, and the crowd leaned forward expectantly as the hand was played . . . and Nicholas lost.

Good-natured catcalls and sympathetic slaps on the back were accompanied by the scraping of chairs as the gathering broke up with a noisy, amiable shuffle toward the door. It was long after midnight, and only a few hours remained before most of them were expected to rise and begin another day of work.

"Off with 'ee now," Mrs. Garroway urged Sara. "Lady Ladbroke won't be none too pleased 'ee stayed up so late."

"Here. You forgot to take this."

Sara turned to find Nicholas holding out his pocket watch. She shook her head. "Keep it."

"But it's yours. Fairly wagered and fairly won."

"It looks terribly expensive."

"It is. It belonged to my father."

Sara was aghast. "And you wagered it in a *card game*?"

"Don't be so prim and proper!" Nicholas taunted. "That's the risk you take when playing by grownup rules. Or didn't you know that, little girl?"

Sara colored indignantly. If there was one thing she hated,

it was being teased about her age. Snatching the watch away
from him, she drew her shawl over her shoulders and went
haughtily upstairs. Only after she had slipped between the
cold sheets of her bed did she remember that she had left her
necklace behind.

"I'll get it in the morning," Sara told herself. And return
the expensive watch, although she'd do so without speaking
a word to that pompous Nicholas Warburton. What in the
world had ever prompted her to think that she liked him?

Chapter Twenty-one

"Miss Sara! Miss Sara, wake up!"

Sara stirred groggily, then opened her eyes. Minnie was
leaning over her, speaking in an urgent whisper so as not to
awaken the sleeping Louisa. "What is it, Minnie?"

"Your grandfather's in the library. He's askin' to see you
right away."

Sara turned her face into the pillow. "So early?"

"It's after ten, miss."

"Ten!" Sara sat up, rubbing her eyes. "Where is everyone?"

"Already breakfasted and gone outside. Mrs. Stours arranged a skating party."

"And my grandfather wants to see me?"

"Yes, miss. Down in the library."

The request was so unusual that Sara came entirely awake.
Shivering in the frosty air, she dressed quickly and stood
fidgeting while Minnie plaited her hair. Whenever Bellehurst
had guests, the library was converted into a morning room
for gentlemen, but when Sara knocked and was bidden to

enter, she found her grandfather there alone. He was standing before the window with his back to her looking out across the snowbound garden.

Sara went to him and kissed his cheek. He returned the gesture with an affectionate caress, but Sara could tell that he was distracted. Her heart squeezed. Something was wrong. Grandpapa never looked so grave. She put her hands to her cheeks and stared at him with eyes that were suddenly wide and frightened. "What is it? Has something happened? Is Grandmama—"

"I'm all right, dear," came London's soothing voice from the doorway. "There's nothing wrong with me."

Sara ran to her, brimming with relief as she pressed her lips to her grandmother's soft cheek. But her grandmother, she realized at the same moment, looked pale and distraught, the same way Grandpapa did. She stepped back, her eyes going from one dear face to the other.

"Sit down, Sara."

She obeyed wordlessly. By now her heart was beating with great, irregular thumps. In the past, whenever she had committed some wrongdoing, she had always been summoned to the library or to her grandmother's sitting room, where one or the other of them had meted out her punishment. But this was different. Something was terribly wrong; something that went beyond last night's late hours and illicit card games.

"The mail made it through today," her grandfather said at last. Sara's gaze fell on the tidy stack of envelopes lying on his desk. "There was a letter from your mother."

Sara waited, her eyes on his face. This was nothing unusual; her mother wrote every Christmas and always sent a gift for her: a doll or a picture book, or sometimes something more elaborate, like a playhouse or a printing set.

"Sara, she wants you to come home."

She stared, uncomprehending. "I am home."

There was a painful pause.

"No, dear," London said at last. "She wants you to go to America to live."

Sara's gaze did not waver. "Why?"

"Because she's worried about you." Rupert gestured toward the letter on his desk. "Because of the situation here in Europe."

"What situation?" Sara was puzzled but not alarmed. She rarely gave any thought to her mother, whom she had never met. Her indifference had apparently always been shared by Gwen, who had married again barely a year after Sandy's death. Archer Lloyd, her new husband, was considerably older, and had brought into the marriage a pair of unruly stepsons who were nearly as old as his bride. Not surprisingly, the family's early years together had been difficult ones, and a convenient time to send for Sara never seemed to arise. Then, with her stepsons finally enrolled in university and the house quiet at last, an exhausted Gwen had shrunk away from the thought of starting anew with yet another child.

But why does she want me now? Sara wondered. Surely the situation wasn't so terrible that she needed to live in America?

Rupert said, "Relations with Russia have been badly strained in recent months. Your mother worries that we may go to war over Persia. Furthermore, she doesn't trust the German kaiser. Do you remember what we talked about last week?"

"Yes," said Sara, who possessed a lively intelligence and whose passion for learning was encouraged by her grandfather in the form of weekly lectures concerning current events. "Nobody trusts him. You said the British government wants to build more warships to protect us because the Germans have started building whole new navy squadrons."

"That's right. But it isn't Germany alone, dear. Russia is increasing the size of her army, and Austria-Hungary has recently doubled her own military expenditures—that's the money the government spends on the military. Do you understand?"

Sara frowned. "I'm not sure."

Rupert said patiently, "Whenever neighboring countries feel the need to arm themselves, the threat of war always increases. At the moment everyone keeps insisting that no hostility exists between our countries, but nobody really believes that. I personally feel the entire situation is a powder keg waiting to go off. Your mother seems to think so too. And she believes you'll be safer in the United States than here in England should anything happen.''

"But I don't want to go!"

"She's your mother, Sara," Rupert reminded her. "You can't exactly disobey her.''

"And you?" Sara challenged, although he had not spoken unkindly. "Do you really mean to send me away?''

Rupert made no reply. Sara whirled. "Grandmama—''

Skirts rustling, London came to kneel beside her. "I'm so sorry, my darling.''

"Then you've already decided!" Sara cried, aghast. "Without asking me—''

"Hush, dear. There's no point in arguing. Perhaps it won't be for long. You can always come back to us once the war, if there is a war, is over. Hush, now, my dearest. Don't cry . . .''

In a state of dumb misery Sara fought her way free of her grandmother's arms. Weeping blindly, she did not see the tears running freely down London's cheeks as well.

It was midsummer 1914 before the necessary travel arrangements were completed and a suitable chaperone was produced for the voyage so that Sara could finally depart for America. By then the political situation in Europe had become genuinely alarming. Archduke Francis Ferdinand, heir to the throne of Austria-Hungary, had been assassinated in Bosnia, an event the *Times* of London warned would shake the equilibrium of the world. Diplomatic relations between Austria and Serbia had been severed, and by the time Gwen's daughter sailed away from England, the two countries were at war.

The eastern United States, meanwhile, was suffering through its second month of a grinding heat wave, and when Sara descended from the train in Morristown, New Jersey, with her stepfather, Archer Lloyd, she found the station grass browned and the summer flowers wilted. A two-horse carriage stood waiting in the shadows of a sprawling elm, and Sara looked at it with interest. "Are those your hackneys?''

Archer glanced at her in surprise. They were the first words the child had uttered since disembarking from the liner *Penn-land* in New York. "Sure are. Schooled them myself. Like horses, do you?"

Sara nodded.

"Know how to ride?"

"Yes."

"Well, then," he said heartily, "we'll just have to see about getting you a pony of your own."

He was rewarded with a smile, Sara's first, and it so transformed her pointed little face that Archer was moved to reexamine his opinion of the girl. When he had first removed her from the noisy circle of British matrons who had looked after her on the way to New York, he had not been particularly taken with her. She was too pallid and still, and because her glorious hair was hidden beneath a wide-brimmed straw hat, there had seemed to him nothing at all remarkable about her.

Now he watched as she leaned forward on the carriage seat, drinking in a rolling landscape that was surprisingly similar to the countryside she had left behind. Her profile was grave, but her blue eyes brightened with interest as she watched the number of carriages and occasional automobiles passing on the busy street.

"Morristown isn't too far from New York," Archer explained. "That's why you'll find a lot more traffic here than you're used to."

"Where do all these people *live*?" Sara wished to know.

He chuckled. "Either in town or out in the country. We've got a lot of summer residents here at the moment. Nearly four hundred of 'em, to be exact." He chuckled. "In fact, that's what they're called: *the* Four Hundred, which happens to be the capacity of Mrs. Astor's ballroom in New York City. Their chief aim for staying here during the summer is to escape the heat and boredom of New York."

By now the carriage was moving smartly down a long, broad street flanked on either side by neatly trimmed hedges and lawns sprawling backward toward breathtakingly stately homes. This, Archer explained to Sara, was Morristown's famed Madison Avenue, also known as the "Great White Way," a four-mile-long showcase of Elizabethan mansions,

Victorian and period houses, and even a few Moorish palaces. He pointed out to her a turreted castle half-hidden by the trees and told her how it had been purchased abroad by a fellow banker, then dismantled and transported, stone by stone, to America.

Sara studied her stepfather curiously as he lifted his hat to greet a pair of ladies in elegantly bustled gowns who were strolling along the avenue, their parasols swinging. Great-aunt Beatrice had told her that he was very, very rich. She had also said that Sara was a lucky girl to be making a new home among neighbors bearing names like Rockefeller, Vanderbilt, Freylinghuysen, and Scribner.

Sara had never heard of them before, and at the time she had been far too heartsick to care whether or not her stepfather had money. Looking at him now, she found it difficult to believe that he was as powerful as Great-aunt Beatrice had said: a shrewd businessman who had made his fortune lending money to shipping firms, railroads, and companies eager to expand their holdings in the west. Sara thought he looked more like Tom Peale, the round-faced, jolly tinker who hawked his wares from the back of a brightly painted wagon and made himself a nuisance at the Millham Agricultural Fair every year by pinching all the ladies' bottoms. Once he had even dared pinch Great-aunt Beatrice and had been resoundingly slapped for his pains.

He must be about Grandmama's age, Sara thought, studying her stepfather with a thoughtful frown. Not exactly young, but not really old either, although his hair was thinning and his bristling mustache was white. On the other hand, he could easily have been as old as Grandpapa, considering that his sons were already—

I mustn't think about Grandpapa, Sara told herself fiercely. *Or Grandmama or anyone else back home.*

All at once her throat was aching, and she curled herself up in a ball in the corner of the carriage, sitting in dry-eyed misery while the bustling streets of Morristown gave way to the rolling hills and sprawling cornfields of Morris County. Presently the carriage bore sharply to the left and the road gave way to a wide, tree-shaded lane.

Archer, who had been dozing in the opposite corner, snorted and sat up. "Well, my dear," he said, smiling kindly at Sara, whose face he saw was pale and strained, "here we are at last. Are you nervous about meeting your mother? Maybe a little, eh? Well, you shouldn't be. I daresay she's changed quite a bit since marrying me. She used to be shy, you see, and scared to death of social obligations. Not anymore." He laughed heartily. "I've seen to it that she's become active in the community, although it took a lot of coaxing at first. She'll be able to show you a swell time." He laughed again, and Sara smiled thinly, not certain what sort of reply was expected from her.

By now they were approaching Haversham, the Lloyd estate. Through the leafy trees Sara could make out a sprawling, three-story brick manor with a porte cochere and a piazza extending along one wide wing. The carriage halted before a pair of massive mahogany doors, and immediately a white-haired gentleman in a black suit hurried down the steps to open the carriage door for them.

"Welcome home, Mr. Lloyd."

"Thank you, Carruthers. I vow it's twenty degrees cooler here than in the city. Carruthers, this is Mrs. Lloyd's daughter, Sara Ashford."

The butler bowed politely. "Charmed, miss. May I also say that I'm relieved you had a safe crossing."

Sara thanked him shyly. Her mother had already written to her that Haversham's butler and estate superintendent were both British, and she was warmed by Carruthers' precise, familiar accent after the bewildering, belligerent diction of New Yorkers.

"Where's m'wife?"

"In the sitting room, sir."

"Fine. See to the luggage, will you? Come along, Sara."

They went together into the house, which seemed very cool and dark after the shimmering heat of the driveway. Archer's footsteps echoed as he led the child through the marble-laid hall past the grand ballroom and into the sitting room. Unlike the cozy comfort of Bellehurst's parlor, Haversham's sitting room bristled with formal elegance, its dark furnishings a priceless blend of Georgian and Chippendale.

Gwen had been sitting on a settee leafing idly through a collection of fashion plates, but at the sound of her husband's voice in the hall she laid them quickly aside. Crossing to the long mirror hanging on the far wall she glanced swiftly at her reflection. She smiled, unable to find anything wrong with the slimly lovely woman in flowing white looking back at her. With her reddish hair fashionably curled and crimped she looked considerably younger than her thirty-two years. Her ivory skin was smooth and unlined, and her admirers—Gwen had plenty, men and women alike,—found it difficult to believe that she had a thirteen-year-old daughter.

A daughter who now appeared hesitantly in the doorway, clutching a netted bag containing the money her grandfather had given her prior to the voyage, and a worn piece of paper on which he had written her mother's address and telephone number in New Jersey. Her straw hat was askew, and one of her stockings had slipped below her knee. Her pinafore was crumpled and stained with the grime of the harbor and the train, but Gwen did not notice the child's bedraggled appearance. All she saw was that solemn little face with its clean-cut features and those wide blue eyes. Sandy's eyes.

Looking at them, Gwen felt her heart do a painful little jig. She clutched dizzily at the back of a chair as old memories disoriented her, spinning her backward so that all at once she was eighteen again and looking across the vast length of a sunny conservatory at a sandy-haired stranger who had dazzled her with the warmth of his smile and the burning blue of his eyes.

"Good God, Gwen, you look as though you've seen a ghost!"

Gwen's racing heartbeat slowed. Archer had appeared beside her, and she gratefully accepted the glass of brandy he held. The fiery liquid flowed down her throat, soothing her and driving some of the shocked rigidity from her body.

"I'm afraid you gave me a start," she said, smiling wryly at her daughter.

"Because I look so much like my father?"

"How did you know?"

"People are always telling me that."

"Are they?"

"Yes. In fact, Grandmama once said—" Sara broke off and bit her lip. Tears welled in her eyes, and for a terrible moment she thought she would disgrace herself by crying.

With a rustling of skirts Gwen was suddenly beside her, her soft, fragrant cheek pressed to Sara's. "There, there, darling, no need to cry. You're home now, Sara, home where you belong. And we're going to be very, very happy together, aren't we?"

Sara turned her face away, her jaw set. Not trusting herself to speak, she merely nodded.

"Of course you are," Archer answered for the child, and dabbed emotionally at his eyes with a silken hankie.

Meanwhile, a thousand miles away and more, the German Empire formally declared war on Russia and France, and, in England, the first recruitment call was sounded in the villages and town halls.

SIX
Women and War

And the talk slid north, and the talk slid south,
With the sliding puffs from the hookah-mouth.
Four things greater than all things are,—
Women and Horses and Power and War.

Rudyard Kipling

Chapter
Twenty-two

1916
New Jersey

At half past four on a warm, overcast fall afternoon, Sara Ashford descended the wide, curving staircase at the front of Haversham Hall. The enormous house was still. Her mother was upstairs resting in preparation for the evening's festivities at nearby Coppham Manor, and her stepfather was not due home from New York until sometime after six. From the kitchen in the basement came the subdued clanking of pots and pans and the low voices of the maids who were preparing Mrs. Lloyd's hot chocolate. Sara knew that neither of them would dare venture upstairs until the bell summoned them to her mother's boudoir.

Both Haversham's stairwell and the entrance hall were laid with Italian Carrara marble, a gleaming white stone, as smooth as ice, that allowed Sara to slip soundlessly into the foyer and out the front door without being seen. The green of the lawn was dazzling and the bees hummed in the clover as she hurried along the manicured walk toward the stand of oaks on the southernmost side of the park. Once there, with the brick walls of the manor house hidden from view by the feathery gold of falling leaves, she considered herself safe.

Halting amid the barred shadows, she expelled a long breath of relief. Settling herself in the grass, she unfolded the newspapers she carried beneath one arm. Her heartbeat quickened as she scanned the headlines.

FIRST APPEARANCE OF BRITISH TANKS AT SOMME
ENGLISH COUNTIES BOMBED BY GERMAN ZEPPELINS
GERMAN GUNS STRIKE DUNKIRK FROM BELGIAN COAST

Oh, God. Shivering, she laid the paper aside and hugged her knees with her arms. Weeks had passed since she had last received word from Kent. During the early years of the war, Grandmama had written often to soothe and reassure her frantic granddaughter overseas, but with the increase of German submarine warfare in British waters, the letters had declined until eventually, ominously, they had ended altogether.

Dashing away the tears that welled in her eyes, Sara turned to the newspapers once again, this time reading them through with great care, although she knew that her mother would disapprove if she happened to find out. Fashionable young ladies were not supposed to trouble themselves with the war in Europe. After all, President Wilson had been preaching American neutrality for years now, and Gwen thought it extremely doubtful that the country would enter the war at so late a date.

But Sara had made enough friends among the male servants of the house to know that most of them would eagerly fight if given half the chance. And only yesterday Mr. Carruthers had declared that it was only a matter of time before the American government became sufficiently enraged by the sinking of its merchant ships to—

"Miss Sara!"

Sara started, then rose and hastily gathered the papers together. A rush of frustrated anger shook her. How like Mother to send one of the serving girls in search of her! When would she ever understand that Sara was not in the least bit like her? That she did not require a long afternoon's nap in order to appear fresh and well-rested for the coming evening's festivities? They had been invited to a simple subscription dance at the Clark estate, for heaven's sake, so how could she possibly—

"Miss Sara!"

Sara hesitated, torn between escape and a resentful sense of duty toward her mother. Escape would have won hands down had the serving girl not appeared at the top of the lawn just then, cupping her hands and calling. Scowling, Sara stuffed the newspapers into the shrubbery, then climbed back up the hill and crossed the flagstone terrace.

"Please hurry, Miss Sara. Mrs. Lloyd is awake and asking for you."

Her mother's suite lay at the far end of the upper floor, overlooking the terraced garden. It contained an elegant sitting room and a private bath, and a smaller room—really no more than a cubbyhole with an iron cot and a tiny window set high in the wall—intended for the maid. The bedroom itself was richly appointed in gilt and cream, the furnishings Georgian and very beautiful. Several priceless clocks kept rhythmic time on various tables and mantles, and a pair of towering lamps with ruby glass shades flanked either side of the four-poster bed. Haversham, like most of its counterparts in the rolling hills surrounding Morristown, New Jersey, had long ago been wired for—and generated its own—electricity.

Sara had never cared for this suite. Like all the rest at Haversham, it had none of the cozy shabbiness of Bellehurst, whose dark, familiar rooms had always been stuffed with well-worn sofas and chairs that were deep and comfortable enough to accommodate anyone, whether that person was wearing elegant, wide-spreading skirts in anticipation of an evening out, or had just come in from a morning's hack, rumpled and windblown and smelling slightly of horses.

Sara found her mother sitting up in bed sipping hot chocolate. Propped up by numerous pillows and looking lovely in a peach silk wrapper, Gwen smiled with a mixture of exasperation and affection at her daughter and motioned her to sit down. "I'm glad I asked Mary to keep an eye on you. I had the feeling you'd try to sneak out while I was napping."

"Do you feel better, Mother?" Sara inquired politely. Over the years she had come to realizé that Gwen, for all her undiminished beauty and robust health, enjoyed playing the role of an invalid. In fact, nothing pleased her mother more than to take to her bed with some complaint—real or imagined—and lie there faint and ailing while the servants fussed over her and Archer brought her flowers, or baubles and candy, and told her how much he adored her. It was, of course, nothing more than a ruse for gaining attention, but one that Gwen seemed to relish.

"I feel much better, thank you, dear. Well enough to keep our engagement with the Clarks tonight."

Sara did her best to look enthusiastic. She was genuinely fond of her mother and always tried hard to please her, but sometimes it was difficult to do so, especially considering that Gwen enjoyed doing everything Sara did not.

Parties, teas, fancy-dress balls, and elegant suppers were Gwen's favorite pastimes, and even though the Lloyds entertained rarely themselves due to Gwen's delicate health, they were highly popular among the Four Hundred, those fabulously wealthy industrialists and financiers whose estates dotted the rolling New Jersey hillsides. In her youth, Gwen had shied away from exactly those functions, but marriage to a sociable man like Archer had made it impossible to continue in the role of the shy wallflower that had so enchanted Sara's father. Furthermore—and much to Gwen's surprise—she had actually come to enjoy the lively season of Morristown socials, mainly because there seemed to be no lack of people willing to fuss over her and treat her deferentially simply because she was Mrs. Archer Lloyd.

Although Sara had not yet made her debut, she was expected to accompany her parents quite often, but it was a duty that sat uneasily on the shoulders of such a high-spirited girl. Nevertheless, she knew better than to let her reluctance show. "What would you like me to wear?" she asked now.

Gwen considered. Although Sara would not turn sixteen until next year, she had blossomed in recent months from the awkward, angular child who had arrived silent and seasick from England, into a slender young woman of exceptional beauty. Gwen had not failed to notice, with considerable maternal pride, that her daughter's glorious red-gold hair was beginning to cause masculine heads to turn whenever she passed, and that her curving mouth and fine, patrician features were perfectly, irresistibly complemented by her expressive blue eyes. Furthermore, the girl's long years in the saddle and her daily walks through the countryside with her English grandfather had molded her long, boyish limbs into a slender and very seductive shape that owed nothing to the padding and corseting often resorted to by her American counterparts.

"The white tulle," Gwen said now, remembering that she must show the proper deference to her daughter's youth. "The one trimmed with French lace. Do you know which one I mean?"

Sara did. And she was dutifully wearing the maidenly white creation when she joined her mother in the foyer later that evening while the carriage was driven round from the stables in order to take the family to Coppham. Archer was the proud owner of an impressive pair of automobiles, but because coaching was considered one of the most elegant diversions of the day and because Archer himself had achieved some celebrity as an amateur whip, both the Panhard and the Ford would be staying in the garage. Tonight, Archer himself was taking up the reins.

"You look lovely, dear," Gwen approved as Sara joined her in the foyer, and it was true. Sara's slim form was clearly revealed in the sleeveless, clinging lines of her gown, and the simple rope of seed pearls adorning her neck drew attention to her slender white throat. But it was Sara's dramatic coloring that provided the real allure to her otherwise unremarkable dress, because in it her eyes appeared almost brilliantly blue, and the shining weight of her hair, drawn back into a soft knot at the nape of her neck, tilted her pointed chin as though with inborn elegance.

Gwen was wearing an azure satin gown with softly draped shoulders and long white gloves. Sapphires glittered in her ears and about her throat and, despite her worry that the drive to Coppham would tire her considerably, she looked sleekly beautiful and very contented as she was handed down from the carriage at the front steps of the Elizabethan manor belonging to Homer and Ethel Clark.

As a young man, Mr. Clark had made his fortune in railroads, and now he owned vast interests in nearly every state west to California. Coppham, his summer home, was vast itself: built of native granite, it contained over forty-five rooms, every one of them elegantly designed by the noted New York firm of William Baumgarten and Sons. The grounds themselves were vast as well: over a thousand acres of woodland and park landscaped with sunken Italian gardens of boxwoods, and reflection pools and tiered terraces decorated with imported busts and urns.

Mr. Clark, like Archer Lloyd, was an enthusiastic whip, and had entered and won the 1912 Olympia Show for International Coaching in London—an unprecedented honor for any American. Ever since, he had established a friendly sort of rivalry with the older Lloyd, and as the two men shook hands in the receiving line, the tubby Homer inquired at once after Archer's newest pair of hackneys. There followed a lengthy conversation concerning the animals' bloodlines, and, with Gwen's attention similarly claimed by their hostess, Sara was able to proceed alone into the hall. Here, a babble of agitated voices assailed her the moment she stepped inside.

"—Give them a goddamned drubbing if they dare show their U-boats in American waters!"

"—Can't accuse American aviators of violating neutrality, can they? Would you mind telling me how?"

From someone else: "I understand they downed one of those German airships in the Thames last week. Any reports on casualties?"

I can't bear this, Sara thought. If there was anything she hated, it was being reminded that London, and perhaps the surrounding counties of Surrey, Sussex, and Kent, were under constant siege.

Slipping through the terrace door, she ran quickly out into the garden. Despite the fact that the Clarks' subscription dance was supposedly informal, well over two hundred guests wandered along the manicured paths or gathered in groups beneath the brightly striped tent erected on the lawn to drink, eat, and discuss the war. Electric candlelight blazed from the ballroom windows, and the orchestra could be heard tuning up to the accompaniment of a fluting soprano—no doubt a current diva invited from the Metropolitan Opera House to entertain.

Hurrying across the lawn toward the welcome darkness beyond the torch-lit pool, Sara shuddered at the thought of the long hours of dancing and dining to come. She hated to admit that she wanted to leave, but it was true. Only just arrived at Coppham and already she longed for nothing more than to go home and enjoy the quiet solitude of her bedroom, her books, and the last letter from England to be taken out of the drawer, unfolded, smoothed, and lovingly reread.

Keeping to the shadows, Sara wandered farther into the darkness along a manicured path that was barely visible in the moonlight. Emerging on the far side of the artificial lake, she paused for a moment to catch her breath. Here, the breeze brought to her the sudden, unmistakable, and sharply familiar scent of cattle.

Sara's head came up, and all thoughts of the war and her grandparents were driven from her mind. How was it possible? Then she remembered that Coppham was bordered on the east by the Twombley estate, which maintained a large herd of Guernseys once described by *Country Gentleman* as the finest in the nation. Twenty-four of them, in fact, had recently carried off every last prize at the Saint Louis World's Fair. Sara remembered hearing that Mr. Twombley had died a number of years ago, but apparently his cattle remained.

Walking slowly down to the fence, she leaned for a moment against the railing listening to their soft, familiar snuffling. As she did so, she felt an unexpected and long-forgotten sense of peace creeping over her. Perhaps it was due to the fact that she had often stood watching Bellehurst's cows like this when she had been a child.

A child. Strange to think that barely three years had passed since she had left England behind, when it often felt as if she had crossed a long and tortuous lifetime in between. Not that she disliked her mother and stepfather or was unhappy with the privileged life they had made for her here in America.

Far from it. But right now, standing in the darkness listening to the cows chewing their cuds, and hearing the far-off gurgling of an unseen stream, Sara felt as though something that had been frozen within her was slowly beginning to thaw, like a tightly furled bud opening at last to the first warm breath of summer.

Eventually the cattle moved away and the night became still. So still that Sara could hear an occasional laugh or a snatch of music from the house far behind her. She supposed her parents were looking for her by now, but she felt no desire to return to them. Seating herself in the tall grass, uncaring of staining her lovely white dress, she propped herself up on her elbows and tipped back her head in order to look at the stars—and all at once found herself staring into the face of a strange man who had come soundlessly out of the woods and was standing directly over her looking down into her eyes.

Alarmed, Sara scrambled upright. At the same moment a hand possessed of surprising strength clamped itself about her arm and she was pulled roughly to her feet. "What in hell are you doing here?"

It was not the rudeness of the question or its accompanying rough treatment that rendered Sara speechless; it was the unexpected Scots accent with which the words had been uttered. Open-mouthed, she stared into the harsh face of the man who held her. He could not possibly be one of the Clarks' guests, even though he was wearing the prerequisite black suit and tie; not speaking the way he did, as though he had arrived only yesterday on a steamer from Dumferline or Ayr!

"Well?"

Sara could feel annoyance kindling within her. No gentleman would dare address a Coppham guest so rudely, not when it was perfectly obvious that she had been doing nothing more suspicious than sitting on a tussock of grass admiring the stars!

"What am I doing here?" she repeated in arctic tones that she didn't know she possessed. "I could certainly ask the same of you! *I* happen to be a guest of Mr. and Mrs. Homer Clark of Coppham, up on the hill."

"Aye. That's obvious."

Sara bristled. For some reason she felt as though she had been looked over, summed up, and dismissed all in a single glance. It was not a familiar sensation for her, nor a pleasant one, and she opened her mouth to tell him so. But apparently he had already guessed her thoughts from the expression on her face, because all at once he gave a soft, knowing laugh. "You're a right proper snob, aren't you?"

Unaccountably, Sara's anger vanished as quickly as it had come. Perhaps it was due to the fact that his softly rounded burr reminded her so much of Nannie's, whose loving arms had rocked her whenever Grandmama's had not, and whose lilting Gaelic words had been among the first the infant Sara had ever heard. Whatever the reason, she had always been the first to laugh at herself whenever the situation warranted it, and, yes, he was right, she'd sounded just like some perfectly disagreeable snob.

"I'm sorry," she said, laughter in her voice. "You're absolutely right. Sometimes I can be a dreadful little prig."

His lips twitched. "What are you doing down here, lass?"

"Looking at the cows."

"Then you'd better find your way back to Coppham right quickly. Young ladies shouldna be traipsing about the woods in the dark."

Sara's chin tipped. "And who may you be, to be giving such orders?"

"Does it matter?"

Strangely enough, it did. Perhaps it had something to do with his soft, familiar burr, which was so at odds with the rugged looks of him. That, or the damp, mossy smell of the meadow and the cows, which, like his voice, gave Sara a strangely stirring sense of nostalgia. Either way, she was intrigued, and wanted to know more about him.

"Well?" she prodded somewhat artlessly.

"I'm Rob Buchanan."

"Are you a guest here at Coppham, Mr. Buchanan?"

"Aye."

Sara waited, but he said nothing more. He just stood there looking down at her from his great height, his expression giving nothing away. He obviously felt no need to explain his presence here among the cows. The silence between them lengthened.

"Do you live in the area? I don't believe we've ever met."

"No, we haven't."

"Well," Sara said, beginning to feel a little embarrassed and not quite certain what to make of the situation. "I suppose I'd better go."

"Aye, that you should."

"Good night, Mr. Buchanan," she said archly.

"You'll not be wantin' an escort back to the house?" he inquired politely, but Sara had the sudden impression that he was amused by her inexperience and youth.

"Thank you no," she said stiffly. "I can find my own way back."

He bowed briefly. "Good night, then."

Tossing her head, Sara went quickly up the hill, but she spoiled her exit by turning around at the summit. She saw that he was watching her still, no more than a burly shadow against the moonlight. Cheeks flushing, Sara whirled and hurried away. What a rude man. Hopefully she'd not have the misfortune of running into him again.

Chapter Twenty-three

Barely two days following the subscription dance at Coppham, the weather turned with the suddenness characteristic of northern climes. When Sara awoke on Tuesday morning, it was to find the wind tossing the tree limbs and sending dark clouds scudding across the sky. Descending, yawning, to the kitchen, she found the big stove roaring to drive away the chill and Mrs. Haverty, the cook, wearing a woolen shawl over her work apron.

"Mornin', dearie. Awful weather, isn't it?"

Nodding, Sara seated herself at the scrubbed central table. She was dressed in a white blouse and navy blue skirt, and her hair was braided and pinned in a neat coil to her head. This was the prerequisite uniform of the preparatory school Sara attended in Morristown, but from her mulish expression it was not difficult to see that she thought little of the prestigious institution which her stepfather had chosen for her.

Mrs. Haverty set a plate before her. "Best hurry, dear. You don't want to be late."

"No, of course not," Sara teased, smiling. She was fond of Mrs. Haverty, who always permitted her to eat breakfast in the kitchen on school-day mornings when Gwen was still abed.

Sara liked the bustling atmosphere down here much more than the cold formality of the morning room. Big as it was, Haversham's kitchen always felt cozy. Its shelves were crowded with copper spice buckets, copper boilers, fish kettles of varying sizes, and richly jewel-colored mason jars. An enormous stone sink shared one wall with the gleaming electrical range that had recently been installed to replace the blackened Carron stove which had been in use ever since Haversham was built. There were tea caddies and numerous small tables, a stool in the corner near the scullery for the kitchen maid, and a larger Windsor chair for Mrs. Haverty, which she now pulled up to the table so that she could settle herself at Sara's side.

"Mr. Lloyd can't drive you to school in the buggy," she said, remembering. "He had Thompson take him to the station in the car. It looked too much like rain. You'll have to get Thompson to run you over when he gets back."

The door swung open just then to reveal the agitated form of Mr. Carruthers. Sara and Mrs. Haverty regarded him curiously as he paced the floor before them, wringing his hands.

"Anything wrong?" Mrs. Haverty ventured politely.

"Mr. Lloyd forgot his briefcase," Carruthers said gloomily. "I just found it in the foyer. How on earth will I get it to him?"

Sara scraped back her chair. "I'll ride down to the station with it."

"You'll never catch him."

"I will if I go on horseback."

"Not cutting across Mr. Gibson's property, you won't," Mrs. Haverty said firmly. "You know he hates trespassing on his land."

Sara grinned. "It's barely seven o'clock. There won't be a soul awake on the place."

"And Mrs. Lloyd? What do you think she'll have to say if you're late for school?"

"She won't be up for hours yet, as you well know. And she'll never find out either unless you see fit to tell her." Sara took a last bite of her biscuit. "Don't worry about me. I'll be fine. Where's the briefcase, Carruthers?"

"Oh, really, Miss Sara—" Mrs. Haverty began disapprovingly, but Sara was already gone. Pausing only long enough to throw a cloak over her shoulders, she hurried outside and crossed the wind-swept lawn to the stables.

Ten minutes later she was riding Archer's big thoroughbred, Copper, at a hard gallop down the elm-flanked lane leading toward the Gibson estate. Clods of dirt flew from beneath the hunter's hooves, and the cold wind whipped color into Sara's cheeks and made the ends of her cloak flap behind her. She rode astride, her skirts hitched beneath the stirrup leathers, her stepfather's briefcase resting before her on the saddle.

It would take too long to reach the station along the main road into Morristown, so Sara turned Copper across the open field edging Mr. Gibson's land, keeping to the line of trees well out of sight of the house. She had taken this shortcut a time or two before, cutting a mile or more off the distance she would have had to travel otherwise.

Nevertheless, she hoped she wouldn't be seen, because Mr. Gibson was a miserably crabbed old man who probably wouldn't think twice about discharging a shotgun in an intruder's direction. At least that's how common gossip painted him.

Earl Gibson was what people liked to call a typical American money lord; a man who had made a sizable fortune in railroads and who spent vast sums of it maintaining his meticulously landscaped, thousand-acre park and the magnificent, Moorish-style palace in which he lived. Sara had seen him from time to time stumping around the grounds in a frock coat and top hat harassing his gardeners, or keeping a watchful eye on the chauffeur who was responsible for washing and polishing Mr. Gibson's prized motorcar, an enormous white Steamer with gleaming brass trim.

Although the Gibson estate bordered Haversham for a mile or more on the south, the two families rarely made contact. Mr. Gibson, a widower of long years' standing, disliked horses and did not belong to either the Morristown Hunt or the Morris County Polo Club, which were, of course, Archer Lloyd's great passions. Instead, he devoted most of his time to horticulture, in particular roses, which were grown in vast outdoor tracts and long greenhouses—known as ranges—that stretched nearly as far as the neighboring town of Madison. Roses were a lucrative source of income, in fact, and every morning a shipment of Gibson's perfumed cuttings left Madison by way of special railway cars for New York, from where they were then shipped all over the country and to numerous ports abroad.

Sara, having made it safely across the open field without being seen, slowed Copper to a trot as she approached the long glass buildings comprising Mr. Gibson's many greenhouses. She knew better than to risk breaking a pane by sending an errant stone flying from beneath Copper's hooves. Expecting to find the place deserted so early in the morning, she was dismayed to see a delivery cart standing before the last of these houses. Quickly she pulled on the off-side rein, hoping to turn her horse aside and so avoid being seen.

Too late. Copper had already caught sight of the shaggy pony hitched to the cart, and now he pricked his ears and neighed noisily in greeting. In response the door to the shed flew open, knocking over a pail that had been left carelessly on the stoop. Caught by a gust of wind, it went clattering across the yard, striking Copper's foreleg and sending him into a paroxysm of panic-stricken bucking.

Feeling the briefcase sliding from her grasp, Sara made a grab for it only to end up losing her own precarious seat. She was aware of an instant of weightlessness as she was pitched over Copper's head, and then she landed with a bone-jarring thud on the ground, her cloak settling like the wings of a dying bird about her.

"Great bloody hell! What the devil's going on?"

Sara looked up, dazed, to find herself confronting a scowling face that, after a dizzying moment, righted itself into the craggy and very annoyed-looking features of Rob Buchanan.

She smiled at him thinly. "Hello."

"You!" he exclaimed incredulously. "I might have guessed! What in blazes are you doing here?"

"I suppose I could ask the same of you," Sara retorted defensively, sitting up and rubbing her aching head.

"I happen to work here," he responded darkly, "and if you ken anything about Mr. Earl Gibson, who owns this land, you'll ken he doesna take kindly to trespassers."

"I know, I know." Rising stiffly, Sara brushed the hair from her eyes and shook the dust from her skirt. Then she gazed up at him suspiciously. "What do you mean, you work here?"

"What d'ye think I mean?"

"Are you saying you're employed by Mr. Gibson?"

"Aye, that's right. Does it matter?"

"No," Sara said stiffly. "Why should it?"

"You tell me," he growled.

Sara's chin tipped. Without another word, she pushed past him and reached for Copper's reins. But the ends of her cloak snapped and flailed in the wind as she did so, and the big animal snorted nervously and moved out of reach.

"Here, let me do it." The burly Scotsman thrust Sara aside and caught at the animal's bridle himself. Wordlessly he held the stirrup for her while Sara mounted and took up the reins. She expected him to be polite enough to avert his gaze while she hiked up her skirt and tucked it beneath the saddle flaps, but no, he simply stood there looking at her steadily.

"Thank you," she said with admirable dignity when she was finished with this task.

"You're welcome, I suppose. Now take yourself off before Mr. Gibson arrives."

"Certainly. As soon as you let go of the bridle."

He stepped back, and Sara wasted no time urging Copper to a trot. His hooves crunched over the gravel as he headed toward the road.

"Miss Ashford."

Startled, Sara pulled up. "Yes?"

"You forgot this."

She waited while he brought her the briefcase. Reaching down to take it from him she asked, "How did you know who I was?"

Unexpectedly, a smile spread across his weatherbeaten face, making him suddenly appear much younger and far less intimidating. "I've heard about you from Mr. Gibson. Seems you've ridden roughshod over his parkland before, haven't you?"

Sara looked at him sheepishly. "I wasn't aware that I was causing damage."

The grin widened. "Och, I'm sure o' that."

"Are you going to tell him?"

He considered this gravely for a moment, then shook his head. "I suppose it'll have to stay our secret." His eyes twinkled as he looked up at her, and Sara couldn't help smiling back.

"Thank you."

"Off with ye now, lass," he urged, and stood watching her, arms folded across his chest as Sara whirled Copper and sent him cantering toward the road.

Because Morristown's Lyceum Ballroom had burned down several years ago, the annual debutante ball for the daughters of Morris County was held every spring at Washington Hall. This year, owing to the worsening war overseas, the ball had been planned for October, traditionally a month when most of the county's residents were preparing to move back to New York for the opening of the Opera and the new social season. No one, however, seemed to mind the delay, considering that the debutante ball was too important to miss.

There was a crispness in the air as the Lloyds set out for Morristown in their motorcar that night. Sara, sitting in the backseat, could not help fidgeting and scowling in the darkness. Though she would not be making her own debut for another year, she was expected to attend, despite the fact that she thoroughly despised doing so. With war raging in Europe she thought the spectacle of young girls in white dresses descending the curving staircase one by one in order to be received by the grandes dames of the reception committee was hardly appropriate. While rationing was a way of life abroad, lavish displays of wealth were de rigueur in America. Tonight there would be dancing and a formal supper. Everyone would be expected to stay well into the small hours of the morning.

Sara stared resentfully at the back of her mother's carefully coiffed head. If she were back in England right now she'd be hard at work helping the household prepare for the annual tenants' supper dance. If she thought about it long enough, she could envision Bellehurst's Great Hall as it probably looked right now, could smell the pungent scent of the beech logs burning in the grate as she helped decorate the staircases and alcoves with sheaves of grain, and the tabletops with bouquets of berries, dried grasses, and the last of the summer dahlias. There would be the more modest display of cold meats, bread, fresh yeast buns, and clotted cream set out for the busy workers to eat, and the maids would be drinking cider, the footmen dipping into the crates of Younger's Special Heavy that had been graciously provided by the baron.

I'm homesick, Sara thought. *Homesick for Bellehurst and Grandmama.*

For some reason, it only seemed to be getting worse all the time. Sudden tears smarted in her eyes, and she bit her lip and peered quickly at the star-dusted sky, wishing with all her heart . . . But where was the use in wishing? She had already learned all too well the futility of yearning for the life she had left behind, as lost and out of reach to her these days as the mountains of the moon. Someday, one day, when the war was over, she would return. But until then . . .

"Put on your gloves, Sara. We're almost there."

"Yes, Mother."

"What about your handbag?"

"I have it right here."

"Did I remember to tell you that Lydia Barton is making her debut tonight? I only hope her mother didn't dress the poor girl in pink chiffon. How unbecoming for Lydia's sallow coloring."

The Ford drew to a halt at the edge of the curb. A liveried doorman hurried forward to help Gwen and her daughter alight. A rush of warm air and the sound of music enveloped them as they went up the steps. Inside, they divested themselves of their shawls. Ropes of greens and autumn foliage decorated the ballroom, and towering palms hid the orchestra that was playing in the gallery. Tiny electric lamps covered with pink gauze hung from the gallery railings, lending the cavernous hall a festive air. Sofas had been set in out-of-the-way corners, and Gwen cheerfully steered her daughter toward the one occupied by Mrs. Geraldine Jenkins, who was one of Gwen's dearest friends and whose daughter, Bella, would be coming out tonight as well.

The usual small talk ensued. Sara sat quietly, knowing better than to reveal her boredom with a fidget or a frown. Better to pretend that she was enjoying herself, if only for her mother's sake. Sara was well aware that Gwen was both puzzled and saddened by her daughter's lack of interest in the socializing that she herself had come to adore. What a shame, Sara often thought, that her mother had grown up to be so very different from the shy, retiring girl Grandmama had so often described. The credit for that probably went to Gwen's mother, Adeline, who had vigorously and tirelessly championed Archer's campaign to "reform" her unsociable daughter and, later, her granddaughter as well.

At least the situation had improved remarkably since Adeline's death two years ago. Sara shuddered, remembering the dissension that had split the family in those days because

Adeline had been, if anything, even more adamant than Gwen to rear Sara in a manner that would prepare her for the role of the wife of some wealthy area scion.

Lawrence, Adeline's husband, had thankfully always taken Sara's side, protesting that his granddaughter was barely fourteen and that there would be ample time to plan her nuptials in five or six years, perhaps even more. Between the quiet old man and the homesick young girl there had sprung up an unlikely but intense affection, and after Adeline died and Lawrence sold his business and retired to a small house on the outskirts of Madison, Sara visited him often.

The debutante ball, drearily enough, turned out to be just the stiflingly formal sort of affair Sara loathed. There was a sober tone to most of the conversations going on around her because, once again, the day's newspapers had been filled with stories detailing the agony of the conflict at Verdun, and the awful fact that the Germans had succeeded in sinking nine Norwegian merchant ships during the last twenty-four hours.

There was no doubt, however, that many of the bankers, financiers, and manufacturing lords present tonight were benefiting enormously from the economic boom caused by the war. Sara could see as much in the glittering new jewels and fashionable Chanel originals worn by their wives, and hear it in their enthusiastic discussions concerning trade, stock markets, and the increased demand for American goods abroad. Listening to their gloating remarks angered Sara. She found these men objectionable because they were making their fortunes from the suffering of people like Grandmama and Grandpapa. Furthermore, the babble of voices and the scraping of the violins was making her head ache. Excusing herself from her mother and Mrs. Jenkins, she made her way quickly to the outer hall, where the cold night air seeping through the opened windows was like a welcome tonic as it washed up and over her. Sara took a deep breath and looked slowly about her.

To her immense relief, she saw that the hall was empty but for a bored-looking attendant and the occasional appearance of a group of latecomers. There was, as well, a gentleman in a gray suit leaning negligently against the downstairs balustrade smoking a cheroot; a man who straightened with a mocking smile as Sara's gaze finally fell upon him.

"Good evening, Miss Ashford. Am I to understand that you have the same lack of interest in this formal gathering as you did in the dance at Coppham? Or is it simply that you always make it a habit of keeping to yourself?"

Rob Buchanan walked toward her across the length of the foyer. He looked far too relaxed in the elegance of Washington Hall for a man who seemed more at home in work clothes and Wellingtons.

Seeing the surprise that showed clearly on Sara's face, Buchanan laughed. "The suit happens to be mine, you know. No faded breeks or gardener's boots for the likes of Washington Hall, I assure you."

Sara couldn't help laughing with him, although she was a little disconcerted by the way he was towering over her, making her feel, all at once, inexplicably young and silly in her frilly dress. The feeling was decidedly odd, considering that Sara had never paid the slightest attention to her appearance before.

"You don't care for this sort of thing, do you, Miss Ashford?" Rob asked unexpectedly.

"No," Sara said, surprised that he had read her thoughts so well. "As a matter of fact, I loathe it. If I had the choice, I'd far rather be—"

"Where?" he prompted as she blushed and fell silent.

She regarded him solemnly, the color of her eyes reminding him all at once of the bright blue of native Scottish harebells. "At home in Kent with my grandparents."

"Ah, so I was right. You're not American, are you?"

"Only half."

"Which half?"

She smiled and told him, starting with that long ago summer of 1900 when her American grandparents had leased the vicarage at Millham Cross, and ending with her father's untimely death in the Boer War. "It wasn't until everyone started talking about the likelihood of this war that my mother decided to send for me," she concluded. "I didn't want to leave. Nowadays I find myself wishing more and more that I

hadn't. I haven't heard anything from them in months, you
see.''

"That must be very difficult for you." He sounded sympathetic.

"What about you?''

"I'm a botanist," he told her. "University trained in Edinburgh. For the past year I've been supervising Whitewood
range, Mr. Gibson's rose range. We currently have six acres
under glass.''

"Then you haven't been in the Morristown area long.''

"No. I spent a number of years out west, designing botani-
cal gardens on the coast. Originally, I left Scotland in 1906.''

"Alone?''

He flicked the stub of his cheroot away and ground it out
beneath his heel. "Alone and outcast, I'm afraid. I'd alienated
my family, you see, by throwing away the perfect opportunity: taking over half the partnership in my father's textile
mills in Glasgow.''

"Didn't you care for the work?''

He shrugged his broad shoulders. "I wanted to be outdoors,
working with my hands.''

"This perfect opportunity you threw away—those sound
more like your father's words than your own.''

He looked at her in silence, his dark gray eyes regarding
her intently. "You're the first person who's ever realized as
much," he told her. Unexpectedly, he smiled at her, and Sara
suddenly felt as if they were friends of long standing sharing
an old, familiar story. The great difference in their ages
seemed to make no difference at all.

A draft blew over them suddenly, and Sara whirled as the
outer door was slammed shut by a gust of wind. The attendant, roused from his lethargy in the corner near the cloak
room, hurried forward to take the coats from the trio of
arrivals the wind had blown inside. Sara recognized them as
James and Alma Wylie and their daughter Belinda, who,
because they spent their winters on Long Island, were understandably late. Sara's mother had attended school in Philadelphia with Alma Wylie, and now Alma's deeply interested
gaze settled on Sara and the tall man lounging beside her.

"Good evening, Sara."

"Good evening, Mrs. Wylie, Mr. Wylie. Hello, Belinda."

"Hullo." Belinda's gaze, like her mother's, flicked curiously over them.

"Is your mother inside, Sara?"

Sara nodded. "She's sitting with Mrs. Jenkins."

"Oh, good. Come along, Belinda, James." Whispering among themselves, the three of them vanished into the ballroom.

"I'd better go," Sara said as soon as they had gone. "Mother will be wondering what's become of me." She hoped the dim light of the hall hid the embarrassed blush on her cheeks.

"Do you know, Miss Ashford," Rob said unexpectedly, "you're not at all what I first suspected."

"Neither are you," Sara shot back calmly.

A swift, appreciative smile lit the gray eyes and softened the harsh planes of his face. "Perhaps I'll see you inside then."

But Sara did not see him again that night, although she looked for him both at dinner and later among the couples crowding the floor to dance. It finally dawned on her that he had left the ball altogether, and this realization bothered her a great deal more than it should have. Why hadn't he told her he was leaving early? Couldn't he have waited long enough to claim one dance with her?

Don't be an idiot, Sara told herself contemptuously. You only fancy him because he's good looking and because he can be extremely charming when he isn't being rude, and because the way he talks reminds you of the people back home. But he's old enough to be your father . . . well, your older brother anyway, and you're far too young to be thinking that way about men. Especially men like him.

Gwen said, "I wonder what happened to that nice young man you were speaking to earlier?"

Sara choked on the cup of punch she had raised to her lips. "Who, Mother?"

"Why, Carr Vanderbilt's nephew, of course. The one who sat with us at supper. Such a charming young man. Archer was quite taken with him, weren't you, dear?"

"The hell I was. Fellow had spots, and obviously no more brains than a terrier. And if you think even for a moment that I'm going to entertain the notion of accepting him as a son-in-law, you're absolutely—"

"Archer!" cried Gwen, shocked.

"Oh, hell, you know what I mean! . . . Here, Sara, they're starting a cotillion. Why don't you dance with your old dad?"

Sara could scarcely contain her relief. "I'd love to." And, under the annoyed gaze of her mother, she allowed him to lead her away.

Chapter
Twenty-four

On New Year's Day, 1917, long-standing tradition found the Four Hundred assembled at 11:30 A.M. at the Grinnell Willis mansion for breakfast. Promptly at 1:30, the noisy crowd dispersed in various carriages and automobiles for the open bar at Ridley Watts's, whose collection of clarets and sauterne punch was considered the finest in the county. Then on to George Marshall Allen's, then the Charles Bradleys', and, finally, with the winter sun beginning to set in a cold gray sky, everyone converged at Red Gate Farm in Harding Township for the traditional New Year's banquet.

All of them were, by then, in jovial spirits. The war that continued to rage across the Atlantic had rewarded the United States—and most of the citizens of Morris County—with the most prosperous period in its history. And at Red Gate Farm, numerous toasts were made to the old year, and the new, which everyone believed should, from all accounts, prove equally as lucrative.

Sara listened to the noisy talk and the laughter, and wished the butler would hurry up and announce dinner. She was hungry and not a little tired, having stayed up late the night before at Gwen's request to see in the new year with a few chosen friends.

Seth Thomas, the amiable owner of Red Gate Farm, had invited a record number of people to the banquet, and Sara felt flushed by the heat roaring from the fireplaces and the crush provided by her fellow guests. She shifted from one foot to another, wondering how she could have been stupid enough to allow herself to be trapped into conversation by Bella Jenkins's older brother, John, a sophomore at Princeton, who was holding forth endlessly on Pennsylvania's chances in this year's Rose Bowl.

Sara nodded occasionally and murmured politely to show that she was interested. At the same time her eyes scanned the crowded room, hoping to come across someone, anyone, who might be able to rescue her. With considerable relief she suddenly spotted Rob Buchanan in a remote corner of the elegant room talking to Dorothy Dodge, a very charming and eligible young lady who had also made her coming-out that fall. Buchanan said something to her, and Dorothy began to giggle, gazing up at him adoringly from beneath long, sooty lashes. Rob smiled as well, his eyes crinkling at the corners, but when his head came up and his gaze fell unexpectedly on Sara, he merely nodded briefly and looked away.

Sara said abruptly, "Why don't we take a walk through the garden?"

John's astonished gaze went to the windows, where the heavy velvet drapes were drawn back to reveal the snow-covered lawn and the barns and stables beyond. The setting sun painted long blue shadows on the drive, and John turned questioningly to Sara. "It's kind of cold, don't you think?"

"Too cold for a walk before dinner?" she taunted with a smile. She did not know it yet, but her smile made her immediately sensual, and for a moment John regarded her in startled silence.

Then he said: "I've got a better idea. Why don't we go for a drive?"

"Do you have a car?"

"No, but your stepfather does."

Archer, whose stocks had soared spectacularly on Wall Street last quarter, had presented his wife with a new fur coat and a Packard motorcar for Christmas. It was this car, sitting sleek and formidable amid the snowdrifts banked before the front door, that had attracted John's appreciative attention.

"I suppose you could take it once around the barnyard," Archer agreed when asked. "Know how to drive, do you?"

John's chest swelled. "Of course, sir."

"Can we go too?" inquired Bella, overhearing their exchange.

Archer grinned. "Don't see why not. No harm in a little fun before dinner."

"Oh, goody." Bella clapped her hands. "Let's go now, before it gets dark."

There were eight of them who ended up fetching their coats and trudging outside into the bitter cold. As the youngest and slimmest, Sara was forced to squeeze herself into the front seat between the angular John and two giggling girls muffled in thick furs and feathered hats. There was no roof and the wind blew icy cold, but no one seemed to care. The car jinked as it moved away from the front walk, and John, whooping, accelerated.

"Don't go too fast," Bella warned from the backseat.

"Yes, do!" crowed the girl sitting next to Sara.

The car sped away down the drive, churning deep ruts in the half-frozen gravel. Ahead lay the barn and stables, snow-covered and picturesque with their gabled roofs and the black lace of barren tree branches rising into the violet sky. It was this same, lovely scene that had been the subject of one of Nathaniel Currier's most popular Currier & Ives lithographs depicting country life, but the young people speeding past the barn were unaware of this, and probably wouldn't have cared.

The Packard was capable of a top speed of forty miles per hour, and this fact held considerably more charm for them than did the scenery—especially John, who could not resist crashing the gears again and gunning the vehicle forward.

"Look out!" screeched the girl next to Sara, and John swerved just in time to miss a flock of honking geese.

"Maybe we'd better go back," Sara suggested, beginning to worry a little. But John merely grinned and sent the Packard spinning around a massive drift of snow—and straight toward a stone water trough that suddenly appeared in front of them as they sped around the far corner of the barn.

Someone gave a shrill scream, and John made a desperate attempt to swerve to the right. There was a deafening thump as the Packard's hood went crashing through the barn wall only a foot away from the trough. The impact threw Sara against the windscreen, and for a moment she sat dazed, not quite knowing what had happened. Then the Packard's occupants piled out, subdued and shaken, to eye each other in frightened silence.

"Is anyone hurt?" John inquired anxiously.

"You've got a bump on your head, Sara," said Bella.

Sara rubbed her brow. "I'm okay. It doesn't hurt very much."

"At least it isn't bleeding," John said, relieved.

"What about the car?"

They all looked at it. In the gathering darkness it was difficult to see how much damage had been done, and their inspection was hampered by the fact that at least a foot or more of the bonnet and bumper was imbedded in the wall of Seth Thomas's barn.

"I guess we'd better go tell Mr. Lloyd," Bella said reluctantly.

"And Mr. Thomas too. It'll take a mule team to pull the car loose."

John's jaw hardened. "I'll tell him. It was my fault, anyway. Come on, Sara."

She shook her head. "We really ought to make sure first that none of the animals inside were hurt."

"Oh, God, that too? Bella, go tell Mr. Lloyd for me, will you? I'd better take a look inside."

Bella pouted. "He's going to have a fit."

"So will my mother," agreed someone else.

"What do you think Mr. Lloyd'll do?"

"I don't know. Poor Sara."

They were all talking at once now, their earlier numbness

wearing off and relief making them feel a little light-headed. Six of them began walking back toward the house, with Bella in the lead, their heads bowed against the wind while Sara, shivering in the cold, waited for John to unlatch the big barn door.

Inside, they were assailed by a blast of warmth and the sweet smell of hay mingled with manure. The barn was wired for electricity, and when John switched on the lights, a pale yellow glare fell from the high, pitched ceiling. From numerous scrubbed stanchions cows turned their heads to regard them—a fine herd of Guernseys with sleek coats and dark eyes.

John minced his way precariously across the stone floor but Sara, accustomed to barns and uncaring of her fine white shoes, hurried on ahead. "Oh, no!"

The Packard's hood had come to rest in the center of a loose-box stall. Splintered boards lay everywhere, and trapped beneath the front left wheel, bawling weakly, lay a bull calf, no more than a few days old.

Sara sank down beside it. "I don't think it's hurt," she said, stroking and prodding gently. "Only trapped. If we could just wedge it out from under—" She broke off as she felt a warm stickiness seeping over her hand. The calf's foreleg, she saw now, was gashed and bleeding. "John! Come here quickly! We've got to—"

Her words were drowned out by a muted thump. Whirling, Sara saw the gangly length of young Johnny Jenkins sprawled on his back in the straw, his face a curious ashen color. A rush of disgusted anger shook her. "Of all the—"

"Sara! Sara, where are you?"

Relief welled in her at the sound of that deep, familiar voice. "I'm in here!" she called. "Hurry, please!"

Footsteps pounded across the stone floor, and then Rob Buchanan was pushing his way into the stall without sparing so much as a glance for the unconscious John. He knelt beside her. "They said inside you'd been hurt—"

"Not me, the calf."

He examined the gash with great care. The little creature had stopped bleating and lay trembling beneath his touch.

"It'll take some sewing, I'm afraid, but we'll have to get him free first. The others are on their way to help." He pulled a handkerchief from his vest pocket. "Move over so I can put some pressure on it."

"I'll do it."

"You'll get bloody."

"No worse than I am now."

Rob watched as Sara skillfully wrapped the silk square around the calf's foreleg, speaking to it soothingly to stop its struggles. "Not squeamish by half, are you?" he asked with a grin.

"Don't forget I was raised in the country."

"Unlike that one there, eh?" Rob jerked his head in the direction of John, who continued to lie sprawled on his back, but was beginning to groan and stir.

"No."

They exchanged an intimate smile. Then, abruptly, Rob's amusement faded, and he seized Sara's shoulders in a tight grip. "You're hurt, lass. Why didn't you tell me? Your forehead—"

"It's only a bump," Sara protested.

He touched it nevertheless, his fingers surprisingly gentle. "Aye, you're lucky. Not feeling dizzy or nauseous, are you?"

"No." Sara raised her eyes as she spoke to find him leaning close, his gray eyes peering deeply into hers. She grew still, and inexplicably a nervous pulse began beating in her throat. Rob looked at her, at the sweet red mouth that hovered so near. The harshness of his features eased all at once as he took her pointed little chin in his big hand and turned her face toward his. "By God, lass—"

"Sara! Sara, where are you?"

It was her stepfather's voice, sharp with panic, and Sara stirred and, rising, went to the door of the stall. "I'm here," she called. "It's all right, I'm not hurt."

She stepped out into the aisle and was immediately surrounded by Archer and the small crowd that spilled into the barn behind him. Minor pandemonium ensued. Someone gave orders to free the trapped calf, while others bent over the moaning John.

Rob Buchanan, helping to hitch up the brace of mules that was to pull the Packard free, paused to watch the young man stagger uncertainly to his feet.

"What happened? Where . . . where am I?" John's face was pale and confused. "I remember a car . . . Mr. Lloyd, what's happened to your car?"

Buchanan turned quickly to hide his amusement. His smile softened when he looked at Sara. He had no doubt that she would have responded to him wholly if he had tried to kiss her. But she was so young, really a child yet. The thought angered him unaccountably.

Ruthlessly he seized the mule by the halter and jerked it toward the barn door.

In an upstairs boudoir of the Thomas house, Sara was sitting on a daybed surrounded by her mother and a half-dozen anxious, chattering ladies all urging her to lie still and rest. Her soiled dress had been removed and a cold cloth applied to the bruise on her forehead. Wrapped in Mrs. Thomas's shantung silk robe, she finally managed to push the patting, prodding hands away and assure everyone once again that she was truly fine.

"But Bella and the others are lying down," Gwen pointed out. "You really ought to do the same."

"No need to act brave, darling," agreed Mrs. Jenkins. "We all know you've had the most dreadful shock."

Sara gave her mother a pleading glance which Gwen, surprisingly enough, understood. Somehow, she succeeded in getting rid of them, until no one remained save Mrs. Thomas and a ladies' maid who had been sent to fetch another dress for Sara to wear in view of the fact that the girl insisted on returning downstairs.

"How very brave you are," Mrs. Thomas said emotionally.

"Just like her grandmother, Lady Ladbroke," Gwen agreed. "Now there's a woman who always loathed any kind of fuss. Hard as iron and just as stubborn."

Sara paid no attention to her mother's remark. She knew that Gwen was secretly proud of the fact that her in-laws were titled, and rarely missed the opportunity of reminding her friends of it either. "Mother, may I please go down now?"

"All right, dear, if you insist."

Mrs. Thomas beckoned to the maid, who helped Sara slip into a softly draped white dress with a fashionably short, ankle-length hem. When she had finished doing up the hooks, she withdrew, and Sara went to look at herself in the mirror. Her forehead was bruised and her cheeks were unusually pale, but Sara did not notice. Gazing dreamily at the dark-eyed girl in the reflection, she saw only the softly parted lips that for a wondrous moment Rob Buchanan had been planning to kiss. A blush crept across her cheeks as she remembered the way she had trembled at his touch, sensing instinctively what he intended. . . . She looked at her reflection again, and for the first time in her life saw herself not as a girl, but as a woman, sensual, lovely, and very much alive.

Downstairs the men had returned to the drawing room to drink port and talk importantly among themselves. The Packard had been dragged free of the barn and, to Archer's relief, proclaimed only slightly damaged. The mules had been returned to their stalls and the cowman summoned to sew up the injured calf. All in all the menfolk considered it a job well done.

Now there was time to discuss the incident at length, to ponder how it might have happened, and to praise the victims for their bravery. Even John Jenkins was spared, Archer being unable, in the face of the boy's shamed apology, to lay any blame upon him. After all, not everyone could take it on the chin the way Johnny had and still manage to retain some semblance of dignity.

There was a stir in the doorway just then, and Sara stepped inside. Everyone who took a look at her fell silent. Even Archer stared. In her borrowed dress Sara looked years older, her smooth shoulders bared, her slim waist prettily revealed by the clinging material. She wore her red hair unbound so that it spilled down her back in a shining cloud, while her lustrous blue eyes scanned the gathering dreamily.

"My dear—" Archer went forward to lay his arm about her shoulders and kiss her cheek.

She turned to him. "Sorry about the car, Dad."

"No harm done. None at all. How do you feel?"

"Oh, fine. Just a little thirsty."

Archer threw back his head and laughed. "Hear that, Seth? How about a brandy for m'little girl?"

"Sure thing. After what she's been through I'd say she deserves it."

Sara did not immediately take the glass he offered her. Instead, under cover of the conversation that resumed, she asked, "What happened to Mr. Buchanan? I don't see him anywhere."

"Buchanan? I think he took himself off for home a little while ago."

Sara's face clouded. "Oh. I wanted to thank him. He . . . he was very kind."

"Good fellow," Archer agreed. "I hear he's a sharp businessman, too. Earl Gibson tells me his profit's gone up fifteen percent since Buchanan came to work for him."

"That's why I asked him over today," Seth admitted. "I'm interested in starting a range myself. Just a small one, mind, but Buchanan's supposedly the best. I may know a lot about dairy farming, but I don't know one darned thing about roses."

Sara excused herself. Setting aside her brandy untouched, she tried not to analyze the intense disappointment that had overwhelmed her upon being told that Rob was no longer here. Or the annoyance that followed close upon its heels. Why hadn't he waited to bid her good-bye before leaving? Surely he must have known that she would want to thank him for . . . for . . . well, just for being there, for taking charge of the situation while poor John sprawled unconscious in the straw, and for making her feel safe and calm and . . . and as though, somehow, she had suddenly become special to him.

"Don't be ridiculous!" she told herself sternly. "One tiny bump on the head and right away you're ready to pronounce yourself in love!"

Which was so utterly preposterous that Sara dismissed the idea at once, and was appalled at herself for even thinking it.

Chapter
Twenty-five

It was February, the most frigid of winter months, and in faraway Russia thousands of striking munitions workers screamed for the end of czarist rule. Closer to home, after renewed attacks by German U-boats on neutral ships in British waters, the United States government severed diplomatic relations with Germany. Regrettably, the measure did not act as a deterrent; by the end of the month, more than one hundred thirty Allied ships had been sunk by the Germans in submarine warfare. Pushed beyond endurance, President Wilson asked Congress for the power to arm American vessels.

March, with its howling winds and drea·y, wearying cold, brought with it the torpedoing by German subs of the American merchant ship *Algonquin*, and, later, the *City of Memphis*, *Vigilante*, and *Illinois*. At precisely 1:18 on the afternoon of April 6, 1917, President Wilson signed into law a declaration approved earlier by Congress. America was at war.

"We're right in the middle of production," Rob Buchanan explained in his heavy Scots burr. "The season runs from September roughly to the end of June. The cycle takes seven weeks, and we work ten hour days every day watering, spraying, and heating the roses to bring them into flower. Then the cutting begins." He held up his hands, which were scarred and leathery from the thorns. "That's what we're doin' the now."

Archer pursed his lips and looked thoughtfully about him. "How many employees do you have?"

"I've twenty-two under me at the moment."

"That many?"

"Aye, sir."

Archer, along with Harold Bascombe, his estate superintendent, and his stepdaughter, Sara, were taking a tour of Earl Gibson's range to learn the process of growing roses. In the last year or so, numerous small, independent rose ranges had sprung up throughout Morris County, the move prompted by the fact that roses had recently begun proving far too lucrative a crop to remain simply a wealthy man's hobby.

Archer, with his eye to the future and fearing, as others did, that the American economy would collapse once the war was over, had resolved to build a dozen greenhouses of his own in the hopes that they would quickly prove productive. "How many did Gibson start with?" he asked now.

Rob pursed his lips, thinking. "Four, but they were timbered rather than steel-framed and na very—"

Sara, restless, stopped listening at that point and wandered away down the aisle, pausing now and again to admire the endless beds with their neat labels, notation charts, and sweetly perfumed roses. Though the temperature outside was brisk on this early April morning, the greenhouse was warm; heated, as Rob had explained, by massive boilers outside in the yard.

Sara halted before a bed of deep red roses whose lustrous color was impossible to ignore, and bent to breathe their sweet fragrance. When she straightened she found Rob beside her, his thumbs hooked into the belt of his trousers, watching her. She smiled at him. "These are truly beautiful."

"They ought to be. They're American Beauties, a specialty developed by your neighbor, Louis Noe. We sell more of these than any other, and get top dollar for them too."

Sara touched a dark velvet petal. "I can see why."

"When Queen Victoria was still alive, a shipment was sent to Windsor every Christmas."

"Was it really? But how did they stay fresh?"

"The stems were stuck into potatoes to keep 'em moist, and the flowers wrapped in Irish moss so they wouldna bruise."

"And these?" Sara gestured to a seemingly endless row of delicate peach flowers. "What do you call these?"

"Katherine Howe. I named them myself."

"Oh?" Sara said casually. "Is that a friend of yours?"

"No. It was Mrs. Gibson's maiden name."

To her immense annoyance, Sara could feel her cheeks begin to burn, but when she looked up at Rob and caught him grinning down at her, her embarrassment faded and she returned his smile. For some curious reason, she didn't feel foolish in his presence. Just ridiculously light-hearted and gay, and comfortable in a way she rarely felt with others outside her family—which was strange considering that she hadn't seen him at all since the New Year's Day banquet at Red Gate Farm.

"It was kind of you to let us come," she said now. "You must be dreadfully busy."

"Easter's a bad time for us," he agreed. "As bad as Christmas. But when your father called I couldna tell him no. Not when he told me you'd be coming on."

Sara looked up at him quickly, but his craggy face gave nothing away. Somehow, it didn't matter. She felt, all at once, ridiculously happy. But perhaps that was only because the warm, loamy smell of the greenhouse was so loaded with nostalgia that she couldn't help thinking of the conservatory at Bellehurst. Surely it had nothing to do with Rob's casual remark, and she cautioned herself not to jump to conclusions. Nevertheless, it was impossible to misconstrue the comfortable silence that fell between them, or to pretend that she wasn't entirely contented to simply continue standing there with him beside her.

"Sara?"

She turned dreamily toward Archer. "Umm?"

"I think we'd better go now. I promised your mother—"

Loud whooping in the drive made them all look up. Through the glass walls they could see a group of men in laborer's aprons and boots running toward the greenhouse. The door burst open.

"It's war, Mr. Buchanan! America's finally at war!"

"Are you crazy?" Archer burst out.

"No, sir. We just heard it on the wire."

"They're planning a parade down Fifth Avenue to celebrate!"

"Mr. Buchanan, could we—"

Rob said quietly, "By all means, gentlemen, you're free to go."

Under cover of their noisy departure Sara turned to him, her eyes wide and frightened. "What will happen now?"

"Military recruitment, of course. You canna fight a war without an army."

"Could you . . . Will they . . . You couldn't possibly . . ."

Rob said, "I'm thirty years old, Miss Ashford. Young enough to meet recruitment requirements, I'm sure."

"I wouldn't worry," Archer put in jovially. "They're bound to start on a voluntary basis."

Rob said gravely, "You misunderstand me, sir. I fully intend to volunteer."

For a moment Sara looked as if the wind had been knocked out of her. At last she said breathlessly, "Dad, we'd better go home. Mother will want to know."

"You're right." Archer held out his hand. "Thanks for your time, Buchanan."

"Anytime, sir . . . Mr. Bascombe." Rob shook hands with both of them. "Good-bye, Miss Ashford."

Not certain that her voice would be steady, Sara merely nodded without looking at him. Outside in the cold sunshine, shivering, she drew her mantle around her. Archer held out his hand to help her up into the car. She stopped suddenly.

"Wait. I forgot something."

"All right, go on. But hurry, please."

Sara ran back into the greenhouse, her footsteps echoing on the hard-packed earth. She found Rob tamping on an acid-stained pipe near the pump, but he straightened swiftly when he saw her. She paused before him, out of breath, her hair disheveled and coming loose from its pins.

"How can you?" she burst out. "You're not even American."

"But, they'll take me all right."

Sara bit her lip. "You'll think it over first, won't you?"

He laughed humorlessly. "I've been thinking about nothing else for months. For *years*, lass! Ever since Scottish regiments began dying like dogs in Turkey and France."

Sara caught at his arm. "Rob, please don't."

He said harshly, "What do you ken of it, lass? The first time you saw me, out there in Homer Clark's fields, do you remember that night?"

She nodded wordlessly.

"What do you suppose I was doing out there?"

"I don't know. I've often wondered."

"Then I'll tell you. I was fighting my own private war, prowling up and down those bloody fields trying to convince myself that England didn't have need of an aging botanist in her army. That it'd be daft of me to enlist. God knows I canna take orders well, or shoot straight for that matter. And it was a battle I thought I'd won, Sara. Until today."

"Then you're going," she said hopelessly.

"As soon as Mr. Gibson can replace me."

"How long will that take?"

"A week, maybe two."

She looked down at the ground beneath her feet, but she couldn't see anything because her vision was suddenly blurred with tears. She felt Rob put his hand beneath her chin, tip it up with a forefinger so that he could look into her face.

"Och, lassie," he protested, when he saw that she was crying.

She looked at him, her great blue eyes as soft and vulnerable as a doe's. Rob's face twisted. With a groan, he pulled her into his arms. Bending his head, he covered her mouth with his own. For a moment Sara resisted him violently; then, all at once, her arms slipped up and around his neck, and the very bones of her body seemed to melt against him. The feel of his mouth upon hers filled her with wild elation and the sense of coming home for the first time in all those long, lonely years since leaving England. She had never known, never realized how safe she could feel in another person's arms.

There was an impatient honking from the Ford outside. Startled, Sara broke free. For a moment she looked up at Rob with wide, shocked eyes, then she whirled and ran, and the soft pad of her feet vanished into the stillness.

He was gone before the month was out. Sara heard the news in a roundabout manner from Mr. Bascombe. Rob was in south Jersey, training at Camp Dix. Sara had not seen him again before he left, nor had he sought her out to tell her good-bye. She told herself it didn't matter. There was so much else to do and to think about. The school year had ended and, despite her mother's disapproval, Sara joined the Red Cross. Three times a week she drove Archer's little buggy to Madison Academy, a preparatory school in town, where she and a number of other volunteers worked hard producing and packaging army supplies for American soldiers overseas.

Though the spring was beautiful that year, with skies of deep, crystalline blue and the fields and gardens bursting with greenery and flowers, Sara saw little of it, for beyond her excursions to the Academy she rarely went out. Most of the Lloyds' neighbors had extended their winter vacations in Palm Beach that year and so were unavailable for entertaining, while others, whose sons had been called up, were in no mood to go calling themselves.

For this reason, spring proved understandably uneventful for those living in Morris County, but this bothered Gwen a good deal more than it bothered Archer or Sara. The fault, Gwen had already decided, lay entirely with President Wilson, who had passed a Selective Draft Act making registration in the armed forces mandatory for all men between the ages of twenty-one and thirty—and thereby affecting a large percentage of families in the county.

"I haven't any idea what to do with myself today," Gwen complained one morning at breakfast. "The Hemphills aren't back from Newport yet, and Geraldine Jenkins hasn't been interested in *anything* since her Johnny was called up. I was hoping we'd be able to plan another dog show at Giralda Farms, which was ever so much fun last year. But no one seems willing." She stirred her tea, looking morose and far too thin in her striped taffeta morning dress.

. "You could come into New York with me," suggested Archer. "I'm only working half a day today. You could do some shopping and visit the cinema. See that new Chaplin film."

"*The Pawn Shop?*" Gwen brightened. "It might be fun. Will you go with me, Sara?"

"I'm sorry, Mother, I can't."

"Oh, that silly Red Cross of yours! Surely you can miss it just this once?"

"Not today, I'm afraid." On impulse: "Why don't you come with *me*?"

Gwen shuddered delicately. "Thank you, dear, I'd rather not."

It was the waiting that turned out to be the hardest part. Waiting for news, waiting for word on the fate of the first American troops to land on French soil. Sara kept herself informed as best she could, often meeting the newspapers as they were delivered in the predawn darkness at the railway station and reading them right there in the buggy, squinting in the weak light of the lanterns. Occasionally she haunted the sidewalks outside Fagan's Hall or Bottle Hill; anywhere that men gathered to drink and grouse and exchange news, although their numbers were dwindling these days because drinking had become prohibitively expensive now that Washington had adopted a whiskey tax as part of the nation's War Revenue Bill.

Then, in July, an unexpected letter came from her grandmother. Eagerly scanning the first of two densely written pages, Sara's heart swelled with gratitude. It must, she thought, be a very difficult time for everyone at Bellehurst, but as usual Grandmama wrote only of the simple things, the news she knew would be comforting to hear.

The planting is, of course, finished by now, and I am immensely pleased with our crops so far. The rain has been steady and the temperature delightfully moderate. Mr. Brockman has managed to till a very large garden and we should be able to put by plenty for the winter. We've three new calves, and the Skeltons' sow has produced a litter of the most darling little shoats you've ever seen.

Everyone here is doing quite well considering. The government has finally granted voting rights to women, although Eugenia was furious that they were limited only to those over thirty. Now that she is divorced from that painter fellow and once again living at home, she has taken this suffragette movement very much to heart. Your grandfather is convinced (resigned is, perhaps, a better word) that she will end up being drawn into politics and so run for a seat in the next elections.

Your grandfather is doing very well, I might add, though it would be unfair of me to deceive you by saying that he isn't beginning to show his age just a little. Nothing alarming: some graying at the edges and the inevitable slowing down of old age, but there is no sign, thank goodness, that his mind is any less shrewd than it always was.

I'm not certain how many of my letters have made it through to you. From the few we've received of yours, it's clear that a number have been lost in-between, so perhaps I should tell you again that Victoria had another baby, her third girl, on 10th December last year and that she was christened Winifred.

Speaking of names: you've surely heard that the king ordered his sons to drop their German titles, and that the royal family is now known as the House of Windsor? I saw little Princess Maud riding her pony in the park when I went to London for Winifred's christening. Such a darling little girl.

As for you, Sara, you are my darling girl as well,
and I pray that you are well and happy. Now that
the United States has joined the war effort I can
only hope you never have cause to experience the
grief we feel when sons and grandsons of friends
we have known all our lives end up as casualties.
Only last month the Skeltons lost their Herbert to
the bombardment at Messines Ridge. It was too,
too cruel for both of them. Take care of yourself,
my darling. I can only hope this letter reaches you
intact.

As Always,
Your loving grandmama.

Sara laid the letter aside and sat for some time looking out
into the lushness of the garden beyond her window without
really seeing it at all. Then she said, as though speaking to
someone else in the room, "No. It could never happen. I
refuse to believe it."

But she knew that it could. She had no idea if Rob was
still in the States undergoing training or if he was already
among the American troops that had, under the command of
General John Pershing, sailed for France early last month.
The worst part of it was knowing that she couldn't expect to
ever find out, considering that Rob owed her nothing. Not a
letter, not a cable, nothing.

Though he might have kissed her passionately that day in
the greenhouse, he was certainly not in love with her. Not,
at any rate, the way Grandmama and Grandpapa loved each
other. Grandmama had always said that the very idea of love
at first sight simply did not exist; that people could feel an
instant, intense sort of attraction for one another, but that
love—*real* love—came later, and then only with time and
intimate knowledge, and a firm commitment upon which to
build a lasting friendship between one another.

On the other hand, how could Sara explain the feeling of
closeness and familiarity that she experienced whenever Rob
Buchanan was with her? It was the same sort of closeness she
felt with her grandparents, with Nannie, Aunt Eugenia, Mrs.

Skelton, and so many others at Bellehurst whom she had known and loved and laughed with in those happy early years of her youth.

Sara was old enough now to understand that her mother had never really been a part of the Bellehurst she herself considered home. Oh, she had quite obviously been fond of Sandy's parents, and Sara knew that they had loved her too, but Gwen was from a different world and had wanted nothing to do with the quiet, orderly life that slipped softly through the hour glass in that secretive corner of Kent.

With Rob, on the other hand, things were entirely different. Sara had no difficulty imagining bringing him to Bellehurst and introducing him to her grandparents. She was convinced that they would welcome him with open arms, while Rob, in turn, would openly approve of them.

Ridiculous. No, stupid, actually. Stupid in the extreme of her to dream even for a moment that Rob Buchanan was the least bit interested in a sixteen-year-old girl. Because if he was, he would have written her by now, if only to let her know where he was and that he was doing well.

Three months had passed since his departure for Camp Dix—enough time for even the briefest of missives to get through. But there had been nothing. Which was exactly what Sara should expect from a man she had met barely three or four times before.

Grimacing, she rose and went to stand before the mirror. The girl in the reflection looked a little thinner than she had three months ago, and was now unfashionably tanned from the many buggy rides to Madison Academy each week, despite the fact that she always wore a hat. To Sara's mind she looked disappointingly awkward and lacking in polish, like a long-legged colt that hadn't quite grown up yet.

Which is what I'll have to do, Sara decided suddenly, if Rob Buchanan is going to take any notice of me when he comes home from the war.

Chapter
Twenty-six

The gloomy gymnasium was quiet but for the sound of ripping cloth. Now and then the subdued voices of the women broke the stillness, but it was far too hot for any real conversation. The long tables were piled with bedsheets that were being cut and divided in a neat, methodical fashion, with six women working diligently on each side. The early September heat was appalling, despite the fact that all of the windows had been opened. When Sara had left Haversham earlier that morning, she had been greatly tempted to wear the pair of bicycle shorts her Aunt Eugenia had recently sent her from England, but Gwen had been both horrified and adamant.

"Oh, Mother, I'm only going out to roll bandages!" Sara had protested.

"With half of our friends and neighbors there helping as well. What do you think they'll say when they see you? I'll not have you labeled some sort of—of militant. You'll wear your peach-striped blouse and gray skirt. They're the coolest things you own."

Sara had grudgingly done as she was told, but beneath the ankle-length skirt her long legs remained bare. Stockings were one item of clothing her mother hadn't mentioned.

"All finished, Sara?"

"Almost." She quickly rolled the last of her strips and secured them with pins under the tight-lipped scrutiny of Miss Lottie Gaines, the Academy's headmistress and now director of the Morris County chapter of the American National Red Cross. Miss Gaines took her wartime job very seriously, and there were not a few among her volunteers who objected strenuously to her authoritarian manner—only never to her face, of course. She was far too formidable for that, and even proud, high-handed Mrs. Rockefeller sprang obediently to attention when Miss Gaines's boot heels echoed in the corridor.

"You've done a fine job, Sara, as always. Now, ladies, I think we should all take a short break. Sara, will you help Miss Felsinger and Mrs. Hughes pour lemonade?"

Sara went outside to wash her hands beneath the pump. The street beyond the schoolyard lay quiet in the heat haze, and, but for a single horse and buggy waiting in front of the drugstore, was completely deserted. Was it because of the heat or the war that there seemed to be less and less people about these days? Sara wasn't sure. All of them had been fortunate so far, as Miss Gaines liked to remind them, that they hadn't as yet felt the real pinch of war by being asked to make genuine sacrifices. The government had recently asked each family to save a pound of flour per week, and that was all.

Overseas, the situation was drastically different, of course. Since June, doughboys had been arriving in France at the rate of fifty thousand a month, and, once their battle training ended in October, they would be among the first Americans to be moved into the frontline trenches. Washington continued to draw numbers for the draft, and resisters had actually been threatened with execution. Recently, President Wilson had even proposed the drafting of aliens who lived in America.

So Rob wouldn't have been spared even if he hadn't volunteered, Sara thought.

Wearily, she dampened her handkerchief at the pump and dabbed her hot brow and cheeks. Beneath the straw boater she wore, her hair curled riotously because of the humidity. Sara brushed it back from her brow with an impatient hand, and as she did so she saw a high-wheeled black carriage with bright-red trim turn the corner and draw to a halt in the shade near the curb. The man driving it wore a blue suit and a bowler. He had discarded the suit jacket on the seat beside him and rolled up his sleeves, revealing deeply tanned forearms.

Catching sight of Sara, he wound the reins about the carriage brake and leaned back, hooking his thumbs beneath his suspenders and stretching his long legs before him.

"Well?" he called, when she made no move toward him but just stood there staring, her hand arrested on the brim of her hat, her heart beating a wild tattoo. "Would you care to go driving with me or not, lass?"

Sara glanced back at the school. Miss Gaines was expecting her to pour lemonade. There were more bandages to roll and various items of clothing to sew. "I—I can't."

"Afraid?" Rob jeered.

She tossed her head. "Certainly not."

"Come on, then. I haven't got all day." And he grinned at her so disarmingly that Sara's heart turned over. She ran to him then, and Rob, laughing, lifted her up beside him. Picking up the reins, he urged the horse away at a spanking pace.

There were dozens of questions that leaped to Sara's mind. Where had he come from? Where had he been? How long was he staying? Why wasn't he in uniform? Had he failed to join the army after all, and had he—she scarcely dared entertain the forbidden thought—come back to Madison because of her?

"You've grown up in the few months I've been away."

"Kind of you to notice," Sara said tartly.

"Still the prickly little thing, aren't you?"

She ignored this. "Where are we going?"

"For a drive. I haven't much time."

"Oh."

He glanced at her averted face, at her proud profile with its womanly curve of cheek and throat, and her lovely, childishly transparent blue eyes. He'd all but moved mountain and earth just to arrange this particular leave, and although he knew he was going to disappoint her, he wasn't about to waste time making amends. "I'm sailing for France next week."

"Oh?" She sounded offhand, but he could sense the effort it cost her.

"Aye. The First American Division's been ordered to Lorraine. I've less than two days to set my affairs in order."

She turned to him, her eyes filled with sudden anger. "And am I to be one of those affairs, Rob Buchanan? Is that why you came here out of uniform? To be more circumspect? Well, at least you were right about that. There aren't many doughboys showing their faces around Morris County these days."

Rob let his breath out in a long, low whistle. "What an unjust accusation, Miss Ashford! That temper must go with that hair. No, I haven't come to take advantage of you. I've come to take you to lunch. Where do you suggest we go?"

Sara, nonplussed, told him.

Off the Morris and Essex Turnpike sat a lovely, two-story farmhouse that had recently been converted into an inn, with boarding rooms upstairs and a number of small, cozy dining rooms below. The establishment was run by Mrs. Homer Whaley, a widow whose hospitality and culinary expertise had earned her inn, Westwood Manor, an impressive reputation and provided her, as well, with a comfortable means of support.

Rob's buggy drew to a halt beneath the towering oaks in the front yard, and Mrs. Whaley herself appeared at the screen door, a smile of welcome lighting her eyes as her gaze fell on Sara. "Sara Ashford! How are you, dear? It's been months since your father brought you in for ice cream." Her lively gaze rested with interest on the burly Scotsman who helped Sara to the ground.

"Hello, Mrs. Whaley." Sara stooped to kiss the soft, scented cheek. "It's lovely to see you too. Dad's been awfully busy, so we haven't had time for ice cream excursions. This is Mr. Buchanan, a . . . a friend."

"How do you do, Mr. Buchanan. Please, come inside. I've taken on three boarders this month, but they've already eaten and gone back to work."

"Oh, dear. I hope there's something left for us?"

"Now, Sara. You should know better than to ask."

They followed her into the dark, raftered hall, where they were assailed by the delicious smell of simmering stew spiced with onions and garlic. Mrs. Whaley led them to the smaller dining room, where the windows opened onto a lovely view of the rolling lawn and the deep green of hemlocks and hickory trees. At her request, they seated themselves at a small table directly beneath it, covered with a checkered cloth and crisp white napkins.

Mrs. Whaley peered twinkling from one young face to the other. "Special occasion, is it? How about a bottle of wine? I'd be glad to scoot down to the cellar for something special."

Sara blushed, but Rob remained calmly in control. "I believe Miss Ashford would prefer lemonade, thank you, and I'll take a beer. Ale, if you have it."

She bustled away, marvelously discreet, and Rob grinned at Sara when they were alone. "She seems very fond of you."

"Oh, no. She fusses that way over everybody who comes in to eat."

"But I get the feeling she doesn't 'scoot into the cellar' for just anyone."

"No, I guess not. She's fond of my stepfather, you know. He was the one who suggested she sell her marvelous pies and ice cream from the front room of her house after Mr. Whaley died. The idea caught on, and now she's got a regular restaurant downstairs and paying boarders upstairs."

"Tell me about your stepfather."

"You've already met him."

"Aye. And he seems a fair enough fellow. Has he got his range established yet?"

"No. With one thing and the other he never got around to it. And he sort of lost interest when you went away."

"You seem to get on well with him."

"Yes. He's always been kind to me, and we've been friends from the start. It helped that we shared some common interests. Horses and the like."

"How old were you when you came to live at Haversham?"

"Thirteen."

"And before that?"

Sara told him, describing Bellehurst the way she remembered it, and painting for him the rich tapestry of her childhood in a manner that couldn't help but bring it alive for both of them. Rob listened quietly, his eyes on her face, and Sara didn't stop talking until Mrs. Whaley bustled in with steaming platters of stew and assorted side dishes, which she set down with a flourish before bustling out again.

"I've probably bored you," Sara said apologetically.

"Not at all." Rob's own childhood had been entirely different. The coldness of his aloof, authoritarian father, and the pitiable invalid who had been his mother had never filled the gloomy, musty-smelling depths of their enormous house off the Royal Mile in Edinburgh with warmth. "No wonder you miss it."

He sounded as though he meant it, and Sara's heart swelled with gratitude. "I intend to go back someday. As soon as the war's over and it's safe to travel again. I thought it would be nice if—" She broke off, because mention of the war had suddenly reminded her that Rob was a soldier now; that he was going away to fight in that war; that this magical luncheon was, for him, just an interlude between the rigors of Camp Dix and the shell-torn trenches of France.

"I forgot," she said, with a slight tremor in her voice, "you're going away." Her eyes, glass-clear and as blue as the sky, turned on him, and they were the eyes of a woman, not a little girl any longer. "Do you really have to go?"

"Aye."

Her eyes continued to hold his, and it was almost as if she could see her own aching loneliness reflected within them. "Why did you come back?" she asked in a whisper.

Rob shook his head, unable to explain to her what he didn't know for certain himself.

"Well, then, here we are."

The arrival of Mrs. Whaley with two enormous slabs of chocolate cake drizzled with rum-flavored cherry sauce saved Rob from having to answer. Grateful for the reprieve, he turned the conversation along other lines.

Later, after they had eaten and were driving down the dusty road in the direction of the Academy, he was filled with an unfamiliar sense of uncertainty. Sara had unwittingly put her finger on the one nagging question he could not have answered. Why *had* he come back? There was really nothing for him to settle in New Jersey before leaving for France. His decision to come back had seemed reasonable, even logical, while he was still away at camp, but now, with Sara sitting in a decidedly awkward silence beside him, he was at a loss to explain why he was here. "Look, Sara—" he began.

"Rob—"

They had both spoken at the same time and now, catching each other's eyes, they laughed easily together. The tension between them was magically gone.

"You go first," Rob said.

"It wasn't really important. I was just going to ask you if you'd mind turning left down that lane there. The one behind the trees."

"And where does it lead?"

"To Powder's Mill. Have you ever been there?"

"Never even heard of it."

"Oh, then you'll love it. If you have the time," she added.

Rob did, and because there was a car trundling toward them along the main road, a car which might very well contain someone they knew or, worse, who would know them, it seemed a timely suggestion to him to turn the buggy down the shady lane Sara had indicated. Moments later they were bumping across an uneven stretch of ground that opened onto a clearing surrounded by statuesque oaks. Here, the sound of rushing water came to them on the breeze, and the horse pricked his ears and nickered longingly.

"I know how he feels," Rob said with a laugh. "I could use a drink myself." Stopping the buggy, he climbed out and held out his hands to Sara. "May I help you down, madam?"

Perhaps it was the beauty of the sun-dappled clearing and the warm smell of decaying leaves and summer wildflowers that had served to replace his doubts with a sudden sense of exhilaration. Sara seemed to have sensed it as well, for she smiled at him without a trace of self-consciousness and held out her hands to him willingly. They strolled together to the bottom of the clearing, where the land dipped dramatically to reveal a view of spellbinding wonder.

A shallow river, flanked by ferns and tangled undergrowth, rushed past them, frothing and churning over massive boulders and beds of bright stones. Downstream stood the mill, a square, raftered building of considerable age built of the same native stone, and set amid a field of wild blooming daisies. The mill's big water wheel spun idly, but from where he stood Rob could see that the water had been dammed off some time ago so that the current no longer flowed through it.

"The mill went out of business a few years ago," Sara told him, following his gaze. "It's a shame, actually. My stepfather used to bring me here to watch them grinding. There was always so much going on. Men and donkeys carrying enormous sacks, dogs barking, and Mr. Ketcham, the miller, always cursing about something."

"You were lucky to have seen it. It's a way of life that is, I think, drawing to an end. Wait and see, soon everything having to do with agriculture is going to be mechanized."

"Is that your professional opinion, Mr. Buchanan?" Sara teased.

"Aye."

"Then what on earth will you do with yourself? After the war, I mean? Will there be work for a botanist to do, or will machines make you obsolete?"

"There will be more than ever for a man like me to do," Rob answered seriously. "Once the war ends we're going to have to feed most of France and Belgium, perhaps even Russia, if Premier Kerensky doesn't succeed in making order out of the chaos. European farmers will have to become a hundred times more productive than they've ever been, and it's going to take university-trained horticulturists like myself to help them do it."

Sara looked at him wonderingly. "Then you're going back to England when it's all over."

"Yes. I thought you were planning to do the same?"

"I was."

"Then why should I come back here?"

Their eyes met and held for a long moment, and all at once Sara was aware of a deep feeling of joy that swelled within her heart and gave wings to her being. It was as if, in that one shared look, they had discussed their future and decided it between them.

"You'll wait for me, of course." The smile that touched Rob's mouth and gray eyes seemed to soften the craggy planes of his face.

"Of course I will," Sara whispered. "But you're the one who's going to have to wait. I'm the one with all the growing up to do."

"No. No, that isn't true." Rob's smile was gone, replaced by an intensity that seemed to shiver through her. Taking one of her hands, he turned it over and kissed the inside of her palm. Gently he closed her fingers around it as though he would have her hold the kiss there forever.

"Now," he said softly, "I think it's time I took you back. Miss Gaines will be wondering what's become of you."

For a moment Sara regarded him blankly, then the color rushed to her face and her eyes grew enormous. She said breathlessly, "Oh, God! Whatever am I going to tell them?"

Rob laughed. "You'll think of something, I'm sure. It's a crafty little beastie you are."

She laughed too, and Rob reached out unexpectedly to take her face in his hands and press his lips to that lovely, laughing mouth. Unashamed, the blood singing through her veins, Sara wrapped her arms about his neck and returned his kiss with a sweet innocence that astonished and disarmed him. They were both of them breathless when they drew apart at last.

"Come on," Rob said gruffly, taking her hand.

Sara held back. "Will I see you again before you go?"

"If you behave yourself, aye."

She heard nothing from Rob the following day or the next. Although she knew that he would keep his word, she couldn't help fretting. Their time together was so terribly important and so terribly short, and she deeply resented Earl Gibson and anyone else who was keeping him from her.

When Rob did show up at last, Sara was hopelessly unprepared for him. Archer had recently purchased another colt from a breeder in Narragansett, a lovely liver bay with a beautiful, flowing gait and a skittish temperament to match his fiery looks. Sara had asked if she might break him, and Archer had agreed on the condition that she school him only

when her mother was away from home. Gwen was, and
always had been, afraid of horses.

On this, a blindingly bright summer morning, Gwen had
asked Thompson to drive her to the train station. Despite the
heat, she intended to spend the day in New York visiting her
aunt Isadora, Adeline's younger sister, whose usual habit was
to shuttle back and forth between her homes in Newport and
Palm Beach. As the widow of a wealthy industrialist, Isadora
rarely took time to visit her niece at Haversham because she
was forever traveling here and there with a great gaggle of
equally well-heeled, widowed friends. Gwen had asked her
daughter to accompany her, but Sara, terrified of missing a
call from Rob, had pleaded a headache and so got out of it.

Later, after Gwen had gone, she appeared downstairs
dressed in a man's cotton shirt and work chaps. In the cool
of the stables she slipped a halter onto the colt and led him
out into the paddock. Here, the sun was climbing into a hot
blue sky, and the air smelled of dust and hay and freshly
mown grass.

For the past two years, Sara had been helping her stepfather
school his horses in preparation for the show driving competi-
tions he loved. She, too, had developed an interest in the
sport after discovering that driving from the box was an art
which required a considerable amount of patience and effort
to learn. It was a challenge she had readily accepted in the
hopes of easing the boredom of the genteel life Gwen expected
her to lead.

The splendid colt, as yet unnamed, was intended to work
in tandem with Bajazzo, Archer's prize hackney leader. Ever
since the summer holidays had begun, Sara had taken over
his longe-line schooling, which was designed to assure the
proper development and strengthening of the young animal's
muscles. Now, letting the line play out between her fingers,
she flicked the whip and urged him into a trot.

For several minutes the colt moved in an obedient circle
around her. Sara used verbal commands to slow him to a
walk, then coax him back to a trot. Pleased with his progress,
she finally urged him to a canter, but the colt responded by

exploding into a fit of bucking, showering her with a cloud of dust.

Coughing and gasping, Sara reeled in the line until she was able to grab the animal by the halter. Aware of her anger, he quieted at once and stood trembling beneath her hand. His beautiful coat was covered with dusty sweat, and Sara, wiping the grit from her eyes, was grimly aware that she looked no better.

"Is this how you keep busy when you're na rollin' bandages?"

Sara whirled with a gasp to find Rob Buchanan leaning against the fence grinning at her. She knew an instant of piercing joy at the sight of him before embarrassed color flamed in her cheeks. For just an instant the teachings of her mother and her Great-aunt Beatrice tolled like doom in her head: a lady did not sweat in the presence of a gentleman. A lady never allowed herself to become dirty. A lady never wore trousers no matter the circumstances.

In the next moment she found herself laughing out loud. This was Rob, not some drawing-room grandee, and one of the many things she was learning to love about him was his complete disregard of her unconventional ways. Indeed, no matter how strangely she might look or behave, she knew that, to him, it would never mátter.

And it didn't. Vaulting the fence in one easy motion, Rob came to stand beside her. Taking the lead line from her, he spoke soothingly to the uneasy colt. "I'm on my way to Chatham. Would you like to come?"

Sara nodded, delighted.

"Then put up this handsome fellow and go tell your stepfather. The ghillie who answered the front door said your mother wasn't home."

Sara laughed. "That was Carruthers, and he doesn't take kindly to being called a servant. And I can't go just yet. I have to wash and change first."

He frowned at her. "What for?"

Sara stared at him, arms akimbo. "Why, just look at me!"

Rob did and, grinning, told her he liked what he saw. But

Sara was adamant. She would not ride in the buggy with him, dressed like a cowboy and smelling of horses. And so Rob was obliged to wait in the cool of the kitchen with the very flustered Mrs. Haverty while Sara ran upstairs to set her appearances to rights.

Her heart was singing as she peeled off her clothes and tossed them into the corner. There wasn't time to bathe; she couldn't bear to be away from Rob that long, so she gritted her teeth and sponged herself off with the cold water in the basin. A vigorous brushing loosened the dust from her hair and gave it the sheen of burnished copper. Twisting it in a knot and pinning it hastily to her head with a pair of tortoise-shell combs, Sara slipped into a crisp white blouse and blue skirt and, lastly, a pair of gloves. On her way out through the bedroom door she grabbed a hat with trailing feathers.

In the kitchen she found Rob sitting in Mrs. Haverty's prized Windsor chair with a chilled tankard of ale at his elbow, looking every inch a man who felt utterly at home. Sara turned her arch gaze in the cook's direction, but for once Mrs. Haverty refused to meet her eye.

Pursing her lips to conceal her amusement, Sara looked at Rob. "Ready?"

The chair creaked as he got up. The pleasure in his gaze as he looked at her made Sara feel as giddy as the blushing Mrs. Haverty. They went out together, walking side by side in companionable silence. As they crossed the drive to the buggy, Rob said, "Did you tell your father where you're going?"

"I left a message with Carruthers."

"That's all you need to do?"

"Yes, why?"

"Well, because—" He frowned. "Because I like to think it isn't every day that you go off alone with a fellow your father hasn't officially received."

Sara was touched. "You're the first," she assured him. "And I promise you it would be entirely different if Mother were home. But she's not, and since Dad's putting one of his ponies through its paces at the track, he won't be back for hours. Even if he was, he'd never object to the company I keep. He thinks very highly of you.''

"As a botanist, yes. Not as a man taking his stepdaughter alone on a drive.''

"Where is it we're going?''

"To the Coleson range on Chatham Turnpike. Mr. Coleson asked if I'd look in on his roses before I left town. They've come down with some sort of blight his foreman can't treat. Since Haversham was on the way, I thought I'd stop in to fetch you first. Do you mind?''

"Of course not.'' Sara didn't care where they went as long as they went together.

It was nearly three o'clock before Rob finished his inspection of Ezra Coleson's range. Sara had waited for him in the buggy beneath the branches of a spreading oak, unwilling to get in the way while the men discussed business. Eventually, tired of sitting on the hard bench, she got out and began wandering up and down beneath the trees, her hat trailing by its ribbons down her back. When Rob finally returned to her, he smiled and gently set it back on her head.

"I'm sorry. I had no idea it would take so long.''

"Well, I'm hot and thirsty now,'' Sara told him archly. "I hope you intend to do something about it?''

He handed her up into the buggy. "Well, there's only one thing a gentleman can do when a lady complains of the heat.''

"What's that?''

"Buy her ice cream.''

Rob halted the buggy in front of the Essex Turnpike Inn, a lovely clapboard building standing on a shady corner lot in Chatham's charming town center. Leaving Sara in the buggy, he disappeared through the screen door and returned a moment later with two wafer cones topped by enormous scoops of peach ice cream.

"Oh, this is heavenly,'' Sara sighed as he got in beside her.

"The ice cream, or being here with me?''

"Both,'' she answered seriously.

There was a brief silence while Rob maneuvered the buggy around a slow-moving truck that was loaded down with grain sacks. When the wide road lay before them once again and the houses and storefronts of Chatham had given way to rolling corn fields, Rob said softly, "I have to go away."

Sara froze. "When?"

"Tomorrow. I'm due back at Camp Dix."

"Are you being shipped out?"

"Aye."

"Will it . . . will it be dangerous?"

"We're not being sent to the front right away, if that's what you mean. We'll spend a month or so training with the French infantry first."

"Will you write me?"

"Of course."

The ice cream, unnoticed, had melted. Sara tossed the cone away. Wordlessly, Rob handed her his handkerchief. She wiped her fingers and then, under the pretense of doing the same to her lips, dabbed away her tears so that he wouldn't see her crying. She kept her head bowed. She did not trust herself to speak.

After a while the buggy bore to the left and began bumping down an uneven road. Sara looked up to see that they were on the deserted lane that led to Powder's Mill. She glanced quickly at Rob, but his face was averted.

Eventually the buggy halted in the shade at the edge of the clearing. Rob wound the reins about the brake and climbed out. His expression was oddly grim as he held out his arms to help Sara down. He did not look at her. Instead, he led her wordlessly into the clearing. The water level in the river bed had dropped considerably during the week. The thundering current was gone, replaced by a gentle murmur.

In the clearing, amid the droning bees and the gently waving flowers, Rob turned Sara to him. Because she still wouldn't look at him, he tipped her chin with his forefinger. She felt him start as his eyes met hers.

"For God's sake," he said gruffly, "don't cry." Putting his arms around her, he drew her closer until her head lay against the curve of his arm. "I canna bear it when you cry."

"I don't know how I'm going to bear saying good-bye to you," Sara whispered.

"Or I to you. Surely you ken by now why I came back. I had no choice. You've never been far from my thoughts since I went away."

"Nor you from mine."

"I was going to write you. You can't imagine how many times I started a letter."

"But you never did."

"No. I thought it would be better to come back and tell you myself that—" His gruff voice trailed away.

"Tell me what?" Sara whispered.

"That I think I'm in love with you."

"Oh," she said. "Oh—" But her words ended on a sigh as Rob lowered his head and kissed her. The moment his mouth touched hers, Sara felt passion stir within her, awakening from the long, dormant sleep of youth. Her mouth softened beneath his and her arms slid up around his neck. Rob groaned as her body melted against the length of his. Tossing aside her hat, he unpinned her hair and let the glorious wealth of it spill into his hands. His mouth found hers again, and as the heated touch ignited dark desire, they sank together into the grass.

The breeze caressed them, the grass buoyed them as they lay together, while the touch of Rob's hands and lips showed Sara the wonder, the enchantment of love and the undeniable pull of two young bodies that had been made to fit together. She wrapped her arms and legs about him, and her lips beneath his became as soft and yielding as the petals of a rose.

She returned his kisses and gave herself over to the pleasure of loving him, of feeling her body rise up in offering, unafraid, unashamed. Looking into his eyes, she knew that he yearned for her as much as she did for him; that he wanted nothing and no one else. He pulled her to him and when he made her a part of him she gave a gasp of mingled pain and pleasure, then arched herself against him. Only the murmurous river was witness to the wondrous ending of her girlhood.

Chapter
Twenty-seven

Sara did her best to keep busy. With Rob gone, there was nothing else left to do. The winter was endless, and because school and the Red Cross were no longer enough to keep her occupied, she signed up for special nursing classes in the auditorium at Drew Theological Seminary. Gwen was not pleased by this, but Archer, surprisingly enough, encouraged her. There was a new dimension to their relationship these days, a maturity that had never existed before, and when Sara calmly announced one morning that she intended to go to medical school rather than waste time making her debut, it was Archer who championed her cause in the face of her mother's bitter opposition.

But the winter was not entirely disharmonious. Sometimes the three of them dined out, or paid visits to friends who like them, had chosen, despite the cold, to remain in the country. Once, Archer took both of them to the cinema to see Theda Bara in her stirring role as Cleopatra, and twice they ventured out into the bitter weather to see Mary Pickford star in *The Little Princess*.

Nevertheless, Archer's enormously flourishing business demanded considerable attention and so, of necessity, he was often away in New York and, occasionally, in Washington. Gwen moped and complained whenever he was gone, and she was sufficiently bored, as the new year turned, to threaten leaving him and withdrawing to Palm Beach. Archer merely laughed at this, while Sara paid no attention to her mother's unending theatrics. There was a considerable difference, she felt, between being deprived of one's man simply because of business commitments and sending him off to the Western Front.

In February, Sara celebrated her seventeenth birthday. Though the weather was ugly and they had been forced for some time now to ration fuel, Gwen insisted on having a party. It would be nothing elaborate, she promised when Sara protested, but hopefully something festive enough to relieve the tedium of winter.

"We'll have dancing, and perhaps a few parlor games to get things started, and as for supper . . . Hmm. I wonder if a buffet would do?"

"How many people do you intend asking?"

"I don't know. We'd better start a list."

"May I invite a few of my own friends?"

"But of course, dear. It's your party."

But Gwen was not pleased with the modest list Sara produced, under considerable prodding, several days later. They were mostly the names of fellow nursing students whom Sara had met at Drew, and were not what Gwen considered a suitable mix. There was no point in arguing the matter, however. In recent weeks Sara had become exasperatingly stubborn about certain things, and Gwen had already learned to recognize the warning signs in the set of the girl's jaw and the spark of anger in her eyes.

She was growing up to be exactly like that English grandmother of hers, Gwen would tell herself with a shake of the head. Adeline, her own mother, God bless her, had often said Lady Ladbroke was one of the most unreasonable women she'd ever met when it came to making up her mind about something. It had to be in the blood, Gwen feared, and blood, regrettably, was something a person could not change.

So Sara went ahead and invited whomever she wished to her party and, as Gwen had feared, ended up turning the affair into an unqualified disaster. First off, they had made the mistake of allowing Alma Wylie to talk them into hiring the Madison Cornet Band for entertainment. While it couldn't be helped, considering that they were the only musicians in the area whose ranks had not been decimated by the draft, the sound of their brass instruments blaring out such popular

revue pieces as George Gershwin's "Swanee" destroyed any
hope of providing the genteel atmosphere Gwen craved. Furthermore, the nursing students Sara had invited were exactly
as gauche as Gwen had expected, and there was a palpable
chill in the air as the privileged daughters and sons of the
Four Hundred dined in clannish silence at the buffet, danced
with each other, and pointedly ignored the rest.

At a quarter after nine that evening, Sara stood beneath the
archway of Haversham's drawing room watching all of this
with a fixed smile on her face. She felt sorry for her friends,
sorry for her mother, and, for once, even sorry for herself.
Oh, what she wouldn't give to be upstairs right now soaking
in a boiling hot bath!

A cold draft lifted the hem of her party dress, and she
turned to see Archer stepping into the foyer, borne in from
the garage by an icy blast of wind. Handing his hat and cane
to Carruthers, he crossed to his stepdaughter and fondly kissed
her cheek. "Happy birthday, my dear."

"I'm so glad you could make it," Sara said, feeling inex-
pressibly relieved to see him.

"I promised I'd be back in time, didn't I?" Archer cast a
swift glance around the gaily festooned drawing room. "Uh
oh. Looks like they've split into enemy camps."

"I had a feeling this would happen, only Mother didn't
believe me. Whatever should I do, Dad? All of my friends
from school look bored, and I never realized before what
horrible snobs the others could be!"

"Don't worry about a thing. I'll handle it."

She regarded him suspiciously. "What will you do?"

"Trust me. I've got a grand idea. Oh, and, here——" He
reached into his vest pocket and withdrew a sheaf of envelopes. "Your birthday mail. I picked it up on my way out
this morning."

Sara leafed through them quickly. There were the usual
greetings from neighbors and friends, and a card bearing
Grandpa Lawrence's spidery signature. Another was from
Howard, the oldest of Archer's two sons, who lived in Boston
and rarely came to Haversham, but who always remembered
to send birthday and Christmas salutations. The other was

probably from Paul, his younger brother, currently fighting the Germans somewhere south of the Somme, and so Sara gave the bulky envelope with the foreign postmark barely a glance. There would be time to read it later. She was looking for a letter from her grandmother.

But there was none. Sara sorted through them once more just to make sure. She knew that Grandmama would never forget her birthday, so it had to be the war. This bloody, stupid, insane war.

Sara put the cards and letters down on the hall table. She might as well rejoin her guests in the drawing room, where, from the sound of it, her stepfather had somehow managed to liven things up a bit. Paul's letter, lying on top of the neat stack, caught her eye one last time. And all at once Sara realized that it wasn't from Paul at all. The postmark read Calais, and the bold, dark lettering was nothing like Paul's haphazard scrawl. Sara picked it up and went quickly into the library, shutting the door behind her. Curling up in Archer's big leather chair, she opened the envelope and unfolded the densely written pages.

Amiens
December 20, 1917

My dearest lassie:

To make certain these birthday greetings reach you in time, I'm sending them early with a mate from the F.O. who's been granted Christmas leave. Hopefully they'll reach you in time to let you know that you are never far from my thoughts, especially now, on your seventeenth birthday.

I can't begin to imagine how you will celebrate such an auspicious day, though I can only hope it won't involve another party like the one on New Year's at Red Gate Farm when that daft Jenkins lad drove your father's car right through Seth Thomas's barn wall. If you only knew how much

I wanted to kiss you that day . . . but no more
than I long to kiss you now, and hold you close to
my heart.

I'm certain you've heard that the Germans plan
to negotiate a peace treaty with the Russians at
Brest Litovsk. We've heard similar rumors, but
they remain, as always, just rumors. We take very
little as truth here in the Allied trenches, although
we're well aware that a German-Russian peace
would bode ill for those of us here on the front
line, since the kaiser would then be free to relieve
the Eastern Front and send his troops to face us in
the west.

I can imagine you now, frowning and fretting
over such news and jumping to alarming
conclusions. You mustn't fear for me, darling
Sara. I'm reasonably well fed, in jovial holiday
spirits, and can't help believing that we'll be
together soon. *In'shallah*, as your wise English
grandmother would doubtlessly say. Remember
always that you promised to wait for me, because
I plan to hold you to your word.
With fondest birthday wishes, my love,
Rob

Down the hall, the Madison Cornet Band had broken into a
raucous marching tune. Sara could hear the enthusiastic
cheers and stomping of feet in time to the lively beat. She
got up slowly and folded Rob's letter carefully away. Out in
the hallway she ran into Bella Jenkins, glowing with exertion,
her curls clinging damply to her face.

"There you are, Sara! They've sent me to fetch you. We're
having such fun! Do you know what your father's done?"

"No."

"Organized a *dancing contest*! Can you *imagine*? With
prizes for the best couple and everything! What a grand idea!
Oh, I do think this is the loveliest party you've ever had."

"I'm glad," said Sara.

Bella looked at her sharply. "You sound strange. Is anything wrong?"

"No," said Sara, and she smiled dreamily. "Everything's perfectly wonderful."

By the end of March, the Germans had moved three million troops to the Western Front. Launching a heavy attack on the fifty-mile line near Cambrai, they managed to push back the Allied forces and capture a number of strategic French towns. The British suffered heavy losses, and the prime minister moved quickly to appoint General Ferdinand Foch commander of the Allied armies.

In May, the Germans dumped fifteen thousand gas shells into American trenches. It was only the beginning of a massive new offensive, and within days the French forces had crumpled at Chemin des Dames while the victorious Germans crossed the Aisne River.

Archer had arranged for *The New York Times* to be delivered to the front door at Haversham every morning, and Sara arose early each day to scan the headlines. Every time, her heart beat with terrible apprehension at what she would find. Nevertheless, she took little notice of the descriptions of civil upheaval in Russia, the discovery of German war mines off Delaware Bay, or the downing of flying aces Raoul Lufberry and Manfred von Richthofen, the Red Baron. The bombing of Paris by the huge German howitzer "Big Bertha" evoked no sympathy either; American doughboys were being slaughtered at Amiens and Cantigny and that was all that mattered. Because Sara had no idea whether or not Rob was among them.

The worst part of it was waiting to find out. And tormenting herself with the thought that if Rob did die, how on earth would she ever know? Once, in a fit of sheer panic, she wrote a letter to his family in Scotland only to tear it up again when she realized that she had no idea where to send it. Finally, she had to acknowledge the awful fact that there was nothing she could do—except keep herself occupied and pray that one of Rob's own letters would somehow make it through.

* * *

June arrived, bringing with it the beguiling sweetness of another summer. Overseas, Germany launched its fourth great offensive of the war, and Archer took Gwen to Washington for the season, wanting her with him while he served time on the War Industries Board, to which he had recently been appointed.

Sara did not accompany them. Frantic at the thought of being away from home should a letter arrive from Rob, she dug in her heels and refused to leave. Gwen, resigned, offered little argument. After all, her daughter had never shown the slightest interest in any of the pursuits that should, by rights, come naturally to a privileged and very lovely girl of upper-class means. The lure of the lively Washington political scene meant nothing to her, and even Archer agreed that they would all be much happier if Sara stayed home.

"She's old enough now, I reckon. We'll find someone to keep an eye on her—your aunt Isadora would do just fine. I bet she'll jump at the chance to get out of Newport for a while, and it's just for a couple of months."

"But what will you do with yourself all summer, Sara?" Gwen asked, unconvinced.

"Why, keep on with the Red Cross and my classes at Drew."

Gwen's lips thinned. It was no secret that she disapproved of Sara's ambitions of becoming a nurse, and had secretly hoped that the girl's interest would wane as her studies grew increasingly difficult and her hours of volunteer work at Morristown's newly chartered halfway house increasingly long. Sara's talk about medical school dismayed Gwen as well.

Maybe I should have left her in England after all, she thought now, gazing into the set face of her daughter. The girl had grown alarmingly thin in recent weeks and seemed unusually quarrelsome. But although Gwen fretted about this, in the end she had no choice but to leave Sara in the care of Isadora—and Lawrence, who gladly agreed to leave his home in Madison and spend a few months at Haversham.

The house seemed much more peaceful with Gwen and Archer gone. Isadora Franklin, Adeline's younger sister, was the sort of person who firmly believed in the rights of privacy, and so she interfered little in Sara's affairs, preferring to spend her days curled on the divan with a scotch and water (never mind that the county had recently gone dry), reading Gwen's fashion advertisements and chain smoking cigarettes. She was a tall, rather alarming-looking woman, as uncaring of her appearance as Adeline had always agonized over hers, and Sara, who found her utterly refreshing, was genuinely fond of her.

Lawrence Parker was now well into his seventies, a tall, spare man, gray haired and very quiet, but of an amiable nature that made him welcome anywhere. He, too, spent most of his days reading books or pottering in the garden, and to Sara's relief, expressed his unqualified approval of her decision to take up nursing. In fact, the three of them—Lawrence, Sara, and Isadora—got on delightfully well.

"I'm off to class," Sara announced one particularly muggy afternoon, appearing in the doorway of the parlor in her calf-length blue and white uniform and sensible half boots, her hair plaited and pinned neatly to her head.

Lawrence, looking up from his newspapers, wished her well, while Isadora, nose buried in *The New Yorker*, merely waved a slim, braceleted arm in farewell. There were no questions, lectures, or veiled recriminations as there were whenever Sara took her leave of Gwen, and she felt a rush of relief and affection as she kissed them both and pedaled off on her bicycle in the direction of town.

Though she never let anyone see it, Sara was hurt by her mother's refusal to accept her decision to pursue a career. Sara longed to confide in Gwen, tell her that she intended marrying a Scotsman when the war was over and that the money she would earn nursing, while not grand in the least, would help make ends meet until Rob could get himself established.

The fact that she was destined to inherit a tidy sum of money herself when she married—inasmuch as both Archer and Rupert had settled sizable dowries upon her—never occurred to Sara. She had never paid the slightest attention to such matters, and, for her, it was perfectly natural that a wife should contribute equally to a marriage—which just went to show how much of her early life had been influenced by her strong-willed grandmother and aunt.

Today, Sara thought as she sped downhill, the tires of her bicycle swirling up clouds of dust, *today when I come home there will be a letter from Rob*.

It was a litany she repeated every day—one that she clung to and never allowed herself to doubt. Propping her bicycle against a tree on the lawn, she unpinned her hat and went into the cool, dark corridors of the Academy. The usual babble of female voices greeted her there. Miss Gaines had already organized several rows of basket packers and set a table or two aside for the seamstresses. Sara, who was hopelessly inept with a needle, went immediately to work stowing provisions.

"We're going to the theater tonight," someone said to her. "It's idle Monday. Want to come?"

"What's playing?"

"What else? Another Chaplin film."

Sara thought about this. "Yes," she said. "I'd like that."

"Great. Dottie's father said she could use the car. We'll pick you up at seven."

"Okay."

The rest of the afternoon was spent discussing the movies, and Sara's high spirits lingered as she pedaled homeward. She could not shake the certainty that today there would be a letter from Ron, and when she went inside, she paused at once at the hall table, where Carruthers always left the mail.

But there was nothing. Biting back her disappointment, Sara went up to her room to change.

Later that afternoon, the telephone rang. Isadora was upstairs soaking in the bath, and Lawrence had fallen asleep in the library armchair, his book slipping unnoticed to the floor. Sara got up quietly and went out to answer it.

"Haversham."

"Miss Sara Ashford, please." A man's voice, tinny and far away. Perhaps an acquaintance of Archer's, calling from Washington?

"Speaking."

"Miss Ashford, my name is Brant, Arthur Brant. I'm the chief horticulturist here at Whitewood range."

Whitewood. That was Earl Gibson's range. Why would anyone—

"Are you acquainted with a Mr. Rob Buchanan?"

Sara's heart froze. "Yes," she said faintly. "I am."

"Well, when he left for France he asked me to look out for you. Let you know if anything happened to him. I'm sorry, Miss Ashford. We got the news this morning. He's dead. Killed in combat somewhere east of Château-Thierry, on the Marne. I thought you'd want to know. Hello? Miss Ashford, are you there?"

"Yes, I'm here."

"I'm really very sorry."

"Yes. It . . . it was kind of you to call."

A long pause.

"Well, then, I'll be getting back to work. Good-bye, Miss Ashford."

"Yes," said Sara. "Good-bye."

Slowly she replaced the receiver. The hall was silent. The ormolu clock on the side table ticked quietly to itself. Sara put her face in her hands and did not stir for a very long time.

SEVEN
Peacocks and Lilies

Remember that the most beautiful things in the world
Are ofttimes the most useless;
Peacocks and lilies, for instance.

John Ruskin

Chapter
Twenty-eight

London awoke with a start. Gray dawn seeped through the open windows, and a warm breeze stirred the chintz curtains. For a moment she lay there confused, until the blurred, sloping ceiling became crystalline, like her memory, and she knew that she was home. Home at Rose Cottage, and today was Friday. Tomorrow, Saturday, was her birthday. She was going to be seventy-five years old.

"Bah." London rose slowly to her feet and spent some time stretching the aches from her joints and muscles. Then she dressed slowly, carefully, in a tweed skirt and gray cardigan and brushed and pinned her hair.

Downstairs, she was surprised to find the silent kitchen in a state of fomentation. The stone sink that had once been Ida Skelton's groaned with tins and buckets of flowers soaking in icy spring water. The kitchen door slammed and Sara came in disheveled, fresh-faced, as lovely as ever.

"Hello, Grandmama." She kissed London's soft, scented cheek. "I didn't wake you, did I?"

"Of course not. What have you been doing? Robbing my garden of its treasures? Does Mr. Brockman know?"

Sara began trimming the stems of dark purple irises, arranging them in an enormous ceramic jug. "Yes, he knows, and I'll admit he's none too happy. But he has no right to complain. Aunt Victoria rang last night and asked if I'd make some flower arrangements and bring them up to the house today. To give the house a festive air for your birthday."

"Bah," said London again. She moved about, brewing tea and setting out milk, scones, and marmalade while Sara continued snipping and arranging her armful of blooms. For a while there was contented silence in the kitchen. Outside the sun was rising higher, burning through the layers of mist, and the air came alive with the songs of birds.

London sat down at the table and spread jam on a yeasty roll. "Who is Victoria expecting today?"

"Louisa, Alice, and Winifred, with their families. And the Stours, I think."

London made a face. "Where's she putting them?"

"At the Paxton Hotel. We're all supposed to meet for supper there tonight. And tomorrow there's going to be a marquee erected on Bellehurst's lawn, so that right after breakfast the grand fete can begin."

"I cannot wait."

"You've grown nasty in your old age, Grandmama, did you know that?"

"For heaven's sake, child, what are you saying? I've been nasty all of my life. Now, put down those shears and have something to eat."

They breakfasted in companionable silence. London poured herself a second cup of tea. "This dinner at the hotel," she said eventually. "Is it supposed to be formal? Victoria hasn't been particularly communicative with me of late."

"She told me last night it was just for the family. A simple gathering so everyone could get acquainted again."

"And she's planned all of this on neutral ground? Well, well. Sometimes I think Victoria deserves more credit than I give her."

"Is there a problem you haven't told me about, Grandmama? Secret love affairs, skeletons in the closet, that sort of thing?"

"No, thank goodness. Diverse as we are, it's a relief to know that we're not the sort of family that—like some whose names shall remain unmentioned—provides constant fodder for the gossip mills." London helped herself to another roll. "As for family feuds, I can recall only one. Clarissa Stours once fancied herself in love with George Warburton's cousin, Archie. When Archie up and married Olivia, she didn't talk to either of them for years. But that's neither here nor there nowadays. Clarissa's long dead, and so is Archie."

"But you've kept in touch with Olivia."

"Always. She's one of my dearest friends, even though I haven't seen her since . . . goodness, I can't remember when."

"Is she coming to the party?"

"Regrettably not. She's far too old. Like me. That's perhaps the most grievous thing about it, Sara. Losing touch with your friends simply because you lack the youthful energy to travel long distances in order to see them. I just hope Nicholas can make it. Victoria said he was dreadfully noncommittal on the phone."

"Because of his work?"

"Yes. He's got a hugely successful veterinary practice up in the Lake District. I've never been there, and I would so like to see it. When was the last time you saw Nicholas?"

"At Grandpapa's funeral."

"What a sad time for a reunion. You were both children still."

Sara laughed. "Grandmama. I was twenty."

"There. You see? Barely out of small clothes."

Smiling, Sara pushed back her chair and began clearing the dishes from the table. "Nicholas and I became good friends the first time we met. That was during my last Christmas at Bellehurst, when Nicholas and his mother came to spend the holidays with us. But at Grandpapa's funeral we— I don't know. Things had changed." Abruptly, she turned back to the sink. For a moment there was silence.

"Are you curious about seeing him again?"

Sara considered. "No," she said honestly. "What interests

me more is seeing how Louisa and Lottie turned out, and meeting Winifred and Alice. And Nelson, the future Lord Ladbroke.''

London laughed, although it sounded suspiciously like a snort. "I'm afraid you're in for a disappointment, my dear.''

"So you've told me before. Now, would you be so sweet as to let me do the dishes? I'll wash them as soon as I've finished with the flowers.''

Gratefully, London agreed. "I'll ring Victoria in the meantime. See if there's anything I can do.''

Alone in the kitchen, Sara stacked the dishes beside the sink and cleared away the jam jars and remains of the bread. Then she returned to her flowers. There was a florist in Temple Lynn, but Aunt Victoria had said that he was hideously expensive and that she saw no reason why she should pay good money for overpriced hothouse hybrids when Rose Cottage's borders were fairly groaning with spring blooms.

Sara, surveying with some satisfaction the brilliant pink, yellow, purple, and white cuttings before her, was forced to agree. Now that the jug was crammed with lovely bearded irises, she set it aside and began filling another. Humming a little to herself, she thought back on the things her grandmother had said during breakfast. Remembering, despite herself, the last time she had been home—how sad and lonely the house had seemed without Grandpapa.

Her humming stopped. She remembered the faces of the mourners who had crammed the tiny church during the funeral, remembered Aunt Victoria's noisy sobbing, Eugenia's white-faced silence, and, especially, the quiet grief of her grandmother, who had seemed to Sara, all at once, to have grown shrunken and unbelievably old.

What had struck Sara too, upon returning home to Bellehurst after an absence of nearly ten years, was not only the change in her grandmother, but the terrible poverty in evidence everywhere. The postwar boom had ended, and England was in the throes of a grinding depression. Moreover, the country was bedeviled by deep political unrest, as characterized by army camp riots, youth movements, and labor strikes.

Sara had returned to a Bellehurst which little resembled the warm, cozy world she had left behind, a world out of time, a way of life that was forever gone, and she had been forced to grapple with this sense of loss equally as much as she mourned the loss of her grandfather. Time, it seemed, left nothing untouched.

First off there had been Aunt Victoria and Uncle William, who had, during Sara's absence, moved their noisy brood of children into Bellehurst and made it their permanent home. None of the renovations had been completed then, and the house seemed to have lost much of its warmth and charm with her grandfather's passing.

Secretly, Sara had resented the intrusion of Victoria's offspring into what had once been her own, private world.

"But that's pure selfishness on my part, of course," Sara had confessed to Aunt Eugenia on the morning of Rupert's funeral as the two of them walked together through the barren garden. "I want things to be just the way they were before I left. Which is ridiculous, I know. Everything in life must change sooner or later."

"But some things never do," Eugenia countered with a faint smile.

"What do you mean?"

"You. You're all grown up, Sara. And quite Americanized, whether you realize it or not. I understand you've taken up nursing in Madison hospital?"

"So?"

"But your feelings for Bellehurst don't seem to have changed one bit."

"Oh, Aunt Eugenia. How can they? This has always been my home."

"There, you see?"

"I only wish—" Sara glanced over her shoulder, through the lace of barren branches toward the house where the black crepe draped over the front portal bellied in the wind. "I only wish I'd made it back in time to see him again."

"I cabled as soon as we realized how serious it was."

"I know. I'm grateful."

"We're the ones who are grateful to you, my dear. Your

being here has made quite a difference to Mum.'' Aunt Eugenia's expression was kind. Now, approaching forty and widowed for the last five years, she was nonetheless still
beautiful, with a gamin sort of beauty emphasized by her
slender, athletic shape and the boyish Eton crop in which she
had cut her hair. Though she was modestly dressed for the
funeral, her dark skirt was fashionably shorter than anyone
else's, and she wore silk stockings, the sight of which had
made Beatrice, upon seeing them for the first time that morning, gasp in disbelief.

The church bell in the valley began to toll. Eugenia put her
arm around Sara. "Come on. It's time to go."

The family drove down to the village in William's big
Daimler. The tiny church was already crowded with mourners, but the Ladbroke pew remained vacant. Sara seated herself between London and Victoria. All the women of the
family, even Eugenia, wore heavy black veils. Through hers,
hazily, Sara could make out the catafalque standing before
the altar, the hatchment blazing with gilding, and, below it,
the deep, ceremonial red of the drapery that covered the heavy
coffin itself. Upon it rested a velvet cushion bearing the late
baron's breastplate and various badges of honor, surmounted
above by the Ladbroke arms.

Sara's eyes burned with sudden tears and she looked away
quickly. The Reverend Thomas Trask, a younger, thinner,
and far more somber version of the long-dead Mr. Wynstaffe,
took his place at the podium. The service began. The wind
moaned beyond the thick stone walls, setting the candles
guttering. Sara shivered and wished she had worn gloves.

During the hymn there was a small disturbance at the entrance of the chapel. A latecomer had arrived, and people
were moving aside so that he could make his way quietly
down the aisle. He slid into the pew next to William, who
sat on the outside to the left of his wife. Victoria, sobbing
noisily into a handkerchief, didn't bother looking up. Sara
glanced toward him discreetly, without moving her head, but
she could see nothing beyond the bowed and quivering form
of her aunt.

It was over at last. Sara helped her grandmother rise, and

London clung for a moment to her granddaughter's arm, as though she needed its youthful strength. The family pew emptied first while the other mourners waited respectfully in their seats. Stepping out into the aisle, Sara came face to face with the latecomer. His green eyes were solemn, his expression unsmiling. With a curt nod to Sara, he took London's arm and led her toward the door.

Sara stared after them, shaken by a rush of bewildered anger. Oh, it wasn't fair! How dare he! How dare Nicholas Warburton grow up looking just like Rob Buchanan? There could be no mistaking those rugged features, the dark eyes and black hair, although there was more to it than just a catalogue of coloring. It was the broadness of Nicholas's shoulders, his mocking expression, even the same, intriguing cleft in the chin. How could it have happened? And to him, of all people?

Outside in the windy churchyard rain had begun to fall. Dark clouds scudded across the lowering sky. Sara saw Nicholas bend his head to say something to her grandmother. Although London was tall, he seemed to tower over her. Lifting her veil, London touched his cheek in a fond caress. She said something in response, and then he was hurrying her toward the waiting car. Angry, bitter, shaken to the core of her being, Sara followed more slowly.

"What do you think of him?" London asked. She and Sara were alone in the parlor. The mourners who had been invited to the house after the funeral had all gone home, while the rest of the family had withdrawn, one by one, to other rooms and other pursuits. Now only London and Sara remained, the one sitting calmly but wearily in a wide-lapped chair, the other gazing with restless eyes out into the wet, windy night.

Sara stirred, lifted her head. "Who?"

"Nicholas. It's been eight years. My, how he's changed. Grown up. You did know he was married?"

"Yes, you wrote. His wife didn't come."

"No. She's in Edinburgh, visiting Livvy."

"They have no children?"

"Not yet."

Sara yawned. Stretching her arms over her head, she came slowly to her feet. "Are you hungry? Shall I ask Mrs. Jakes to bring you a snack? Or something to drink?"

"No thank you, dear. I'm going to sit here for a little while longer and then go to bed. What about you? We've hardly had a moment to speak together since you came. Are you comfortable up there in your tiny room?"

Sara smiled. "Oh, Grandmama, how can you ask? It's wonderful being home. Even . . . even under the circumstances." She walked around the small table separating them and kissed her grandmother's cheek. "Good night."

"Sleep well, my darling."

In the doorway, Sara hesitated. Glancing over her shoulder, she saw that her grandmother had closed her eyes and was leaning her head against the back of the chair. Something in her still face made Sara's heart skip a beat. Softly, she closed the door behind her and stood for a moment in the dark corridor grappling with her tears. When she looked up again, Nicholas Warburton was standing before her. She hadn't heard him approach, and she had no idea how long he had been watching her.

"Is she all right?"

"I think so. Just very tired."

"Why didn't you persuade her to go to bed?"

"Impossible. Her rooms are right below the nursery, and with all the iced cake Aunt Victoria's children had today they'll be up for hours yet."

"Do you mind if I give it a try?"

Sara smiled at him with considerable relief. "As a matter of fact, I'd be extremely grateful."

Giving her arm a reassuring squeeze, Nicholas went past her into the parlor. Sara stood for a long moment staring thoughtfully after him. How kind he was, and understanding, too. Regrettably, she knew that she would always resent him a little, no matter how friendly they might become, if only because of the way he looked.

The following afternoon the family gathered in the parlor for the difficult task of reading Rupert's will. The children were sent to the nursery with the stern admonition to behave themselves while the servants cleared away the remains of the funeral tea and whispered among themselves in the subdued manner that is usually reserved for a house visited recently by death.

Sara was surprised when Mr. Thornby, the family solicitor, asked her to join them. She knew that Grandpapa had left everything to his wife and daughters, and couldn't imagine why she should be included. But there was a special bequest for her after all, one that brought tears to her eyes, because it was so like Grandpapa to remember how much they had enjoyed reading and studying together when she had been young: he had left her the contents of his library.

"But some of those books are valuable first editions!" Uncle William had protested.

Sara cast an embarrassed glance at her grandmother, but it was Nicholas who said calmly, "Surely Lord Ladbroke had his reasons, William. Sara is enrolled at university in America. The rest of us can't claim similar intellectual pursuits, can we?"

William had made what Sara considered a very aggressive retort, but no one really took offense, because all of them knew how upset he was that the Ladbroke baronetcy had been passed to Rupert's brother, Charles. As well, Bellehurst and most of the baron's personal fortune were included in the jointure that now belonged to his wife. Both Victoria and Eugenia had inherited some twelve thousand pounds apiece, but William's sulky expression made it obvious that he did not consider this enough. All of them were more than a little relieved when the meeting ended at last.

Later, after the family had dispersed following a silent supper in the chilly dining room, Sara drew Nicholas aside in the hall. "It was kind of you to speak up for me this afternoon. Thank you."

"No need to thank me," Nicholas said gruffly. "William was completely out of line. Somebody should have confronted him about his behavior long before this. It was utterly inexcusable to act that way in front of your grandmother."

"You care about her, don't you?" Sara asked wonderingly.

Nicholas's face lost its harshness. He smiled. "Doesn't everyone?"

They stood and smiled at each other, and in that moment they were close, drawn together by their mutual love for London.

It was the last time Sara was to see him. When she appeared downstairs the following morning he was gone, driven to the station by William's chauffeur to catch the early train.

At that moment the peace of the early morning was shattered by a loud explosion, and Sara was hurled back into the present by the unexpected blast. She had dropped the flower jug she had been holding, and now all thoughts of the past, of Grandpapa, the funeral, and Nicholas, promptly flew from her head. Peering out of the window she saw Eugenia's ancient motorcar chugging down the hill from the direction of the manor house. As it drew to a halt in the drive it backfired again, and Eugenia emerged, coughing and cursing. Grinning, Sara wiped her hands on a towel and went outside to meet her.

"Good morning, my pet. Is your grandmama awake?"

"Yes."

"Oh, I'm glad. How is she feeling? The weather's so perfect that I thought I'd take her walking with me."

"The house must be filling up," Sara observed maliciously, "because I can't think why else you'd be so anxious to leave it."

"Cheeky brat," Eugenia said cheerfully. "You're right. Henry and his family arrived last night, bringing Isobelle Ashford with them. She's got a nurse companion who is, I think, even more ancient and confused than she is. And Beatrice! What a creaking Victorian relic! I feel as if I'm surrounded by corpses." She laughed. "What about you? Care to join us?"

"Sorry, I can't. I've got to take some flowers up to the house for Aunt Victoria."

"Know how to drive, do you?"

"Yes."

"Then take my car."

"Gosh, thanks. I was going to hitch Jessamine to the cart."

But by the time Sara had loaded the flowers into the boot and turned the tiny car around, she was wondering if perhaps it would have been wiser to refuse Eugenia's kind offer. Clanking, shuddering, and groaning, the ancient vehicle chuffed uphill, wafting bluish smoke in its wake and disturbing the rooks from their perches high in the chestnut trees with intermittent backfires.

Strangely enough, the entire household hadn't collected in the courtyard to witness Sara's noisy arrival. The front door remained closed, the heavy drapes drawn. Bearing an armful of flowers, Sara juggled open the latch and went inside.

"Hello! Anybody home?"

Silence, and the cool, lavender smell that was Bellehurst's alone, welcomed her. Sara crossed to the back corridor, her footsteps echoing on the bare wooden floor. Surrounded by silence, she was struck all at once by the thought that this was the first time she had been alone in the house since her arrival. What a wonderful feeling, because you could never really experience the soul of a house until it was empty and still. And it was wonderful to discover that nothing had changed; that the feeling of coziness and comfort the house had always given her remained.

In the pantry that had once been part of the stillroom, Sara set down her flowers and dusted off her hands. She poked her head down the flight of stairs leading to the kitchen. "Mrs. Jakes? Curwen?"

"I think they're both upstairs, serving breakfast to our guests."

Sara whirled, startled by the strange masculine voice. A tall young man was lounging in the doorway behind her. He was good looking in an ill-kempt sort of way, with a lock of fair hair tumbling over a very aristocratic brow. His baggy flannel trousers and moss-green tweed jacket sat naturally on his youthful frame, and there was much of the Ashford about him: the deep blue of his eyes, the chiseled features, the easy grin that lifted one corner of a disturbingly sensual mouth. It was not hard to see why this carefree young fellow had already earned himself the reputation of a masher.

"I never imagined you'd look so much like Grandmama," Sara said wonderingly.

He arched an eyebrow at her. "Then you know who I am?"

"Yes. You're Nelson Warburton, the disobedient Ladbroke heir."

He laughed. "Now that blunt remark immediately identifies you as Cousin Sara. A tart tongue like that could only belong to someone raised by Gran."

Smiling, they shook hands. Then Nelson crossed to the big wooden table to examine the enormous bouquets. "What have we here? Flowers for the birthday girl?"

"Yes. What are you doing up so early?"

"Same thing as Aunt Eugenia. Fleeing for my life from all the ancients upstairs." He tugged at his necktie and smoothed back his hair. "I'm off to forage for greener pastures."

"At Rose Cottage?"

Nelson's handsome face assumed an expression of mock horror. "Whatever for? I'd only be roped into holding Gran's yarn while she knits. Thank you, no."

"Grandmama isn't into that sort of dotage yet," Sara said defensively.

"Of course not. But such are the remarks I'm expected to make, seeing that her jointure is the despair of me, the Ladbroke heir." He laughed, and the richness of the sound took the sting from his words.

Sara couldn't help warming to him. "Then where is it you're fleeing to?"

"I'm not certain yet. Perhaps the Beckwiths. Nora was going to take me riding, but I've no wish to sit astride that foaming beast of hers. I'm beginning to suspect that he relishes nothing more than rubbing me off against the nearest tree. I'll be back in time for supper, of course. It won't do to send Mum into a decline."

"Heavens, no."

"Then you'll tell her where I've gone?"

"Certainly."

Nelson flashed her a very bright, very charming smile. "Top hole. See you tonight."

The house door slammed. Amused, Sara turned back to her flowers, which had suffered a little during the turbulent climb uphill in the Austin. She had barely succeeded in rearranging the first bouquet before she was interrupted again, this time by Nora, who clumped inside wearing a tailored riding jacket and canary breeches. Her hair was arranged in sausage curls beneath a velvet crash cap, and her face took on a suspicious look when she saw Sara standing alone at the table.

"Where's Nelson?"

"Gone to the Beckwiths. You just missed him."

"Why, that grotty little . . . He knows perfectly well we were supposed to go riding! How does he plan to get there?"

"He didn't say."

"There'll be hell to pay if he's taken Daddy's car."

"I'm not sure—" Sara began, but Nora brushed past her, her whip slapping ominously against her thigh.

Sara shook her head, smiling. Small wonder that Grandmama viewed this family reunion with something less than utter enthusiasm. Petty squabbles seemed to be the order of the day, and she wondered as she went back outside to fetch the rest of her flowers what other surprises awaited her.

Chapter
Twenty-nine

By late afternoon the flowers had been successfully distributed, various relations appeased and fed, and preparations for tomorrow's mammoth birthday buffet completed. The only disagreement to arise that day seemed to concern the order of priority in queuing for the bathroom.

By then, fortunately, Sara was already back at Rose Cottage dressing for dinner. The weather was warm, and she had chosen a dark green voile dress that suited her fiery hair and was of a length to reveal the shapely turn of her ankles and the buttons on the straps of her high-heeled shoes.

London, too, had donned unaccustomed finery. She wore the dark blue of the Bedouins, though the cut of her skirt and jacket was smartly French rather than Arabic. Her hair was carefully pinned beneath a veiled hat trimmed with blue ribbons, and she had screwed dangling earbobs into her ears and wore about her throat the double strand of pearls Rupert had given her on her fiftieth birthday. Crocheted gloves, a lavish cloak, and her straight-backed posture gave her the regal demeanor of a queen. Sara, delighted, clapped her hands as the two of them met in the raftered hall.

"You look wonderful, Grandmama!"

"But you far outshine me, darling, which is as it should be. Turn around and let me look at you. Oh, there's Eugenia, honking in the drive. Are you ready? We'd better go. It won't do for us to be last."

The Paxton Hotel, formerly a fifteenth-century coaching inn, stood amid a stand of towering elms facing Millham Cross's tidy market square. Part of its original, half-timbered walls and worn, cobbled courtyard remained, although the rest of the building, with its warren of cozy rooms and raftered dining nooks, had been remodeled during the burst of prosperity following the turn of the century and the Boer War's end.

In order to smooth over any ruffled feelings possessed by those Ladbroke guests who had been relegated to the hotel rather than Bellehurst itself, Victoria had arranged for the family's first formal supper to be held in the hotel's largest and most elegant dining room. Here, a number of family members had already gathered to await London's arrival, while being plied with cocktails and hors d'oeuvres by waiters in crisp black uniforms.

London was surrounded the moment she stepped inside, but Sara hung back, her hand on Eugenia's arm. "Wait a moment, will you? I'm afraid I don't recognize anyone."

"Nonsense. We haven't changed all that much. There's Winifred over in the corner with her husband, Albert, talking to Alice and Louisa. Your cousin Nora is there near the window with Henry and Abigail Stours—"

"*That's* Henry?"

Eugenia made a face. "Yes. I'm afraid he's put on a bit of weight. Wallace and his wife haven't come down yet—I imagine they're putting their children to bed. But here comes William with your great-aunt Isobelle—you met her briefly at the house this morning."

"Yes." Sara had been struck then by the tiny old lady's resemblance to her grandfather. "I still can't believe she came all the way from Leeds for Grandmama's birthday. She's well over ninety, isn't she?"

"It's more a tribute to your grandfather than anything else. He was always her favorite brother."

"And who is that over there talking with Aunt Victoria?"

"That? Your great-aunt Edith."

"And the other one?"

"Your cousin Charlotte."

"She's lovely."

"Yes. So she's always reminding us."

"Eugenia! Yoo hoo!"

"Oh, lord, it's Miss Wagstaff. I'll bet she's got a list as long as her arm of the things we've overlooked. Can you manage on your own now?"

"Yes, of course."

Eugenia grinned and plunged into the crowd. Knowing better than to remain, Sara made her own escape as well. Having already been subjected to the tiresome criticisms of Aunt Beatrice's companion herself, she had learned to avoid her assiduously. Miss Wagstaff was tall and rake thin, and her old-fashioned views were championed by Aunt Beatrice. Dressed in an outmoded, corseted gown, Beatrice was currently holding forth in a corner of the dining room, surrounded by nephews and nieces who wore upon their faces the unmistakable signs of desperate boredom.

One had to marvel at Grandmama, Sara thought, for having put up with Beatrice all these years and never, to the best of Sara's knowledge, losing her temper with her. It couldn't have been easy, because Great-aunt Beatrice was the most overbearing person Sara had ever known, even worse than Grandmother Adeline when she had been alive.

Lost in thought, Sara wandered into the hall just as the front door opened and a man in a trenchcoat hastened inside.

"Excuse me," he said breathlessly to Sara, "am I late?"

"No. You've only missed the drinks."

He paused in the midst of removing his hat to give Sara a second look. "Good lord, you're Sara Ashford, aren't you?"

"Yes."

"Is it still Ashford, or have you married?"

"No, it's still Ashford."

Nicholas Warburton handed his things to the hovering attendant, then turned to face her. He was just as tall and dark as Sara remembered, but perhaps the years had softened his resemblance to Rob Buchanan or time had simply dimmed her memory of the man, because there was no longer anything in his rough-hewn face that aroused within her such bitter resentment and longing. Instead, she felt only a sense of relief that he was here, knowing how much her grandmother had been counting on seeing him.

"Grandmama's inside," she told him. "She was afraid you wouldn't come."

"I wouldn't have missed it for the world."

He sounded sincere, and Sara smiled at him, her grandmother's smile. "She's in the dining room. I'll take you to her."

"Thanks."

She glanced beyond his wide shoulder. "Your wife and mother didn't come?"

A muscle twitched in Nicholas's jaw. "I'm alone."

Feeling oddly chastened, although she couldn't imagine why, Sara led him into the dining room. It pleased her to see how her grandmother's face lit at the sight of him. She was moved to wonder all at once if perhaps her grandmother might not be lonely—which was absurd, considering that Grandmama was perfectly content to live alone at Rose Cottage and that she was constantly surrounded by a large and loving family. Nevertheless, the smile she had given Nicholas had been different somehow.

She smiles at him the way she does at me, Sara realized suddenly. As though in some strange way we are special to her.

Dinner was announced, and the family made its noisy way to the long table. Sara found herself sitting between Uncle William and Winifred's husband, Albert Creighton, a balding little man whom Eugenia, in her usual, unkind, and disparaging fashion, had nicknamed Albert Cretin because he seemed so incomprehensibly dim-witted to her.

Indeed, Sara found that there was little he cared to discuss other than his business, which was a small, moderately successful shoe company quartered in a crumbling Bayswater warehouse. Regrettably, there was little help to be solicited from Uncle William, who was, as usual, being fussed over by his devoted stepmama, who was seated to his left. Sara was eventually prodded by sufficient desperation to seek her escape in the food, which was actually quite delicious.

Like many of the other restaurants, pubs, and hotels in the country, the Paxton had been suffering in recent months from a slow but increasingly noticeable scarcity of expensive foods and ingredients. Its adventurous kitchen staff had therefore begun improvising with local produce and game, and the surprisingly pleasing result that evening was a splendid brace of pheasants stuffed with liver pâté, a fish terrine flavored with garden herbs, and accompanying vegetables bought at Tuesday market and braised lightly in butter. There was a fine Stilton at the end of the meal—which had included several ambitious courses of wines—and a cream-slathered fruit compote for pudding.

William had made a brief speech at the beginning of the meal, and afterward numerous toasts were drunk to the dowager baroness, who received this noisy homage with her usual good grace. During the lengthy applause signaling the end of dinner, Sara looked down the table at the many faces. Poor, ancient Isobelle had fallen asleep, her wrinkled cheek resting lightly on the shoulder of Miss Carmody, her paid companion. Nelson was tipped back in his chair, arms crossed indolently behind his head, wearing a look of long-suffering boredom.

Victoria's married trio of daughters, Louisa, Alice, and

Winifred, were dressed in the varying degrees of high fashion their husbands' incomes allowed; all of them were smoking cigarettes and attempting to look very haughty and chic. Victoria herself, sitting between Nicholas and Wallace Stours, was looking immensely pleased with herself, which she had every right to be. The dinner had been an enormous success.

The big hall clock chimed eleven, and as if on cue, the family broke up amid a babble of good-natured voices and the scraping of chairs.

"What are you planning to do now?" inquired Nora, coming up behind Sara.

"I hadn't thought about it. What about you?"

Nora shrugged. "I don't know. Albert and Tony are staying to play darts. Louisa and Winifred want to watch."

"You don't care to?"

Nora made a face.

"Come up to the house with us, Sara," Nelson suggested, grinning at his sister as he joined them. "We could always use a fourth for bridge."

Sara said apologetically, "I've no idea how to play."

"Good heavens," Nelson exclaimed in mock horror. "You can't be serious!"

Nora shot him a contemptuous look. "See? Not everyone in the world lives for the game the way you do. Daddy says we can play records."

Now it was Nelson's turn to pull a face. "You and that bloody gramophone."

"I'm sure we'll think of something," Sara said hastily. She was tired and would have preferred going home to bed, but thought it would be best to avoid a quarrel between Nelson and his sister.

William solved the problem by inviting everyone who wasn't interested in darts up to the house for drinks. London declined, as did Beatrice and Isobelle who were, they insisted, longing for bed. Coats and hats were collected from the front hall, and the older ladies, along with Victoria, Miss Wagstaff, and Miss Carmody, were driven away through the darkness toward home.

In the hall, London put her arm about Sara's waist. "Eugenia is going to take me back. Go on up with the others. Enjoy yourself a little.''

"I will.'' Sara kissed her grandmother's cheek and then climbed into the Daimler, which Francis had drawn to a halt before the front door. Lights twinkled through the trees as they turned up Bellehurst's long drive, and a brisk northerly wind ruffled the leaves of the chestnuts towering above the garage. The dogs in the kennel set up a wild barking as the car coasted to a halt.

"No loud music, please, children,'' cautioned Victoria, meeting them in the hall. "Aunt Isobelle and Mother Warburton have gone upstairs. Poor dears, they were exhausted.''

"Cards, then,'' Nelson said promptly. "Though we'll need an extra hand. How about you, Charlotte?''

"Gracious, no. I loathe playing cards.'' She turned to Nicholas, who had entered the hall behind her. "What about one of those drinks Papa promised?''

They went into the parlor, which was cozily illuminated by floor lamps shaded in ruby-colored glass. With a groan of pleasure, Nelson sank onto the sofa and stretched his long legs before him on the Turkey rug. Curwen appeared and began serving drinks, while William turned on the wireless. The strains of "Blue Skies'' floated softly through the room.

"Anyone remember how to foxtrot?'' he asked.

"I do,'' said Aunt Edith promptly. "Come on, sonny, give me a spin.''

Everyone laughed and applauded. Aunt Edith was enormously fat, but there was nothing she enjoyed better than dancing—even with partners who were unable to put their arms around her. William, with his head of thinning blond hair reaching barely to her shoulder, was no exception, but he handled her manfully enough to keep her giggling as they whirled about the room. Some of the others got up to join them while Nelson, alarmed at the prospect of being pressed into duty by one of his unattached female cousins, hastily organized a game of cards.

Victoria alone declined to join the merriment. She was wrestling with the dilemma of Nicholas Warburton's unexpected arrival, because she had no idea where to put him.

The Paxton Hotel was booked up with family as well as the out-of-town guests who would be attending tomorrow's party, and she wasn't certain if it was proper to give him Louisa's old room, which, although it was the only one left unoccupied, lay directly across the hall from Charlotte's.

Nicholas was married, but he'd come without his wife or mother, and Victoria wasn't sure if it would be wise to put him on the same floor as Lottie, considering that the girl had gone to no pains to hide her interest in him.

"I just don't know what to do," Victoria complained to Mrs. Jakes, by now thoroughly vexed and ridiculously close to tears.

"We could always make up the daybed in the Red Room sitting room, ma'am," the housekeeper suggested.

"But Mother Warburton has already taken over the entire suite."

"Perhaps if we explained that it was needed for Master Nicholas—"

Victoria brightened. "You're right. She'll simply have to understand that it couldn't be helped."

Mrs. Jakes made what sounded suspiciously like a snort.

"You may go up and tell her what we've decided," Victoria added, just to punish her.

Mrs. Jakes's lips thinned. "As you wish, madam."

Concealing her triumph, Victoria returned to the parlor. Her guests, she saw with considerable satisfaction, had made themselves comfortable during her absence. Some of them were dancing. Others were drinking and talking together. Nelson, Charlotte, Nicholas, and Nora were deeply involved in a game of whist. William had abandoned Aunt Edith and was sitting on the sofa next to Albert Creighton's sister Delia, wearing what Victoria called his bounder's look. A Woodbine dangled artfully from the corner of his mouth, and he held a drink in one hand while the other stretched across the back of the sofa very nearly brushing Delia's bare shoulders. Delia was giggling at something he had said.

Pointedly ignoring them, Victoria seated herself near the fireplace and motioned Curwen to bring her a drink. She felt immeasurably pleased with herself. The dinner had been enormously successful, and she had managed to handle the crisis of Nicholas's appearance in a most professional way. Now, if only the weather would hold for tomorrow's party, and the caterers and musicians and the extra help she had hired from Temple Lynn arrived as instructed, she could consider herself fortunate indeed.

"It's been a wonderful evening, Aunt Victoria."

Victoria looked up. "Oh, Sara, it has, hasn't it? I'm ever so pleased. How pretty you look tonight. I hope you've been enjoying yourself?"

"Yes, of course." Sara seated herself next to her aunt and tucked her legs comfortably beneath her. She looked relaxed and very lovely, Victoria thought, in a bottle-green knitted jersey dress that was softly belted at the waist. A slim girl, tall, and very dashing with those deep blue eyes and that reddish-gold hair. But as yet unmarried and, despite her youthful looks, Victoria suddenly realized, certainly no longer what one would consider young.

"Why is it you've never married, dear?" she asked, in her usual, artless fashion. "I confess I've always wondered. This obsession of yours to have a career—is it something that American girls are raised to want, or did you simply inherit Eugenia's odd notion about a woman's right to vote and work?"

"Perhaps a little of both," Sara admitted, smiling. "But the important thing is that I really enjoy what I do. I've been drawn to medicine ever since I rolled my first bandages back home during the war."

"But a husband and family. Surely you can't say you've never longed for either?"

Sara's smile faded a little, and her tone grew wistful. "Oh, certainly I'd like to have children someday, but I've never met anyone who made me feel the way I did when—I mean, the way I *imagine* one should feel when finally meeting the man you'd like to spend the rest of your life with."

Victoria looked surprised. "Is that what you've been waiting for? But, my dear, things never happen that way! Not in real life. Only in films and novels. Devotion, respect, and a commitment to duty—not love—should be the touchstones of a strong and happy marriage.''

"Like yours and Uncle William's?"

Victoria looked sharply at her niece, but there was no hint of sarcasm or unkindness in that soft, guileless voice. "Yes," she said uncomfortably, "that's exactly what I mean. And now you must excuse me. I should mingle with my other guests."

"Poor Mum." Nora had come to stand behind the sofa. "How she does like to fool herself! Devotion and duty! Ugh! Sometimes I wonder why she wasn't born Mother Warburton's daughter instead of Gran's. They're so horribly alike, don't you think?"

Sara smiled wickedly. "Lost badly at cards, did you?"

Nora scowled. "God, yes. I made a bloody hash of it, in fact, and now Nelson's furious. Sara, do you think Nicholas will dance with me if I ask him?"

"I can't answer for him, you silly goose. Try it."

"I wonder why he didn't bring Lillith with him."

"Why don't you ask him that, too?"

"I wouldn't dare."

"What's she like?"

"You've never met her? No, I suppose you haven't. She's a wonderful little thing, so sweet and airy that it's impossible to dislike her. We're all very fond of her, especially Mum. It's too bad she and Nicholas never had any children."

"Perhaps they didn't want them."

Nora's mouth sagged open with surprise. "Doesn't everyone?"

Sara couldn't help laughing. "Oh, my dear, no! Look at Aunt Eugenia. She's been married twice before, happily enough, but I'll wager you half a crown she's never been happier than she is now. Don't you envy her a little, being able to travel wherever and with whomever she pleases? She'd never have that kind of freedom with children in tow."

"I've never really thought about it before," Nora said slowly. In her world, there was no room for alternatives. One did one's duty, as Mum and Daddy always said, and took care to marry well. But supposing she *wasn't* happy with that? Edward VIII certainly hadn't been content to do his duty, and his abdication last year to marry the woman he loved had made quite an impression on Nora's vulnerable heart.

On the other hand, she had no wish to work—not the way Daddy or Sara did. Her nose wrinkled as she recalled Sara's description of her long commute into New York City every morning to the laboratory where she spent all day mixing together smelly medicines. Surely keeping house for a handsome husband and cooing babies was greatly preferable to that?

Still, one did have to envy Sara her freedom. And Eugenia and Charlotte, though everyone knew Charlotte would leap at the chance to marry the first acceptable man who asked her. It wasn't Charlotte's fault that her looks couldn't compare with the other girls who had made their debuts with her and managed to snap up all the eligible young men not killed in the war.

She said unexpectedly to Sara, "Do you suppose I might be able to come visit you when I'm in the States?"

"Of course," exclaimed Sara, remembering that Nora had mentioned something about a trip to Boston during summer hols. "I'll take you to the city. We can do the theater and museums. Better yet, my mother can take you. There's nothing she loves better than Manhattan. Ever since my stepfather died she's become the unofficial 'extra' for sight-seeing excursions to town."

"It sounds lovely. Will you show me where you work, too?"

Sara was surprised. "Yes, if you'd like."

"I'm told you're involved with patent medicines," came Nicholas's voice from behind them. Without waiting for an invitation, he settled himself beside Nora, his long body sprawled comfortably across the sofa cushions. "How did you land a job like that?"

"My stepfather arranged it the year before he died. He was friendly with Frederick Humphries, the president of the company."

"Which is—?"

"The Homeopathic Medicine Company."

"I've heard of it." Nicholas laughed, seeing Sara's astonished expression. "Why should that surprise you? I have a dispensary at my clinic, you know, and use a lot of the same medicines you professionals compound for human patients. Chlorodyne, Formalin, Hexamine—"

"Have you been following Sir Alexander Fleming's work with *Penicillium notatum*?" Sara inquired eagerly.

"Of course. Anyone who doesn't sit up and take notice is an utter fool. I've a friend at Oxford working on plant diseases, designing therapeutic practices based on the phenomenon of antibiosis. It closely parallels the work Fleming has done culturing penicillin as an antagonist."

Sara's heart leaped. She had never come across anyone outside of her company knowledgeable enough to discuss a field she considered immensely exciting. They talked on. Neither of them noticed when Nora, bored, drifted away or when Curwen discreetly refreshed their drinks.

After a little, Sara glanced at her watch and was astonished to see that it was long after one. She looked around her, a little disoriented and unsure of her whereabouts, like a sleepwalker awakening from a drugged sleep. The wireless had been switched off and only Uncle William and Delia remained, talking quietly in the far corner. Curwen hovered nearby, wearing that look of weary boredom that made it clear he was ready for the guests to retire so that he could lock up and go to bed himself.

She said, "I think it's time I went home."

Nicholas rose with her. "I'll drive you. My car's in the garage."

"There's no need. I can walk."

"Would you rather I came with you?"

"I'm not afraid of the dark."

"That isn't why I asked."

Sara smiled at him. "It's really not necessary. Thank you all the same."

Outside the moon was hanging low amid the trees, and the sky was a soft mantle of darkness. No clouds obscured the horizon, and the sweet warmth of the night wind promised continued fine weather for tomorrow's party. Stepping into Rose Cottage's tidy front garden, Sara paused for a moment at the gate to savor the stillness. Through the budding trees she could make out the bulk of Bellehurst's roofline soaring into the sky behind her. The parlor lights were still on, and she could just picture Curwen and Mrs. Jakes tidying up together in haughty silence. A light continued burning in the small upper room that was Nora's, although the rest of the house was dark. Even in darkness, however, it hadn't lost its sense of slumbering security; something, Sara suddenly realized, that Haversham had always lacked.

Rose Cottage, too, enveloped her in cozy warmth the moment she stepped inside. The hall lamp had been left burning, and a pool of comforting light spread through the raftered gloom. Sara switched it off and went quietly upstairs, being careful to avoid the creaky places that would awaken her grandmother and her aunt.

In her own room a light continued burning as well. Someone—Grandmama no doubt—had turned the bed linens back. Sara undressed, brushed her teeth, and washed her face. With a glad sigh she slipped between the cool cotton sheets. Propping her arm beneath her head she lay on her side thinking back on the evening, and wondering about Nicholas, who had, long ago, aroused within her such pained resentment because he had looked so much like the man Sara had loved. For better or worse that resemblance was gone, or perhaps it was simply that it didn't matter anymore. In a way, Sara was glad. Nicholas was charming and kind. It would have been unfair to dislike him simply because he reminded her of someone else.

She found it impossible to imagine what Lillith Warburton looked like from Nora's vague description. Perhaps there was a photograph of her crammed among the countless others in the desk drawer in Grandpapa's old study. Sara thought it odd that Nicholas had left his mother behind, but even as she contemplated the reasons behind this odd event, she found herself slipping easily into a deep and untroubled sleep.

Chapter
Thirty

London was floating, floating above the bed in which she lay. She had lost her balance and fallen down the terrace steps during her birthday fete and lain unconscious in the grass for a minute or two before her senses had returned. She must have twisted her ankle when she fell, because the moment she opened her eyes she became aware of the pain. That, and other things: the brilliant blue of the sky above her, the softness of the grass in which she lay, and the sound of someone close by weeping. It sounded like Victoria.

"Stop it," London had said crossly. "I'm not dead yet."

"Of course you aren't, darling."

That was Nicholas, and London turned her head to find him kneeling beside her, smiling at her as he examined her ankle. London remembered being greatly reassured by his calm, practical manner.

"No broken bones," he had said at last.

"Are you sure? I'm not a milch cow, you know." Pain had made London peevish.

Nicholas laughed softly. "Some human bones are remarkably similar to animal bones, dear. Now lie still and we'll get you to bed."

He and William had carried her upstairs into one of the hastily vacated guest bedrooms, and the doctor had come and given her something to take away the pain. London couldn't remember what it was, but it left her groggy and uncaring and drifting in a state that was neither wakefulness nor sleep.

She was glad that she felt this way—so impervious to everything. It made her guilt less difficult to bear. She knew that she had frightened everyone by falling, and ruined the elaborate birthday preparations Victoria had made. At least she had maintained enough presence of mind to order everyone back outside so that the party could continue without her.

Judging from the noise floating up to her window, it was still a rousing success. The band Victoria had engaged was playing every imaginable dance tune, and from the babble of voices and the shouts of the children it appeared as though the guests had taken her advice to heart and were enjoying themselves tremendously. As well they should. The weather was glorious, the food and drink the finest available, the lively music impossible to resist.

"Grandmama?"

Slowly London turned her head to find Sara's face floating into view, framed by that glorious red hair, her blue eyes wide and uncertain. "Did I wake you?"

"Not at all. Come in. I'm glad to see you."

"Aunt Victoria said I shouldn't come up. She said you were resting and it would be better not to disturb you."

London patted the bed. "Nonsense. Come sit by me. I'm a little bit vague, I'm afraid, but I still want to hear what's happening. Is the party a success?"

"Enormously. You can't imagine how many people have come. Mr. Brockman has been engaged merely to show the cars where to park."

"Then I'm glad, especially for Vicky. What have you been doing, dear?"

Sara laughed. "What do you expect? Duty dances with all the uncles and cousins and half the male population of Kent. My feet are killing me, which is why I decided this would be a good time to steal away. Do you know, they've gone through all the crates of champagne already and four bowls of Uncle William's punch, and now they've started on the ale that was sent up from Paxton's."

"And it's barely four o'clock," London murmured, shaking her head. "What else?"

"Oh, the usual Warburton nonsense. Henry's boy, George, fed Aunt Beatrice's Pekingese all the leftover blancmange.

The poor little thing was dreadfully sick all over Mrs. Beckwith's shoes."

"Good heavens. What else? Nothing so awful, I hope?"

Sara grinned wickedly. "Well, Nelson made a wager with Noel Olwyn, daring him to walk through the marquee in that old suit of armor that used to be Grandpapa's."

"And did he?"

"Yes, and nearly frightened Great-aunt Isobelle half to death. The helmet got stuck when he tried taking it off. Curwen had to work for twenty minutes with the wire clippers before he was freed."

London's lips twitched. "And you, dear? Are you enjoying yourself?"

Sara's expression softened. "Very much. If only you could be there, Grandmama."

"Oh, I don't mind." She was actually quite content to lie there, feeling for all the world immensely fortunate to have missed the mayhem Sara described.

"The only one not enjoying himself is, I think, Colonel Packer. He's been looking dreadfully lost ever since they brought you upstairs."

"Poor man. Tell him you've been to see me and that I'm recovering quite nicely."

"He wants to marry you, Nora says."

"Yes. Dreadful thought."

"You never cared for anyone but Grandpapa, did you?"

"If you mean, did I fall in love with anyone after he died, no."

"But do you think it's possible?"

"What?"

"That people can fall in love, really in love, more than once."

Careful, London warned herself. Her head felt very thick and strange from the medication. No telling what she might blurt out in such a groggy state. But she said, firmly, "I not only think it, I know it."

"You seem very sure of that."

"I am. The human heart is very adaptable, Sara. Never forget that."

"I won't." Sara leaned over and kissed her. "Now you really should try to sleep."

"I will," London promised. But she lay there for quite some time after Sara had gone, ruminating on the girl's question and wondering what on earth had prompted her to ask it. *Khuda ke malum.* God only knows.

She realized she must be groggy indeed to be thinking aloud in Hindustani. Not that she remembered much of the language anyway, but it was an expression that Alex had used when they had crossed the desert together.

Alex. For the first time in a great many years, perhaps thanks to the drugs she had been given, London was able to see his face clearly before her, not clouded as it usually was by incredible time and distance. She remembered the dark lock of hair that had tumbled over his brow, and the way his rough-hewn features had softened with passion and longing as he had looked at her that last time on the pier in Algiers.

She closed her eyes and made a sharp movement as though of denial, and a shaft of pain shot through her injured ankle. Behind her closed lids, Alex's features had shifted; changed into those of another man: Nicholas Warburton. But Nicholas's eyes were green, and Alex's had been blue . . . as blue as Sandy's—and Sara's, whose clean-cut features now imposed themselves easily, perfectly, over Alex's in her mind. Her thoughts moved back to Nicholas and immediately settled upon an idea so unlikely that London thrust it contemptuously aside.

"Go away," she told it aloud, "I will not hear you."

When Sara returned outside she was immediately pounced upon by Colonel Packer, who must have been lying in wait for her behind the shrubbery edging the terrace. Taking her arm, he inquired hoarsely after the baroness. Sara assured him that her grandmother was recovering nicely.

"Glad to hear it," said the colonel, thumping her happily on the shoulder. "Though I suppose she won't be coming downstairs again today?"

"No, sir. I rather doubt it."

"Ah ha. I see." He looked so woebegone that Sara felt sorry for him.

"Don't worry. I'm certain she'll be well enough to attend the Millham Music Society meeting on Wednesday."

But he surprised her. "Talk her out of it if you can. Too much too soon can't be good for a body. Won't be missing much anyway. A bunch of boring old women listening to horrid music and charging three pence for cold tea and soggy biscuits."

"Then why do *you* go?" Sara asked, surprised.

His ruddy complexion deepened in color. "Ahem. Well, yes, you see—" He faltered and fell silent. The time had, quite obviously, come for him to change the subject, and so he seized with some desperation on the condition of the roads between his home and Bellehurst and the difficult time he had had traveling between the two. The county council was entirely to blame, and after proceeding to lambaste them for several minutes, his embarrassment faded and he found himself warming to other subjects, in particular his favorite theory of how the war had finished England's old, quiet days and left everyone rushing around with no time for simple pleasures anymore, and what in bloody blazes did Sara think should be done about it?

By now Sara was chafing to get away, but she forced herself to murmur a polite reply. She understood now why Nora had called the colonel a cracking bore, but of course she couldn't be so rude as to simply walk away from him.

"Colonel Packer!"

Sara turned and, with some relief, saw Nelson crossing the lawn to join them, a drink in one hand and a pretty girl hanging adoringly on the other. "Talking scandal once again, I assume? You'll give my American cousin the wrong impression about us, sir."

"Nonsense," said the colonel vigorously. "I never truckle to foreigners."

"Oh, but I'm not a foreigner," Sara protested.

Nelson's eyes twinkled. "Thinking of moving back to this side of the duck pond, are you?" he teased.

"I don't know," Sara said, surprised. "I've never given it any thought."

"Ooh, they've started a three-step," exclaimed the girl as the band on the lawn broke into a rousing country tune. She turned eagerly to Nelson. "Dance with me, poodle pie?"

"Okay loo." With an indulgent grin, Nelson allowed himself to be dragged away.

"Insolent pup," muttered the colonel. "Would've benefited enormously from six months in the trenches." He looked around expectantly to see if Miss Ashford agreed and was startled to find her gone. Scanning the crowd, he caught sight of her at last whirling about in the arms of her uncle, the earl, who had, apparently, led her away for the dance without so much as begging the colonel's pardon.

Not that it really mattered. Colonel Packer had a game eye for pretty girls, and Sara Ashford looked pretty indeed, revealing an appreciable length of her shapely legs whenever her skirt flew up in response to the rousing movements of the dance.

"I suppose I might as well leave the celebrating to the young ones," the colonel decided, and went off to help himself to another drink.

"Mama?"

Awakened from sleep, London slowly opened her eyes. The drapes were drawn across the casement windows, but a shaft of golden sunlight poured between them, illuminating the tidy guest room in which she lay. Her daughter stood hesitantly in the doorway, and London smiled a greeting.

"Victoria. Come in. What time is it?"

"Almost six."

"Good heavens!" London pulled herself upright on the pillows. "I can't believe I've slept so long. Dr. Lowery's draft must have been stronger than I thought. Are the guests still here?"

"Yes. And showing no signs of wanting to go home. If things keep up, Mrs. Jakes and I will have to offer them something for supper." Victoria crossed the room and drew back the curtains so that the waning sunlight spilled inside. When she turned around, London noticed the puffiness beneath her daughter's eyes. She bit back a sigh. Victoria's capacity for weeping was legion, and heaven help her for being a negligent mother, but at the moment she truly didn't feel up to enduring what would probably amount to a very emotional outburst—doubtless having something to do with Beatrice, whose presence in the house never failed to reduce Victoria to tears.

"What is it, dear?" she inquired nonetheless.

"Oh, Mama." Victoria's face crumpled. She looked, all at once, very defenseless, plain, and middle-aged. What had happened, London wondered, to the lovely young girl who had enjoyed such a splendid Season not so many years ago? "I'm thinking of leaving William."

There was silence.

"Whatever for?" London asked at last.

Victoria uttered a choked sob. "There are so many reasons—"

"Tell me about them," London said softly.

Victoria mopped at her eyes with a crumpled handkerchief. "Oh, Mama, I'm sorry. I know it's a terrible time to bring this up, but I can't stop thinking about it. It has to do with Nora, mainly. She told me this morning that she wants to attend boarding school after all, and after she goes, the house will be much too large for William and me."

"But I thought you had both decided against sending her abroad. The times are so dreadfully uncertain. Look at Germany. And Spain. If there should be another war—"

"There won't be. Albert says Mr. Chamberlain won't allow it. And Nora isn't going to Switzerland. She wants to go to America."

"To America?"

"Yes. I've already talked to Sara, who says there are plenty of excellent girls' schools to choose from."

"But America is so far away!"

Victoria's lower lip trembled, and her eyes swam with fresh tears. "Yes, I know. But Sara feels certain her mother will permit Nora to stay at Haversham during the holidays so she won't be entirely alone. There's plenty of room. And she can always come back to Kent for summer hols."

London watched her daughter keenly as she vigorously blew her nose. She found it difficult to believe that Victoria would agree to such a thing—and give her consent so soon. Victoria always took forever to mull over anything new, especially something as important as this.

Of course, it went without saying that spoiled, silly Nora would benefit enormously from several years abroad, but on the other hand one simply didn't desert one's husband of twenty years because the last of one's children had finally flown the nest.

"And the other reason?" London prodded.

"Mr. Herbert."

London stared. Dear God, an affair. The last thing on earth she would have expected from Victoria. She found she had to clear her throat before she could speak. "Who—who is Mr. Herbert?"

"You know." Victoria's voice was muffled by her handkerchief, for she was once again blowing her nose. "You're always reading the newspapers."

Comprehension dawned—and with it a wild impulse to laugh. "Oh, my dear! Do you mean Mr. A. P. Herbert? The one whose marriage bill is presently being debated in the House of Lords?"

"Yes, that's the one. Eugenia told me all about him last night at dinner."

London said quietly, "What did she tell you?"

"That Mr. Herbert's bill proposes to extend the grounds for divorce. To make it easier and more acceptable."

"Victoria. Divorce is never easy, and I doubt that even Mr. Herbert will succeed in making it acceptable. The new bill merely advocates extending the grounds for divorce to include cruelty, insanity, and desertion."

"Oh." Victoria's face fell. "Oh, I see." She was silent for a moment, thinking. "I suppose I can't really accuse William of being any of those." She sounded almost disappointed.

London closed her eyes, then opened them again. "How

does William feel about this? I mean, you must have discussed it with him . . . What? You haven't? But, my dear, surely it's not too late to work things out between you? Whatever made you decide the situation was so hopeless?''

Victoria shrugged. ''I can't really say. I just know that it is.''

''You've given up on the marriage.'' London spoke flatly, although she knew that she really shouldn't be surprised. Victoria had never been one to work hard at anything difficult. And marriage to a man like William had certainly never been easy.

She felt all at once enormously weary and annoyed. How like Victoria to make such a momentous decision today of all days, and throw it in London's face when scores of guests were milling about downstairs and she herself was lying in bed with a painfully twisted ankle, feeling fiendishly woozy from the medication the doctor had given her.

''Victoria.'' She mustered all of her strength to sound calm and supportive. ''If leaving William is really the thing to do, then you'll know it inside. Of course, you won't be able to help feeling a little frightened and very sad, but also enormously relieved. And nothing anyone says can persuade you otherwise. Is that how you feel? Please, don't answer now. Think it over first. Carefully. And, for heaven's sake, wait until you have more time. The last few weeks have been hectic enough, to say nothing of what's going on downstairs right now.''

''All right. I promise I'll consider it again.'' Victoria dabbed her eyes and blew her nose one last time. Then she smiled, and in her swollen face there suddenly appeared a glimmer of her father's looks and his great charm. ''I love you,'' she said tremulously.

''And I you, my darling.''

They kissed, and Victoria went back outside, feeling for all the world much better about everything. London, meanwhile, fell back against the pillows feeling drained and exhausted.

At almost the same moment there was a knock on the

bedroom door. London stifled the sudden urge to laugh. "Come in," she called.

This time it was Nicholas, and she smiled at him, taking pleasure in his company and in the way he looked. She had always approved of tall men who could wear the fashions of the day with ease, and in his gray coat and flannel trousers Nicholas looked more like a man heading off to his London club than a country veterinarian come to dose her herd of cows. The confused emotions Victoria's visit had aroused within her were suddenly stilled. Her drumming heartbeat slowed, and with it her head ceased to ache.

"Come in and kiss me, you wicked boy."

Smiling, Nicholas obliged. "I was hoping I'd find you awake. I've been wanting to come up and see how you were feeling. Better, I hope?"

"Yes, indeed. And I'm glad you're here. I was just thinking to myself that I've never been so bored in all my life."

"Then you must have led an extraordinary existence, with nothing more serious to complain about than sickbed woes."

"I *have* led an extraordinary life," London agreed tartly, "and was blessed and cursed by it in turn. Regrettably, the girl I used to be has vanished far, far into the distant past. Do you know, I read Wodehouse now, and Mr. Evelyn Waugh, and I couldn't quote you a single *sura* from the Koran to save my life. It's depressing to think how very, very British I've become."

Nicholas pulled up a chair and, straddling it, grinned down at her. "You? British? How can you say that? You know perfectly well that most of your views and beliefs aren't the least bit British at all."

"And what do you know about my views and beliefs?" London inquired pointedly.

"I've heard them all from my mother, who has shared with me the contents of the many outrageous letters you've written her over the years."

"I see. Should that make me feel flattered or annoyed?"

"The Warburton women," Nicholas observed, "get annoyed about everything. Why is that, I wonder?"

"I'm an Ashford," London reminded him.

"Ah, yes. I'd forgotten. Ashford women tend to split into different camps. On the one hand you have those stern Victorian critics, like your daughter Victoria and your cousin Beatrice, and then the more forward-thinking ones—"

"Yes, yes, I know. I've heard all this before. Like my daughter, Eugenia, who smokes cigarettes and wears bicycle shorts and once scandalized the entire county by teaching a Roman Catholic priest to dance the Black Bottom. Tell me," she demanded as Nicholas laughed, "which of us do you prefer?"

Nicholas's eyes twinkled as he looked at her. "I think you know."

"But my dear boy! You married a girl from the opposite camp."

He did not reply to this, and London looked at him searchingly. Almost two years had passed since she'd seen him last, and he seemed older and more careworn to her these days, although he was still a good-looking man whose rough-hewn face bore the not unpleasing lines of strength and character. She said abruptly, "Why is it that Lillith didn't come?"

His eyes met hers. "She's in Edinburgh."

"Doing what?"

"The Lord only knows."

"Is the marriage over?"

"Would you be surprised if it were?"

"No. Your mother's recent letters have hinted that something was amiss."

"And it doesn't bother you?"

"Why should it? I've never believed a couple who are unhappy together should remain together. And I still believe it was silly and priggish of all our small-minded countrymen to criticize Edward VIII for abandoning his duty in order to marry a divorced woman. But, my dear, it hasn't really gone as far as that between you, has it?"

"It might just as well. She's been living with her mother for the past four months, enjoying all the things I can't give her in rural Calverdale: theaters, restaurants, streets crammed with chic little dress shops. I suppose you could call it an unofficial separation.''

"With no hope for a reconciliation?''

Nicholas shook his head. "It doesn't seem likely. Each of us has been waiting for the other to make the first move, though how I shall get around to it is bloody well beyond me. I'm too damned busy. Let her take the time away from her silly friends and her shopping excursions.''

"You sound terribly bitter.''

"Do I? I'm not. Not really. Only bloody weary of the whole thing. I can't even remember when we stopped caring for each other, it happened so long ago.''

"Oh, Nicholas, I am sorry. But I'm grateful that there aren't any children involved. Think how difficult it would have been for them.''

"Yes, I know. That, in fact, has been the root of much of our disagreement all along.''

"Don't tell me Lillith wanted children!'' London exclaimed. She found it impossible to envision childlike, frivolous Lillith saddled with a noisy brood of offspring.

"No, Lillith wasn't the one who wanted a family.''

London looked at Nicholas in some surprise, but he rose abruptly and crossed to the window. Leaning against the sill, he folded his arms across his chest and peered restlessly outside. From where he stood he could make out a corner of the crowded marquee, and the countless cars parked far down the hill. The lawn and the garden paths were filled with guests, the women wearing flowered spring dresses and elegant hats, the men in formal coats, though some had stripped down to their shirtsleeves because of the warmth of the day.

A group of children, shrieking with laughter, passed beneath his window in pursuit of a galloping hound, presumably an escapee from William's kennel. Behind them lumbered Mr. Brockman, Bellehurst's ancient gardener, with a lead in his gnarled hands. Judging from the expression on his face, he wasn't enjoying himself too much.

Smiling, Nicholas turned around to look at the old woman in the bed behind him. He was greatly fond of her; had always

admired her, and was grateful to her, too, for the kindness
and friendship she had shown his mother all these years—
and for the fact that he himself had always been made to feel
so welcome beneath her roof.

"I'm sorry," he told her now. "I came up to see how you
were feeling, not to burden you with my personal problems.
I don't know how you do it, but it's always been so bloody
easy confiding in you."

"The Tuareg were always good listeners," London said
impassively. "Perhaps I learned it from them."

"I want to thank you, too," Nicholas said gravely.

"For what?"

"For what you've meant to me all these years."

Absurdly, she felt tears sting her eyes. She was not normally a woman given to crying easily, and it frightened her
a little. "Go away," she said gruffly. "And for heaven's
sake tell the others I'm not up to receiving anyone else. I'm
tired and old and I want to go to sleep."

"I'll post a guard before your door," Nicholas promised.

"Oh, you." She threw her pillow at him, but he merely
dodged it and, laughing, kissed her cheek before closing the
door.

Chapter
Thirty-one

The ten of them, Victoria, William, their daughters, son,
sons-in-law, and Nicholas, rose like guilty schoolchildren
when London entered the dining room the following morning.
That was probably due to the fact that they had been talking
about her, London thought irritably. Her annoyance faded,

however, when all of them scrambled upright like a flock of geese and bolted around the table toward her.

"Gran! Should you be up so soon?"

"Mama, how could you? Why didn't you ring for Mrs. Jakes?"

"You look marvelous, considering," Nelson added gallantly, kissing her hand.

London smiled at them. She was wearing the same blue dress, refined in taste, that she had had on at yesterday's party when she fell; she had brought along no other. Her silver-blond hair was brushed back into a neat chignon and, although she was pale and walked with something of a limp, she appeared to have recovered surprisingly well from yesterday's accident.

"Sit and have some breakfast," William urged, guiding her solicitously toward the chair on his left. "Coffee?"

"Tea, thank you."

She allowed him to serve her and watched silently as the others resumed their places. "Eugenia and Sara are still at Rose Cottage, I suppose."

Victoria answered. "Yes. Eugenia rang earlier to see how you were. I told her you were still asleep."

"Well, I wasn't. I've been up since daybreak."

"Doing what, for heaven's sake?"

"Lying in bed, thinking."

"About what, Gran?" Winifred wished to know.

London had wanted to wait a little longer before dropping her bombshell on them, but this suddenly seemed as good a time as any. "I've made up my mind to go to Edinburgh. I want to visit Olivia."

No one knew quite what to say. William spoke first. "When?"

"As soon as can be arranged. Tuesday or Wednesday, it doesn't matter."

Victoria's eyes bulged. "Tuesday? But what about your guests? Your family?"

"What about them? Most of them will have gone home by then."

"But how do you propose to get there?"

"In the usual manner. I'll catch the 8:13 to Paddington and from there—"

"But Mama, you can't be serious! Only yesterday Dr. Lowery recommended you stay in bed for at least a few more days—"

Now all of them were talking at once, offering advice or berating her for what London supposed was seen as the irresponsible behavior of a mad old woman. She could tolerate the thought for only so long.

"Be quiet, all of you." She had not raised her voice, but her tone was one that all of them knew. An obedient silence fell. Laying down her butter knife, London regarded each of them in turn. "I've quite made up my mind to go, and I won't allow any of you to change it. My ankle is fine. My spirits are fine. But I'm old. Seventy-five. It occurred to me last night that I haven't the luxury of putting things off much longer. I want to see Livvy. Having Nicholas here reminded me of how long it's been since I've seen her. So instead of trying to talk me out of it, perhaps you should be deciding which of you would be generous enough to accompany me?"

"I'll take you, of course," Nicholas said at once. "It isn't too far out of my way, and Mother, I think, would be delighted."

"And how do you propose to get home?" William demanded. "We can't let you travel back to Kent by yourself."

"That's precisely why I would like one of you to go with me," London said.

Everyone stared down at their plates, as she had half expected them to. She looked at her daughter. "Victoria?"

"Oh, Mama, how can I? Don't you remember our conversation yesterday?"

"I most certainly do. And you're right. You've your own affairs to put into order. Charlotte? Nelson?"

But both of them suddenly remembered other commitments. Winifred, Louisa, and Alice pleaded familial duty. London listened quietly to their apologetic explanations, her expression aloof, letting none of them see that she was hurt.

Perhaps she *was* being churlish and demanding, but, for heaven's sake, how often had she ever asked favors of them?

"Eugenia will come with me," London thought. Eugenia was always ready to travel at a moment's notice, and the money she had inherited when her second husband died had left her marvelously independent. No doubt she'd find a trip to Edinburgh a lovely diversion after the dull rigors of this birthday reunion.

When London returned to Rose Cottage, she asked Eugenia, but her daughter surprised her. "Oh, Mum, I'm sorry, but I can't."

"What do you mean, 'you can't?' "

"The Welchels have asked me to accompany them to Florence. It's already been arranged. They've never been and of course I'd love to act as their guide. Who knows? Maybe I'll even hunt up an old lover or two at the Doney café." Her teasing smile faded. "Oh, Mum, I was only having a bit of fun with you. Tell you what. Why don't you wait until I get back? I won't be gone above three weeks. We could go in July. Think how lovely Edinburgh will be in high summer."

"I want to go now." London didn't care how petulant she sounded. Oddly and inexplicably, a sense of urgency had settled over her during the night, when sleep had eluded her for hour upon dragging hour and she had lain like an invalid in her bed without the will or the strength to move. For some reason, that had frightened her—made her realize that she was becoming vulnerable, frail, *old*.

The kitchen filled with an awkward silence. Half an hour earlier, William had driven London home, and she had confidently put her request to Eugenia the moment she had come across her eldest daughter sitting at the table spreading jelly on a fat raisin scone. Now London lifted her chin and squared her shoulders and told herself it didn't matter. She'd simply go alone, or borrow Miss Wagstaff or Miss Carmody for the trip and hope she'd be able to endure their dry-as-dust personalities for as long as it took to get to Edinburgh and back.

The kitchen door opened and the awkward silence, mercifully, was broken by Sara, who entered whistling, a laundry basket tucked beneath her arm. She stopped in front of them and stared. "Grandmama! When did you arrive? I was just thinking that I'd have some lunch, walk up the drive, and pay you a visit. How are you?"

"Much better today, thank you. Eugenia and I have been having a chin-wag."

Sara set the basket in the corner and poured herself a glass of milk from the icebox. "About what?"

"Your grandmother," Eugenia said crisply, "has decided that she cannot wait to throw off her invalid's bonds in exchange for a wild fling to Edinburgh."

"Eugenia, stop dramatizing. It isn't a wild fling, just an impulsive one. I want to pay a visit to Livvy. With Nicholas here and willing to accompany me as far as Carlisle, there's no reason why I shouldn't. I just need someone who will accompany me back home, that's all."

"After the fall you took yesterday it's out of the question."

"I am not so old," London snapped, "that I can't take a train home from Scotland."

"Is that so? When you haven't traveled farther than Temple Lynn in years? The last time you went to London, for heaven's sake, was for Abigail's christening, when you weren't even seventy yet. Don't you remember? You were thoroughly exhausted when you got back."

London said nothing, but her lips thinned.

Frustrated, Eugenia turned to her niece. "Couldn't you go with her, Sara?"

"I'm sorry, it's impossible. My ship sails from Southampton on the eighteenth."

"That's quite all right, dear," London said calmly. "Eugenia, what time does Victoria intend serving dinner today?"

"Around one, I think."

"Very good. That should give me plenty of time to ring Mr. Clavering at the station." Without another glance at either of them, she went out. Sara and Eugenia exchanged a long look.

Finally Eugenia said, "I hate it went she gets like this. As pig-headed as a bull terrier and twice as foul-tempered. Would you mind telling me why she can't delay the trip for three short weeks? I'd be more than happy to take her when I get back from Italy. And what makes her so certain the time will be convenient for Olivia?''

Sara didn't know what to say. Stepping into the larder, she took out the ham and a wedge of cheese, then sliced the end off a brown loaf of crusty bread. After a while she said, ''I don't know why, but I feel guilty.''

Eugenia patted her arm. ''Don't feel bad, pet. You've your own life to live. It's her fault, really. Stubborn old besom.''

Sara was awakened during the night by the sound of thunder pealing across the hills. Lightning flashed beyond the panes, and then the rain came, drumming on the roof while the wind lashed the treetops and snapped the flowers in the garden. Slipping quietly downstairs to make sure none of the windows had been left open, Sara was startled to come across her grandmother standing in the darkness by the terrace doors and gazing out into the stormy night.

''Even after all these years,'' London said, turning and becoming aware of her granddaughter's presence, ''I've never stopped marveling at English rain. How often it falls, and keeps on falling, till you'd think the earth couldn't hold any more. For some reason it never fails to remind me of Algeria.''

''Algeria? Why?''

''I'm not certain. Maybe because of the contrast. Watching the rain and the wind, I can't help remembering how the sun looked sinking over the salt mines of Bilfha. The way the desert shimmered in the heat. Sometimes, when I lie awake at night listening to the rain tapping on the glass, I find myself dreaming of the nomad's freedom.''

''Oh, Grandmama.'' Sara's voice throbbed. ''I never knew you cared so much, even after all these years. You never said, not once. Why didn't you go back?''

''What for? Ali Wad Zarim always said that a wise man never opens the wounds that God has cleanly healed.''

''You never wrote them, either.''

"For much the same reason. My foster father was the only one in the *zariba* who knew how to read and write. But even if I had written, it would have been fiendishly difficult getting the letters through. And it doesn't really matter anymore. He's probably been dead for years now. All of them would be."

A flash of lightning tore through the darkness. For a brief moment London's face was illuminated in haunting contrast, and what Sara saw in it made her put her hands to her heart. "Oh, Grandmama," she said helplessly. Then, impulsively: "Let me come with you."

A soft laugh. "To Algiers?"

"No, to Edinburgh. Uncle William can change my ticket for me, don't you think?"

"What about your work?"

"Forget my work! It's been *sixteen years* since we saw each other last. I can't think of anything I'd rather do than go to Scotland with you. If you'll have me, that is."

London, who rarely wept, could feel the sudden prick of tears in her eyes. Angrily, she blinked them back. Crying was for the very young . . . and the old. Still, it was a long moment before she trusted herself to speak. "I'd like that very much."

They ended up traveling first class, which came as something of a shock to Victoria and William, considering the cost. But when William tried to talk them out of it, he found his mother-in-law exasperatingly deaf to his arguments. This was to be her first trip to Scotland, London frostily maintained. She intended to go in style.

And stylish it was. The three of them, Nicholas, Sara, and London, had a compartment all to themselves with steam heat and blankets and soft little cushions for resting their heads. The W.C. was right next door, and the dining car directly behind them boasted fine linen and tableware from Spode.

The train departed London in a downpour, chuffing north through the wet, outlying slums and hamlets and towns. Fascinated by the changing scenery, Sara spent the first few hours at the end of the carriage, while Nicholas read and London dozed contentedly in her seat. For tea that afternoon, Eugenia had supplied them with a bulging hamper from Fortnum & Mason, and, along with a lovely bottle of Gamay presented to London on her birthday, they treated themselves to a most satisfying celebration.

As well, Eugenia had seen them off at the station with an enormous bouquet of flowers. These, along with the fashionable hats, gloves, and tailored dresses worn by London and her granddaughter, gave their compartment an elegant atmosphere. The sense of adventure was strong, and London's spirits were high.

Still: "I've noticed you're not being very charitable to Nicholas," London remarked after tea. She and Sara were momentarily alone, Nicholas having volunteered to dispose of their trash in the receptacle at the end of the car.

Sara looked surprised. "What do you mean?"

"You don't seem to have much to say to one another."

"He's not a talkative man."

"No, but you seem rather reserved yourself, dear. Don't you like him?"

"Yes, of course. But I'm afraid we exhausted our mutual interests on the night before your party. I really believe we don't have much else in common."

"What a shame. I had hoped . . . Oh, look to your left, dear. What a charming cathedral. What town is this, I wonder?"

It was still raining when, two hours later, the train halted in York. The pavement glistened, and on the platform people jostled one another with wet luggage and umbrellas. The spires of York minster were shrouded in mist, and Sara, peering through the window, expressed disappointment at the lack of a proper view.

"We'll come again," London assured her.

Will we? Sara thought. It seemed unlikely, and terribly sad.

Eventually, the station master blew his whistle, and the locomotive groaned to life. Sara returned to her seat and picked up her book. After a while, she looked up and saw that London had drifted to sleep with a rug over her knees, for the temperature had been dropping little by little as the train sped north.

"What are you reading?" inquired Nicholas, who had been silent until now.

Sara held up her Penguin edition of *A Farewell to Arms.* "What about you?"

"Nothing so ponderous." Nicholas turned over the cover of the *Illustrated London News*.

They smiled at one another. Then silence fell again. Both of them were a little embarrassed to realize that they had run out of things to say.

The rain ended toward evening, and the sunset proved spectacular: a fiery orange sun breaking free of the millrace of clouds to bathe the rugged landscape in ethereal color. The train had already passed through the northernmost reaches of North Yorkshire, and as the mist lifted, the landscape was seen to be made of brilliant purple moors and deep green hills rolling higher and higher toward mountainous uplands.

London, accustomed to the storybook neatness of Kent, was enchanted. "I can't believe this," she said over and over. "I never dreamed anything could look so wild."

"Then perhaps you should come with me when I change trains in Durham," Nicholas teased. "The Lake District, where I live, is even more spectacular."

Sara noticed that he did not say "we." Did that mean he no longer lived with his wife? Pondering this odd likelihood, she very nearly missed the sudden inspiration that brightened her grandmother's face.

"Why, Nicholas, what a splendid idea! I should love to have a look at the Lakes. Wouldn't you, Sara?"

"No," Sara said at once, appalled. She cast an appealing glance at Nicholas.

"Sara's right. Don't forget you're ticketed through to Edinburgh."

But London was unperturbed by this. "We can always purchase a return from Newcastle and continue to Edinburgh tomorrow."

"Mother's expecting you tonight," Nicholas tried again.

"We can always ring her and say we've been delayed. I'm certain she won't mind."

"I've no place to put you—"

"Surely there's an inn nearby that's clean and moderately priced?"

"Well, yes. The Kennemeade Lodge. It's a small hotel about a mile or two down the lane from my clinic."

"There, you see? It sounds marvelous. What do you think, Sara? Should we spend a night in Wordsworth country?"

Regrettably, Sara could think of no reason why they shouldn't.

"Then it's settled." Suddenly London found herself feeling as happy and irresponsible as a young girl. Free for once of the oppressive atmosphere surrounding Victoria and William's decaying marriage and their constant complaints about money, servants, and the terrible realities of the present, she realized that she had, of late, allowed herself to be drawn too deeply into their difficulties. She was seventy-five years old, for God's sake. Time to stop worrying about her children, time to indulge herself a little. Where had she been since Rupert's funeral? Eugenia was right: no farther than Temple Lynn.

I've come full circle, London thought happily to herself. In her youth she had traveled often and extensively. Ali Wad Zarim had always laughed at her restlessness but had never attempted to curb it. How could she have allowed herself to become so complacent during the long years of marriage to Rupert? Of course, their life together hadn't been entirely easy. The war, the lengthy depression, Rupert's scholarly pursuits, and the difficulty of raising three very different and energetic children had robbed them of much of their freedom.

I'm glad, London thought, *so glad I'm here now. I'd hate to be pushing up daisies without this one final fling.*

Still smiling, she glanced over at her young companions. Neither of them seemed pleased with this sudden, impulsive adventure. Sara was staring out the window, chin in hand, her expression glum beneath the brim of her smart little hat. Nicholas was bent over the cricket reports, but London saw that he was frowning, as though his thoughts lay elsewhere.

Bah, she thought. Tossing aside the rug across her legs, she came energetically to her feet. "I am," she announced, "going to the dining car for a drink. Would either of you care to join me?"

Both of them declined. The compartment door slid shut on her tall, regal figure. Almost immediately Nicholas gave a low whistle. "Is she always so impulsive?"

"Oh, no," said Sara. "Sometimes she's much worse."

"I'm sorry."

"So am I."

He gave a soft laugh, which made him seem all at once more approachable and kind. "I don't mean I'm sorry that you're coming to Calverdale with me. I hope you don't think I'd be so rude."

"I know. And I didn't mean to make it sound as though you were the reason I didn't want to come."

"I know what you meant," Nicholas said. He grinned at her. "Pax?"

Smiling back, Sara shook his outstretched hand. "Pax."

Chapter Thirty-two

"I don't believe I've ever slept so well in my life. How about you, Sara? How do you feel?"

Groaning a little, Sara sleepily opened her eyes to find her grandmother standing, fully dressed in a gray skirt and blue cardigan, at the open window of their room in Kennemeade Lodge. A cool breeze, fragrant as only mountain air can be, wafted inside, making Sara burrow deeper beneath the downy covers of her bed. "Grandmama," she groaned, "how long have you been up?"

"Hours. Long enough to take a walk through the village and down the lane to the prettiest stone bridge you've ever seen. Straight out of a Turner painting. Then I had a lovely chat with Mrs. Quint, our hostess, and rang Nicholas at his surgery."

Sara raised herself up on one elbow. "My, you have been busy. Did he get in touch with his mother?"

"He did. And Livvy was so delighted to learn we were here that she decided to come down herself. She'll be with us around suppertime, I think. I hope you don't mind. I know you've never been to Edinburgh, and if you've really set your heart on seeing it—"

Sara sat up and brushed the hair from her eyes. For a moment she regarded her grandmother in silence, then she smiled. "You are the most exasperatingly unpredictable person I've ever known. No, I don't mind missing Edinburgh, if the Lake District is what you want to see. I just hope Nicholas warned you that this glorious weather won't last. He told me yesterday that the area rarely sees any sun."

"I know. I don't mind. Do you?"

Despite herself, Sara had to laugh. "No, I guess not. At least you're right about that good night's sleep." She got out of bed, stretching and yawning. Crossing to the dresser she rummaged through her valise. "I only hope I brought along the proper things for trekking. I assume you want to go trekking?"

"But of course. What else does one do here in the fells?"

"No twenty-mile hikes, Grandmama, do you promise?"

"Sara. I am neither a professional mountaineer nor an idiot. I'll leave the ascent of Scafell Pike to the young. But a turn around the moors after breakfast would be just the thing. Now, where are my woollies? I could have sworn . . . Ah, here they are. You'd better dress warmly too. There's a chill in the air."

"Yes, Grandmama," Sara said dutifully. "And how about breakfast? I'm starved."

Nicholas Warburton, M.R.C.V.S., screwed the cap onto a tube of ointment and handed it to the elderly gentleman across the examination table. "Here you go, Mr. Coggins. Use it twice a day and that rash should clear right up."

"Thank you, Mr. Warburton." The ointment was tucked carefully into a patched trouser pocket. "I'll ring you at week end and let you know how he's farin'."

"Yes, do that."

Mr. Coggins picked up the small black dog that cowered on the table and tucked it beneath one arm. The surgery door closed softly behind him. Nicholas washed and dried his hands before crossing to the inner door leading to the waiting room. "Next, please."

A young woman in dark slacks, boots, and a thick guernsey sweater rose and came toward him, smiling. Unaccustomed to such revolutionary attire here in the remote Cumbrian fells, Nicholas couldn't help staring, before his gaze traveled upward to the lovely, smiling face. With something of a shock he recognized Sara.

"Hello," she said. "I hope you don't mind my being here."

"Not at all. How long have you been waiting?"

"Since the orange tom with the torn ear."

"That was quite some time ago. You should have announced yourself."

"It didn't seem fair, cutting in front of your patients. You've got a very busy practice."

Nicholas glanced past her into the empty waiting room. "I'm finished for now. Where's your grandmother?"

"Off on a tour of her own. We couldn't agree on where to go, and finally Mr. Quint offered to drive her to Grasmere."

"To see Wordsworth's cottage?"

"Yes."

"What about you? What did you have in mind?"

Sara's bright blue eyes dropped from his face, and a faint blush stole across her cheeks. "I'm interested in your dispensary. I was hoping you'd have time to show it to me."

"I just happen to have a few minutes before I leave on my rounds. Come on."

Nicholas's surgery was located on the ground floor of an eighteenth-century farmhouse built of native gray stone, with a weathered slate roof. The barren hills rose steeply behind it, but the garden was lush and green, and flowering fruit trees were scattered amid the chestnuts and pines. The village road ran nearby, separated from the house and the outbuildings by a tidy yard. Beyond it lay a small pasture enclosed by stone walls filled with numerous bawling, black-faced sheep.

Nicholas led Sara on a tour of the surgery, with its narrow passages and numerous small rooms smelling strongly of ether. He showed her his instruments, the calipers, forceps, firing irons, calving hooks, scalpels, and syringes stored neatly on sterilized cloths or hanging from the whitewashed walls. The dispensary was small but well-stocked, and Sara wandered among the shelves of colorful glass bottles and the mortars, pestles, scales, and graduated beakers, feeling very much at home.

"Do you practice alone?" she asked.

"No. I've a partner. We share the work, large and small animals alike. Actually, the house and surgery are his. I came into the practice eight years ago, when I was first newly qualified."

"Do you live here too?"

"Yes. My wife and I have . . . had a suite of rooms on the second floor. Francis, my partner, is unmarried." Nicholas was busy collecting tincture bottles and syringes as he spoke. Dropping them into a metal case he said, "I'm due at Harold Shopes's for some tuberculin testing."

Sara hesitated. "Would you mind if I came along?"

"It'll take most of the afternoon. He's got nearly sixty head to be surveyed. It's long, smelly work."

"I don't mind."

He smiled at her grudgingly. "Okay. But don't say you weren't warned."

Pausing long enough to notify the housekeeper of his departure, Nicholas led Sara around to the garage where an ancient Morris was parked amid the straw bales and a dusty collection of antique farming tools. The car was so tiny that Sara had to tuck her long legs beneath her and sit hunched over so that her head wouldn't hit the roof. The car rattled and groaned as Nicholas backed it out into the drive, but when he apologized she merely laughed.

"Don't worry. After riding in Aunt Eugenia's Austin I can tolerate anything."

Nicholas laughed, and it occurred to Sara that the awkwardness that had existed between them ever since his arrival at Bellehurst had faded. Yes, he was a quiet man, but she no longer felt as though she had to deliberately think up things to say in order to dispel the silence between them.

Harold Shopes's farm was nestled in a quiet valley between two towering mountains, which the locals called "tops," at the very end of a winding, isolated road. The lovely white farmhouse sat near the banks of a thundering stream, and the mountains rose dramatically behind it, their gold-green peaks crisscrossed with mile upon mile of wandering stone fences.

Mr. Shopes came out to meet them as the Morris coughed loudly and died in the cobbled yard. When Sara got out, the sharp, familiar scent of cattle came to her on the wind. She could hear their plaintive lowing from inside the byre, the sound mingling pleasantly with the rushing of the water.

"Na, then, good day to thee, Mr. Warburton," said Mr. Shopes. He was small, lean, and shaggy-haired, and was staring unabashedly at Sara's slacks as he spoke.

Sara tossed her head and smiled at him while Nicholas, lips twitching, introduced her. "This is a cousin of mine, Mr. Shopes. Sara Ashford, from America."

The faded eyes in the weatherbeaten face continued to regard her with deep interest. "Pleased to meet you, miss."

"Has the herd been put up?" Nicholas asked.

Instantly Mr. Shopes became brisk and business-like. "Got ten in t' fold yard, twenty in t' barn, and the eighteen young be together in t' stalls."

"Right. Then we'll start with the big ones, shall we?"

Mr. Shopes's son and younger brother met them outside the barn, and they, too, stared pop-eyed at Sara when they were introduced.

"Why don't you sit here?" Mr. Shopes invited, dusting off a milking stool for her.

"Thank you."

Nicholas set aside his instruments, took off his jacket, and rolled up his sleeves. Stooping, he scrubbed his hands in a bucket of soapy water. Sara noticed that his arms were nearly as browned and muscular as Mr. Shopes's, who spent his life outdoors involved in heavy labor.

The cattle, a herd of shaggy Shorthorns, were mingling nervously against the far wall of the barn, their nostrils dilated, the steam rising from their bodies. It was up to the Shopeses to catch them by the nose and halter them quickly so that each in turn could be held still while Nicholas administered an intradermal injection. Some of the creatures were docile, others bucked and kicked and bellowed in panic, and still others were so wild that all three men were forced to wrestle them into submission.

By the time they were half way through they were all sweating heavily, and the temperature in the barn had risen uncomfortably. As well, the Shorthorns' diet of new spring grass had loosened their bowels, and when Nicholas and his helpers had finished with the last of the calves they were all but covered with brownish-green muck.

"Thank God," Mr. Shopes grunted at last. "That be the last of 'em."

The barn was suddenly, miraculously, still. All of the bawling creatures had been released back to pasture, and now only the bull stood alone in his stall, eyeing them with his dark, unperturbed bovine eyes.

Nicholas came around the enclosure, but when Sara got up from her stool he waved her away. "You'd do better to wait outside. We none of us smell very good." He was stripping off his grimy shirt as he spoke, and Sara, laughing, obliged.

The sun was still shining when she stepped outside, but the wind was cold, and she shivered and folded her arms across her chest as she leaned against the Morris waiting for Nicholas. After a moment he came, his box of instruments in one hand, an apologetic smile on his face as Sara straightened and walked toward him.

"I tried cleaning up a bit, but a bucket and brush rarely do justice to the worst of it."

"It's a hot bath you'll be needing," Sara agreed, wrinkling her nose.

"Mr. Shopes invited us to lunch, but I hope you don't mind that I begged off. Mrs. Coulson will have something hot waiting back at the surgery, and I'd like to change before I eat."

"Yes, I think you'd better." It was difficult for Sara to keep a straight face. To her, Nicholas no longer resembled the well-dressed veterinary surgeon who had arrived at the farm several hours ago. Now he looked more like a wrestler who had challenged his opponent to a mud skirmish and lost. His boots, shirt, and trousers, and even a bit of his hair, were caked with mud—or manure. (Sara wasn't sure and she had no desire to find out.) There were bruises on his arms and a tear in his pant leg where one of the struggling animals had kicked him.

"So this is how you fill your days."

He grinned. "Not always. Most of the time it's sheep, and they're a sight more docile."

They drove back to the surgery, where Nicholas went immediately upstairs to wash and change. Left alone in the hall, Sara found her way to the big, whitewashed kitchen and asked the housekeeper if she could help with the lunch.

Mrs. Coulson was at first inclined to refuse, for she was unable to help viewing Mr. Warburton's visitor with considerable disapproval. However, she quickly discovered that, trousers notwithstanding, Miss Ashford was made of the same, unpretentious stock as herself, and she thawed visibly.

"I've nothin' to offer but mash and bangers," she said apologetically, placing a tureen of steaming sausages on the dining-room table. "I wasn't told to expect an American for lunch, and I'm not sure you'll care for them—"

Sara assured her, quite truthfully, that she had been raised on such provincial fare at Bellehurst and that she had never lost her taste for the dish no matter how long she had lived in America. Mrs. Coulson thawed further and even began to smile a little; she was a dour woman not usually given to intimacy with either her employers' patients or guests.

"Sit down, miss, sit down. Mr. Warburton should be along right shortly."

"Well," said Nicholas, entering the dining room as if on cue, "I trust I'm presentable now?"

Sara sniffed the air experimentally and assured him that he was. They ate together in companionable silence. Sara was surprised how much the crisp mountain air had affected her appetite—or perhaps Mrs. Coulson's talents as a cook had something to do with the number of helpings she ate.

Nicholas watched her with some amusement. Lillith, his wife, had the same slim figure as Sara, but tended to pamper it considerably more than Sara did. In fact, it was rare for Lillith to eat more than a few bites at any given meal, and he wondered suddenly if her self-imposed habit of starvation wasn't partly responsible for—

Sara's soft voice interrupted his thoughts. "You're frowning. Is something wrong?"

"No," he answered honestly. "I was just thinking about my wife."

Sara waited for him to say more, but when he did not, she looked down at her plate and toyed for a moment with her potatoes. "Does she live here with you?"

"Not anymore. She left for Edinburgh several months ago."

"Does she intend to come back? I'm sorry. Perhaps I shouldn't—"

"No, it's all right. And, no, I don't believe she will." Nicholas refreshed his glass of lager, drained it, and set it aside. "Lillith was born a MacCrae, a name you'd recognize if you were familiar with Edinburgh. Her mother was the granddaughter of an earl and a considerable heiress in her own right, while her father made a fortune building ships during the war. I met her at a party while I was still at university and we got married the year I accepted this position here with Francis. At first Lillith was enchanted with the countryside, but after a few dismal years of continuous bad weather and nowhere to go but church or the local pub she became, I think, excruciatingly bored. Naturally the district has its charms, but not when you crave the excitement of the city.''

Sara said, ''I'm sorry,'' and meant it.

''It doesn't matter. Not really. I think, looking back on everything now, that we stopped loving each other a long time ago.''

Sara was suddenly embarrassed. She sensed that Nicholas was telling her things he rarely told anyone else or even, perhaps, admitted to himself. And all at once her heart went out to him, and she felt a sudden, unexpected surge of animosity toward this unknown Lillith, who had seen fit to hurt such a kind and gentle man, a man who had doubtless tried his best to do right by her and make her happy.

She set aside her fork and folded her napkin. ''I think it's time I left. Grandmama will probably be back from Grasmere by now and will be wondering what's become of me.''

Nicholas glanced at the wall clock. ''I didn't realize it was so late. I've got to keep surgery hours from four to six. Do you want me to drive you?''

''Oh, no, that isn't necessary. I'm happy to walk.'' She rose and gathered up her dishes, but Nicholas waved her away.

''Leave them, please. Mrs. Coulson would have a rugger of a fit. One rule here at the surgery is never to invade her territory.''

''If you insist . . .''

''I most emphatically do.''

He accompanied her out into the hall. Catching sight of her reflection in the mirror, Sara gave a mock shriek of alarm and turned accusingly to Nicholas. ''Why didn't you tell me I looked so—so rumpled?''

''Because I didn't think that you did. You looked quite charming to me.'' He smiled down at her as he said this, and Sara was suddenly aware of how tall he was. Unexpectedly she found herself at a loss for words.

''It was kind of you to let me tag along,'' she managed a last. ''Thank you.''

''We'll do it again, if you like.''

''Yes, I would.''

"You didn't mind the heat and the dirt?"

"Not at all."

"And the manure?"

She laughed. "It's a fact of life for a veterinarian, isn't it? Why should I mind?"

His eyebrow arched in surprise. "Really?"

"Really."

She went down the steps to the drive and turned to wave at him before starting down the road. He watched her walk away, a tall, graceful woman, not a girl anymore, in slim trousers and a heavy knit sweater. A woman who had, he remembered suddenly, once stood up to the combined menace of her bullying cousins and who had nearly broken his nose with a cricket bat. A woman who had not, apparently, changed at all, for she had taken the lewd ogling of the Shopes men in stride; even laughed about it and then proceeded to sit quietly in the midst of bellowing calves, cursing, sweating men, and an endless fusillade of vile green manure. Obviously a woman in a million, just like that tough, wonderful grandmother of hers.

He saw that Sara had disappeared around the bend in the road. Turning, he went back inside, where he found Mrs. Coulson washing dishes at the kitchen sink. She looked up, saw him, and immediately began berating him for having let his guest go home without offering her dessert.

"Good manners is good manners," Mrs. Coulson reminded him pointedly, "and a proper dinner ain't never finished without proper pudding."

"I'm sorry, Mrs. Coulson. I didn't realize you had anything prepared for dessert."

"I baked a fruit tart while you were gone at the Shopes's."

Nicholas regarded her with some surprise. Mrs. Coulson's fruit tarts were rare treats at the surgery. Sara probably didn't know it, but somehow she had managed to earn the housekeeper's respect—rarely given to strangers—and managed it quite effortlessly, slacks and all.

Chapter
Thirty-three

That evening, Livvy Warburton arrived on schedule and was picked up at the station by the amiable Mr. Quint. She came loaded down with baggage, smartly attired in a dark blue suit and giving off the delicious essence of patchouli powder. Sara had only a very dim memory of the grief-bowed widow who had shared the Christmas holidays with them at Bellehurst so many years ago, but at any rate this older Olivia no longer resembled the shy, unsure creature she had been then.

Although she had aged and was decidedly frail, she had retained much of the charm and effervescence that had first made Archie Warburton sit up and take notice. When they were introduced that evening in the parlor of Kennemeade Lodge, Sara was treated to a warm embrace and a barrage of compliments that seemed genuinely meant.

Livvy had also managed to retain the slimness of her youth, and her chestnut hair, done up in fashionable sausage curls, bore only a few traces of gray. It was plain to see that she was delighted to see London and that the feeling was warmly reciprocated. Sara sat listening as they caught up on news, talked of old times, and generally behaved in such a girlish, giggling manner that she found herself fascinated. Nor did they come up for air until they heard Nicholas's aging Morris groaning up the drive.

And then, all at once, Livvy became grave. "Oh, my dear," she said to London, "I *must* ask your advice. Before Nicholas comes in. It's about Lillith."

Sara rose politely to her feet. "I think I'll meet Nicholas in the hall. He'll be wondering where we are."

Livvy smiled at her gratefully. "Thank you, dear."

"Now, what is it you wanted to tell me about Lillith?" London asked when they were alone.

Livvy leaned forward. Her tone became grave. "I saw her yesterday. I made a point to stop off at her parents' to let her know I was coming here. You'll never imagine what she told me. London, she's met someone else."

"By that do you mean another man?"

Olivia's eyes brimmed with sudden tears. "I'm afraid so."

"Is she in love with him?"

"From what she said, I imagine she is. He's an older man, a business partner of her father's, and apparently quite wealthy. What on earth am I to tell Nicholas?"

"Nothing."

"But—"

"Livvy, darling, it's really none of our business. You've no right to say one word, not unless Lillith specifically asked you to. Did she?"

"No. She said she was going to tell Nicholas herself, but I do feel I should warn him."

"You've *got* to leave it up to her. Pretend you're unaware of a thing, no matter how difficult that may be."

Olivia sighed. "I suppose you're right, but I do so hate sitting by and doing nothing to help."

"At the moment it's the kindest thing you can do," London said gently.

"But—"

"Hush, darling. Here they come."

Olivia smoothed down her dress and did her best to assume a bright smile. When the parlor door opened she sprang to her feet. "Oh, Nicholas, darling, there you are!" She hurried across the room to embrace her tall son and to kiss, in turn, the proffered cheek of the short, balding man behind him. This, as Sara had already learned in the hall, was Francis Whister, Nicholas's partner. He had a pleasant face, a small, neatly trimmed mustache, and a very courtly manner that she had liked at once.

"Shall we go in to dinner?" London asked brightly.

The dining room of the Kennemeade Lodge had a pleasant

bar with an open fire and oak settles at one end. Because it was so early in the season, they were among the only guests, and were treated to an enormous country meal of home-grown produce and fresh vegetables from the inn's small glasshouse garden. As well, there was seafood salad and Cumberland sausage, the local specialty, and a surprisingly good ale that loosened their tongues and kept the conversation flowing all evening.

Sara, in fact, had never seen Nicholas so talkative. It was obvious to her that he was greatly fond of his mother and her grandmother, and she wondered how often the three of them had visited together while she was far away in America.

"What shall we do tomorrow?" inquired Olivia, when the last of the pastries and the fresh-ground coffee had been consumed.

Francis said, "I've given Nicholas his freedom for the day."

"How kind of you, Mr. Whister! Now, London, you and Sara must tell us if you have any special wishes."

London said thoughtfully, "Perhaps, if the weather permits, we could take the ferry to Hawkshead."

"That would be grand. Both of you *must* see Windermere while you're here. It's the largest and quite the loveliest lake in England."

They all agreed that this was an excellent idea, and plans were drawn up as to where and when they would meet in the morning. Nicholas suggested that they take the local bus to Windermere because the four of them would never fit comfortably into his car, but Francis protested, fearful that the older ladies would become too fatigued if they were forced to wait at the stop.

"You can take my car and I'll use the Morris to make my rounds. Now, now, Mrs. Warburton, there's no need to thank me. I'm quite happy to do it."

Sara inquired softly of Nicholas, "Has he driven your car before?"

"Not recently. I can't think why else he'd behave like such a gentleman."

They exchanged a knowing smile, and then Nicholas pushed back his chair. "See you in the morning, then."

Olivia held out her cheek to be kissed. "Good night, my dear. Sleep well."

The three of them, Olivia, London, and Sara, remained at the table while the Morris crunched away down the drive, and all was at once very cozy and still. Yawning discreetly, London rose and announced that she intended to retire. The others agreed that this was an excellent suggestion, and Sara slept deeply that night with the fresh mountain air streaming through the open window.

Breakfast was an enormous Lakeland tradition that included black pudding, Cumberland sausage, haggis, and an eye-opening variety of fresh breads and scones and even a platter of smoked rainbow trout. Sara could not remember when she had last eaten so well—or so much.

The weather was overcast, with a chill to the air, and she had dressed warmly in a heavy skirt and sweater, with thick stockings beneath her walking shoes. After breakfast she went back upstairs to brush her teeth, comb her hair, and draw a line of lipstick across her lips. Then she settled herself on the bed and leafed through a magazine while she waited for her grandmother.

"There's no need for you to wait here," London protested, emerging from the bathroom. "The downstairs parlor is much cozier. Oh, isn't that a car turning into the drive?"

It was, and London, crossing to the window, recognized Francis's well-tended Hillman. "Why don't you go down and meet Nicholas?" she said to Sara. "Tell him Livvy and I will be down in a moment."

By the time Sara got to the landing, Nicholas had already crossed the porch, opened the front door, and stepped into the hotel's pleasantly appointed hall. Looking up and seeing her on the stairs, he said without preamble, "I'm afraid we're going to have to delay our departure for a bit. I've gotten a call, and with Francis already gone, I had to take it."

"Oh, dear. Nothing serious, is it?"

"Probably not. A fellow near Rydal has a farrowing sow in a bit of difficulty. I shouldn't be too long."

"Do you mind if I come?"

He looked surprised. "If you'd like."

Mr. Quint, who was working at his ledger behind the front desk, waved them toward the door. "Go on, then, Mr. Warburton. I'll tell the ladies you've been delayed."

"Thank you. I am in a bit of a hurry."

They went quickly down to the car. A soft mist hung over the dells as they passed beyond the village and sped toward the open pastureland. They did not speak as Nicholas turned south down the Keswick road and, passing a lumbering tractor, drove on for another mile or so before bearing sharply to the left. Then they were bumping down a plain dirt track running alongside a river with high, grass-grown banks. On the opposite side, in a wide green pasture, grazed a flock of the ever-present sheep.

"That's the Rothay River," Nicholas said.

"It's beautiful. In fact, the whole countryside is breathtaking. I'm truly glad I came."

"You might not be, after we get to Walter Soames's place."

"Why not?"

"Ever been around pigs before?"

"Not really."

"Then just wait and see."

The Soames farm consisted of a rambling stone cottage with a green slate roof, surrounded by sagging barns and smaller outbuildings. Leaning fence posts and lichen-covered walls attested to the farm's great age, which Nicholas said numbered at least two hundred years, if not more. The setting was bucolic, wildly remote, and, as well, permeated with the unmistakable tang of porcine manure, a sharply acrid smell that assailed Sara the moment she got out of the car.

Nicholas took off his tweed jacket and tossed it on the front seat. "You'd better wait here."

"Why?"

He looked her up and down. "If you value your clothes, you'd better."

"Don't be silly," Sara retorted, laughter in her voice. "I'm sure there's nothing inside that barn that a good laundering can't cure.''

He was surprised, but did not show it. Lillith had always been considerably more particular about her wardrobe. But there was the laboring sow to be thought of, and he left her to make her own way slowly across the urine-dampened floor to the end of the barn where Mr. Soames waited in the glaring light of a single bulb.

Sara looked across the partition at an enormous pink sow lying on her side in the straw. Her flanks were shuddering and heaving, and she was making soft grunting noises that could only be interpreted as sounds of distress. Nicholas had already stripped off his shirt and was washing his hands and forearms in a bucket of soapy water the farmer had provided.

"How long has she been like this?"

"Since eight this mornin'. Been strainin' all along and doin' herself no good."

"It's not her first litter, is it?"

"Nay, Mr. Warburton. She's had two others and not a problem with either."

Nicholas stepped over the uneven boards that sectioned off the sow's pen from the rest of the barn. "Probably a malpresentation. It shouldn't be too hard to help her out." He patted the sow's trembling flank as he spoke and, kneeling beside her, inserted his arm into the birth canal. Sara and Mr. Soames watched in silence as he palpated carefully, frowning a little, the dark hair falling into his eyes.

"Aye, that's what it is. The first little fellow got turned around, that's all. He'll probably be dead, I'm afraid—" Nicholas withdrew his hand as he spoke, and a tiny, pink-snouted piglet emerged that, to their surprise, was kicking feebly. Nicholas worked quickly to clear the fluid from its mouth and nose and, massaging it with a rough burlap sack, finally placed it within reach of a milk-engorged teat.

"There be the next 'un!" exclaimed Mr. Soames excitedly as another piglet emerged, kicking and struggling, entirely on its own.

Nicholas said, "I think she'll be fine now. I'll give her an injection just to make sure."

The pitocin worked quickly, and once the contractions became sharper and stronger, the exhausted sow was able to deliver the rest of her litter with gratifying ease. Half an hour later, ten healthy little piglets were grunting and tugging eagerly at her teats.

"I've seen it so many times," Nicholas said softly, breaking the long silence, "but it still seems like a miracle." He gathered up his belongings and grinned at Sara. "Now comes the fun part."

"What's that?"

"Driving back with me in the car."

"You'll be wanting some tea, you and the missus," said Mr. Soames.

"Thank you, no. We're already late for another appointment." Nicholas was scrubbing his naked arms and chest as he spoke. Pulling on his shirt, he shook hands with Mr. Soames and went with Sara out to the car. They both climbed in, but even with the windows rolled down the smell stayed stubbornly with them.

Sara made a face. "Whew! I see what you meant."

"It's nearly impossible to wash off. I'll have to bathe and change before I can even think of taking my mother and your grandmother to Windermere."

"I'll have to do the same," Sara said, because the smell seemed to have permeated her own clothing as well.

"Nicholas," she said after a moment.

"Umm?"

"Do I look anything like Lillith?"

"What? Oh, because of what Mr. Soames said? Actually, you're just the opposite. Tall and titian-haired, while Lillith is very small and blond."

"Then why—"

"Mr. Soames has never met my wife. Neither have most of my other farming clients. Lillith has never, in all the years of our marriage, accompanied me on my rounds. Nor would she dream of frequenting the places the local farmers go to of an evening."

"I see," said Sara. Although Nicholas had spoken without emotion, she couldn't help feeling sorry for both of them.

By the time they reached Kennemeade Lodge, the awkward reference to Lillith was forgotten. Instead they were involved in a lively discussion concerning the farrowing and the merits of pitocin. Indeed, Sara had forgotten all about the way the two of them smelled until London, coming down the walk to meet them, let her outstretched arms fall to her sides as she backed away in mock horror.

"Oh, my dears! There's no need to ask where you've been! You'll have to clean yourselves up, otherwise they won't allow you on the ferry."

"You've never been one to hesitate about hitting from the shoulder, have you?" Nicholas teased. "You might have put that more discreetly."

"Indeed not." London's aristocratic nose twitched imperiously. "No other words could describe what you are. Off with you now, my boy. I'll see that Sara is ready by the time you return."

Laughing, Nicholas caught Sara's eye. *I told you so*, he mouthed.

She saluted him as London herded her up into the hall. In the end nothing remained for Sara but to undress completely, slip into the bath, shampoo her hair, and lather herself vigorously with a bar of soap. When she emerged at last, scrubbed clean, dressed in a new gray dress and matching sweater and sprayed sweetly with some of her grandmother's cologne, she presented herself downstairs and was pleased to earn their unqualified approval.

Regrettably, it turned out to be a waste of time. While Sara had bathed upstairs, the weather had taken a nasty turn, and neither Livvy nor London declared themselves willing to brave the icy wind on the open deck of the ferry.

"We'll sit here by the fire and warm ourselves with tea," Livvy said. "And chat until dinner. What do you think, Sara?"

But Sara felt restless, although she was unable to explain why, and it was with a feeling of deep relief that she saw Francis's Hillman turn into the drive and Nicholas's tall, oilskin-clad figure come striding up the walk.

Inside the door he paused, shaking the rain off him. Stepping into the parlor he laughed at the sight of London knitting contentedly in an armchair and his mother curled on the sofa drinking tea. "Looks like you're settled in for the afternoon."

"Yes. Do you mind? It's much too miserable for an outing."

Nicholas turned to Sara. "What about you? Still interested?"

She nodded, her spirits soaring. "If you are."

"You're not going on the ferry, I hope," Olivia said worriedly.

"No. We'd do better to drive down to Grasmere. Tour some of the studios and craft shops," Nicholas said.

"That would be nice," London agreed. "I visited some of them yesterday. Will we see you at dinner?"

"Of course." Nicholas looked at Sara. "Ready?"

She was, and it took only a moment for them to dash across the wet grass to the car and rumble off down the road. Although the sky pressed ominously low and the rain continued to pour, the landscape had lost none of its charm. If anything, the stark hills and tumbling rivers appeared even more dramatic, shorn of the sunlight's softness, as the scenery unfolded, dark and brooding, before them.

"It's lovely," Sara exclaimed, peering through the dripping windscreen. "Even in the rain."

"You won't be saying that if we happen to get a flat."

"Are you always so positive?" she chided.

"You're right," he said, "I'm sorry." And he smiled at her in a way that made the heat creep to Sara's cheeks.

"Here we are," Nicholas said after a moment, and Sara looked up to find that the car was bumping into the village of Grasmere which, despite the weather, still possessed an Old World charm that was enhanced by its lovely stone houses, quaint streets, and antique pubs.

Nicholas parked the car near a whitewashed storefront whose sign board proclaimed it the studio of Heaton Cooper, an artist, Nicholas explained, who, like his father before him, spent most of his summers on the tops sketching the beauty of the lakes.

"Why, this is Mr. Soames's old farm!" Sara exclaimed,

stepping inside the neat, well-lit studio and halting before a lovely watercolor that was instantly recognizable. "I can't believe he'd paint something so ordinary, and make it look so beautiful!"

"Because you're seeing it through the eyes of a painter who lives in the very landscape he paints," Nicholas explained, joining her. "The local artists have been doing it for at least two hundred years. Some of the early paintings by Turner, for example, could easily be used as maps today."

"May I help you?" A young woman wearing glasses and a heavy sweater was coming toward them, smiling in welcome. Sara asked the price of the Soames painting and was disappointed to discover that she lacked the money to purchase it.

"No problem," Nicholas told her. "I'll buy it for you."

Sara was delighted. "Oh, that's sweet of you! I'll pay you back as soon as—"

"No, I said I'd buy it for you. I want you to accept it as a gift."

"But I couldn't!"

"Why not?

"Because . . ." She didn't know why.

Nicholas dug into his pocket. "Think of it as a commemoration of your first trip to a farrowing house." To the salesgirl: "Wrap it up well, please. I'd hate for it to get wet."

Later they stopped to warm themselves in a crooked-fronted old pub with leaded windows and a sloping roof facing the market square. Stepping through to one of the back rooms, they settled themselves comfortably in a booth near the fire. The ceiling was low-beamed, the atmosphere one of unvarnished warmth and character. Nicholas ordered tea for them both, and, as well, a pint of ale for himself.

"In Kent, this would be called an inglenook," Sara said, looking about her.

"And in America?"

She frowned. "I don't know. The pubs—bars—are so different there. They lack the . . . oh, coziness that your English pubs seem to have."

"Do you make it a habit of frequenting bars back in the States?"

Sara laughed. "No, I don't."

"Then what do you do? When you're not working, I mean?"

"I'm something of a homebody," Sara confessed.

"You still live at Haversham with your mother."

"Yes. Though the house has become something of a white elephant since my stepfather died. Much too large for the two of us and too costly to maintain. Mother is considering selling it and moving to a smaller house."

"Will you go with her when she does?"

Sara smiled wryly. "I'm not sure. Sometimes I tell myself I'm too old to go on living with my mother, and I'm certainly earning enough to afford a place of my own. But still . . ." Her voice trailed off. For some reason, her life sounded terribly shallow and pointless when described to Nicholas that way. Which was odd, because she'd never thought of it like that before. She could feel Nicholas's dark, intense gaze upon her.

"Any plans to get married?"

"Heavens, no!"

"Never been serious about anyone?"

She looked down at her hands. "Yes, once."

"What happened?"

"He was killed in the war."

"You must have been very young."

"I was. Barely sixteen. He was much older."

"I'm sorry."

She looked at him. His expression was open, kind. She realized that he meant it, and was deeply touched. "You're the first person I've ever told."

"He must have meant a great deal."

Absurdly, she felt tears sting the back of her eyes. "Yes, yes he did. No one—no other man—has ever made me feel the same way he did."

"No one?" Nicholas sounded doubtful.

Sara laughed weakly. "Well, there were one or two others. I was very fond of my mentor at university. We were . . . close for a number of years."

"But not close enough to get married."

Sara shook her head. "I almost did get married once. Strangely enough, he was one of the many 'eligibles' Mother was always throwing at my head. He loved horses the way my stepfather did, and I suppose that's what served to make him special to me. That and the fact that he believed there was more to life than debutante balls and making the social register."

"What happened to him?"

"Nothing. He married someone else and moved to Newport."

Nicholas's wise, dark eyes rested briefly on her face. "You were afraid to make a commitment, weren't you? Because of this other man. The one who was killed in the war."

"Yes," Sara whispered. She smiled thinly. "I suppose that's why I'll always be an old maid."

"A pity," Nicholas said.

Sara looked at him, but he was drinking his beer, and his face was turned away from her so that she couldn't see the expression on it. She sipped her tea, wondering silently how he had managed to understand her so well. It made her feel grateful toward him and made her wonder, too, why on earth Lillith Warburton had decided Nicholas wasn't the sort of man worth holding on to.

She was startled when Nicholas set his empty glass down with a bang and said, "Let's go," in a taut voice that she had never heard him use before. In silence she followed him to the bar, waited while he paid, and then went out with him into the gray, dying day.

Neither of them spoke during the drive back to Calverdale. Glancing now and again into Nicholas's set face, Sara realized that he was angry, but she couldn't understand why.

When the car jerked to a halt in front of Kennemeade Lodge, she gathered up her belongings. "Would you like to come in?" she asked brightly. "Your mother would probably appreciate seeing you."

"I've got to get back in time for evening surgery," Nicholas said curtly.

"Oh. I see." She opened the door, got out, and leaned down to speak to him through the window and thank him again for the painting. But Nicholas shifted gears and sped away, the tires crunching across the wet gravel. Sara stared after him, feeling thoroughly bewildered and not a little hurt.

Chapter Thirty-four

"Grandmama?"

"Sara?"

London finally found the light switch. She sat up, blinking like a cat blinded by headlights, and gave her granddaughter an apologetic smile. "I must have dozed off. Silly of me, but it was so warm in the parlor, and when I came upstairs I thought I'd lie down for just a moment." Her eyes narrowed as they rested on her granddaughter's face, then moved to the bulky package under her arm. "What have you got there? Did you buy something in Grasmere?"

"Yes, a painting. Actually, Nicholas paid for it."

"May I see it?"

"If you like."

There was silence as London broke the seal and took off the thick brown wrapping. "Oh, my dear, it's beautiful. What a lovely keepsake of your trip!"

"Oh, Grandmama, I think I'd much rather forget today's outing, thank you."

London carefully returned the watercolor to its wrapping, set it down on the small table between their beds, and, pushing the hair from her eyes, regarded her granddaughter in silence. At last she said, "You've quarreled with Nicholas."

Sara gave a hollow laugh. "More to the point, Nicholas quarreled with me. Or at least I think he wanted to. On the way home in the car he was so quiet, as though he were angry with me, and for no apparent reason.''

"No reason? Are you sure?''

"None that I know of. We were in a pub in Grasmere, talking about nothing important . . .''

"It couldn't have been unimportant.''

"Well, it was,'' Sara insisted.

"Perhaps not to Nicholas.''

Sara said scornfully, "Grandmama, you're dramatizing!''

"And you seem angry all of a sudden,'' London observed. "Would you mind telling me why?''

Sara tossed her head. "If you must know, we were discussing my past.''

"Do you mean your past as it pertains to men?''

Sara's chin tilted. "I do. Nicholas was so kind and understanding in the pub and I thought . . . Oh, it doesn't matter what I thought!''

London's expression softened with sudden understanding. "Oh, my dear, are you telling me you've been in love before? With whom? You've never told me anything about it.''

"I know.''

"Would you like to tell me now?''

Sara's voice trembled. "No.''

"Very well.'' The mattress creaked as London got to her feet. "It's probably high time we joined Livvy in the dining room. As for Nicholas, I can't begin to help you understand what happened when I have no idea what the two of you were talking about.''

She crossed to the mirror as she spoke and, unpinning her hair, began to brush and plait the shining, silver-blond strands. It was a familiar gesture to the watching girl, bringing back the long-ago nights of her childhood, when she had crept down to her grandmother's bedroom to kiss her good night and always found her brushing her hair in much the same way.

"Oh, Grandmama.'' Sara's voice throbbed with sudden pain. "I don't want you thinking I've been keeping secrets from you all these years. I haven't. But there was someone, a long time ago, and what happened between us wasn't anything I'm ashamed of. It's just hard to talk about him, that's all. I suppose because he was killed in the war.''

''Oh, my darling,'' London said softly. She laid aside the brush and held out her hand. ''Sit down and tell me.''

And Sara did, dashing the tears from her cheeks as she spoke and talking about Rob in a rough, halting whisper that tore at London's heart.

''So that's why you never married,'' she said at last. ''I suspected all along it wasn't for lack of offers. But I find it difficult to believe that you were never strong enough to put this man's death behind you.''

''Oh, Grandmama, it isn't that. There were others after Rob, and I cared for them very much, but none of them made me *feel* the way he did.''

''My poor Sara! First loves are always special, passionate, filled with an unalloyed happiness that can't quite be duplicated the second or even the third time around. But that should never diminish what comes after—''

''No, Grandmama, you don't understand. It wasn't like that at all. Not really. Being with Rob meant being with someone who made me feel cherished and safe. Complete. As comfortable and cozy as slipping into a well-worn pair of shoes. I know it sounds silly—''

''No,'' said London. ''It doesn't sound silly at all.'' She was silent for a moment, thinking. Then she said, ''Is this what you told Nicholas today? Just before he became so silent and withdrawn?''

Sara nodded unhappily. ''I can't imagine why.''

''I think he may be in love with you,'' London said slowly.

Hot color rushed into Sara's cheeks. ''Grandmama! Don't be silly!''

''Well, it would explain his odd behavior in the car. Perhaps your words made him realize that you've never quite gotten over your first love. It's hard to compete with a ghost, Sara.''

Sara said nothing.

''Perhaps if you made it clear to him that you *have* gotten over Rob Buchanan—''

''Why should I?'' Sara asked, surprised. She looked at her

grandmother sharply. "You're not trying to push us together, are you?"

"Why, no, dear. But Olivia did confide in me that Nicholas's wife intends to marry someone else. It will only be a matter of time before Nicholas himself is free."

Sara stared at her, incredulous. "But, Grandmama, I'm not in love with him!"

London smiled into her granddaughter's puzzled eyes. How very young she still was in some ways. "Are you sure of that, my darling?"

Sara colored indignantly. "Of course I am! He's good and kind, but—"

"Yes?" London prodded as Sara fell silent.

Sara rose and began to pace around the room. Her manner had become agitated, as though she were struggling to come to terms with something inside herself. After a moment she said stonily, "I'm not going to fall in love with anyone, Grandmama." Her expression changed, and all at once she said hopelessly, "It just hurts too much."

A great weariness seemed to settle over London. Her eyes closed. How wrong the child was, she thought feebly. She felt her heart squeeze with pain for her granddaughter, and suddenly the pain grew, clawing at her insides until London gasped. "Sara—" She reached out a trembling hand, saw her granddaughter's shocked face tilt crazily before her, but she was powerless to touch her. Her heart beat wildly and she writhed with the spasm before it stopped, abruptly, and blackness roared up to engulf her.

"Sara."

Sara stood up so quickly that the blood rushed from her head. She saw Nicholas coming toward her down the long, dim corridor of the tiny county hospital. She stumbled as she started toward him and would have fallen but for his arms reaching out to catch her. She clung to them, and her face when she looked at him was white and frightened. "Grandmama . . ."

"She's all right, Sara. I've just spoken with the doctor. She's going to be fine."

"Then it wasn't——"

"Yes, it was a heart attack, but fortunately not a bad one. She should be discharged in about a week." He peered at her closely, his hands on her shoulders. "Are you all right? You look awful."

"I've been crying all afternoon."

Nicholas's hands tightened reassuringly. His expression was tender as he looked at her. "It was probably the excitement of her birthday and the trip up here. She simply undertook too much."

This sounded so calmly reasonable that Sara's trembling stopped. She scrubbed at her eyes and tear-stained cheeks. "When can I see her?"

"Not just yet, which is probably a good thing. It'll give you time to decide what to do."

"About what?"

"Will you be staying here until she's discharged?"

She stared at him, astonished. "Of course!"

"Then we'll have to bring your belongings up from Calverdale. And make arrangements to send my mother back to Edinburgh."

Sara's mind was beginning to work once again. "I'll have to phone Bellehurst too. Let Victoria know what's happened."

"Leave that to me. You've endured enough today."

Sara smiled at him, deeply grateful. Ever since she had rung him up from Kennemeade Lodge, crying and babbling incoherently, and he had appeared, calmly in control, driving her the twenty-odd miles toward Carlisle in pursuit of the ambulance that carried her grandmother, she had been glad, so terribly glad, to have him there.

The feeling didn't diminish as they spoke with the on-duty nurse, rang up Olivia in Calverdale, and went down to the parking lot to collect Nicholas's car.

"We were discussing you, you know."

It was very dark by now, and she felt rather than saw Nicholas's start of surprise. "Me?"

"Yes. I was upset because you seemed so angry when you dropped me off at the hotel. And when I told Grandmama, she seemed to think it was because I'd told you about Rob Buchanan." Sara gave a hollow laugh. "Isn't that ridiculous?"

Nicholas slowed the car and, shifting gears, made a sharp left turn before accelerating smoothly. The rain had stopped, but the roadway was wet. The tires hissed and, in the weak beam of the headlights, the shadows of trees and farmhouses slipped silently past. "Yes," he said after a moment. "It's certainly ridiculous."

"There's more."

"Is there?"

"I think Grandmama was trying to play matchmaker. She kept insisting that you and I should be together." Sara's voice quavered. "I was short with her, and now I feel so ashamed. I know it wasn't what she intended at all."

"Your grandmother's no fool," Nicholas said quietly.

"No. Besides, you're already married."

"Not for long," he said wryly.

"Oh, then you know—"

"Yes, my mother told me. She's always been a miserable liar and even worse at keeping secrets."

"How do you feel about it?"

"At the risk of sounding callous I feel, in one word, relieved. High time the bloody thing was over."

There seemed nothing else to say, and so they drove the rest of the way to Calverdale in silence. Sara leaned her head against the soft leather of the Hillman's seat, feeling utterly drained. As well, a feeling of unreality was beginning to creep over her. She felt as though she had been plunged into the middle of a bad dream. Grandmama had had a heart attack. Somehow, even the words didn't make sense.

Olivia met them at the front door of the lodge, pale and distraught, and kissed them both out of sheer relief that they were back. Mr. and Mrs. Quint were there as well, still shaken by the fact that one of their guests had suffered a heart attack on their premises. Yes, they were greatly relieved to hear that Lady Ladbroke had been pronounced out of danger. Yes, of course they would drive Mrs. Warburton and Miss Ashford back to Carlisle once their belongings had been packed, if it meant saving Mr. Warburton another lengthy drive.

Sara agreed that this was an excellent suggestion. Nicholas, she thought, was looking very weary. Doubtless he'd be called out on a number of veterinary emergencies during the night, and his appointment book for tomorrow was already overfilled—he'd told her so himself. He needed rest, not another long drive back down those wet, winding roads.

"Thank you," she said, standing on tiptoe to kiss his cheek. "You've been wonderful."

"Yes, well, I'm only sorry it happened." He didn't look at her, only ran his hands through his dark, disheveled hair. "Go on up and pack your things. You, too, Mother, if you insist on going with Sara."

"I most emphatically do! You can't expect me to abandon my dearest friend at a time like this!"

Nicholas smiled at her gently. "I know. I'll ring Bellehurst in the meantime."

"Come on, Sara," Olivia said kindly, and the two of them went quickly upstairs.

Victoria Warburton sat hunched in the front seat of her husband's Daimler, which had no heater and so was very cold. Rain beat against the windscreen, and she shivered and drew her fur-lined coat more tightly around her. Through the darkness the tarmac showed wet and deserted. She said tremulously, "Can't you go any faster?"

"For God's sake," William answered irritably, "do you want me to put the bloody car in the ditch? I'm driving as fast as I dare." He threw her a look of intense dislike. "What's your hurry, anyway? Nicholas said your mother was doing fine."

"Fine?" Victoria shrilled. "Fine? She's had a heart attack, for heaven's sake! She's seventy-five years old! People that age rarely get over heart attacks!"

William did not respond. Victoria had been all but hysterical ever since Nicholas's telephone call from Cumbria. She had insisted on leaving immediately, no matter the time, and badgered William relentlessly until he had agreed, even though he hated the thought of the long, wet drive ahead. To make matters worse, they had had to leave Francis behind because there wouldn't be enough room for everyone on the return trip, which left William to do all the driving himself.

"I wish Eugenia were here," Victoria said suddenly.

"Whatever for?" asked William, annoyed. "She's the most undependable person I know in a crisis."

"Not one like this!"

"Oh, really? How can you be sure she won't start an affair with the clinic doctor or, worse, set your mother's room on fire with those Turkish cigarettes she smokes?"

You are the most undependable person I know, Victoria wanted to say, but of course she didn't. Nevertheless, the situation with Mama was so dreadful that she felt compelled to defend her side of the family. "Eugenia is always dependable whenever it really counts."

"Oh, is she? Then how do you explain her behavior at your mother's party? Organizing those unseemly dances, arguing with my mother, showing Nelson how to cheat at cards, and putting those blasted ideas about America in Nora's impressionable head?"

Victoria, closing her eyes, felt the tears trembling on her lashes. "William, please."

He retreated into a sulking silence, and the next few hours passed without a single exchange of words between them. At least it gave Victoria the time to think, which was gratifying, because she was never any good at it whenever there were distractions. Although she was deeply shaken by her mother's illness, in a way she was relieved that it had happened. It would, she decided, give her just the excuse she needed to finally make her break with William.

Mama was ill, she'd say, and would need round-the-clock care for at least the next few months. And since she, Victoria, was obviously the best suited to do so, then she might as well move into Rose Cottage to be with her. Obviously, Bellehurst would then be nearly empty, and Victoria could see no reason why it shouldn't be sold—which was something she knew William had been considering anyway.

Of course, the house was legally Mama's, but heart attacks

had a funny way of making people aware of their own mortality. Surely Mama would readily agree that selling the burdensome property would be in everyone's best interest. Although the market was currently depressed, Victoria felt certain that the sale would still bring in a sufficient sum to make a generous settlement for William and provide Nora with tuition for her schooling. Nelson would be finishing soon at Oxford anyway and would, so Victoria devoutly hoped, show an interest in entering his father's firm.

The scandal would be huge, of course, when word of the Ladbroke divorce broke in the newspapers, and that was the only point that gave Victoria any real qualms. Nevertheless, she made up her mind to go through with it, and none of their friends, so she piously believed, would dream of faulting her for giving up her marriage in order to care for her dear, ailing mama.

"I shall hate living in that poky little cottage," Victoria thought, but it just couldn't be helped. Hopefully there would be enough money left over from the Bellehurst sale to buy a pleasant little town house for herself and Mama somewhere in London once Mama was well again.

In fact, the thought of owning a Belgravia address was so enormously comforting that Victoria leaned back against the seat and allowed herself a smug little smile which William, fortunately, could not see in the darkness.

Chapter
Thirty-five

It was dark and very still. London felt herself drifting slowly upward through the black layers of consciousness. She knew, without really knowing how, that something terrible had happened. What? Vague memories nibbled at the edge of her mind. She'd been struck down by a carriage, she recalled, and then Eugenia had been born . . . No, no, that was all wrong. That had happened years ago. Annoyed, she struggled weakly to shake off the last vestiges of sleep, and slowly opened her eyes.

She knew at once that she was in hospital. There could be no mistaking the clinical smell of camphor mixed with ether, or the stark look of the room, unfamiliar though it was. A vase crammed with wildflowers stood beside her bed, and the institutional curtains covering the tiny window had been drawn back to reveal a gloomy, overcast sky. Edinburgh. Was she in Edinburgh? It always rained in Scotland, Livvy said. But Livvy wasn't in Scotland; she had come to Cumbria to see her. Then this must be—

She became aware of movement beyond her bed. Slowly, she turned her head and saw her granddaughter's face floating toward her through the shifting shadows. There was the sound of a sharply indrawn breath, and then Sara's jubilant voice. "Grandmama! You're awake!"

"Of course I'm awake." She meant to sound peevish, but her voice came out all wrong. Weak and quavering, like an old woman's. *Bah*, London thought. *I am an old woman*. And if memory served her right, she'd suffered a heart attack. And survived.

Another face appeared beyond Sara's shoulder. With a start, London recognized Victoria, red-eyed from weeping, an absurdly flowered hat sitting comically awry on her head.

"What are you doing here?" London asked.

At the sound of her mother's hoarse voice, Victoria succumbed to a rather distasteful flood of tears. Only after Sara had brought her some water and London had made a number of soothing noises did she regain sufficient control of herself to blow her nose and attempt a watery smile.

"I'm so very tired. We drove all night," she explained. "I don't believe I've slept a wink. Now, don't you worry about a thing, Mama," she added, putting away her handkerchief and warming to her role. "William is booking us a room in town, and we'll stay as long as it's necessary. William can put Sara on the train when it's time for her to leave and we'll bring you home in the Daimler. I'll ring Mrs. Jakes this afternoon and tell her to have my things moved down to Rose Cottage.''

"Whatever for?" London asked, alarmed.

"I've made up my mind to move in with you. You can't live alone now that you've had a heart attack.''

"But what about Nora? William?''

"Don't worry about them," Victoria soothed. "Nora will be going away to school, and you know how things stand between William and me. Once we put Bellehurst on the market—''

She was interrupted by the nurse, a very formidable specimen clad deceptively in angelic white, who informed them in a tone that brooked no argument that her patient needed rest.

"Sara—'' London began, but the nurse ushered both women out.

Exhausted, London closed her eyes. Her heart was pounding in a frightening manner, and it was an enormous effort simply to draw a breath. She had never felt so tired, so drained, so utterly defeated. Victoria, in a misguided belief in her own goodness was leaving William to *move in with her*. They were going to sell Bellehurst. Sara, it seemed, was returning to New York.

Alex, I'm sorry. London wished that she had told Sara the truth about Sandy long ago. Perhaps if she had never kept secrets from her Sara would understand herself better. And now it might be too late. *What will happen if I die tonight?* London asked herself. Who on earth would convince Sara that she was falling in love with Nicholas Warburton? It was hard fighting a ghost. Rupert must have suspected it, and Nicholas, perhaps, had realized it as well. *Oh, gracious*, London wondered, *whatever shall I do? Alex, I'm so tired.*

Sara sat at the pockmarked table in the hospital waiting room. She was writing a letter to her mother. Outside, the rain beat against the glass and the sky was dark and menacing.

There were subdued voices at the nurses' station down the corridor, and the sound of approaching footsteps. The door swung open. Sara looked up.

It was Nicholas. Rain beaded on his coat and hat and dripped to the floor. She laid down her pen and looked at him. For a moment neither of them spoke.

"Are you here alone?" Nicholas asked at last.

Sara nodded. "Victoria and William have gone to the inn to catch up on sleep. Your mother went out for the evening paper. It was nice of you to come up in this weather to check on Grandmama."

"How is she doing?"

"About the same. I had the chance to speak to her doctor earlier. He thinks he'll be able to tell us more about her condition tomorrow. How long she'll have to stay and that sort of thing."

A nurse appeared in the doorway. "Miss Ashford?"

The color drained from Sara's face. "What is it?" she asked, coming swiftly to her feet.

"It's all right. Lady Ladbroke is asking for you. The doctor says you may go in for a moment."

Sara's eyes went to Nicholas's face. "Go on," he said reassuringly. "I'll wait here."

Her grandmother's room was dark. The bleak daylight beyond the window was fading into night. Sara switched on the light, then wished she hadn't. Her grandmother looked so pale, so small and diminished, lying in the bed.

"Oh, Grandmama," Sara breathed.

London's eyes opened. She gave a thin smile. "Sara . . ." Her voice was faint, but she plunged on determinedly. "I'm so glad you're alone. I wanted to tell you there wasn't . . . I didn't intend to interfere between you and Nicholas earlier."

"It doesn't matter," Sara said quickly, but London shook her head.

"The idea only came to me after we arrived. When I saw the two of you together, I realized how right you were for each other. I can tell he's in love with you. And I care so very much about the two of you. I want you to be happy.

And to stay here in England, not go back to New York. But I was wrong to meddle. I'm old and thoughtless and selfish . . .''

Sara quickly laid a hand on her grandmother's shoulder. "It's all right, Grandmama. Hush now. Try to rest. I'm here. I'm not going to leave you."

"I'm glad," mumbled London. Her eyes closed.

Sara looked down into the still, white face, and told herself that there was no reason to be frightened. Just because Grandmama looked so terribly frail didn't mean she wasn't going to recover. Still, it was awful to suddenly try imagining a future without her, to envision how empty the world would be when Grandmama was gone.

I can't stand this, Sara thought desperately. Her lip trembled and tears stung her eyes. Fiercely, she dashed them away.

"Sara?"

She took a deep breath, trying to calm herself. It wouldn't do for Grandmama to see her crying. "I'm here. What is it?"

"You heard what I said, didn't you?"

"Yes, yes, of course. Now, please—"

"I want you to promise me something."

"What?"

"To think about what I said. Look into your heart. Maybe you'll find that you love him after all."

"Grandmama—"

"No!" The thin, cold fingers seized Sara's hand and clasped it tightly. "I want you to listen to me because I know. I know! I made the same mistake myself, you see. I had everything, everything, but I gave it all away. And all for some misguided sense of duty, a stupid belief that fate could not be rubbed out however much one might wish to change it. And I paid for it. At first. But I was lucky. I was given another chance—with Rupert, as fine a man as any that ever lived, though it took me many, many years to realize it."

"Grandmama, what . . . what are you saying?"

London's blue eyes blazed, and for a brief moment a splash of color crept into her sunken cheeks. "Only that you hav the same chance to be happy. Few of us are ever that fortunate. Don't throw it away, Sara. Promise me you'll think about it first. It won't do to find your way into Eden and then deliberately leave it. If you go, you may never find your way back.''

London's eyes closed and her hand, which had been clutching Sara's tightly, slipped onto the sheets. Terrified, Sara sprang up, but even as she rushed toward the door to summon help, the thin, rasping voice came again.

''Sara.''

''I'm here, Grandmama.''

''There's something else I want to tell you.''

''Can't it wait? I'd much rather you rested.''

''No.'' London's voice was agitated. ''If I die tonight you'll never know the truth.''

''Don't be silly.'' Sara's voice quavered. ''You aren't going to die. The doctor said so.'' She saw the tears well beneath the closed lids and trickle down her grandmother's cheeks. Picking up the thin, parched hand, she said softly, ''All right, Grandmama, I'll listen. What is it you wanted to tell me?''

Nicholas was leafing restlessly through a well-thumbed magazine when Sara appeared in the doorway. Taking one look at her ravaged face he sprang up and seized her by the shoulders. ''Sara! What is it? Your grandmother—''

''She's fine,'' Sara assured him tonelessly.

''Then what is it?''

''Nothing. I . . . I just feel . . .'' Her words trailed away. How could she explain to Nicholas how she felt when she didn't even know herself? When her whole world had been turned upside down?

''Sara, look at me.''

She lifted her eyes to Nicholas's thin, unshaven face and saw the kindness, the tenderness there. ''Don't,'' she whispered, ''don't look at me like that.'' To her horror, she burst into tears.

In the next moment she found herself in Nicholas's arms. Her face turned into his shoulder as the very bones of her body seemed to melt into an embrace that shook her with its sweet, voluptuous ease. She wasn't sure if she lifted her face to his or if it was Nicholas who bent his head to hers. She only knew that his mouth was suddenly upon her own, and the rightness of it, the sense of belonging, shook her to her very soul.

An outer door slammed somewhere nearby, and it was this that broke them apart. Not hurriedly, but slowly, with a sense of lingering regret.

"Why, Nicholas! What are you doing here? I thought you were at the clinic." Olivia was coming toward them, a newspaper tucked into the pocket of her raincoat. Her eyes went from her son's impassive face to Sara's bowed head. "Well," she said briskly, "I'll just look in on London for a moment. Can you stay for supper, Nicholas?"

"I'm not sure. I've got to be back early. I'm on call tonight."

"I won't be long," Olivia promised.

Silence fell once she was gone. After a moment Nicholas said, "I really don't think I should stay. Normally, I could ring Francis and ask him to take over for me, but he's been called out of town unexpectedly."

"I see."

Nicholas thrust his hands into his coat pockets. "When are you leaving for the States?"

"The twelfth of June. Eugenia arranged it. I was just writing Mother to let her know."

Nicholas nodded. Again the silence fell. The rain beat against the glass. At last he stirred and said, "Well, I'd better be off. The roads will be pretty much impassable."

Sara looked up at him searchingly. "Then why did you come?"

He withdrew his hands from his pockets. "Actually, I wanted to give you this before you left. I found it in my desk drawer the other day. It must have been sitting there for years."

Sara looked up to find Nicholas holding out his hand to her. Wrapped around his finger was a gold locket she recognized instantly as the one her grandparents had given her on her twelfth birthday, the locket she had wagered in a card game

on a Christmas night so many years ago. She had forgotten
its existence until now.

"Thank you." Warily, she took it from him, being careful
that their fingers didn't touch. She was afraid to look at him
because she didn't want him to see how close to tears she
was. Seeing the locket again had suddenly made her poi-
gnantly aware of how much Nicholas was a part of her past,
a part of Bellehurst and the happiness—now so long gone—
that she had known while living there.

But he was letting her go. He wouldn't have returned the
locket otherwise. And she knew now, suddenly and inargu-
ably, that her grandmother had been right. She didn't want
to go. Since Nicholas had kissed her he had suddenly become
as necessary to her as breathing. The obvious had roared up
and over her the moment their lips had met.

Nicholas said softly, "I really can't wait any longer. Will
you tell my mother that I had to go?"

She nodded without looking at him.

"Good-bye, Sara. I probably won't be seeing you again
before your grandmother is discharged. I'm going to be tied
up at the clinic for the next few days."

There was a lump in her throat. She had to swallow twice
before she could speak. "I understand. Good-bye."

"You'll keep in touch, won't you? Once you're back in
America, I mean?"

"I will."

Looking down at the floor, she heard him hesitate, then
turn and walk out of the room. A door slammed. Moments
later came the sound of an engine being cranked far too
roughly, then tires squealing on wet gravel. Then that, too,
faded into the steady roar of the rain.

London and Sara sat in the garden at Rose Cottage under
a warm, summer-blue sky. From where they sat they could
watch the butterflies and the bees bobbing insatiably from
flower to fragrant flower. The garden was bursting with color.
In their absence, spring had arrived full-blown. Mr. Brockman, resplendent in a new overcoat and balaclava despite the
warmth of the day, was scratching happily at a distant border.

London, thinner, grayer, but behaving considerably more vigorously than one would have thought for a woman whose heart attack lay barely a fortnight behind her, bent and plucked a fat pink blossom from the bed near the terrace. Tucking it into the buttonhole of her cardigan, she smiled at her granddaughter. "How beautiful the weather is. I can assure you that it's raining in Cumberland."

Sara laughed. "I'm sure spring will get there eventually."

"Has it arrived in New Jersey yet, I wonder?"

Sara's laughter stilled. Her young, lovely face lost much of its charm. "Probably. I'll know next week."

London's gaze went to the old stone wall, to the vines, heavy with drooping petals, growing upon it. "Then you're still leaving tomorrow?"

Sara looked away. "I can't change my plans a third time, Grandmama."

"I know you can't, my darling. I was just hoping—" She broke off and laughed self-consciously. "Silly of me."

"What?" Sara asked unwisely.

London's calm blue eyes went to her granddaughter's face. "I was hoping you and Nicholas might change that."

"How can we?" Sara asked angrily. "If he hadn't wanted me to leave, then he would have said *something*."

"And would you have stayed?"

Sara did not answer. London leaned back wearily in her chair. She still tired very easily these days, and she was finding this exchange—the first serious one between them since their return—utterly exhausting. Perhaps she ought to take one of her pills. Eugenia was in the kitchen preparing lunch. Surely she could bring them?

London looked again at her granddaughter's bowed head. With unsteady fingers, Sara was shredding a flower she had plucked from the border. The petals fluttered onto the bricks. London said bluntly, "Well, are you in love with him or not?"

Sara's head came up. "Would it matter?"

"It would, and don't you go scowling at me like that, Sara Ashford, or I'll slap the scowl right from your face. I have every reason to hope things will work out between you and

Nicholas, because I've made up my mind to make Bellehurst over to the two of you.''

Silence.

"I thought . . . I thought Uncle William was planning to sell it!''

London said tartly, "That's not his decision to make. The house belongs to me, and now that William and Vicky are ending their marriage, I've decided to leave it to you.''

"Grandpa Lawrence once said he wouldn't take Bellehurst on a platter. That the death duties alone would bankrupt him.''

"Do you think I'm so old and senile that I'd hang some cursed albatross around your necks? Neither of you are young, Sara, you're not children anymore. You deserve the luxury of enjoying yourselves without the constant worry over money. I happen to have enough, you see, all of it quite prudently invested. William knows nothing about it.''

"And what about the war? There's going to be one, you know. Everyone says so. No one can do anything to prevent it, Grandmama, not even you.''

"And if there is? So what? We've lived through war before. Why should that worry you? Wars are fought by young men, not those Nicholas's age. And especially not family men.''

"So now you've got us married with children.''

"It's something I feel in my bones, Sara,'' London said crisply. "Karma, in the manner that Ali Wad Zarim used to believe in it. I know for certain that you and Nicholas are destined to grow old in this house surrounded by a large and loving family. It's waiting for you, darling, *if* you truly love him.''

Sara was silent for a moment. Then she said, slowly, "I do love him, Grandmama. Only I never realized it until you told me about . . . about Alex.'' It was the first time she had ever acknowledged him or said his name aloud. "You were right. It is possible to love twice.''

"Or perhaps simply to share the same love with a different man.''

With her palm, Sara brushed away the tears on her cheeks. "You're forgetting one thing, Grandmama.''

"What's that?"

"It takes two people to make a marriage."

London smiled. "I wouldn't worry about that. It's been over two weeks since we left Calverdale. Just enough time, I'm willing to bet, for Nicholas to swallow his stubborn pride, drive to Edinburgh, and confront his wife with a divorce. And as soon as he does, he'll show up here at Bellehurst, without a word of warning, to find you. But you, impetuous, stubborn thing that you are, won't do him the courtesy of waiting."

"Oh, Grandmama." Sara shook her head and tried to smile through her tears. "What makes you so sure Nicholas is willing to give up his practice and start over in Kent?"

"*In' shallah.* It's all in the hands of God, my darling."

Scowling, Sara came to her feet. "Now I've heard quite enough, thank you. Maybe you believe in that sort of mystical claptrap, but I certainly don't."

She went stiffly across the lawn and up the terrace steps. She halted at the murmur of voices coming from inside. She heard the sound of footsteps, and then someone was lifting aside the heavy drapes and opening the parlor door. Sara looked up.

And saw that it was Nicholas.